Welcome to Gold Valley, Oregon,
where the cowboys are tough to tame, until they
meet the women who can lasso their hearts.

Cowboy Christmas Blues (ebook novella)
Smooth-Talking Cowboy
Mail Order Cowboy (ebook novella)
Untamed Cowboy
Hard Riding Cowboy (ebook novella)
Good Time Cowboy

In Copper Ridge, Oregon, lasting love
with a cowboy is only a happily-ever-after away.
Don't miss any of Maisey Yates's
Copper Ridge tales, available now!

From HQN Books

Shoulda Been a Cowboy (prequel novella)
Part Time Cowboy
Brokedown Cowboy
Bad News Cowboy
A Copper Ridge Christmas (ebook novella)
The Cowboy Way
Hometown Heartbreaker (ebook novella)
One Night Charmer
Tough Luck Hero
Last Chance Rebel
Slow Burn Cowboy
Down Home Cowboy
Wild Ride Cowboy
Christmastime Cowboy

From Harlequin Desire

Take Me, Cowboy
Hold Me, Cowboy
Seduce Me, Cowboy
Claim Me, Cowboy

Look for more Gold Valley books coming soon!

For more books by Maisey Yates,
visit www.maiseyyates.com.

MAISEY YATES

Good Time Cowboy

HQN™

HQN™

Recycling programs
for this product may
not exist in your area.

ISBN-13: 978-1-335-47461-2

Good Time Cowboy

Copyright © 2018 by Maisey Yates

The publisher acknowledges the copyright holder
of the additional work:

Hard Riding Cowboy
Copyright © 2018 by Maisey Yates

www.HQNBooks.com

Printed in U.S.A.

CONTENTS

Good Time
Cowboy

To Jackie, Megan, Nicole and Rusty.
Thank you for being my support system, my panic button and my OMG PLEASE SOMEONE READ THIS AND TELL ME IF IT MAKES SENSE crew. You have no idea how much I appreciate you.

CHAPTER ONE

LINDY PARKER HATED the rodeo. Just in general. The sights, the smells, the cloud of testosterone that covered everything.

She hadn't always hated it, but now it all reminded her of her ex-husband. Damien was so firmly part of that world to her. Whenever she'd gone to rodeo events, it had been for the sole purpose of seeing Damien's work. To see the results of PR campaigns he'd run and to rub elbows with possible sponsors.

The rest of it didn't much appeal to her. Dirt and bright lights and overly loud announcers.

But if there was one thing she hated more than the rodeo itself, it was the bull riders.

Cocky. Arrogant. Jerks.

Even her younger brother, Dane, suffered from a bad case of it when he'd been out on the circuit for too long.

But there was no bull rider who irked her quite like Wyatt Dodge. Her dear ex's favorite rider. A man who'd made Damien tons of money and inflated his ego beyond the telling of it, which, in her humble opinion, had contributed to the flagrant affair her husband had engaged in with a woman who had—at the time—worked at Grassroots Winery, and had been young enough that she still probably remembered how to get to Sesame Street.

Not that it was Wyatt Dodge's fault. No, Damien was

responsible for his own body parts and where they wandered. He was the one who had made vows to her, and even if she did feel like perhaps his prolonged exposure to a pack of manwhores hadn't helped her marriage, she knew exactly where the fault lay for what had transpired.

With Damien.

She'd caught him kissing an employee of their winery. A much younger employee. Sarabeth, who Lindy had considered a casual friend. A woman she'd invited into her home. A woman she'd paid an hourly wage to. And apparently some of those hours had been spent in bed with Lindy's husband.

And Lindy could hold a grudge. And had. All the way to court, where she had managed to get full ownership of Damien's family winery, Grassroots Winery.

Jamison Leighton and his wife had been unsurprisingly angry at the way all that had gone. But, they shouldn't have left the entire thing to a son who didn't know how to keep it in his pants. Particularly not a son who had signed a very foolish prenuptial agreement, designed only to protect *him* from *her*. Which had meant that all bad behavior stipulated in said agreement had been based on the assumption that she would be the one to do all the very bad things.

And so, she had emerged victorious. She'd given more power back to his sisters, who had not had a chance to claim any part of the property from his parents, but who had stood by her side through the ordeal.

She was close to Sabrina and Bea, in spite of the fact that they were blood-related to Damien. They were the sisters of her heart, and they all worked together even now.

She loved the winery, but unfortunately it was that work that brought her to the Get Out of Dodge ranch now—and was bringing her into contact with a man that she liked less than cooked carrots.

Bull rider. Manwhore. Friend of her ex-husband.

Wyatt Dodge.

Lindy gritted her teeth and parked her little red car in the gravel lot. She questioned her decision-making sometimes. The fact that she'd come to Wyatt with the idea of the joint barbecue that would hopefully increase business at both Grassroots and Get Out of Dodge. A barbecue that would showcase the grounds of the dude ranch and the wines from Grassroots, and educate people on the different activities available at both locations.

But it made sense. Business sense, anyway. And she'd felt like it would be shortsighted to let her feelings for Wyatt—both her irritation and the strange tightening she felt in her stomach whenever he was around—hinder an important business decision.

Back in the day, Get Out of Dodge had been a thriving dude ranch, bringing people in for miles. But then, Quinn Dodge had lost his wife, and the tragedy had made it difficult for him to continue running the place at that capacity. Since then, the ownership had passed to Quinn's son, Wyatt, who had retired from the rodeo circuit. He was working on bringing it back to its former glory, modernizing it and creating a place that would cater to what guests wanted now.

Lindy felt like she was very much doing the same with Grassroots. Now that it was in her control she was doing all the expanding she had wanted to do when she and Damien had been married. He had been just happy to live in a big house and let the winery bump along, making income as it had always done.

Not Lindy. Lindy had come from nothing, and she didn't take a thing for granted.

All that mattered was the future.

And getting through all of it without killing Wyatt.

"Now," she muttered to herself. "If I were a pigheaded asshole where would I be?"

Seeing as it was lunchtime, he would probably be in the aptly named mess hall.

Lindy had to admit that the ranch was charming. All the little cabins that had been redone over the past few months, as well as the large communal dining hall, filled with picnic bench-style setups and with more seating outside by the river.

There were arenas with fresh dirt, both covered and uncovered, where people could ride, and learn to do some rodeo basics. They did a roping and barrel racing primer, and they were beginning to do trail rides of varying lengths and skill levels.

That was one of the big joint ventures happening between Grassroots and Get Out of Dodge.

They were offering a ride through the winery that took people through the vineyards and ended in a farm-to-table dinner in one of the revamped barns on her property. If you were staying at the ranch, you got a discount. And it was Jamie Dodge who was leading the ride.

It didn't do them any good to see each other as competitors—they weren't. He had people coming to stay on his property, and she had booze. That meant they were natural bedfellows.

When it came to business.

Lindy forced a smile as she traipsed into the mess hall. "Good afternoon," she said, taking a chance that it would be Wyatt who was sitting inside.

She wasn't disappointed. But, along with Wyatt were his younger brothers Grant and Bennett.

"Good afternoon," Wyatt returned, leaning back in his chair and tipping his cowboy hat back on his forehead.

"I'm here to discuss brochures," she said, feeling her lips tighten up as she spoke the words.

It was weird. Standing in front of them in a pencil skirt, wearing high heels and standing like she had a rod bolted into her spine.

She'd trained herself to be this way. She'd grown up in a trailer park with hand-me-down clothes and a mind-set of fending for herself. She might not have learned how to be fancy growing up, but she'd learned to take care of herself.

When she'd met Damien, she'd put her survival skills to good use. He'd paid attention to her, given her the kind of love she'd imagined a girl like her could never earn. In return, she'd figured out how to blend into his world. She'd wanted to be an asset to him, not a disadvantage. So she'd put this sleek, beautiful armor on.

She was still doing it now. But she ran a winery, so honestly, the learned behavior was on theme.

"You could have just sent me an email," Wyatt said.

"I did," she responded, through clenched teeth. "I sent two emails. A week ago. You didn't respond to them."

"Sorry, I don't check my email all that often."

"Then why did you suggest that as a method of communication?"

"Better than any other."

"I have brochures," Lindy said, reaching into her purse and pulling out two of the aforementioned items.

They had decided that they were going to do two-sided brochures that would be placed in the cabins at Get

Out of Dodge and in the tasting rooms for Grassroots. But, she needed Wyatt to approve them before she had them printed.

"Lindy, I really don't care about the font or whatever is on a brochure."

"Well, I need you to care."

Grant, who she had always liked, extended his hand. "I'll have a look," he said.

She shot Wyatt a triumphant glare and walked across the room, placing one in Grant's hand. "That's option one," she said.

"Let me see," Bennett said.

She had always liked Bennett too.

Bennett was the youngest of the Dodge brothers, newly engaged, and a veterinarian, well respected in the community of Gold Valley.

Grant worked on the ranch. A widower, he was talked about often in hushed tones the moment he left the room. But then, his romance with his late wife had made literal headlines at the time. A teenager marrying his dying high school sweetheart. It made for a great story. Though, it had been something of a crushing reality. And one that seemed to follow him wherever he went.

She had an inkling of how that felt. Not the grief part. But the being a topic of conversation part.

She was *the divorced one*. People whispered about her behind their hands, talked about what a shame it was that husband of hers had turned out to be a no-account. Or they talked about how that had been her plan all along. A gold digger. Nothing but trailer trash who had married above herself and hadn't been able to keep the man happy. Who had taken him for all he had, and had ended up with money she hadn't earned.

The honorable Leighton family should never have been parted from their family property. Obviously. Regardless of the fact that a judge had disagreed with that assessment.

Yes, she knew what it was like to be whispered about.

Sadly, she could find no such connection, empathy or respect for Wyatt.

But then, in fairness, he didn't try to earn it.

Finally, Wyatt stood up, slowly. And as he did, her mouth went dry. He was tall. Very, very tall. The tallest of all of the brothers, which was saying something, as they were all over six feet. She was used to large, strapping men. Hell, her brother was one.

But Wyatt Dodge was not her brother. He was infuriating. He was obnoxious. He was friends with Damien.

He was definitely not her brother.

And not ugly. Regrettably.

Not even close.

Wyatt Dodge was one of the most magnetic men she had ever met.

Grant and Bennett were handsome like movie stars. Grant bearded, Bennett clean-shaven. Symmetrical. Brown eyes and square jaws and all of that. Wyatt was *rugged*. He had a scar running through his chin that she was sure he had gotten doing something stupid, because bull riders never did much of anything smart.

He always had just a little bit of stubble on that firm jaw of his, and it looked like it would be prickly if she touched it. His boots were always dusty, and his jeans usually had holes. Unless he was dressed up, and then he put on some slightly nicer jeans and boots that she suspected were made from snake. She wished she didn't know that. She wished that she hadn't retained those details.

She knew that he had more than one black cowboy hat, though you could be forgiven for thinking they were all the same. And that he had one that was tan, which usually went with his nicer clothes.

She also had the first moment they'd met branded into her memory.

She knew way too much about him, having seen him from afar over the years when Damien was doing PR for the circuit and she was still his wife.

And then, she had relearned a lot of it over these past couple of months while the two of them had been forging something of a business relationship.

None of it made her feel at ease around him. She was decidedly easeless in his presence, and she didn't know what to do about it.

He reached out and took both brochures from his brothers, his large, weathered hands making the brochures look…well, wrong.

Like maybe he needed information carved on a stump of wood with some kind of sharp, rudimentary object.

Damien had been something of a rhinestone cowboy. He dressed the part, but that was so he fit into his surroundings. He didn't do ranch work.

Wyatt was as real as it got.

And it shouldn't matter to her at all. Only in the sense that it was probably good for business. And the more business that came out to the ranch, the more traffic it would drive to Grassroots.

Plus, they had a deal. Get Out of Dodge was going to serve Grassroots wine exclusively, and that would draw people in to buy more as well.

He turned the pamphlets over, examining them, and for some reason, Lindy felt that examination in a close personal way. She shifted awkwardly, attempting to ignore the strange, hollow feeling between her thighs.

"It all looks good to me, *Melinda*," he said, using her full name, which *no one* ever did. He only knew it because they had gone out drinking once after a big win for Wyatt had resulted in a good endorsement deal that Damien had helped Wyatt net. And the subject of middle names had come up, which had brought up the subject of her full name.

And now, years on, he sometimes used it to irritate the hell out of her.

"Thank you," she said, keeping everything smooth and serene on the surface, while internally she was flipping him both middle fingers.

That was what she did now. It was how she played this game. She had perfected her polished exterior to the point that no one knew there was a little grit left beneath.

She did. Because it was the grit that kept her going.

"Why don't we walk outside a bit?" he asked, his eyes connecting with hers and lighting her insides on fire.

Lord almighty.

"I want to show you some things," he continued.

She squared her shoulders and followed after Wyatt, giving Grant and Bennett a small wave before heading outside.

"Something we need to do in person?"

"Yes. Otherwise I would have emailed you. I have your address." His handsome face was a study in sincerity and she wanted to punch it.

She bit the inside of her cheek. "Right. *Anyway*."

"I just wanted to talk a little bit about the Fourth of July shindig that we're having."

"Right. The shindig." Grassroots would be providing wine, and they would also be serving Donnelly cheese. Plus, they would be touting the virtues of both Grassroots and Get Out of Dodge. It was an important event, one that they were heavily advertising for in surrounding communities.

"I was thinking we would do some rodeo demonstrations," he said. "Over there in the main arena." He gestured broadly across the way at a grand, covered area, with two sets of bleachers on either side. The bleachers were new.

It looked like Wyatt figured that if he wasn't traveling with the rodeo he might as well bring it back here.

"Really?" she asked.

"Yes. I was wondering if Dane was going to be around?"

"I doubt it. Anyway, it's not like you're outfitted to do a bull ride here." There were bleachers, but they were missing the heavy gates and fencing needed to keep people safe if they were going to bring those animals out.

"Not bulls," he confirmed. "I figured we would do some roping. Not going to go crazy. You're right. We don't have the facility for it. But it would be damned cool if we did."

"I'm not going to have my brother get himself injured doing a stunt to benefit your ranch, Dodge."

"Your brother rides often enough. He can get injured anytime."

"Right." She pursed her lips. "But *competing*. Not messing around here." Dane's ability to earn a living was everything to him. His way of escaping their upbringing. He didn't need to put it at risk messing around here. "Anyway. I'm pretty sure that Dane is solidly booked in competition for the next few months."

"That's a shame. I like him."

Heavily implied in that sentence was the fact that he did *not* like *her*. But, that wasn't her problem. It also wasn't fair. Dane was different. His life was different. He got rewarded for being a good old boy. For being a reckless redneck.

She got no such rewards from life. She had to prove that she was capable. She was strong and smart. That she belonged in the world she'd married into, and divorced out of.

Dane got to be fun and dangerous and get rewarded for it. But then, that was her experience of all these rodeo idiots. Their life was a big party. They didn't do responsible things like keep to their commitments or honor their vows. No. And her husband had jumped right into that.

But, that was beside the point.

"Sorry. *He* didn't quit."

"I *retired*," he pointed out. "I didn't quit. Midthirties is a rough time to still be flinging your body around like that. Other guys do it, but…not me. I'm done." A smile tipped the corner of his mouth upward, and she noticed some lines crease his skin right by his eyes.

He had aged since they'd first met all those years ago but that didn't make him less attractive. Instead, those weathered signs of aging, of years lived, only made him more attractive in a strange way. She had to wonder if it was some kind of weird female survival instinct. That this man who had taken all these risks was here, had made it well into his thirties in spite of those risks, was sending signals to her body that he was a good provider, or something.

But her body was terrible at correctly identifying men's true natures. Even if it wasn't, she didn't want to know Wyatt or his...nature. So, she wasn't even going to ponder it.

"Well. Whatever. So you're thinking roping events?" She pushed the conversation back on track.

"Yes. I got all the approvals from insurance. As long as we don't have any guests participating, or anything like that, we are cleared for it."

"Glad to hear it."

"I was also thinking Jamie could lead a ride during the barbecue."

She nodded. "Sounds good to me."

"Will it be all right with you if we take the group over to the vineyard?"

"Should be fine."

Their eyes caught for a moment, and for some reason it felt significant. More so than the moment before. He was not the kind of man she normally liked.

Granted, she'd been with *one* man. And in the end she hadn't liked him very much at all. But still.

He nodded, then smiled. Slow and lazy. It licked through her like fire and she did her very best to ignore it. "Good."

She cleared her throat. "Good."

"So, just the brochures? Were there any emails that you needed me to read?"

She curled her hands into fists, irritation coursing through her, saving her from the heat. "Can't you just... check your email?"

"Can't you just…tell me what you need?" He smiled. Enigmatic. Infuriating.

"There's nothing, but if I need anything else I'll be sure to send you an email. And maybe I'll add a follow-up phone call."

"Sounds good. Could you arrange for 6:00 a.m.? A wake-up call? That would be pretty fancy. Haven't had that since I was on the circuit."

"You stayed at *motels* that gave you wake-up calls when you were riding on the circuit?"

"No. The women that spent the night usually woke me up early when they were sneaking out, though."

He was such a jackass.

"Right. Well. I will not be giving you a wake-up call. Of any variety." Her lips twitched, and heat flooded her cheeks.

"Noted."

She turned away, her heart hammering hard. She had the inescapable feeling that she had made a deal with the devil in forging an alliance with Wyatt Dodge. But the devil was infinitely preferable to her ex-husband, and the devil currently had what she needed.

And so, a deal with the devil it was.

WYATT WATCHED LINDY's figure as she retreated, the wiggle in her hips transmitting her irritation while also sending some signals to his body that he could do without, thanks.

He let out the breath that he felt like he had been holding for the past fifteen minutes, feeling the tension ease out of his body, down along his spine. That woman got under his skin, no denying it.

Under normal circumstances he *wouldn't* deny it. He

would have just had her by now. But there were complications to that. Big ones. Like the fact that she was the ex-wife of a man he had once considered a good friend.

Like the fact that she hated him.

Oh, and the fact that he had wanted her from the moment he'd met her, when she had still been hitched to the aforementioned friend.

The fact that he hadn't made a move on her was a relief only in that it indicated he had learned to think with something other than his cock since he was sixteen years old.

Lindy Parker was a particular kind of thorn in his flesh.

He remembered the moment he'd met her with a distressing amount of clarity. He had been in a bar after one of the events, and she had walked in looking prim and uncertain, her hands clasped in front of her, holding on to her handbag, her blond hair swirling around her as she took stock of the rabble and ruffians in the room.

And he had…he had felt the floor of that bar fall out from underneath his feet.

He had wanted her, immediately. Viscerally. It had been an instantaneous and deep desire unlike anything he had ever felt before.

Then, he had seen the diamond ring sparkling on her left hand. It had only loomed larger in his vision as she had walked over to where he was sitting. He'd had all those seconds, those long moments of watching her make her way across the room to decide he didn't give a damn who had given her that ring or what it meant. He wanted her. And if she was going to let him have her…well, then he wasn't going to waste a thought on the poor bastard who'd given her the diamond.

He'd thought that right up until she'd walked up and kissed his friend right on the mouth.

She was Damien's wife. Of course.

Because the first woman to make him feel like he couldn't breathe in longer than he could remember was obviously going to be married to a friend of his.

Even if she hadn't been married to Damien…they were not meant to be. She had been unfriendly to him from the beginning. It wasn't even her divorce from Damien that had triggered the unfriendliness.

He still wanted her. Dammit.

And he didn't do that stuff. He didn't *want* and not *have*. Sex, as far as he was concerned was a recreational activity. People didn't need to make such a big deal out of it. But, he also preferred to like the women he banged. And he preferred it if they didn't want to decapitate him.

Lindy fell into that category.

The divorce…

Yeah, that was complicated, but it had a little bit more to do with her not liking him rather than him being concerned about preserving a relationship with Damien.

As far as he was concerned Damien was a dickhead. Cheating on Lindy had been an asshole thing to do. There was no defending it. Wyatt wouldn't even try. Some men shouldn't get married. Wyatt was one of them. But, he *hadn't* gotten married. Damien had. And he had owed it to his wife to be faithful to her. The damned man hadn't even tried as far as Wyatt could tell.

It had all come out later, when Damien had drunkenly slurred over a beer about the end of his marriage that he had cheated on Lindy multiple times over the years. Being on the road with all that temptation around was too much for him, he'd said. When the buckle bunnies couldn't find a cowboy to get laid with they would always take him.

And it was all Wyatt could do not to ask him if he was screwed in the head. Because what the hell man would want another woman when he had that one in his bed? Wyatt sure as hell wouldn't.

Of course, he had never tried monogamy, so he supposed he couldn't actually judge. But he did.

Still, the fact that he didn't exactly want his friend to know that he had illicit fantasies about the other guy's wife was one reason he had held back on lecturing him too much. The other being that he just wasn't the right man for that job.

A shiftless manslut who had never had a committed relationship in his life was the last person on earth who should hand out lectures on marriage.

"She does *not* like you."

Wyatt turned around and saw his brother Grant standing there, looking amused with the situation.

He supposed he should be happy to see Grant looking amused at all, since his brother rarely did. But, he wasn't. Not when it was at his expense.

Wyatt had never claimed not to be a selfish bastard.

"She doesn't," Wyatt agreed.

"And you want her."

"She's a shrew," Wyatt said, by way of answer, crossing his arms, watching as that little red car of hers drove away.

"A hot one," Grant pointed out.

"*You* sleep with her then. I don't want to have to dig her fingernails out from under my skin after."

"It's my understanding you end up with fingernails

embedded in your skin when it goes well," Grant said, his tone dry.

"Unless she does it because she wants to mortally wound you."

"From where I'm at right now, I'm not sure I see a drawback either way."

"Go." Wyatt made a shooing motion with his hand. "Get some. Refresh your memory."

Grant lifted a brow, the lines on his forehead deepening. "Not likely."

Wyatt locked eyes with his brother. "Get out of town. Find a woman who doesn't know you and your entire life story."

"You know," Grant said. "I tried that once. She remembered me. From the news."

"Damn."

His brother's marriage had ended up famous.

An eighteen-year-old who married his high school sweetheart even knowing she wouldn't live long had been a tragic and wonderful gesture, as far as the world was concerned.

As far as poor Grant was concerned, it had just been life and love. In the end, he had suffered a hell of a lot. But that's what he was famous for. Being true-blue to a woman who was long gone.

No one had asked if he wanted to get famous, of course. It had been one of the last things Grant wanted. Second only to his wife dying.

Which had thrown Grant right back into the headlines. Wyatt was sure that made hooking up…complicated.

Wyatt Dodge did not like complicated. It was just one of the many reasons that he was not going to follow the road his attraction to Lindy wanted to take him down. Nope. And hell no.

Anyway, getting things off the ground with Get Out of Dodge was too important.

If he succeeded, then no one would ever have to know the reason why.

And that was the ideal situation.

"I appreciate you being here," Wyatt said. "I hope you know that."

"I do. But, it's not like I had anything truly amazing that I was leaving behind. A job at the power company for little more than a decade…sure. The retirement was going to be good…" Grant shook his head. "How long can you possibly live for the future? I mean, socking away money, punching a time card all to invest in years you might never even see? What the hell is the point of that? Can you answer me that, Wyatt?"

Wyatt rubbed his chin. "I've been riding bulls for the last…fifteen years? I am not the person to ask about thinking ahead. If I had been thinking ahead I never would have done that."

His spine sure would've thanked him, and unlike so many others, he had never even sustained a serious injury. He was lucky. Lucky as hell. The guys that ended up getting seriously trampled often never walked in a straight line again. Wyatt had gotten out more or less intact. Just a couple of scars. Even still, at thirty-five his body had taken the kind of beating most guys his age couldn't imagine.

"I'm glad to be here," he said. "That's what I meant by the speech. That's all."

"I'm glad, too," Wyatt responded.

Grant turned and walked away, leaving Wyatt standing there, looking around the property. It was all coming together nicely. The landscape in front of the main house, the gravel paths that led between the buildings, raked clean and neat.

Wyatt hadn't taken anything this seriously for the past twenty years.

The cabins had been restored and redecorated, and he was actively working on finding a cook who could provide something more than basic food.

He had to reach his goal of getting the ranch to full occupancy by the end of the summer, and he had to reach total financial solvency in the following year. Otherwise, he was going to fail at Quinn Dodge's ultimatum.

And that meant his father was going to sell the ranch.

That was the thing his siblings didn't know. Wyatt wasn't the owner of the property.

It was still Quinn's. And unless Wyatt succeeded in a very short amount of time, it wasn't going to be in the Dodge family anymore. Instead, Get Out of Dodge would be nothing more than a stack of cash divided between the siblings, and Wyatt couldn't allow that.

He knew that his father expected him to screw up.

Wyatt was determined that he wouldn't.

There was no other option.

Of all the reasons not to sleep with Lindy Parker, that was the best one.

He didn't need her as a distraction, he didn't need her as a friend and he sure as hell didn't need her as a lover. He needed her as an ally.

Because if he didn't have that, he might lose.

And if there was one thing Wyatt Dodge did not do, it was lose.

CHAPTER TWO

LINDY'S COMPUTER MADE its special email chiming sound and she bent down to look.

Wyatt Dodge.

Her heart slammed against her sternum like a hammer going down on iron.

She braced herself. She didn't know for what, except that obviously if he was actually emailing her now after making a big deal out of the fact that he didn't need to email her, he was being an ass. That much she was certain of.

She clicked. Surprisingly, it was a comprehensive commentary on the brochures that she had sent.

"Leave it to you to be on topic when I expect you to be an asshole." She muttered to herself as she straightened, then she turned and startled when she saw her brother Dane's form filling the doorway.

"Talking to yourself?"

"I wasn't talking to *you*." She thought about pulling him in for a hug. Then didn't. They weren't really a hugging kind of family. Sometimes she wished they were. But she didn't know how to change it now. "I didn't think I was going to see you until September."

"I was heading up from Red Bluff, going to an event in George, Washington. This is a little out of my way, but I figured that I would stop in for a bit."

It was difficult to believe sometimes that Dane was her little brother. He towered over her by at least a foot. Broad-shouldered, rugged and with the kind of smile that made women weak in the knees. She was proud of him. And always a little bit nervous about just how he used his good looks and charm.

He was a bull rider.

All adrenaline, here and now and no thought for the future. Constantly living for the action, never worrying about the reaction.

But she loved him.

They'd had it rough growing up. Their dad had been in their lives only intermittently until he'd finally left for good, their mom making it impossible for them to have a relationship with him. Not—she supposed—that he'd tried that hard to change it.

They'd grown up in a single-wide trailer, a small space for three people, and yet Lindy had always felt like there were walls between them. Their mom was a proud woman. So proud she could hardly bend down to give her children a hug.

Distance. That was what she and Dane had both learned, and learned well. To rely on no one but themselves.

"How long are you going to be here?" she asked.

"The rodeo starts in two days. So really, I need to get out of here tomorrow. I don't want to hassle with the traffic. Lots of people are going to be coming in on the highway."

"This is one of the big ones, isn't it?"

"Yep," he said.

"Do you have any breaks after this?"

"I've got a few small events down South, just things

to build up points. But there's some downtime in July, before the big stuff. Sisters, Pendleton and Vegas."

"I have a feeling that Wyatt is going to ask if you want to do some things over our Fourth of July event that we're planning. I don't actually know if he's going to have you ride bulls."

"Well, I'm not going to barrel race," Dane said, as if that was the most ridiculous thing in the entire world.

"I'd pay to see that," she said.

"It's for girls," he said.

"Right," Lindy shot back, crossing her arms. "And mostly, you're afraid that you'd get beaten."

"Hell yeah," he said. "You need precision for that. A connection with your horse. Do you know what you need to ride bulls? Big balls and the subtlety of a blunt instrument."

Lindy knew that you needed more than that, particularly to get where Dane had gotten in life. Where Damien had helped him get. She resisted asking about that. Asking about Damien. She knew that he was still around, managing various aspects of different riders' careers. But not Dane's.

The minute that Dane had found out about Damien's infidelity, Dane had gone scorched-earth-no-survivors on his brother-in-law.

In fact, he had done what he could to break off Damien's relationship with the professional association. He hadn't been entirely successful, but she knew that he had convinced several riders to start working with outside PR people and refuse to work with Damien.

Whatever she thought about her brother's day-to-day morality, he had come through for her in the end. The two of them against the world.

"So, basically you're crashing on my couch over-night?" There would be no crashing on her couch. She lived in a gigantic house all by herself. There were more than enough bedrooms for Dane to have his pick.

In point of fact, she would be surprised if he ended up spending the night at her place. It was more likely that he would end up in the Gold Valley Saloon picking up a new conquest.

"That's about the size of it," he said.

"You know you're always welcome."

She sighed heavily, and then lifted her hands above her head, locking them together and flexing them back-ward, stretching herself upward from the center of her chest, drawing her shoulder blades down and trying to release some of the tension in her body.

"I think you're doing too much," Dane commented, following her out of her office and into the main dining room of Grassroots Winery.

Over the past couple of years Lindy had overhauled the facility and opened a satellite tasting room in the town of Copper Ridge.

The dining room—where they hosted lunches, wed-dings, parties and pretty much anything else—was a converted barn that had been on the property for years, now carefully crafted into a rustic and elegant setting.

They had a few guests, sitting and eating cheese plat-ters while drinking wine flights and visiting.

The vast, wooden chandeliers that hung down at the center of the high, arched ceiling were blazing with a golden glow, bathing the room in soft lighting.

It was beautiful. Perfect.

Hers.

The kind of thing she never could have imagined when

she was a girl growing up in a Gold Valley trailer park on the dying edge of town.

A place with more empty buildings than businesses.

Her former sister-in-law, turned sister by choice, Sabrina Donnelly was standing behind the counter scribbling on an order form.

She and Sabrina had always had a lot in common. From the moment they'd met, Lindy felt like she'd found the sister of her heart. While her former mother-in-law and father-in-law had given her a less than welcoming reception into the family, Sabrina had been warm and open.

Of course, that had been due in part to the fact that Sabrina had been estranged from her father—over something to do with Liam Donnelly.

Liam Donnelly who now, finally, some fourteen years later, was Sabrina's husband.

"Hey, Sabrina," Dane said.

Sabrina looked up, smiling. "Hi yourself." Then, her eyes fell to Lindy, and Lindy must have been telegraphing something because Sabrina's expression changed to one of concern. "Are you okay?"

"I'm fine."

"She's doing too much," Dane said.

"I am not *doing too much*."

She was doing things, yes. Making changes. But they were all good, and she was happy with them.

It was likely that if she looked taxed it was because her mind kept going over and over the fact that Wyatt had finally sent her an email after resolutely ignoring her emails. And that it was clearly connected to the conversation they'd had yesterday.

But there was nothing she could do about any of that.

She had the exact amount of things to do that had to be done, and she had to deal with Wyatt Dodge.

All of that was regrettable in some form or another, but it was better than being impoverished. Better than being married to a man who was sleeping with other women behind her back.

All things considered, life was great.

It didn't mean that her muscles weren't tired and her neck wasn't stiff, but still.

"I know that she is," Sabrina said. "But, this looked like something might be going on in addition to that."

"Nothing is going on," she said.

Sabrina and Dane continued to stare at her.

"There isn't," she said, defensively. "I mean I'm navigating the Wyatt Dodge situation, but other than that…"

"What Wyatt Dodge situation?" Dane asked.

"The one I mentioned to you earlier," she explained. "You know. Rodeo events and all the other various crap he's trying to add to our event. That in and of itself is a whole thing. That's what I meant by that."

"Is he giving you a hard time?" Dane asked.

"Does he ever *not* give someone a hard time?"

Dane smiled. "Not really. That's kind of his thing."

"Well, good to know that I'm not special." Those words seemed to echo inside of her, reverberating and lingering and in general just not going away.

She seemed to be the only one who noticed that, however, which was welcome. She didn't want anyone studying her too closely. Didn't want anyone trying to get a read on her thoughts. Or her feelings.

She was violently opposed to most of the thoughts and feelings she had surrounding Wyatt Dodge that didn't involve pushing his head through a wall. And sadly, those thoughts and feelings existed.

She had always prided herself on her ability to hold two thoughts in her head at one time. She was a dreamer, and she was a pragmatist. She had experienced a life of poverty, and a life of plenty, and she had always imagined those things had given her the capacity to understand that reality was complex.

She was a lot less self-congratulatory about the fact that she found Wyatt simultaneously infuriating and sexually compelling.

And she was downright ashamed of the fact that there seemed to be a part of her that had hoped that Wyatt's teasing was something reserved just for her.

She knew better than that. Knew better than to want that. Particularly from someone she didn't even like.

As if your judgment when it comes to men is good enough to consider liking them a decent litmus test?

She gritted her teeth. "Anyway. Nothing out of the ordinary. I mean, at least, nothing out of the ordinary in terms of the last couple of years. Expansion is..." She lifted her hand and rolled her wrist in a physical indication of the march of time. "Expansion. The future."

"Right," Dane said, grabbing hold of her hand and shaking it gently before drawing it downward. "But if you work yourself into an early grave you don't get to enjoy that future."

"I am not about to be lectured on longevity by a bull rider."

Dane opened his mouth to say something smart-ass, no doubt, and was stopped by a slamming door coming from the back room of the converted barn.

Lindy didn't have to ask to know who it was. "Are you all right, Bea?"

"Fine," came the cheerful reply.

Lindy's other former sister-in-law, Beatrix Leighton—usually called Bea—came in to the room, breathless and smiling. That smile only got bigger when she saw Dane standing there.

"I didn't know you were coming to town," she said, her cheeks turning an extremely obvious shade of pink.

Dane, for his part, seemed oblivious to the pinkness of Bea's cheeks. Which was just as well. Bea was one of the most caring, good-natured people Lindy had ever met. She'd been thirteen when Damien and Lindy had gotten married, and just like Sabrina, she felt like a sister to Lindy.

When the dust had settled, and the ink had dried on the divorce papers, there was a reason Sabrina and Bea had stayed loyal to her. They were family by choice.

Sadly, Bea didn't have familial feelings for Dane. Though, Lindy knew Dane only had brotherly feelings for Bea.

Dane was a player. He was all smiles and easy banter on the outside, but beneath that he was like Lindy. A little bit hardened by life. A little bit cynical.

Bea didn't have a cynical bone in her body.

"Just for the night," he said.

"We should do something," Bea said, nodding.

"Should we?" Dane asked.

"I'm tired," Lindy said.

Bea looked at her with large eyes. "Lindy," she said, "Dane's here."

"Yes," Lindy responded. "I had noticed. He's kind of difficult to miss."

"That doesn't sound like a compliment, Lin," he said.

"It wasn't."

"I can see if Liam wants to go out tonight," Sabrina said.

Sabrina's husband was an integral part of managing the business of the tasting room in Copper Ridge, and he was also a rancher, working the Donnelly family ranch, the Laughing Irish. Lindy would be surprised if he had any more energy to go out than she did.

"I'm going to be in Gold Valley," Bea put in. "I'm starting up work at Valley Veterinary with Kaylee Capshaw."

Valley Veterinary was the clinic that Wyatt's brother owned along with his best friend turned fiancée. She had generously offered a job to Bea, who was forever bringing small animals in need of tending back to the winery, much to Lindy's chagrin. This was going to be a much better way for Bea to channel her bleeding heart, as far as Lindy was concerned.

It would give her something to focus on, a life away from the winery. Bea might be part of the same family as Lindy's ex-husband, they might have the same genes, but Bea was not cut from the same cloth.

Sabrina was different, but she did have some of that Leighton reserve. Bea didn't seem to have it at all. She was open, energetic and willing to forge paths where most people would see none. Her optimism was almost boundless, and that was one of the things that made Lindy worry on her behalf.

Especially when it came to her very obvious crush on Lindy's brother.

Just another reason Bea needed to get out and get a life beyond Grassroots.

"He might not want to come out that far," Sabrina said. "But I will see."

"I'm game." Dane smiled.

"Me too," Lindy added quickly, before she could stop herself. But honestly, she was not going to send Dane and Bea out to a bar together.

Dane would end up hooking up with some random woman, and Bea would just sit there in the corner by herself like one of the wounded raccoons she often rescued from desolate roadsides.

Lindy could not stomach that.

Bea would grow out of her crush naturally. She didn't need it bludgeoned to death in a small-town bar with an audience of gossips ready to spread it around like wildfire through pine trees.

"Great," Dane said. "I'll go toss my stuff in the house. Then we can head over to the bar after work."

"Work for the rest of us," she pointed out. "Some of us here never got real jobs."

"Hey," Dane said. "If you can get work being a cowboy, I highly recommend it."

He winked and walked out of the room, and Lindy couldn't help but notice the way that Bea's eyes followed his every move. Okay, that gave her something else to worry about at least. She didn't have to think about her issues with the upcoming barbecue and all the work that there was left to do as long as she focused on being a buffer between her poor, lovelorn sister-in-law and her brother.

One thing was for sure, it was a welcome change from thinking about Wyatt Dodge.

CHAPTER THREE

WYATT NEEDED A stiff drink and some meaningless sex.
There were a couple of barriers to the sex. There was
the fact that his younger sister, Jamie, had accompanied
him to Gold Valley Saloon tonight. There was the fact
that his brother Grant had come along as well. And then,
there was the lingering issue of the fact that he couldn't
get one particular woman off his mind.

There were no barriers to the stiff drink, however,
and he was headed right that way.

Jamie and Grant went to claim a table, but Wyatt
wasted no time heading straight over to the bar.

"Laz," he said, signaling the owner of the bar. "I need
a drink."

"Feeling picky about what?"

"I'd say it's your choice, but you'd pick something
aged and expensive. I just need something strong enough
to burn the day off."

"Cheap swill it is," Laz said smiling, turning and
grabbing hold of a bottle of whiskey and pouring Wyatt
a measure of it.

He slid it down the scarred countertop and Wyatt
caught hold of it, tipping his hat before lifting it to his
lips. "Put it on my tab," he said.

"Will do," Laz responded.

Wyatt turned and surveyed the room, leaning back

against the bar for a moment as he did so. It was pretty empty now, considering it was early in the evening. But as the night wore on it would fill with people who were looking for the exact same thing he was.

All day long on the streets of Gold Valley, you could walk down the sidewalk and run into friends. Neighbors. They would ask you how your day went, and he would say good. And all along you would both continue with smiles pasted onto your face.

But in the saloon, when darkness descended on the cheerful streets, that was when you met your neighbors for honest conversation. That was when they finally wore their cares on their faces while they tried to drink them away.

Here, there was honesty. Here, there was alcohol, and a good game of darts.

Wyatt preferred it to daytime small talk every time.

He was something of a bar aficionado. Having been to a great many towns, large and small, in his travels with the rodeo, he had been exposed to a whole lot of different scenery. A whole lot of different people.

And it was in his experience that the bars were the great equalizer. That was where everyone went. Young, old, rich, poor. To celebrate, to commiserate.

That was where, in essence, everyone and everyplace was the same.

He looked down into the whiskey glass. "Damn," he commented. "This is good stuff."

If he was feeling philosophical already, it had to be pretty strong.

He pushed away from the bar and walked over to the table where his siblings were waiting.

"You didn't get a drink for me?" Grant asked.

"I don't know how the hell much you had to drink today," Wyatt returned. "I'm not enabling you."

"I don't drink too much," Grant said, but they both knew that wasn't true.

Wyatt knew for a fact that his brother had to have a drink every night before he went to bed, or he couldn't sleep. But that was one of those things they didn't discuss. At least not at length. They made jokes about it, they could mention it in passing. But they could never get into what it actually meant.

The Dodges were a close family, but it was a stretch to call them emotionally well-adjusted.

"You know I haven't had too much to drink today," Jamie said, leaning back in her chair and crossing her arms.

"Yeah, I also pay you enough that you can go get your own."

Jamie scowled. Then she sat up, planting both booted feet on the ground, pushing herself into a standing position. "All right. I'm going to get a drink."

Grant stared at her. She stared back. And then she sighed heavily. "What do you want?"

"Whiskey," he responded.

"Of course." She shook her head, her dark ponytail swinging with the motion, and then she headed over toward the bar.

A few of the men sitting at tables around them followed her movements, and Wyatt was sure to give them his deadliest glare. Jamie was twenty-four, certainly old enough to have her own life and date and all of that. But age had nothing to do with the fact that none of the assholes in this bar—hell, none of the cowboys in this town—were good enough for his younger sister.

Jamie, for her part, seemed oblivious. That suited him just fine.

"So," Grant said, leveling his dark gaze on Wyatt. "What crawled up your ass and died?"

"Excuse me?"

"You're in a crappy mood."

"I don't think that's true," Wyatt said, folding his arms over his chest.

He was conscious of the fact that he was mimicking his sister's body language from a moment ago.

"I do," Grant said.

"Right. And I'm supposed to take commentary on my mood from a guy who has been in a crappy mood for the past decade?"

"I wasn't criticizing. I was just asking."

"Just got a lot going on," he said. Because he wasn't going to say that he was stressing out about whether or not he was going to be able to fulfill their father's directive.

That he was afraid he was going to let them all down. That Jamie was going to end up out of work and Grant was going to have left his boring but long-running career at the power company for nothing.

It was easy for him to convince himself that his father wouldn't actually sell the ranch. Because the fact of the matter was, Quinn Dodge was a hard-ass, but he was a hard-ass who loved his kids.

That was the conclusion that Wyatt would come to if it were any of his other siblings in his position.

But it wasn't Grant. It wasn't Jamie. It wasn't Bennett.

It was Wyatt Dodge spearheading this project. And deep down he had a feeling that his father might just let him fail. Not just himself, but his brothers and his sister.

That was something he could never explain to Grant. Nobody else had the relationship with Quinn that Wyatt had. And it was his own damn fault. It was a situation he created. A relationship that he'd earned.

He couldn't even be pissed about it.

Except he was.

"Oh," Grant said, looking somewhere past Wyatt.

"What?" Wyatt shifted in his chair.

"She's here."

Wyatt didn't have to ask who. He froze in his chair, his jaw hardening. He felt like...he felt like he was in damned high school, and he resented that. His younger brother telling him not to look. And him resolutely not looking.

To hell with that.

He lifted his glass and swallowed it down in one gulp. "I'll be back."

He pushed away from the table and stood, turning and seeing Lindy standing there. And it was like someone had put their fist through his stomach, grabbed hold of his internal organs and twisted hard.

It reminded him of that first time. But then, every time he saw her it reminded him of the first time.

He gritted his teeth and began walking toward her. And he knew the moment she saw him. Her eyes didn't meet his, no. And she very resolutely did not look in his direction. But she knew that he was there. He could see it. In the way that her shoulders suddenly went stiff, in the way that her whole body got ramrod straight. To the casual observer it might look like she simply had a neutral expression on her face. One that hadn't changed in the past ten seconds. But he was not a casual observer.

No, her face had changed too. There was a firmness to

the corners of her mouth. Intent. The absence of a smile or frown, totally and completely purposeful.

"You didn't respond to my email," he said. "I'm wounded."

She tilted her head slightly, looking up at him. Then, she faked surprise. As if she truly hadn't realized he was there until right then.

That shouldn't get him hot. Nothing about her should get him hot. But everything did. Everything damn well did.

"Sorry. Were you expecting a same-day response? I didn't think that you engaged with such newfangled technology all that often."

"Nice to see you too."

"Right."

He grinned. "Most people would say that it was also nice to see me. That's manners, Melinda."

The light behind her eyes indicated that she wanted very much to tear his throat out. But her expression betrayed that not at all. "We didn't go over how to handle infuriating cowboys in deportment."

She hated it when he called her Melinda. He knew that. He also loved saying it. Because no one else did. It put him in the mind of other things he might do to her that no one else was currently doing.

Unless he had the read of it wrong. Maybe she had a different lover every night. It was possible, for all he knew.

Just because his balls were all bound up in wanting her, didn't mean her body was similarly bound up in wanting him.

"Now that's a shame," he said. "How are you supposed to go on if you don't know whether or not you're supposed to hold your pinkie out when you tell me to go fuck myself."

"Oh, I know which finger to hold up when I tell you that, Wyatt Dodge. Don't you worry about that."

"What brings you out here tonight?"

A moment later, his question was answered when in came her brother, and a friend of his from the rodeo, Dane Parker. Followed by her former sister-in-law Beatrix Leighton.

"They were parking," Lindy said, by way of explanation. "I mean. They were parking the truck. They weren't out parking."

That made him think of all the things he might be able to accomplish if Lindy went parking with him.

Yet again, he felt like he was back in high school.

He really did resent that.

"Dane," he said, reaching around Lindy to offer his hand to the other man. "Didn't know you were going to be in town."

"I live to be a surprise. Lindy mentioned that you might have a job for me coming up in a few weeks."

"If by job you mean being unpaid entertainment for a mob of people. Yes."

"For the big launch event for Get Out of Dodge?" Dane asked.

"Yes. But, it benefits Grassroots Winery too," Wyatt put in. "You know, since we have such a cozy partnership now."

Lindy's perfectly placid expression slipped. Just for a moment. "Right. I guess we'd better go find a table."

"There's one right next to us," he said, because the hell if he was going to let her avoid him. The hell if he was going to sit in the same bar as her and let her pretend he wasn't here. The hell he was going to spend all night trying not to look over at her.

"Thanks," Bea said, her tone bright. Dane thanked him too, both of them clearly oblivious to the fact that Lindy wanted to scream.

Wyatt led the way back over to his table, and he ignored Grant's assessing gaze. It didn't escape Wyatt's notice that Lindy took the seat at the table that put her farthest away from him.

A moment later Jamie reappeared, smiling broadly when she saw the new additions. "Bea," she said, sliding her chair over slightly and putting herself next to her. "Good to see you."

It surprised Wyatt that Bea and Jamie were friends. Though, they were the same age. Just about. But still, Bea was softer, fine-boned and possessing the femininity of a vaguely feral fairy. Jamie was tall, no-nonsense and, as far as Wyatt knew, resolutely allergic to dresses.

Bea started talking with broad hand gestures about some of the animals she had cared for at the clinic today, and suddenly Wyatt understood the connection. Animals. Jamie had practically been born in the saddle. Horses were her passion. And Bea seemed to like anything with four legs.

"I'm going to get a drink," Lindy said.

"I'll go with you," he said.

He ignored the look earned from Grant as he and Lindy walked toward the bar.

"Let me ask you a question," Lindy said. "Do you try to get on my nerves?"

"To be perfectly honest with you, angel, I don't have to try. You make it too easy."

"So you were that boy."

"What boy?" he asked, as the two of them sidled up to the bar. Lindy pressed her delicate hands down on that scarred wooden countertop, and he pressed his down alongside hers.

For a moment, all he could do was stare at the contrast the two of them made. Her smooth hands, with long, fine-boned fingers, not a single scar to be seen. His own, weathered, with more than a few chunks taken from them.

If he were to take hold of her, his hand would cover hers entirely.

If he were to pull her up against his body, the contrast would be much the same. Soft. Hard. Smooth. Weathered.

"The one that pulled pigtails," she said, not looking at him when she spoke.

Something stirred inside of him, and he just couldn't stop himself from saying what he said next. "I still pull pigtails," he said. "If the lady asks me nicely."

She looked at him, a cautious expression in her blue eyes. Like she was about to give the answer to a math problem she'd done in her head, and wasn't entirely certain of. "I doubt that's ever happened."

"Sure it has." He grinned and waited. For her to get mad. For her to blush. Something.

Except, now he was going to end up thinking about that for far too long. Usually, she met him barb for barb. But this particular innuendo didn't seem to resonate. Maybe that was because she wasn't standing there mired in sexual tension. Maybe it was because she didn't think of him that way.

But it might just speak to other things. Inexperience he wouldn't have thought a woman who'd been married for a decade could possibly have.

That forced him to wonder. To wonder about her marriage, which he shouldn't do. Especially because she had been married to a man that he considered a casual friend.

"Whatever, Wyatt. I want a drink, not more of your inane commentary." She turned away from him, clearly frustrated by that interaction. Maybe because she hadn't managed to verbally maneuver her way to the top of it. "Hi, Laz," she said as the bartender approached them. "I'd like an IPA."

"An IPA," he said. "Wow."

"Do you have a commentary on my choice of beer?" she asked as Laz turned and retrieved a bottle for her.

"I made my commentary." He turned his attention to the bartender. "I'll have whatever you've got on tap that isn't an IPA."

"I imagine you have opinions on the masculinity of that beer?"

"Not particularly. I didn't ever figure beer had a gender."

"You know what I mean," she said.

"I just think it's bad beer. And if I wanted to lick a pine tree I would."

"I would almost pay good money to watch you do a wine tasting."

"Why is that?"

"Because I imagine that your palate is as unsophisticated as the rest of you."

He chuckled. "And I imagine you think that's an insult. But, in order for me to feel insulted by that I would have to care."

"Thank you," she said to Laz, ignoring him completely.

"You can put her terrible drink on my tab too," Wyatt said, turning away from the bar.

"Don't put my drink on your tab," Lindy said. "Don't put my drink on his tab," she said to Laz.

"Put the drink on my tab," Wyatt reiterated.

"I'll pay for the drink if you don't knock it off," Laz said.

"I can pay for the drink," Lindy said, through gritted teeth. "Put his drink on my tab."

"This isn't a contest," he said.

"I'm not a charity case," Lindy said. "We are in a business partnership."

"I wasn't treating you like a charity case. I was just going to pay for your drink."

She lifted her chin, her expression defiant. "And I don't need you to."

"I'm not really sure why you're intent on making all of this a battle. We're working together, remember?"

"I know," she said, but she sounded slightly more subdued than she had a moment ago.

"I swear, I enjoy getting on your nerves, but I'm not actively trying to start a fight with you."

She looked skeptical. "Is there a difference?"

"Yes. I like to tease you. I don't actually want to make it so the two of us can't have a conversation."

"I don't like to be teased," she said, looking at him from beneath blond lashes.

She looked younger right then. He didn't know why. It made him want to be nicer. To try to be a little bit more sincere.

"That's going to be a problem," he said. "Because I am what I am."

"I didn't sign on to be teased," she said. "I just want to make this work."

The two of them stepped away from the bar, but didn't

head back to the tables. "So let me ask you this," he said, a thought occurring to him for the first time. "Did you approach me to make this partnership to get back at Damien?"

Her expression turned mulish. "Why would you think that?"

"Because. He's my friend. You're his ex-wife."

"Do you really consider him a friend?"

Wyatt shrugged. "I'll be honest with you, I haven't talked to him in a couple of months. I'm not part of the rodeo circuit anymore, so we're not really running in the same circles. Some people you hang out with mostly because of the proximity. Not because you choose to. And I'd be lying if I said his behavior during the end of your marriage didn't impact my opinion of him."

She blinked. "Really?"

"Yes. What he did was a jerk move."

She frowned. "I wouldn't have thought you would care much either way."

"Turns out I do." He let out slow breath. "Fact of the matter is, I've never done commitment. But hey, maybe that's because I know myself well enough to know I'm not cut out for it. I figure if a man makes vows he ought to keep them."

"So, you think he's a jerk?" she asked, her fingers shifting over the bottle of beer, making him think of what it would be like to have those fingers on him.

"Oh, honey, I *know* he's a jerk," Wyatt said.

"Well, that's mildly placating, I have to say."

"I'm a lot of things, Lindy," he said, not using her full name, seeking as much of a truce as they could continue to have. "But I'm a man of my word. That means I don't give it very often. But a man only has his word, as far as

I'm concerned, when all is said and done. If I can't promise something, I don't. That means I have no respect for
a man who can't do the same."

She narrowed her eyes, her blue gaze roaming over his
face as if she was seeing him for the first time. "I value
that in a business partner. It has to be said."

"Good. I can't promise that I'm not going to irritate
you after this, you understand that, right?"

"Now you're forcing me to respect that. Since you're
refusing to say something just to placate me, and you're
standing by that honesty thing." She sighed, as if she
was intensely aggrieved. "But, I guess I have to accept
that, don't I?"

"You don't have to. But it would make things easier."

"Fine. Anyway, thank you for your comments on the
brochures."

"I still don't really care about the brochures."

"If you want then I can go ahead without asking you
for your opinion on things like design."

"I'd kind of like that," he said, then he frowned. "But
I don't want you to feel like it's all on you either."

The crease between her brows relaxed, and he realized this might be the first time he had ever seen her
without it. "Really?"

"You're doing a hell of a lot, Lindy. It doesn't seem
right to put it all on you."

"You're the one basically reopening his business right
now. The winery has been slowly expanding, but I've
never had to do a full relaunch. I think right now your
plate is probably a little bit fuller than mine."

"Okay. We can't be too nice to each other either. I
don't like it."

She smiled. A small smile, just the corners of her

mouth turning slightly upward, but he would take it. "I'm sure we'll relapse eventually."

"Fair enough. Any other business stuff you want to cover?"

She tapped the side of that beer bottle, his eyes drawn again to the way she held on to the slender neck. His blood burned in his veins.

"I imagine that much like I had you take a few bottles of wine so that you had some idea of the product you were going to be pushing on your willing victims, I'm going to need to have some idea of the trail rides happening at the winery. Do you think that Jamie could... Do you think she would mind taking me out?"

"I'm sure she wouldn't mind at all," Wyatt said. In fact, he had a feeling Jamie would love nothing more.

"Okay. Maybe we could set something up in the next week, then?"

"Okay."

"I'm not a very experienced rider."

Those words were like the burn of a match being struck against his skin, a flame put to his already heated blood.

"Is that so?"

"No. I haven't... I haven't been on a horse in years."

He clenched his teeth. "I don't think it's a very challenging ride."

"Good," she said, looking relieved.

"We should head back over," he said, jerking his head in the direction of the tables where Bea and Jamie were still talking, and Grant was looking sullen.

"Right," she said.

Reflexively, he reached out and pressed his fingers to her forearm, as if to guide her back toward the table.

And that was a big mistake.

The press of his fingertips against that soft, bare skin of her arm was like an explosion.

He jerked his hand back, as if he'd been burned. Because he felt sure that he had been.

Her gaze flew to his, something sharp in them now. Worse, he could see the heat that was still burning his fingertips reflected there.

She wasn't unaffected by him. Not at all.

"Before we go back over there," she said quickly. "Grant isn't interested in dating again, is he?"

CHAPTER FOUR

SHE WAS AS stupid as she was transparent. She didn't care if Grant wanted to date again. She wasn't interested in Grant like that at all. But she had to do something to... something. To diffuse that very obvious moment that had just happened between herself and Wyatt.

She didn't like this. Not at all.

She didn't like feeling like she didn't have the upper hand on a social situation. Didn't like feeling as if everything around her was so far beyond her she could never reach it.

That was her entire experience in the early days of dating Damien and being his wife. Feeling like she had just walked into the room in the middle of a conversation and had to spend every moment thereafter playing catch-up.

She hated that feeling. More than anything.

Well, that wasn't true. Actually, she hated finding out that her husband had been having an affair for years and years even more. Although, it was a different side of the same coin. Being out of the loop. Being ignorant. Being small.

Somehow less than everyone that surrounded her.

Wyatt didn't make her feel like she was *less*, but he made her feel something. And she didn't like it.

She'd gotten her balance in a small sense when she had demanded that Laz put Wyatt's drink on her tab.

But then, he had touched her.

He had touched her, and she hadn't been able to disguise her response to it. She could see it in his eyes. That he thought he knew exactly what she felt. And even if it was true, even if he did, she was not going to let him have that.

She enjoyed this. That hesitation in his eyes. The tightening in his jaw. The fact that she had him on his back foot. Yeah, she liked that a lot better than feeling like she was on hers.

He tilted his head back. "Grant, huh?"

"He seems like a nice guy. Good-looking too."

"Right." His teeth were clenched so tight she'd be surprised if he didn't chip one. Maybe that shouldn't satisfy her. But it did.

"Just wondering if you have the inside track on that." She tried to look both cool and interested at the same time.

He lifted a brow. "I expect you could ask him yourself."

"Oh, I expect I could." She kept her tone light but steady. She had a feeling it was that lightness that had him caught so off guard.

"Then why ask me?" He was trying to sound casual too. Unlike her, he was failing.

"Everyone could use a good wingman, Wyatt. If you wanted to be mine, I would hardly say no." She smiled, and he didn't.

"I'll pass."

She lifted her shoulder. "Suit yourself. But, I would have returned the favor."

"Wingmen are for amateurs, honey," he said. "I've never needed one yet."

He walked away from her, heading back over to their shared corner of the saloon. She was captivated watching him. Even angry at him. Even with him angry at her.

Those broad shoulders, narrow waist. His ass in those jeans.

She didn't know who she was when she looked at him. The things she noticed. What it made her want.

She stood for a moment and took a breath trying to get a hold of herself. It was only then that she realized her hands were shaking. Dammit.

She crossed the room, making her way back over to the table. "Why don't you sit next to Grant?" Wyatt asked, giving her an evil smirk from his position in his chair.

And that made her suspect that he didn't believe her at all. Asshole.

"Sure," she said, easily, casually. She took a seat next to Grant. "We haven't had a chance to talk much," she said, turning to the other man.

Grant was looking at her, somewhat blandly, and she felt a small twinge of guilt. She wasn't interested in him. She didn't want him to think she was. Not when she wasn't going to actually follow up.

That was a new low. Using a widowed man as a pawn in her control game.

But, his extreme and apparent lack of interest made her feel less guilty immediately.

Somehow, they stumbled through the rest of the evening making conversation. And she could feel Wyatt's eyes on her the entire time. But she refused to look back at him.

WYATT WAS IN a foul mood by the time he got home. It was late, and he was slightly drunk. He, Grant and Jamie had all had a bit too much to drink to drive home, and they'd had to call on Bennett to come and pick them up. Bennett had muttered about their poor planning, and the fact that he'd had to leave his fiancée and home to come bail his asshole siblings out because they hadn't chosen a designated driver.

Wyatt had *not* told him about the fact that the three of them had discussed using Bennett as a designated driver before they had gone out for the evening. The fact of the matter was, they had known that their more responsible brother would be on hand to deal with them.

Hell, the man had the benefit of going home to his fiancée and son every day after work. He could deal with his siblings who were single and alone.

Not that Wyatt had ever felt like marriage and kids were the goal for him.

Still, he was in a bad mood, and he wasn't supposed to be. A night of drinking had been intended to cure his ills, not add to them. But that encounter with Lindy, her asking about Grant, yeah, that had all added some ills.

Then, the phone rang.

"Dad," he said, doing his best to keep the whiskey slur out of his voice. "You know it's midnight, right?"

"I know," his father responded.

"To what do I owe the pleasure?"

"Freda and I were on the road all day. This is the first time I've had a chance to call."

He also had a feeling that his father was standing outside of their camper. That he had waited until Freda had gone to sleep, because Wyatt's stepmother would undoubtedly not approve at all of the situation.

The woman his father had married was one of the kindest people Wyatt had ever met. She had embraced Quinn Dodge's kids like they were her own.

When Bennett's son that he hadn't known he'd had had shown up out of the blue, she embraced him as a grandson. Not that Quinn hadn't, it was just that it never failed to amaze Wyatt that this woman who hadn't raised them treated them like she had.

That she was in many ways much easier than Quinn never would be.

But then, maybe that was part of it. She didn't know him. Not really.

His father did.

"Right. But, it's not like you called to say good night."

"You know I didn't," Quinn said, his tone firm but gentle. "I called to check on the project."

"Right. The ranch. The one that you're going to sell out from underneath me if I don't get my stuff together."

"It's not like that. Ranching is hard business, Wyatt. I barely kept our heads above water all those years. Hell, if it weren't for the money you earned riding in the rodeo we would have gone under. You know that."

Yeah, his rodeo money. Money that landed somewhere between trying to atone for a sin he wasn't sure he was sorry for and a big middle finger. His dad had wanted him to stand on his own, to get on without support… and the money had been nice proof that he'd gone and done that. "I know. But doesn't that make the place even more mine?"

"It makes you even more invested, sure. Invested in pouring money into a pit. I've done it for a lot of years. I don't want the same thing for you, unless it looks like it will be more than a pit. The problem with ranching is it gets under your skin. You get addicted to it. You can't let it go even when you should."

"Right. I'm sure that's it," Wyatt said. "You being concerned that I'll take another hit of this dusty brand of heroin we call being a cowboy."

His head was starting to hurt and his mood was just getting meaner. They'd had this talk at least four times, and Wyatt didn't like it any more now than he had the first time.

"You can be angry at me if you want," Quinn said, "but that doesn't change the reality of the situation. If you can get it off to a good start, then I'm more than happy to let it go without interfering. But take it from someone who spent his whole life working that land. It's not that easy. You think it is, because you managed to skip off and make money as a performing cowboy, Wyatt, but being a real cowboy is not that easy. And it's not that fun. Grant's been through enough. Jamie's been through enough. If we can't get it together to save the place… We can't get it together."

Wyatt gritted his teeth. "There's no *we*," he said. "We're not in this together. We—you and me—we're working against each other."

"That's where you're wrong," Quinn said, his voice rough. "Whatever you think, I'm on your team. I know it didn't feel like it when you were a kid, getting his butt whupped for letting the cows out and causing trouble. I know it didn't feel like it when you were in high school and I grounded your ass for sneaking out. But this is the same."

Right. A team. A team where Wyatt had been left all on his own.

Be a man.

As if that was advice. As if that was enough.

He supposed neither of them were in the mood to discuss why Wyatt had left home in the first place. Not in the mood to talk about the first time his father had fallen in love after Wyatt's mother's death and had brought home a woman he'd intended to marry.

A woman who had ended up in Wyatt's bed.

They were *never* in the mood for that.

"You can see it however you want," Wyatt said. "It doesn't change what I have to do. It doesn't change that I'm working against the clock because of you."

"You're a bull rider, Wyatt. Working against the clock is what you do. So do it now. Complete the ride. If anyone can do it, I think you can."

Wyatt hung up the phone then. Because he didn't think his father really believed that.

And there was no amount of whiskey-laden late-night phone calls that could change his assessment of that.

He should go to sleep. There were no decisions made past midnight under the influence of alcohol that were good. That was an absolute fact. There were no scientific breakthroughs, no cures for any diseases, or anything else that came out of this hour and level of sobriety.

But then, even sober, Wyatt Dodge wasn't going to accomplish any of that. So none of it mattered anyway.

He picked his phone back up and stared at it for a moment.

He was not going to call her. It was late. And he had manners.

But he opened up a new message box and typed in a text.

If you have time tomorrow, we can go for that ride.

He sent the message.

Yeah, he had told her that Jamie would take her out, and he had meant it then. But, now, he was going to do it. This was his business. This was his ranch. His partnership with Grassroots.

And hell, if Lindy could take that winery and make it something bigger, something better, after Damien, there was no reason why he couldn't make Get Out of Dodge something better than his father had made it.

Maybe his dad didn't think he could. And hell, maybe Wyatt had never given him a reason to think that he could. But that was going to change. That was going to damn well change.

What time?

The response surprised him. As well as the lack of questioning over why Jamie wasn't going to be the one leading the ride.

Lunchtime.

Okay.

He groaned and threw his phone down on the couch, heading up the stairs toward his room. There. He had made a decision.

It was about the ranch. He refused to believe that it had anything to do with spending time alone with Lindy. That something about that conversation with his father had riled up the devil in him.

As long as the devil was productive, he didn't much care.

CHAPTER FIVE

EARLY THE NEXT morning Lindy couldn't figure out what had possessed her to agree to go on a trail ride with Wyatt Dodge today.

Originally, the plan had been for Jamie to take her. They had discussed that. But somehow, when she had still been awake, tossing and turning, her phone had dinged, and she had looked at it. She had seen his name and she had...

She didn't know what she had wanted. Didn't know what she had hoped.

She hadn't expected an invitation to go riding. But she had found herself agreeing.

And then she had fallen into a fitful sleep, where she had dreamed of weird arguments with Wyatt, where they were bickering over where Grant was going to take her out to dinner.

Then she had woken up, relieved that she wasn't actually going to dinner with Grant, but not all that relieved that she was going for a ride with Wyatt.

She scrubbed at her face and rolled out from beneath her down-filled duvet and grimaced as the chill in her bedroom settled over her skin.

One of the first things she had done when she had thrown Damien out was get a new mattress and a whole new bedroom set.

First of all, because she had always wanted a lovely, white bedspread with some artful accent pillows, and Damien had insisted they have something that was "for both of them and not just her." Which had clearly meant, for him. Darker colors, to go with the heavy, dark wood frame that had gone with the bed. As he had gone, so had that.

But, she had also needed a new mattress, because she had very little confidence that he had never taken another woman to their bed, and she would be damned if she was spending one more moment sleeping on a mattress her husband had had sex with someone else on.

There were a great many chances to experience indignity in life, and she had been on the receiving end of that a few times. Damien was just lucky she had offered him the mattress instead of burning it like she had initially wanted to do.

She knew people didn't believe it. Even her own mother thought she had just married Damien for his money. And that she had happily cut and run when she'd discovered his infidelity in part because she had never wanted him.

But she had. She had loved him. She had believed that he had loved her too. That he hadn't cared where she had come from. That she had been enough for him.

What an idiot she'd turned out to be.

She wasn't sure what was worse: letting everyone know just what an idiot she was, or letting them continue to believe that she was a heartless gold digger.

She had a feeling that public opinion on her was split down the middle.

But Wyatt thought that Damien was an idiot.

Which was perhaps why she felt even the tiniest bit

charitable toward him. Was perhaps why she wasn't so completely opposed to going on a trail ride with him today.

She ruminated on that while she got dressed. She found a pair of nice jeans—much more casual than she would normally wear—and a dark-colored button-up top that wouldn't show any dirt she might pick up during the ride.

She pinned her blond hair back in a low bun and looked at her reflection critically. She was hardly recognizable as the person she used to be. The person she'd been before she had started dating Damien.

She was sleeker now. Much more sophisticated.

She used to be proud of that. The distance she had put between herself and what she'd been. Now, it felt a little bit like a poisoned chalice. After all, she was partly who she was because of Damien. And she… In the end, she despised what he stood for. What he could allow. What had been acceptable to him.

He had asked her one time to forgive him. Had told her that she was making a big mistake throwing their marriage away over a physical relationship.

He had said that sex didn't matter.

But sex had mattered when she'd been a twenty-year-old virgin, cautiously giving him her body. He had said that it meant the world then. And that even though he had been with a couple of other women they didn't matter, not in light of what sex between them meant. Because he'd said that with her it had been love. It had been everything.

After being married to the man for ten years she was supposed to believe that sex could also be nothing. As long as it was shared with someone else. Even though he had made vows to her.

She had wanted to scream. She had wanted to cry. To let her inner trailer park out, throw something at him, call him a string of foul names. But she hadn't been able to. She'd been frozen. Frozen inside the body, inside the image that they had created together.

She hadn't shed a single tear. Not then, not after.

She had simply told him no. That there was nothing left for them. That there would be no future for the two of them. Not after a betrayal like that.

He had gotten angry after that. He had blamed the dissolution of their marriage on her.

And after that…he had told her there was no other chance to get back with him. That he was leaving her for the other woman. That he was in love with her, and it didn't mean nothing. That she was the most important relationship in his life.

Not Lindy.

She sighed heavily, turning away from her reflection. She wasn't going to bother with any makeup beyond a tiny bit of mascara and some clear lipgloss anyway.

Odds were high that she'd end up with allergies, and she didn't need a whole ton of eye makeup running down her face thanks to the horse and the pollen that would no doubt be swirling around them in the vineyard.

It was warm out, but still, she debated whether or not she should put out a pair of boots or a pair of tennis shoes. Ultimately, she decided on the tennis shoes, even though they did not make her outfit look as sharp as the boots would have.

She made her way downstairs, walking through the large, empty house, taking in the details. They spoke to the fact that it was now her house, and not a shared dwelling.

Her foot hit the landing and she made for the front door.

"Good morning," came a scratchy, male voice coming from the direction of the dining area.

She jumped, pressing her hand to her chest. Then she remembered that she wasn't alone.

"Dane," she snapped, making her way from the entry and into the dining room, where her brother sat, his hat on the table in front of him, a cup of coffee on his left. The table was long, and always far too formal-looking. But with Dane at it, it bordered on ludicrous. "I forgot you were here."

"Sorry."

"Then don't look so amused."

"Sorry," he said again.

"When are you heading out?"

"In about an hour. It's a bit of a drive."

She nodded. "Yeah," she said. "I know."

"Where are you headed? In jeans," he said, lifting his brows.

He had known her when they were kids. When holey jeans and sneakers were her uniform. If even Dane was surprised to see her dressed down now, she truly had changed.

"I have to go in to my office." Her office, which was just across the property in the back of the Grassroots dining room. "And then I'm going for a sample trail ride."

"A sample trail ride, huh?"

"Yes. I need to know exactly what we are offering our guests, after all."

"Very responsible."

"I like to think I am."

"Are you happy?"

She blinked, regarding her younger brother closely. "What does that mean?"

"Exactly what it sounds like it means. Are you happy?"

"No," she said. "I mean… What's happiness, Dane?"

"If I remember back to what they taught us in kindergarten, it's a feeling."

"You know what I mean. I'm tired right now. This has been a stressful couple of years. I'm not going to lie to you about that. But I'm accomplishing things. I'm taking this… I'm making it mine." Suddenly, she realized how important that was. To be more than Damien's creation. For this winery to be more than his creation.

For her *life* to be more than his creation.

"Sure," Dane said, reaching out and pressing his hand over the top of his cowboy hat. Then, he lifted it and put it on his head. "Just don't forget to have fun sometimes."

"You have enough fun for the both of us, I think." She tried not to sound bitter about that, she really did. She was pretty sure she failed.

"No one said you couldn't have fun, Lin," he said, standing up and moving over to where she was rooted by the doorway.

"I …" She sighed, feeling defensive and hating that she did. "It's not the same. For me. You've made success out of being kind of a rebel. That's not going to work for…"

"For someone who wasn't a bull rider."

"For a *woman*," she finished. "Anyway. I already have enough working against me. I can't go out and be crazy. I just… I want to make this place so successful that people forget what I used to be. I want to go so far beyond what Damien ever would have done that no one will think of it as something I took from him. Because they'll know that he could never have achieved all of this."

"That's a tall order."

"I've never been afraid of a challenge."

"Now, that is true," Dane said. "If you were a rider, the bulls would be afraid of you."

"Thank you," she said, not caring if he meant it as a compliment or not. *She* took it as one.

"You're scary."

She sighed heavily. "Thank you. Again." She edged toward the door and Dane took that as a solid cue.

"See you later," he said.

"See you." She hesitated for a second, and then she stepped forward and gave him a hug. "Be careful, okay?" Dane went tense for a moment, then rested an uneasy hand on the center of her back, his interpretation of a hug, she supposed.

"Lindy, I can't be careful. It's literally my job to go out and do something stupid now."

"I know. I love you, Dane. I want you to be safe."

"I'll be as safe as I can be."

He tipped his hat, and she shoved his chest. That was about as sincere as they got.

She walked out of the house, and made her way down the beautifully manicured cobblestone path that led to the main grounds of the winery. A place like this… It would have been beyond her wildest dreams to even visit when she was growing up. Now, she lived here.

The fact that she lived here alone was something she preferred not to focus on.

She took a deep breath, inhaling the scent of pine, the cold, fresh smell of the river beyond the grove of trees that enclosed Grassroots Winery.

The sun filtered through the tops of the evergreens, making the needles look like tinsel. Like Christmas in June.

This place belonged to her, not just legally, but in some real, inextricable way. The way that it wound around her soul, the grapevines entwined with who she was… The exhaustion she had felt a moment before when she had been talking to Dane seemed to vanish. By the time she got down to the dining area, it was gone.

Sabrina's car was already in the parking lot when Lindy arrived, and she pushed the door open to find her friend sitting at one of the tables working on inventory.

"Taking orders down to Copper Ridge?" Lindy asked.

"Yes, ma'am," Sabrina said, looking up and smiling. Then, she got a look at Lindy's outfit and frowned. "You're wearing jeans?"

"Weirdly," Lindy said, "it's only 8:00 a.m. and you're the second person to comment on that."

Sabrina's eyes widened further. "I'm the second…"

"*Dane* is staying at my house," she said. "Whatever you're thinking…stop it."

"Okay. I was wondering if I had missed more not going out last night than I thought."

"You didn't miss anything," she said.

"We were going to come," Sabrina said. "We got… distracted." The word was laden with meaning that was impossible to miss.

Lindy rolled her eyes. "Spare me."

"If you're jealous, you could always find someone to deal with your physical frustration…"

"I'm not physically frustrated enough to deal with the emotional frustration that comes with having a man in your life."

That much was true. Anyway, she was so exhausted she couldn't fathom trying to make room in her life for a lover.

She gritted her teeth, trying to keep visions of Wyatt out of her brain.

Wyatt Dodge, and the fact that she found him attractive, had nothing to do with that.

"Indulge me," Sabrina said. "Why are you wearing jeans?"

"I'm going out for a trail ride," she said crisply.

"A trail ride?"

"I know that you are aware of the route and everything that's going to be used for the ride that Get Out of Dodge is going to conduct on winery property. But I haven't actually seen it."

"So, Jamie is going to take you out?" Sabrina laughed. "I would pay to see you on a horse."

"I do know how to ride. And, Jamie isn't taking me."

Sabrina lifted a brow. "Who *is* taking you?"

"Wyatt," Lindy said, trying to sound casual.

"So, you're wearing jeans. For Wyatt."

"No. I'm wearing jeans to ride a horse, because a pencil skirt would necessitate me riding sidesaddle. Which isn't happening. I don't even think they make sidesaddles anymore."

"I'm sure they do," Sabrina said, "but that's beside the point."

"No, it isn't."

"He gets under your skin," Sabrina pointed out.

"Yes," Lindy said, "he does. Because he's that kind of guy. That cocky, arrogant asshole that thinks he can get away with anything. That thinks a smile and his easy charm is going to cover up any mistake he might make."

"He's not Damien," Sabrina pointed out.

That forced Lindy to compare. Damien's slick charm versus Wyatt's rough, down-home variety. Damien would never give a woman a hard time, never tease the way Wyatt did. He'd only lie. Pretending to love, honor and cherish while he snuck around.

She couldn't imagine Wyatt sneaking.

Wyatt was a full-blown hurricane. And hurricanes didn't sneak.

She didn't like that they weren't as similar as she wanted to pretend they were. Because as long as Wyatt was just Damien in different clothes, it was easy to convince herself she wanted nothing to do with him.

Well, *easy* was a stretch.

"Too similar," she said anyway.

"Is there any man you wouldn't think was too similar right now?"

"No," Lindy said. "I'm not in the market. Like I said, I have too much to do."

"Right. I mean, I get you. I was you."

"That's different. You didn't date because you fell in love with Liam Donnelly fourteen years ago, and it never changed. Even when he left. I'm not still in love with Damien. I'm not hung up on him. I'm trying to make my way on my own for a while. When I have a handle on that…then maybe I'll worry about bringing someone else into my life."

"A physical relationship doesn't have to intrude on that," Sabrina said, looking innocent.

"If I want to place an ad online I'll remember that."

"Why place an ad?" Sabrina asked, her tone saccharine. "You're going on a trail ride with Wyatt later."

"Did you not hear me the first time? I'm immune to

men like him. Anyway, I have to work with him. That puts him squarely off-limits."

Sabrina shrugged. "Suit yourself. But whenever you two are in the same room it feels like there is literal electricity in the air. If I were you… I would be tempted to see where that might end."

"I know where it ends," she said. "Divorce court."

"It was like that between you and Damien?"

It wasn't a leading question, but a genuine one. And Lindy wished that she could say it had been. That the strange undercurrent that existed between herself and Wyatt was just old hat to her. Nothing she hadn't navigated before.

But it was like something else entirely. So different that most of the time she tried to pretend it was irritation, that it wasn't attraction at all.

But then…

Then she was reminded of that first moment she'd seen him. Five years ago. With her husband's ring on her finger.

They'd been traveling together that year for Damien's work with the rodeo, and that had meant more nights in honky-tonks than she cared for. But she'd gone anyway.

She'd gone to meet Damien after an event one night. And *he'd* been there, sitting on a bar stool across the room. He'd looked at her. Which was nothing. Nothing new, nothing extraordinary. People looked at each other every day.

This had been like a lightning strike. Electric. Immobilizing.

Lethal.

She'd had to force herself to keep moving forward, and the whole time he'd stared.

His brown eyes locked on to hers, his expression filled with a kind of intensity she had never seen before.

It had been like her entire body had been hollowed out, making room for this feeling that he had created and placed inside of her. There had been nothing but that. For a full thirty seconds. Nothing else existed outside of it. Not her life. Not her marriage.

Then Damien had stood up, smiled, grabbed hold of her and introduced her as his wife.

It had been like watching a train she had been meant to catch move away from the station, far ahead of her, going somewhere she would never be able to follow.

After that, she felt like she'd been slapped in the face by reality. And whatever feeling she had felt moments before had been replaced completely by anger. Resentment.

At him. As unfair as it was.

"Yes," she said, her throat dry. "It's just a little bit of a spark. I'm a woman. He's a man. It's nothing…" Again, she flashed back to that first moment in that bar, when the earth had shifted beneath her feet. "Nothing I haven't felt before. Nothing I won't feel again. If you don't catch one train, another will always be by," she said, in defiance of that earlier metaphor that had passed through her mind.

"If you say so."

"I do. And I have work to do."

"Okay," Sabrina said, writing on the order form in front of her with a flourish. "I have to get down to town. Enjoy your ride."

Lindy clenched her teeth. "Oh, I will. I will."

CHAPTER SIX

WELL, HELL. HE had anticipated how much he'd want her if she showed up in a little pencil skirt, the kind he wanted to shove up her hips so he could step between her thighs. He had expected her hair to be in a prim little bun. Had expected that he would want to take it down and run his fingers through it. He always did.

What he *hadn't* expected was for her to be wearing jeans. Jeans that molded to her long, slender legs and showcased her figure in a new, tantalizing way, that the styling of her skirts didn't.

Neither was better than the other. Not really. But it was a new look at her body, and his own body reacted favorably to that.

The damned pervert.

She still looked prim in her way. She was wearing a button-up shirt, and all those tiny little buttons made his fingers itch to undo them. But she had on a pair of tennis shoes, and that made him smile.

He got out of his truck, his boots hitting the gravel in the drive, the rocks crunching beneath his feet. And she was standing there, her arms crossed, her blue eyes sharp and assessing.

She was trying to get a read on him. Trying to figure out what he might do, so she could figure out what she should do.

If there was one thing he'd figured out about her—besides the fact that her ass had the most delicious curve to it—it was that she liked to be in control.

Too damned bad for her. Because so did he.

"Let's get this show on the road," she said, affecting an impatient tone.

He damn near shook his head.

He had expected better from her. She had gone and shown her hand. She was already eager to get this over with. And he didn't have anywhere else in the world to be. Which meant he was gonna take his sweet-ass time.

He closed the door to the pickup truck slowly, then made his way around the back to the small horse trailer that was hitched up there. "It'll take a couple of hours to do the whole trail," he commented.

"I know," she said. "When Sabrina and Jamie worked out the route, they discussed that."

He nodded. Also slowly. "Right."

Only a man who'd made a study of Lindy Parker would have any idea how agitated she was. But, he was a man who'd made a study of her.

The way her blue eyes flashed when she was angry. The way she pursed her lips together and pressed her mouth into a flat line to keep from displaying any emotion she hadn't damn well chosen to display.

The particular set of her shoulders, the way she squared her hips. Like she was ready to face an opponent in battle.

He saw all those things contained in her still form and placid expression.

Because he was a fool.

A fool who was really enjoying drawing all this out.

He undid the latch on the horse trailer, then slid it

open. He climbed up inside and encouraged the two horses they were taking out on the ride—Emmy Lou and Trixie—out into the lot.

All the while very aware of the fact that Lindy was standing there, stiff-necked and anxious. Her very non-casual mood at stunning odds with the outfit she'd chosen to wear today.

No. She was not more relaxed than usual at all. But then, he wondered if that was *him*, more than it was anything else.

Unless it was Grant.

Annoyance kicked him in the gut.

He didn't believe that she wanted to date Grant. But, clearly she wanted him to think that she did.

Mostly, he was confident in the fact that she *did not*. Mostly, he was confident in the fact that the kind of heat and fire he'd felt when their skin had made contact last night could not be one-sided.

He wasn't sure if that was a victory or defeat, but he was certain of it nonetheless.

"Grant says hi," he mentioned offhandedly, getting the tack out of the horse trailer and beginning the process of readying the animals.

"Does he?" she asked, keeping her tone as smooth and placid as the expression on her face.

She was a beautiful, accomplished little liar, that woman.

"Yes," he said. "I told him that you...expressed some interest last night."

"Did you?" There was a small break in her composure. A slight twitch to her brow, a little hitch in her breath.

If she wanted to lie, then two could play that game.

"Yes. He was very interested."

"Well. That's…good. Very good. Because, I also am very interested."

He stood there for a moment, the lead rope to the horse in his hands, his eyes fixed on hers. And he watched as the color mounted in her cheeks. Pink. Tempting. He wanted to kiss those blush-stained cheeks. Hell, he wanted to kiss her everywhere.

He had a feeling that that was written on his face as clearly as the blush was written across hers. "You are shameless, Lindy Parker," he said, bending down and tightening the girth on the horse's saddle. Gratified when he could feel her eyes moving over his body as he worked.

"I am not," she snapped.

He straightened and turned to look at her. "My brother is a grieving man. And you would use him to get at me?"

Lindy's mouth dropped open, then closed, like a fish. "I am not trying to…get you."

"I mean to irritate me."

She sniffed. "Well. If you didn't think that I wanted to go out with him why did you tell him I did?"

"I didn't," he said. And then he winked, because he knew it would enrage her. "But, this was a fun little play we just acted out."

She treated him to a very teenage facial expression and he couldn't help but smile, imagining how she might have been when she was younger. Less polished. Less careful. "You're such an ass."

She reached into the small purse she was carrying and pulled out a pair of sunglasses, jamming them over her eyes.

As if that would protect her.

He could read her every emotion on that pale skin. He

wondered if she knew that. He wondered if anyone had ever told her that anger made her flush a certain shade of rose, that desire made her flush creep down her neck, intensifying the color.

He knew.

He knew, because he had been watching her for the past five years.

There was no way on earth that didn't sound creepy as hell, but it was the truth.

"Sure. I never said I wasn't." He kept staring her down, even while he got the second saddle on the other horse, while he bent down to tighten the girth. "And you started it. You were the one who asked me about Grant."

"I have a feeling you think there's something going on here," she said, her shoulders going even stiffer. "But there isn't. I wanted to make that clear."

"All you had to do was say it," Wyatt said, except, that was a lie too. Because he knew, whatever she said, that she felt this thing that existed between them.

"Okay. There's nothing happening here," she said, waving a well-manicured hand, her eyes still shielded by the large, dark glasses.

"All right," he said. "Saddle up, cowgirl," he said, gesturing to Trixie, the more placid of the mares.

"All right," she said, snippy. She placed her foot in the stirrup and hauled herself up on the back of the horse. She wasn't an experienced horsewoman, not as far as he could see, but she'd definitely been on the back of one before.

With ease, he put himself in the saddle, and maneuvered himself so that he was in the lead position. "How long has it been since you've ridden?"

"Oh," she said, sounding slightly thrown at the change

of topic. "I don't know. Not since I was in high school probably? So...a long time."

"It's like riding a bike," he said. "I assume. I've never gone a significant amount of time without being on the back of a horse. Also, I imagine you're a hell of a lot more saddle sore than you are when you pick up bike riding after a good number of years."

She huffed out a laugh. "Good to know. I look forward to the screaming muscles. And as I limp around the house, I'll remember that you're the reason I can barely walk."

He thought about letting the moment pass by. But then, he thought no. He was going to take it. "Honey, you are not the first woman to say that to me."

He couldn't see her face, but if stiffness was something you could feel in the air, he was certain he felt it now.

"You're disgusting," she said.

"That is not the general consensus."

"See, this really does make me want to go on a date with Grant," she commented, keeping her tone light. "Because I doubt he would ever say things like that to a lady."

"Grant has barely spoken to a woman in eight years. I'm not sure he knows what he would say to a lady at this point in time."

That little bit of unexpected honesty made his chest turn a little bit.

"So he hasn't... He hasn't gone out with anyone since his wife died?"

"No."

"I can understand that," she said, slowly. "I imagine any experience with marriage makes you think twice about jumping in again."

"You don't want to get married again?"

"Right now? No. And I can't imagine ever willingly submitting myself to that ever again."

"I don't think his reasoning is quite the same as yours," Wyatt pointed out.

"No. I expect it isn't. But it's just… More than even the not trusting someone else, it sounds like a lot of work. I was married. I was married for a long time. It's like, I've done it. I've seen what that life is like. I've seen what it can give me. I'm not really interested in checking it out again."

"Been there, done that?"

"Yes," she confirmed.

Damien had a lot to answer for, and that was the damned truth. No, Wyatt wasn't any more interested in marriage than Lindy was, but she was the kind of woman who should be. The kind of woman who deserved better. Who should have gotten a hell of a lot better than she had. If she didn't want marriage, it should be because there was something better and brighter out there for her. Not because she was exhausted emotionally. Not because her heart had been battered, ground into the dust underneath the heel of some jackass's boot.

"I've always thought marriage seemed pretty overrated myself," he commented.

She surprised him by continuing the topic. "Why is that?"

"One woman for the rest of my life," he said, the lie slipping out easily. "I don't think I could handle that."

As if it all came down to him being afraid he couldn't control his dick. As if it didn't have anything to do with the hard, sharp truths he learned about himself when he was seventeen years old. The hard, sharp truths about what it cost to care for someone. Loss and betrayal and defiance, all mixed up together.

"Well, I admire you for knowing that about yourself." She didn't sound admiring in the least.

"So, we figured we would take the guests down by the river," Wyatt said, changing the subject.

All of this was getting a bit too close to places he kept well guarded for a reason. It was one thing to try to get under her skin a bit. It was another to cut his own skin away from the bone and scrape it raw.

Anyway, the sun was shining and he was out on a horse, in the middle of a Tuesday. Another thing that drove home the fact that he had made good decisions in his life, in addition to a hell of a lot of bad ones. But, for now, he was going to go ahead and enjoy the ones he'd made that weren't terrible.

Working outdoors, being able to spend the day out in the wilderness, with a beautiful woman… Well, it wasn't all bad.

He maneuvered his horse down the narrow trail that cut through the thick, green grass and behind a copse of pine trees that shielded the river from the rest of the winery grounds. He knew—because Jamie had given him a map to look at last night—that the trail would take them to where the grapevines grew.

On the other side of the river was a thicker, denser grove of trees, and back in the distance, shaded beneath the firs, he thought he could see a little cabin.

"Is that your property too?"

"What?"

Clearly, Lindy had been thinking about other things too. "There. Across the river."

"Oh," she said. "Yes. Right now, Bea lives in the little cabin."

"Really?" The spread was bigger than he'd initially thought. Which made Lindy's ownership of the place even more of a triumph than he'd realized. "So, your in-laws lost all of this land. To you."

"For the want of a better prenuptial agreement, yes."

"Do you ever feel guilty about that?"

He turned and looked behind him, examined the stricken expression on her face. "I'm not suggesting you should," he added.

"No," she said. "I don't feel guilty. Because Damien had ownership of the winery at that point, not Jamison and his wife. I think, if they'd had it still… Well, first of all, it wouldn't have gone to me. Second of all, I might feel bad. But the fact of the matter is I was doing a good portion of the work when Damien and I were married. I was the one trying to lead new initiatives, initiatives that I've put in place now. He was mostly preoccupied with his work for the rodeo. And that's fine. But this was my passion project, not his. And I don't know…maybe it's not…strictly fair. Maybe assets should be divided directly in half. But he wasn't left with nothing."

"Do you wish he had been?"

"What kind of question is that?" Her tone was sharp.

"An honest one. He cheated on you, Lindy. How long were the two of you married?"

"Ten years," she said softly.

"Ten years," Wyatt reiterated. "Ten years you gave to that man. He cheated on you. He ruined it. And somehow, managed to walk away with enough of a dent in his pocketbook that he looks like a victim. I think that's messed up. I want to know what you think. Honestly."

For a moment, she said nothing. The only sound was the plodding of the horses' hooves on dirt, and the rushing river alongside them.

"I think... Yeah, I think he should have lost everything," she said finally. "My honest answer. I'm angry that he was able to walk away with anything. Not because I wanted it all. Just because I wouldn't be that sorry if his life had been reduced to rubble. Or...maybe that's more how I would have felt two years ago. I don't really care now."

"Really?"

"Mostly," she said. She sighed heavily. "I'm not heartbroken anymore. I mean, how much time can you waste feeling heartbroken over a husband who slept with other women?" She laughed, but there was no humor in the sound. "I guess you could waste a lot of time on it, but I don't want to. He's not worth it. The man I loved doesn't exist. I think that's the hardest thing to come to terms with. The person I thought I was married to... If he was ever that man he's not anymore. I can't waste my time grieving over someone who's basically dead. Wondering what I did to make that happen? That's another story. And anger... Anger over wasted time, over wasted tears. That's something else entirely."

"Makes sense."

He might not know about the dissolution of a marriage, but he'd experienced heartbreak. And he sure as hell knew about regret.

"Maybe it does," she said. "Maybe it doesn't. But it's true enough."

They rode on in silence for a while, as the trail wound around the riverbank, and then separated from the water, heading a different direction, where the trees thinned out and the sky opened up, the sun shining down on row after row of twining grapevines.

"This is a helluva place," he said. "You should be proud of it."

He meant that. He might be an asshole of the highest order, he might find it tough to be sincere at the best of times, but she had done a great job here. She was a damn fine businesswoman. And she was right about what she had said about Damien. She had done more with this place. She had done better. In his opinion, she deserved everything she got.

"It's beautiful," she said, her voice suddenly soft. "I remember the first time I saw it. The first time Damien brought me out here. And I just… I didn't think that I was the kind of person who would ever be allowed to have something so lovely."

Something twisted inside his chest. "Why not?"

He was surprised she'd shared that with him, and the look on her face told him that she was too. Almost like she didn't understand the words that had come out of her mouth.

"I don't know." She looked away from him. "I guess… you know. Some people have beautiful things. Some people have beautiful lives. Some people don't. And when you've lived an entire life of dirty and ugly it's hard to imagine you could ever have anything else. That you could ever deserve anything else. I used to think of him like that too."

Wyatt swallowed hard. He related to that a little more closely than he cared to admit. Even to himself. That feeling of being someone who could have a life that looked a certain way. Or being someone who could never aspire to such a thing. Someone who didn't deserve it.

"It must feel more real now," he said, unable to keep the gravel out of his voice entirely.

"I don't know." She paused for a moment. "It didn't last, did it?"

"This place is going to last," he said, knowing that she meant her marriage, but moving on to the winery anyway. "What you're doing here? It's going to last. You can't control what other people do. They're going to cheat." He gritted his teeth, hating that when it came to his own experience with this kind of thing he couldn't stand on the right side of the line. "But this is different. It's not a person. It's land. It's not going to betray you. It's not going to hurt you."

"Now that's spoken like a cowboy," she said. "I imagine the other faithful things in your world are your horse and your pickup truck."

"Damn straight." He took a breath, doing his best to dispel the pressure that had begun to build in his chest. "Speaking of horses, how are you doing on that one?"

"Good," she said. "You're right. It is like riding a bike. In that, I remember how it's done."

"Well, and Trixie here is a pretty easy ride."

"Funny. I think I read that on a bathroom wall about a girl named Trixie once."

"If it was in the Gold Valley Saloon I might've written it there."

She laughed, the sound unexpected and bright, splitting through the relative silence around them. "I don't believe for a second that you would do that."

"You don't?" He shook his head. "Clearly I haven't done a very good job of convincing you that I'm a jackass."

"Oh no," she said. "You've done a fantastic job with that. It's just… I don't think you're that kind of jackass."

"Truth be told," he said. "My name is carved on the wall in the saloon."

"Tacky," she commented.

Before Laz had taken ownership of the Gold Valley Saloon, it had been the thing for people to carve their names outside the bathroom door if they had scored inside. And back in his twenties, when he had been more of a drunken asshole than he was in his thirties, he had put his name up there thinking it was damned good fun.

But then, she was right. It was different than writing down a woman's name and promising she'd give someone a good time, he supposed. As long as the only person you were exposing was yourself, it didn't seem half as bad.

Of all the things he'd done, that wasn't even close to being one of the ones he was most ashamed of.

"Yeah, well," he said finally. "I'm a little tacky."

"I believe that."

They rode on through the rows of vines, the sun casting long shadows across the path as they went. It was a spectacular ride. If they paused for some wine tasting, it would be the kind of experience people would go home and tell their friends about.

The kind of experience that would make Grassroots Winery and Get Out of Dodge prime tourist destinations.

And right now, he didn't care about that. He could hardly think about it.

He was supposed to be out here thinking of exclusively that. But then…but then there was Lindy.

He tightened his hold on Emmy Lou's reins and stopped her midgait. "We figured that right up here would be a great place to stop for a picnic."

He'd force himself back on track if he had to.

There was more grass at the end of the grape vines,

a few picnic tables set out there, with the glorious view of the mountains around them. Back behind them was the row of pine trees, the river now completely obscured. There were no buildings in view. And it gave the sense of being wholly and completely closed in. He paused his horse.

"It's serene out here," Lindy said. "I get so caught up in doing all of the office work that I forget to come out here."

"Well, you'll have to come out on the tours sometimes."

"I don't know if I'll have time."

"It's a double-edged sword," he said, to her or to himself he didn't know. "You make the thing you love your work, and often that means you start neglecting the parts of it that you loved most."

"I guess that's true."

He dismounted, looking back at Lindy. "Why don't we stop here for a minute?"

Lindy's eyes were still covered by her sunglasses, but he could see the hesitation move through her entire body. The subtle twitch in her shoulders, the way her hands choked up on the reins, as if preparing to double down about staying on the horse. About not stopping with him.

He could almost read her internal war with herself. To make a big deal out of it and let him know that she was battling anything at all, or to give in and subject herself to a greater amount of time in his presence.

He'd casually dated women he couldn't read as well as the woman in front of him. And for some reason...he could see through her, clear as day.

Which seemed more curse than blessing in general.

"Okay," she said, getting off the horse quickly, as

though the moment of hesitation before hadn't happened at all.

"So, you actually make the wine here?" he asked, turning away from her and surveying the grapevines.

"Yes," she said. "All of the equipment is housed in one of the other barns on the property. Before my in-laws bought the place years ago, it was a big, working ranch. So, a lot of the original buildings are intact. We've just repurposed them."

"I see," he said. He turned to face her then. She wasn't looking at him. At least, he was fairly certain she wasn't looking at him. Her eyes were still obscured by the sunglasses. Purposefully so, in his expert Lindy opinion.

"What changes have you implemented?" he asked.

She jerked, as if in shock, and then she did look over at him. "Since the divorce?"

"No. All of it. How much of it is yours, Lindy. I want to hear about it." He did. God knew why, but he did. He was fascinated by her. This prickly, inaccessible woman. Maybe that was why. Because she didn't bat her eyes and try to get his attention. No. She was hell-bent on running from the attraction between them. Not tempted to lean into it at all. Maybe he was that simple. Enticed by someone who didn't want him back.

Because it was a novelty.

Because he was a man, and men were pricks.

Or at the very least, led around by them.

"Damien didn't really want it," she said. "In fact, when his parents decided to retire, and they turned the place over to him he immediately started trying to figure out how he could pawn the work off on someone else. That's fine. I mean, he did have a career that was separate from the business. I think to a degree he felt like his father was forcing his hand. Either way, he never wanted anything to do with it. But I… I did." The corners of her lips turned down into a frown, and he could see a slight pleat forming between her brows, right above the edge of the sunglasses frame. "I never really had dreams. I mean, nothing that was above myself. Until I met Damien, and suddenly so many other possibilities were opened up to me. Money doesn't buy happiness, Wyatt, but it sure as hell changes your opportunities. Suddenly…there were a lot of different ways for me to figure out how I might find happiness. Damien was done with school, so, that was never really on the table. Anyway, I hadn't spent a lot of time thinking about what I would study in school. It was one of those things that was never an option for me."

She paused for a moment, tilting her head to the side. "It's a funny thing. You move in certain circles, and it never occurs to anyone that you might not have gone to college. Which was crazy to me, heading into that social circle. No one in my family has gone to school. I would never…assume that someone had. Now, it seems like more often than not I never meet people who assume someone might not have. Class creates interesting divides, even in small towns. I never really realized how complicated it was until I had lived on both the green side of the fence and the dirt side."

"I didn't go to school," he said, lifting a shoulder. "Nothing beyond the school of getting thrown off an angry animal onto my ass. Grant got married. Bennett… He had a goal, and he figured out how to make it happen. I used to envy him a little bit."

"You did?"

He had never said those words out loud before, and he had no earthly idea why he was saying them to her now. "Yeah. Both of them, actually. They both found something they wanted and went for it. I... I kind of fell into rodeo."

"I don't believe that," she said. "I have too deep of an appreciation for how difficult the work is. For how competitive it is. You forget, my brother does it too."

"No. I didn't forget. But I'll be honest and say that I fell into success there. At first...at first I wanted to get away."

She looked interested in that, but she didn't press. And that was good. He didn't really want to talk about the circumstances that surrounded his leaving home for the first time. Not with her. Not with anyone.

"I understand that," she said softly. "Damien was like a nice escape from my real life. When he first showed interest in me... I couldn't believe it."

"If you don't mind me asking, how did you meet him?"

"At the winery," she said, looking around them. "I applied for a job here. I thought it would be a step up from what I was doing. I was working swing shift at a fast-food restaurant in Lola. I was getting tired of the hours and everything else. He did my interview for the winery and then when it was finished... Well, he didn't offer me a job, because he said his father would have to approve that. But he asked me on a date, which he said his father would not have to approve."

"That seems like a mess of human resources issues waiting to happen."

"Probably," she said. "But, it's a family-run business. And anyway... I couldn't believe that someone that handsome and accomplished would want to go on a date with someone like me. I didn't think it would last. I didn't think it would turn into anything. We were different. Different experiences. Different interests. Different friends. But, I worshipped the ground he walked on. All of the things that he showed me that I'd never had the chance to experience before. And I think… Well, I think he liked that. I can't really blame him. What guy isn't going to like that?" She frowned. "I mean, I would probably like that, honestly."

He laughed. "True enough."

"Everything with him is complicated. And always will be. Because there is that scorched earth and destruction desire, like I mentioned earlier. But then…being with him made me want more. Because I could see a potential future where I could have more. And when he made it clear he didn't want to do any work on the winery… I put myself forward."

"How did that go?"

"Not well," she said, smiling tightly.

He could imagine. He didn't know Damien's family, but he'd heard stories from the other man over the years. Imagining Lindy, fine-boned and soft, standing in front of her stodgy, snobby in-laws and making a case for the fact that she should be the one to run the winery…

If he didn't have a healthy heap of respect for her already, he would have gotten some in that moment. As it was, it doubled.

"I figured out how to make a business plan," she continued. "And I presented Jamison with one. He still wasn't happy, but he couldn't argue. When Jamison officially passed ownership on to Damien, Damien resisted a lot of my new efforts. But, I still moved forward with some of it. I had the barns remodeled to make dining areas. To make a venue for weddings, for dances. I started pursuing partnerships with people like Alison Donnelly. To have her bring her baked goods to the winery. And, since the divorce I've started doing farm-to-table dinners biweekly over the summer, and I've opened the tasting room in Copper Ridge. I hope to open one in Gold Valley in the next couple of years. Then, there's this partnership with you."

She took a deep breath, her shoulders rising and falling with the motion, and she walked on ahead, leaving the horses behind as she drifted through the grass, the breeze ruffling her blond hair as she looked out toward the velvet patchwork of the mountains. "That's the thing about people like Damien. He had all of this handed to him. Possibility is something he takes for granted. Achievement is something he takes for granted. I live every day amazed that I have all these resources. And I don't want to waste them. It feels limitless to me. It feels new and exciting. No, I didn't get to go to school and learn about business in a classroom. I rolled my sleeves up and I started doing it. I've made mistakes. I've done things inefficiently. I've overpaid for services. I've had contractors walk out on me and not fulfill their obligations. But for every bit of ground I've lost I've gained more. And I haven't given up. I didn't give up when my marriage dissolved. I won't give up now."

He nodded slowly. "That's damned impressive."

"Do you know…" She paused for a moment, shaking her head. "You're the first person to ask me all of that. To ask how much of this is mine. I think so many people assume that I took this from him. From them."

"Anyone with half a brain can see that isn't true. Just based on the fact that his sisters rallied around you. That says a hell of a lot right there. If people can't respect you, then they should respect Sabrina and Bea's loyalty to you, don't you think?"

"I would like it if they would just respect me. But, I take your point."

"I'm not sure anyone respects me," Wyatt said. "But then, I'm not sure I care."

"That's the difference," Lindy pointed out. "You've never even tried to get people to respect you, have you?"

"Seems overrated to me. I prefer to come up from behind and win before anyone realizes I'm a contender."

At least, that was what he hoped to do with Get Out of Dodge. The alternative was… The alternative was failing. Failing himself. Failing Grant and Jamie. Bennett.

"I've spent too many nights standing in groups of people who think that I'm beneath them. Who think I'm not as smart. Who think I don't deserve to be standing in the spot I'm in. I want…better. I wish I didn't care. But I can't help it. I do."

"It's not a bad thing to care," he said, taking a step toward her, close enough now that the slight breeze carried her floral perfume toward him, the impact of those flowers like a battering ram. "I wish I remembered how." She appraised him closely, and he smiled. "Well, sometimes I wish I remembered how. A lot of times I'm happy I don't."

She was quiet for a breath. "You care," she said, finally.

And for the first time, he was glad that she still had her sunglasses on. Because right about now he didn't want to know what she saw.

It had never occurred to him until that moment that if he could read her, every movement, every minute expression, that she might be able to do the same thing with him.

"About the ranch. Remember, I'm nothing more than a bad cliché of a country song. My horse, my truck, my land."

"Right. Don't forget your beer."

"And my woman?"

She stiffened. "Is there a woman?"

"In a manner of speaking," he said, taking another step toward her, unable to help himself. "Right now, she's not so impressed with me."

"Well, it's not hard to understand why."

He appraised her for the space of three breaths. Watched as her breasts rose and fell with each one. Color stained her cheeks. She was blushing. And still, even with the sunglasses, he knew she was looking at him like she wanted him to turn to stone.

Well, hell, he was hard as stone. Had been from the moment he'd first seen her.

She'd always been there. In the back of his mind. Ever since that first moment.

Yes, he'd been with other women in the past five years. Of course he had. But the more he spent time with Lindy, the more she overtook his senses.

When she had been married to Damien it had been the gentlemanly thing to go off and sleep with other women, to do something to keep himself from fantasizing about his friend's wife.

But, in the time since the divorce... That rationale had become a lot more difficult to maintain, seeing as she was no longer his friend's wife. Or anyone's wife.

Since her divorce... Yes, there had been other women. In the past year...not so much.

And acting like it was a game. Light and funny banter… That was getting harder too. Along with the rest of his damned body.

He liked a game, he liked to flirt, but he was getting tired of this one not going anywhere. He was getting tired of her acting like it didn't mean anything.

It did. She wanted him. He could see it. And he didn't know what the hell her investment was in acting like she didn't. They were grown-ass adults. She didn't want to get married, neither did he. But damn he wanted to burn off some of this electricity that sparked between them every time he saw her.

Yeah, they were working together, but in his mind, that was only making it worse. Ignoring it, continuing to go on like it wasn't happening… That wasn't working. Not for him.

It wasn't going away. It wasn't getting better. It was only getting stronger. And he didn't know what to do with that.

He didn't know what to do with this beautiful, gorgeous brick wall standing in front of him. One that made him crazy, one that made his skin itch and his blood feel like it was on fire.

He didn't know how to want and not have.

Sex wasn't that big of a deal, it never had been in his life. Apart from the one time it had been. But that had been about feelings. It had been about betrayal. And he'd done his damnedest to make sure that feelings never came into it. He'd also made sure that he never poached on another man's territory, not again.

He liked sex without strings. And he and Lindy had no strings between them.

What they had was heat. What they had was need. A kind he'd never felt before.

Her pretending it was nothing…

He was done with it.

Completely done.

"Lindy," he said, addressing the smooth angle of her jaw, the edge of her sculpted cheekbone. "Look at me."

She did, but those sunglasses were still in place, and he couldn't see enough of her.

He reached out and pulled her sunglasses away from her face, revealing wide, blue eyes that she immediately did her best to narrow into a hardier, more guarded expression.

"Give me my sunglasses back," she said.

"I just want to look at you."

"And I just want my retinas to not get scorched."

"I think a few minutes without sunglasses will be fine."

He looped the earpiece of the sunglasses over his shirt. He reached out and took hold of her chin, angling her face upward. "What would it take for you to be a little more impressed with me? Because let me tell you, I've got quite a few skills to recommend me. I might have lucked into success in the rodeo, but some of that is due to the fact that when I set out to do a task, you can be damn sure I'll complete it, honey. If I get on for a ride, I'm not getting off till… Well, till everyone gets off."

"You haven't realized by now that your clever sexual innuendo doesn't impress me?" she asked, but even as she spoke the angry words color bled into her cheeks.

"What would impress you then?" he asked again.

"Honesty. Stop trying to be clever. Stop being a jerk. Tell me what you want."

Desire kicked him in the gut, the anger in her eyes sparking something else entirely. Whatever he had thought he'd felt for her before… It was more now. It was more dangerous, more destructive than anything else that had ever come before it.

"I don't think you want that," he said.

"You don't scare me, Wyatt Dodge," she said. "I'm a strong enough woman to stand on my own two feet even when you're trying to sweep me off them. I was married for ten years. I know where this kind of thing ends up. That girl I told you about earlier? The one who got asked on a date in a job interview and saw that as a gift? She doesn't exist anymore. She's as dead as the man I thought my ex-husband was. I don't think a nice date is a gift, not anymore. My due, maybe. But not a gift. So go ahead. Try me. Give me one ounce of sincerity, and let's see where we get."

She was doing what she did best. Staying in her comfort zone. Throwing down a challenge. Setting the tone. Because she thought he would falter. Because she thought…whatever she thought. That he was messing with her? That he didn't mean it when he said he wanted her? As if the electricity between them could be faked.

"Maybe I should scare you," he said, his voice rough. "Because this? This thing between us… I don't know what the hell it is. If I kissed you right now, if you kissed me back… I think we would light this whole vineyard on fire. All those pine trees would go up like a lit match and dry tinder. We'd start a whole forest fire, baby. I don't want to give you a gift. I want to burn out this thing between us until there's nothing left but ashes. Ashes aren't a *gift*. They're evidence of destruction. That's what I think might happen if we touch. That we may well ruin everything around us, but it might be worth it."

Her eyes widened, and she let out a slow, shuddering breath. Her chin moved imperceptibly between his thumb and forefinger, and he tightened his hold on her, forcing her to keep on looking at him.

"Did I scare you? Good. You wanted sincerity, you're getting it. I want you. You. Not sex. You. That's different. And it bears mentioning, because let me tell you, usually I'm not so picky. I'm not going to pretend that I'm anything other than what I am. But you should know, I don't care about much, but the one thing I've cared about in a long time is that I want the next woman I take to bed to be you."

He released his hold on her and took a step back. "That doesn't need to impress you," he said. "But it's the truth. You can do whatever you want with it. But if I can't be the thing that keeps you up tonight, I sure as hell hope that will."

CHAPTER SEVEN

THOSE WORDS ECHOED in Lindy's head all the way around to the end of the trail, where she dismounted from the horse and mumbled some excuse about having somewhere to be before beating a hasty retreat to the tasting room, where she barricaded herself in her office so that she didn't have to face Wyatt again. Or anyone, for that matter.

Because every filthy thought that had flitted through her mind the moment he had spoken those words had to be clearly written across her skin.

They had to be.

She felt them, radiating from her like a beacon. It was all so clear. All of it. She couldn't pretend that what was between herself and Wyatt was anything other than raw, sexual attraction.

Sure, she had tried. Because she felt like the woman she had become wasn't susceptible to that kind of thing.

Not her.

She had schooled herself into becoming a sophisticate. Had made her life about her professional achievements. Had gotten rid of all that wide-eyed, hopeful newness that she'd had before her marriage.

And really, even then, she hadn't been...

She liked sex fine enough. But it hadn't been a driving force in her relationship with Damien. She had felt soft things for him. Fuzzy things.

Like the slow unfolding of possibilities, the easy rise of the sun over the top of the mountain. A gradual dawning of possibilities that she hadn't felt had been open to her. A kind of relationship she had never seen before. Something caring, with two people who actually liked each other.

Nothing like that bitter, acrimonious, tumultuous relationship her parents had had.

She hadn't wanted anything like that. Like passion.

Passion was overrated.

And she had decided very early on that it was fake anyway. An excuse for people to behave like immature children when they were well past that point. An excuse for people to behave selfishly, to go around doing nothing to control their urges or their tempers.

Passion.

An excuse to stay in an unhealthy relationship.

She frowned. Of course, her relationship had been steady, and it had still gone to hell in a particularly fiery handbasket.

She stared at the back wall of her office.

All of this was moot. She wasn't going to do anything with Wyatt. She wasn't. Not at all.

They were working together. She wasn't going to risk any professional achievement that might be obtained by... distracting herself right now. Particularly with a man she was trying to get business things done with. If you were doing business things with a guy you really shouldn't do naked things with him.

At least, that was her newfound resolution.

She thought of Liam and Sabrina, who had started

out doing business things together for the winery and for Liam's ranch, the Laughing Irish. They had certainly started doing naked things together. But that was different. Sabrina and Liam had a history with each other.

Lindy's only history was with disappointment.

She wasn't going to make the advances she was trying to make with Grassroots any more difficult than they needed to be.

Wasn't going to make them any harder.

And being with Wyatt Dodge… Like that… Would definitely be…harder.

Just thinking those words made her cheeks flush with heat.

He was turning her into the ridiculous, hormonal teenager she had never been.

Another reason to find him irritating.

Yet again, she bemoaned the fact that he wasn't hideous. And then, further still, bemoaned the fact that she couldn't be attracted to his brother, Grant, who was a perfectly decent human being, not working directly with her, and vaguely resembled Wyatt. So, you would think, that she would be more interested in him.

Except, in part, she wondered if that was why she wasn't. Because he was a nice guy, and there would be a chance for a relationship. And she didn't want a relationship.

Other things… She was starting to want other things.

But not a relationship.

Chemistry. Maybe that was the other element of it. Something else that she hadn't paid much heed to in her days of not acknowledging passion as a major issue.

Whatever the conclusion, it ultimately didn't matter because her actions weren't going to change. She knew what she wanted. She knew what was important to her. The fact that Wyatt made her feel a little bit...warm, was no reason for her to lose her head.

She was thirty-four years old. She knew who she was. She had already gone through the dissolution of a long-term relationship and had come out the other side stronger and more balanced.

She was more than able to stand up to a little ill-advised sexual attraction.

That didn't bother her. It obsessed her a little, but didn't bother her. The fact she'd talked to Wyatt so easily about so many things she usually kept shoved down deep...that bothered her a little.

It was weird. Sometimes she felt uneasy with him. Like he was a live electrical wire and getting too close could electrocute her. And other times he felt... Well never like an old friend. But like there was something in him she recognized.

Something like her.

And it made her want to tell him about how she'd changed herself, and about her marriage. Made her believe he might be the only person who could understand.

There was an urgent knock on her office door. "Yes?"

The door opened, and Bea appeared, looking wide-eyed. "Lindy," she said. "My brother is here."

"What?"

"Damien is here," Bea said, closing the door behind her. "I don't know why. I mean, he said something about how he missed me. But, I don't really believe that. I don't think he cares about me at all. He wants to see you. That's what he said. Well, he said he needed to talk to you. I guess that's different."

Lindy's mouth went dry, the moisture leaching from

her body entirely. She felt like a husk. Fragile and withered, frail and easily cracked if the wind blew wrong.

Damien. Here.

She had seen him since the divorce, obviously. In court, mostly.

It had been an assault each time. To have to look at a man she'd shared a life with, a home with, a bed with, and have him stare at her like he hated her.

To feel like she hated him.

Like this space in her heart had been carved out, the love torn away, filled with all this hideous bile she hadn't given her body permission to take on board.

Turning her emotions into strangers.

But that was two years ago. She didn't care now. *She didn't care.*

Except, Bea was right about one thing. He wasn't there to see his sister. And if he needed to see Lindy, it wasn't going to be anything good.

Lindy stood up, pressing her fingers down on the surface of the desk and bracing herself. "I'll see him out there. I'm not going to invite him in here."

"Lindy…"

"What?"

Bea was looking at her like she might regard a small, wounded animal. Which was not good at all.

"Sarabeth is with him."

Oh great. Sarabeth. Of the mystical, magical vagina that had been just so enticing, not to mention ten years younger, that Damien had not been able to prevent himself from falling right into it.

Sarabeth, who had worked at the winery. Who Lindy had considered a friend.

She really, really didn't want to deal with all of that.

She wasn't jealous. Far from it. But it was something she didn't like thinking about. And this... It forced her to think about it.

She had been told, by more than one well-meaning person that she simply needed to put it all behind her. But it had been two years. She had been married to Damien for ten. Maybe when the amount of years between the marriage and where she stood matched the length of the marriage...it would be easier. But until then... Even knowing she didn't want him back, even feeling nothing that was even remotely like jealousy...it stung.

Like an old stab wound being opened right back up.

It didn't make her long for the person who had knifed her, but it did make her aware that it had happened. All over again.

"That's fine," Lindy said, squaring her shoulders. She wished that she weren't wearing jeans. She wished that she didn't look like she had been out for a trail ride. Wished that she didn't have all of her Wyatt thoughts stamped all over her face.

But then again...maybe it was good.

Maybe, Damien showing up and her not looking at all like she typically did was a good thing.

She might just tell him she had been out on a trail ride with Wyatt Dodge, and see what he thought about that.

That almost made her laugh. As if he would care. Seriously, she had reverted to being a teenager.

"Lindy..." Bea was talking to her again, using that same cooing tone that she used when coaxing animals out from under a porch. But, Lindy had had enough. She wasn't a wounded creature to be bandaged by Bea. She was a grown woman. In charge of her own thoughts, her own desires and her own life. And she would be damned if her ex-husband was going to walk into her place of business, walk onto her property, as if he had a right to be there and get into her head.

She strode out the door to her office and into the dining area. And stopped in her tracks.

Because there was Damien, tall, broad-shouldered and pleasant-looking as ever, his blond hair pushed back from his forehead, standing next to a small, dark-haired woman who was thin, petite and sporting a very obvious baby bump.

Pain exploded behind her breastbone.

Why did that hurt? Why *the hell* did that hurt?

I'm just really busy with my career right now...

You're really enjoying your work at the winery...

It's not the right time...

Dammit. Dammit. It didn't matter. It did not matter. She didn't want to have had a child with him. And anyway, it was later. His life was in a different place. It was completely normal that he would be having children with his child bride.

Of course, now it made perfect sense that Bea had been talking to her like she was a wretched raccoon.

She was trying to warn her.

And she knew that when all was said and done Lindy was going to feel like a wretched raccoon.

Like an aging crone standing next to a glowing, youthful, pregnant woman while her own eggs were threatening to turn to dust.

"To what do I owe the pleasure?" she asked, forcing her thoughts to come to a screeching halt, forcing the pain in her chest to halt its progress. She wasn't going to show it. She wasn't going to let her face change. Not even one bit.

"I need to get a few things from the house," Damien said, his tone measured. "As you can see, Sarabeth and I are expecting. And that means that I'm going to need to access my parents' storage. I believe some of it is still on the property."

"I'm not sure if any of your things are still here," Lindy said, trying to keep her tone neutral.

"Dad said that they were. He said that there were quite a few of my childhood things still in one of the old barns. I'm going to need it, because I have a son to pass it along to."

Heat rolled over her in a wave, followed by a ripple of cold, leaving her forehead clammy. But, as long as she didn't show it in her face, he wouldn't know.

Hell, Damien had never been able to tell when she was upset with him when they had been married. When she had made an actual effort to telegraph her feelings. Why would he be able to read her now?

"Well, I'm sure Bea can help you find it. I'm not sure why you felt the need to come and tell me."

Except, she did know why. It wasn't Damien, with his cool, gray eyes, who gave it away. No, he was too practiced for that. A PR man down to his core. He never let that ease slip. But Sarabeth, looking like a gloating frog next to him… This was all some kind of big show.

You got the winery, but I got your life.

The life that Lindy had wanted with Damien. The one that he had spent years denying her in the name of his career.

He had gone and given it to someone else. That was the point of all this.

Screw him.

"Actually, I'm more than happy to take you over to

the barn. Would you like me to drive you or would you like to follow me?"

"Following you is fine," Damien said, his tone cool.

A few minutes later, Lindy found herself behind the wheel of her little red car. Her divorce gift to herself. A fun, zippy little vehicle the likes of which Damien had deemed impractical. He could eat her damned dust all the way over to the barn for all she cared while he trailed behind in his sturdy, luxury SUV.

They compare the best of everything to Cadillacs for a reason, Lindy.

That lecturing tone, filling her head. That way that he had of communicating to her that she didn't know as much as he did, and never could. Not when she was simply a poor trailer park girl from the wrong side of the tracks with no real education.

Everything you know is because of me, or some connection I have. Everything you have is because of me.

She gritted her teeth, squeezing her eyes shut tight as she stopped the car in front of the barn she had a feeling he meant. She needed just a minute to compose herself. Just one.

She took a breath.

And then she got out of the car.

"Follow me," she said brightly. She ostentatiously held her keys out and unlocked the door.

I have the keys, bitch. Not you.

And she could tell that wasn't lost on him.

It was lost on Sarabeth, who was twisting her wedding ring and looking at it smugly, as if Lindy gave a damn about having that diamond shackle on her hand.

She had become more, done more, in the two years

since her divorce than she had done in the ten with Damien.

So there. Maybe she didn't need ten years between herself and her divorce to move on.

Actually, standing there, looking at what an ass he was, at what a ridiculous couple he made with Sarabeth, at the life she was so proud of having that Lindy knew for a fact could so easily crumble around her in the next few years, and likely would…

Yeah. It was far easier to feel *moved on* than it had been a moment ago.

She'd been shocked when she'd seen Sarabeth. Shocked that Damien was here. Thrown off, because she hadn't expected to have to deal with either of them—today, or ever, really—and that had made it all feel bleak for a moment. But that was done now. Past.

"What have you been out doing, Lindy?" Damien asked, his tone crisp. "I can't remember the last time I saw you in jeans."

"I was on a trail ride," she said.

Oh good. He'd asked. She'd been hoping he would. That was the thing about Damien. He was predictable.

"You?"

The lock clicked and she pushed the doors open wide. "Yes," she said. "I'm in a little bit of a business arrangement with Wyatt Dodge."

Damien began to walk into the barn, but paused midstride. "Wyatt Dodge?"

"Yes."

"He's a friend of mine." He said this as though it made her previous statement an impossibility.

"Do you still speak to him?" She affected a genuinely perplexed look. "That's so funny. We haven't talked about you at all."

That little lie tasted sweeter than any candy she'd ever had.

She breezed past him, making her way into the barn. "Feel free to have a look around. I have no idea what any of this is. I've been too busy to go through any of it, I might have had it hauled away. I'm surprised that your parents haven't made time to come out and get it."

"I'm making time now," Damien said.

Their eyes caught and held for a moment. And Lindy was overcome with the strangest sense of... Well, strangeness. She had seen this man naked. The only man she had ever seen naked in person. And there he was, standing in front of her in a crisp button-up shirt and charcoal-colored slacks and she felt...nothing.

Not a twinge of old desire. No nostalgia.

Nothing like what she'd felt those times she'd had to deal with him at hearings.

She had just been out with Wyatt, and he had made her feel...hot and reckless. Angry. Damien made her feel...nothing.

She felt annoyed, at his attempt to goad her. She felt the remnants of that initial pain, that initial shock she felt when she had seen that Sarabeth was pregnant. But she felt so detached. From him. From whatever she had felt back then.

She looked at Sarabeth, and she felt even less. Now that the shock was easing.

Lindy wouldn't say she felt sorry for the other woman. After all, she had most definitely made her own bed, after making it in Lindy's. But she certainly wouldn't trade lives with her. Even if Lindy hadn't ended up with the winery in the divorce, Lindy would have made something of herself. She would have a better life. One that wasn't tied to a man like Damien.

She had done her fair share of trying to figure out what her stake of the blame was in the divorce. And yeah, a lot of it came down to the undeniable fact that they didn't have enough passion. That Lindy did love the winery more than she loved her husband.

But she had done what she could. And she hadn't been distant. He was the one who had traveled. And in the end, he was the one who had broken their vows.

It was…clarifying.

She stood there, and watched while Damien and Sarabeth collected things. The frame to an old crib, some toys and some miscellaneous bags. An old trunk that she imagined had been a toybox.

She had never seen these things. How funny.

She had never asked him to see anything from his childhood. But then, she had never offered to show him anything from hers. Of course, she doubted that her mother had saved anything from her childhood. Or that anything she'd had had been worth saving.

She waited until they had everything loaded up in their SUV, and then she watched as he drove away, exchanging few words with him in the process.

She let out a heavy breath, and got behind the wheel of her car, driving back to the tasting room. When she pulled into the lot, she saw that Damien was gone. So, he hadn't stopped to visit with Bea at all.

She shook her head. He was such an ass. It was one thing to come and play games with her, but to play them with Bea, to conceal the fact that he was trying to get one up on her was beyond the pale.

Lindy walked into the tasting room, where Bea was standing. "I'm sorry," Lindy said, walking up to her former sister-in-law and putting her arm around her shoulders. "You deserve better than he is."

Bea smiled, small and sad. "I know. I got you instead. I chose you instead." She sighed. "For what it's worth, you deserved better than him too."

"I appreciate that. All of it. The fact that you're here with me." Lindy smiled. "I'd rather have you any day."

"Same."

"I'm going to finish up some work." Lindy walked back into her office and closed the door behind her, and it felt like whatever had been holding her spine straight, whatever had been supporting her had been pulled away abruptly.

She sagged down into her chair, her knees completely giving out.

She couldn't believe she had just…done that. Couldn't believe it had just happened.

But her past had come over and rummaged around in her things.

And that as strange as it had been, as stressful and kind of awful as it was… The things Wyatt had made her feel on the trail ride still burned hotter inside of her.

She had faced down her ex-husband and his pregnant wife. But she knew beyond a shadow of a doubt that tonight, when she closed her eyes to sleep, the only thing echoing across her dreams would be Wyatt Dodge, and all the things he'd whispered in her ear.

CHAPTER EIGHT

WYATT FELT LIKE he had been trying to work out the tension that had seized up his muscles for the past three days. Since that trail ride with Lindy, his shoulders had been knotted up hard as a rock.

Frankly, it wasn't the only part of him that was rock hard, thank you very much.

But he hadn't decided what the hell he was going to do about it yet.

It had been one thing to try to prove his point with her on the trail ride, something he thought he had done quite effectively. It was another to figure out what happened next.

Oddly, pounding fenceposts into the ground wasn't doing a thing for his muscles. Or for anything else.

"Are you trying to build a fence? Or are you fantasizing about killing a vampire?" His sister, Jamie, shouted over the sound of his post pounder connecting with wood.

"Is there something you want, Jamie?"

"I came by to help," his sister said, walking over to him and planting her hands on her hips.

"You don't need to help with fencing," Grant said, straightening behind Wyatt. "This is…"

"If you say men's work I'm going to plant a boot up your ass."

"I wasn't going to say men's work," Grant said. "I was going to say it's heavy lifting."

"I can lift heavy things," Jamie said, her dark eyebrows drawing tightly together. "I can sure as hell buck hay, and handle pissed-off horses. Putting in a new fence is hardly going to break me." She lifted her hands, revealing more than a few cuts and scrapes, and short fingernails. "It's not like I'm worried about damaging my manicure."

"If you want to help, Jamie," Wyatt said. "By all means."

"Why are you so pissed off?" Jamie asked, grabbing a roll of fencing and some tools.

"I'm not pissed off," Wyatt said.

"Yes you are."

"I'm not."

"He is," Jamie said, looking over at Grant. "Do *you* know why?"

"No," Grant said. "I didn't ask because I don't actually care about Wyatt's moods."

"I'm not sure that I *care*," Jamie clarified. "But I'm nosy."

"You're both a delight," Wyatt interrupted, gritting his teeth so that he wouldn't say something really asinine.

"No I'm not," Grant said.

"He isn't," Jamie agreed.

"I'm stressed-out," Wyatt said, pivoting to more comfortable territory. He wasn't going to give them the low-down on the entire situation, but in fairness, they did need to know that the grand opening of this place was important.

He'd been trying to handle it all himself. And while he wasn't convinced he couldn't, it seemed fair enough to let them know that it was essential. After all, they were invested in this too. Up above their waders.

Wyatt was past his eyeballs.

"I know there's a lot to do…" Jamie trailed off.

"There's a ton to do. We have to get this place looking good. We need to make sure that the bookings are full. Beyond the opening weekend. I want… I don't want this to be a dead end for either of you. You both threw your hats in with me. Totally. I respect that," he said. "I take it seriously."

The degree to which he cared about Get Out of Dodge wasn't really in keeping with his reputation, and he wanted to make sure it was clear to them. That he did care. That he wasn't taking their loyalty for granted.

"It's not like I left a good job or anything," Jamie said. "I was working part-time at the Gunslinger. I'd rather be heading up trail rides."

"And I can go back to the electric company anytime I want," Grant put in. "I mean, not in the same position, but they would give me a job. I worked there for fifteen years."

"Right. Well. Now I like both of you less because you made your sacrifices seem a helluva lot less impressive."

"Neither of us are very sacrificial. That's not the Dodge way. We care a hell of a lot about our own skin. But, handily, we've all put our lots in together. So, it forces us to care about each other's." Jamie said all of this as if it were an obvious fact.

"She's not wrong," Grant said. "That's how this family functions. No one's a martyr."

"We wouldn't respect anyone who was."

Except, Wyatt was starting to feel like a martyr to the whole damned enterprise. The fact that he was going toe to toe with his dad after all the unspoken tension between them for so many years. The fact that it was forcing him to deny his attraction to Lindy...

Yeah, he was starting to feel a hell of a lot like a martyr. And for a guy who had spent so long chasing glory it was a strange position to find himself in.

He wasn't sure he had liked his life as a bull rider, not when all was said and done. It was fine for a while, but it was a lot like drinking. Oblivion. Moving so fast that you couldn't create connections. That you couldn't think. All that was fine, but it was a bit of a younger man's game.

It earned money, but there weren't achievements he could hold on to.

Maybe his dad was right in one respect or another. Maybe Wyatt did romanticize the idea of working the land. But, running a dude ranch was hardly the same thing as being a straight-up cowboy. And anyway... He was ready to make something with his hands that would last. Something that took more than eight seconds to call complete.

Something that might make him feel like he'd done something. Something other than cause his family pain. Something other than screw up good things when they came along.

He was trying. But if there was one lesson he learned from his former life as a rodeo cowboy, it was that there were no points for trying. Everyone put in their best effort. But you only got points if you finished the ride.

He had to finish this damn ride.

"What can we help you with?" Jamie asked.

"This fence," Wyatt responded.

"That isn't what I meant, and you know it. I meant, how can we help you handle the pressure that comes with reopening the ranch? What can we do to help with the stress?"

"What you're doing," Wyatt said. "I didn't mean to make this your problem. But that's the thing. I want this place to be solvent for all of us. As long as it's mine, my responsibility, I should be doing the heavy lifting. You should be able to come and be confident in the fact that it's going to work out for you."

"That's not how any of this works," Grant said. "Everything's a risk. Everything in life. I get that, maybe better than most."

Silence fell between them. Yeah, Grant did know the ways that life could bite you in the ass. But, in Grant's case, it hadn't been that surprising either. Not that that made it less painful, but Grant had known about his wife's illness before their marriage. He had chosen to marry her even knowing the outcome wouldn't be good.

Wyatt sure as hell wanted to give his brother something better than that when it came to the ranch.

"This will all be fine as long as we don't do a half-assed job," Wyatt said.

Jamie shook her head and carried the bundle of fence down a few yards away from Grant and Wyatt. Just out of earshot.

"What's really going on?" Grant asked.

For a second he considered telling his brother what was going on with their dad. That this was a trial period, and if Wyatt didn't do something pretty damned amazing they were all going to lose everything.

But he wasn't going to let that happen, so he didn't need to confide in Grant. End of story.

"Nothing."

"Sexual frustration."

Wyatt lifted a brow. "You're projecting."

"Am I? I don't think it's a coincidence that you came home acting like you are ready to pick a fight with a bear after you went out riding with Lindy Parker."

"I'll pick a fight with anyone for a good time," Wyatt said dryly. "You know that."

"Sure. I won't lie. You're a contrary son of a gun. But you like to light fires for fun. You're not usually angry. And you've been mean, Wyatt. That's not like you."

Grant just looked at him. Waited.

"I *can't*," Wyatt said. "Because we are doing business together."

"Yeah. You said that." Grant shook his head. "But, you're still fixated on her, so clearly it's not done you any good to go ahead and decide to abstain."

"Doesn't matter either way. It's the right thing to do."

"Since when do you care about that?"

Grant's words struck him right in the chest, went clean through, like a particularly vicious arrow shot out of a compound bow.

"What?"

"I didn't mean that as an insult," Grant said, and Wyatt could tell that he meant it. "I only mean that it's one of the things that I always admired about you, Wyatt. You do what pleases you. You don't worry about higher callings and things like that. You took off when you were seventeen and pursued your dream in the rodeo."

Wyatt could only stand there stunned. Shocked that his brother thought that about him. That he was convinced that Wyatt had left because it was something he wanted more than being with his family.

But then, he had dealt with some similar things with Luke Hollister, his friend and surrogate brother, a couple of months ago, when they'd fought about Wyatt abandoning the ranch.

Luke had felt like he held the place together while Wyatt had gone off and done whatever he felt like.

It made him wonder if everyone thought he was just a raging asshole who did whatever he felt like and he didn't consider anyone else. He supposed he had never done anything to combat that assumption, but he wasn't really sure what he was supposed to do either. Things were complicated, and for whatever reason that all shook out to *look* simple to everyone around him.

He didn't know what in hell to do about that.

"I tried to do the right thing," Grant said, his voice wooden. "Don't get me wrong—I *wanted* to. I really wanted to be there for Lindsay. I wanted to marry her. But… I also didn't see another way. That life… That life that we had… That was all the life she was going to get, Wyatt. At the end of the day, it was her only chance at being married. I don't know what it's left me with. That's the problem. I knew how to center my life around her. How to center things around a limited amount of time. But I didn't know what the hell I was going to do with myself after." Grant shook his head. "Sometimes I would look at your life, and I would think…what must that be like? To walk around not caring at all? For it to not matter whether or not anyone else thinks you're a good guy. I don't know why you would start worrying about it now."

Anger burned in Wyatt's gut, but he didn't know what to do with it. He didn't want to get into discussions of all the skeletons that he had in his metaphorical closet. Didn't want to confess to Grant that he'd done about the worst thing in the entire world to their father and had spent half a lifetime making up for it. That he had to leave. He certainly hadn't chosen to because he wanted to. And what was the point in trying to convince his younger brother that he was a good guy? His younger brother who was—in kind of an awful way—trying to give him a compliment. Trying to tell him that he envied him.

"This isn't about doing the right thing," he said, and that at least was true. "This is about not screwing up what I'm trying to build here. I think I need Lindy's help to make it all go."

"Okay," Grant said. "And you think that a fling with her would prevent you from doing that?"

"I don't know. But it's a generally bad precedent."

"I'm kind of disappointed," Grant said.

"Why?"

"You're my bad behavior idol. I was hoping that you would keep on with it."

Wyatt didn't know what the hell to do with that. Not at all. And he stewed on it for the rest of the time he was out with Grant and Jamie working on the fence.

And then he wondered, if maybe this all wasn't the problem he thought it was. Maybe he was trying too hard to fight his nature. Maybe there was no damned point.

He was acting like Lindy was some fragile ornaments set up on a shelf. She'd been under his skin for five damned years, and now there was no barrier to touching her except the ones that he'd created. And why? Because he was trying to be a nice guy?

He didn't think that was the case, but now he wondered. And hell, if his own brother thought that wasn't a good look on him, it probably wasn't.

So here he was, caught in this hell of trying to deal with what his father had set out before him. Trying to make something of this place, and trying to limit his sexual urges all at the same time. And to what end?

If sex wasn't a big deal, then sex with Lindy wasn't a big deal either. There was no point treating her like she was special. Treating her like there was a tall fence built up around her. No point at all.

Maybe that's why he was having difficulty figuring out how to handle all this. He was trying to be something he wasn't.

And maybe some of it was that he had placed Lindy in an untouchable category a long time ago. That was pointless too. It was a game he wasn't going to play, not anymore.

He knew who he was. His brother had just recited his list of sins to him, and Grant only knew the half of it.

Maybe that was the problem. This total reinvention. Maybe that was why his teeth were set on edge. He might have left the rodeo, but he was still himself. Working toward something permanent here didn't change that.

What he wanted with Lindy… That was something temporary. Something hot and temporary.

It wasn't enough to simply make sure she acknowledged the heat between them. Wasn't enough to make her dream of him. No.

He was going to seduce her.

And he was going to have a hell of a good time doing it.

GOING TO THE Gold Valley Saloon for the second time in as many weeks was not generally Lindy's thing. But as clarifying as the other day had been for her, she still felt like she needed to drink off some of her tension on Friday night.

This time she had managed to rally Sabrina to accompany her, Bea and Olivia to the bar.

Though, even by 7:30, Olivia was looking a little bit worse for wear, her pregnancy making it difficult for her to stay out late. Or to stay out at all. But, she had agreed to make an effort, since they didn't see her as often now that she wasn't working at the winery.

Her morning sickness was making it too difficult for her to be on her feet all day, and she was neck deep in helping her husband, Luke, get their new ranching operation up and running. Which included...fencing and cows, so it seemed to Lindy.

Lindy had never seen Olivia happier. In fact, before she had ended up with Luke, Lindy wasn't sure she had ever seen Olivia truly happy. She had always been uptight, tense and brittle. Being with Luke brought out a different side to her. That was the kind of thing that Lindy couldn't even imagine—a relationship bringing out something better in you.

She could imagine a relationship expanding horizons. She'd had one of those. But she wouldn't say that Damien had made her a better version of herself. Sometimes she thought he had schooled her into a much more difficult version of herself than she needed to be.

Someone stiff and confined, someone she was just now beginning to shed ever so slightly.

She was starting to find that middle ground, she thought. Between her past, trailer trash self and the little Stepford wife Damien had molded her into.

But, she wasn't going to think about that. Not now. She wasn't going to think about him at all. She was having a girls' night out, and she was going to enjoy herself. Thinking about Damien pretty much ensured that she wouldn't.

"Okay," Sabrina said, returning to the table with three bottles of beer and a Diet Coke. The Coke was for Olivia, who didn't drink even when she wasn't pregnant, so it didn't make Lindy feel terribly guilty about imbibing in front of her.

"I'm glad that you were able to come out," Sabrina said. "You usually avoid things like this."

"I'm usually too busy," Lindy said. "There's a difference between being too busy and avoiding."

"Is there? I feel like your busyness is pretty artful."

"It's not artful," Lindy said. "It's just that I like work, so letting myself get consumed with it is easy. But I really, really needed to get out tonight. So. Thank you all for being here."

"Cheers," Bea said, grabbing hold of the beer bottle and holding it out.

The others followed suit.

"Is this related to Damien?" Bea asked.

Lindy shot her a deadly glare.

"I already know," Sabrina said, looking down into her beer bottle. "Sorry."

"Know what?" Olivia asked.

"That Damien's new wife is pregnant." Bea put it out there simple and matter-of-factly, as Bea was wont to do.

Lindy winced. Except, it didn't hurt, so the wince had been reflexive more than necessary. "Well, I thought you might know," Lindy said, directing that to Sabrina. "Considering he's your brother and all." She sighed heavily. "You know, this is really messed up. Because you should be happy that you're having a niece or nephew. And it's really not the baby's fault that Damien sucks."

"I know," Sabrina said, grimacing. "And I am. But it's... I'm mad at him, you know? He really hurt you. And whatever I know logically doesn't make that not true. But we're the baby's aunts either way."

Bea nodded. "Yeah. But, for what it's worth, I still like you better than I like him."

"You don't have to do that either," Lindy said. "You don't have to choose between us."

"I know that. But the truth is we're stuck with him," Sabrina said. "We chose you."

"And I thought I had created a tangled family situation," Olivia marveled.

"Right. How are Luke and Bennett navigating each other now?"

"It's fine," Olivia said. "Really, I think the two of us were only together because we were trying desperately not to be with the people we were supposed to be with. I knew... I always wanted Luke. I just didn't want to acknowledge it. And Bennett and Kaylee... I think they were always meant to be together."

"See," Lindy said. "You didn't cause family drama. You brought two people together who needed to be together, while finding the person you were meant to be with."

"It felt a lot like drama when it happened," Olivia said.

"Well. I can see how it did."

They were silent for a moment. It was funny to all hang out. She was Sabrina's boss, technically. Olivia's ex-boss, and Bea was quite a bit younger than she was. They didn't normally hang out socially like this. But, it wasn't bad. It was good, in fact.

That was another thing that Lindy had lost over the course of her marriage. She had lost friends. Friends it turned out had only been with her because she was a Leighton. Who had only liked her because of Damien and the connections that he brought. And who—when it had all gone down—had sided with him.

Yes. She had kept the house. The winery. But in so many ways it had been like starting over.

For some reason, that made her think of Wyatt. And the fact that there were certain other things she was starting to miss. Things that would also be starting over.

Not relationships but…

As if he had been summoned by the force of her thoughts, the bar door opened and in he strode. Wyatt Dodge. Followed by Bennett, and Luke Hollister.

And it was like… Like the first time.

She hated to think about that first time. Because it made her feel…imbalanced. Because it reminded her that there was something between her and Wyatt that went beyond explanation. That went beyond anything she had ever felt before.

Their roles were reversed, as opposed to their first meeting. He was the one walking in the door, and she was the one sitting there. But, just like that night five years ago their eyes met.

It didn't matter that there were two equally good-looking men flanking him. Wyatt was the one that reached inside of her and turned things all around.

Wyatt was the one that made it hard for her to breathe.

That made her breasts feel heavy and the space between her thighs feel hollow. Instantly. Maddeningly. Wyatt was the one who made her feel ruined with an upward tilt of those gorgeous lips of his. Wyatt was the one who made her feel destroyed by one hot look from those dark brown eyes.

She had been married for ten long years. Her husband's body had become familiar. She'd thought that was a good thing.

But now...now she was suddenly obsessed with the possibility of something new. The first time she'd met Wyatt, being enticed by someone new had felt like a failure. She was married. And her prenuptial agreement had been structured the way it was because her mother-in-law had been convinced bad blood would win out, in the end.

That she would be inclined to stray if there were no repercussions, because that was what low-class women did.

Ironic, now that she knew a little bit more about her mother-in-law's infidelities. Of course, that made some things make more sense. It was always the failings in yourself you judged most harshly in others.

It was better to put all that on Lindy. On a no-account piece of trailer trash.

It was one of the many reasons her visceral reaction to Wyatt five years ago had felt so very, very wrong.

Why she was resisting the feelings now. But what if she didn't?

What if for a moment she didn't?

What would it be like to be with another man? To touch an unfamiliar body.

Wyatt was...unknown. Lindy was normally too much of a control freak to be enticed by the unknown. She didn't like feeling out of her league either. Not now. Not now that she'd learned how to adapt. How to hide it when she was feeling insecure or confused.

If Wyatt touched her, she wouldn't be able to think, let alone keep up an act.

She wondered what she would find if she peeled that

shirt over his head? If she undid his belt buckle, slid the zipper down and…

"Are you okay?"

Lindy looked over at Sabrina and blinked. "Fine."

"You looked like you were on another planet."

Not on another planet, just entrenched deeply in a fantasy that she had no business having.

"I didn't… It's fine."

Olivia had brightened considerably at the sight of Luke. And Luke's presence made Lindy wonder if this was coincidental at all.

Granted, in small towns chance meetings happened frequently. But…

This didn't feel like chance.

But then, for some reason the first time she had met Wyatt didn't feel like chance either.

It had felt like lightning. Like a convergence in the road. But it hadn't felt like chance.

The men wandered over to their table, Bennett looking somewhat sheepish, Luke grinning at his wife and Wyatt still staring right at her.

He didn't do anything to minimize the intensity. Didn't pretend he didn't have his sights set directly on her.

"Hi," he said.

"Hi," she returned, lifting her beer bottle to her lips.

And then, she inhaled it. She choked, slamming the bottle back down on the table and lurching forward, coughing uncontrollably and inwardly cursing as she hacked and hacked and tried to get control over her body.

But then, there was a large, warm hand placed in the middle of her back, certain, sure fingers sliding down the length of her spine. Oh lord. If the coughing didn't kill her the shame from having a full-body reaction to fingertips brushing down her spine would.

He'd touched her face on the trail ride. But that was the only time. Until now.

It was...

And then he patted her.

Like she was a dog.

"Breathe, honey," he said.

She turned her head slightly, her face a couple of inches from his. "I *am* breathing," she said, her throat convulsing one more time.

"Yeah, the trick is to breathe *after* you swallow the beer. Not while you're taking a sip."

"*I will end you*," she said, the threat falling flat as she wheezed through it.

"I don't doubt you." But the patronizing tone and the cocky grin on his face said that he did.

"Mind if we join you?" Luke asked, but they were already pulling up chairs and sitting down around the too-small table.

"Seeing as I'm your wife," Olivia said, "I would be slightly offended if you didn't."

"No," Sabrina said. "Rules of girls' night. No husbands. Mine is sulking at home."

"That's cute," Luke said. "Yours minds."

Olivia made an exasperated noise. "I'm sorry. Mine isn't house-trained."

"There's one room of the house I'm pretty well trained in." His grin turned slightly feral. "The rest... Not so much. But...what I'm good at keeps me out of trouble."

Olivia turned beet red. "This is what I have to put up with."

"If I would have known this was an ambush," Bennett said. "I would have brought Kaylee."

"It wasn't meant to be an ambush," Wyatt said. "Just a chance meeting." But, Lindy could tell that he was lying.

Bennett went off to procure drinks and the others were making conversation. Lindy lowered her voice, so that only Wyatt could hear her. "Own your own BS, Dodge," she said. "Or you're not half the man I was led to believe you were."

"Honey, I have a feeling I'm twice the man you're imagining I am."

"Can you let one double entendre slide by?"

"No, I can't. It would be a disservice to the conversation. Just think, some people get together and spend the entire evening on bland, dull exchanges. When you're with me, you can be certain that'll never happen. Nothing with me is bland or dull."

"Right. Neither is it simple chance. Are you stalking me?"

"Yes," he said, grinning.

She did not know what to do with that, and rather than making her angry, his answer sent her stomach tumbling down to her toes. She took a deep breath, as if the force of the suction might call it back up. "That... I don't know what I'm supposed to say to that."

"Say you're flattered?"

"Why would I be flattered by...*that*."

"Because, secretly, I think that's what you want. You want me to have arranged to meet up with you here. You want this to be on purpose. But, you'd like to sit there and act indignant, pretend you're irritated with me. It excites you."

"It...it does not excite me."

"Yes it does."

"Do you see any confetti? Have I blown up even one balloon, Dodge? There are no signs of excitement anywhere."

"Sure there are," he said, leaning in, his brown eyes intense on hers. "First of all, your pupils are dilated, your breathing is kind of shallow. I can see your pulse—" He lifted his hand, pressed his thumb to the base of her neck. She inhaled sharply. "Careful," he said, his voice soft, almost a whisper. "Don't want to choke again."

No one was watching them. Thank God. She looked around furtively, taking great comfort in the fact that Luke seemed to be entertaining the entire table, and that Bennett had not yet returned from the bar.

"What are you doing?" she asked.

"I just told you."

"Stalking me isn't an answer. Particularly when we both know it isn't true. But, I do think that you're here on purpose at the same time I am."

"Guilty," he responded. "Luke knew that you'd be here. Because of Olivia."

"Great. I have a Benedict Arnold in the ranks."

"In fairness she didn't mean to. But, Luke came by earlier and he happened to casually mention that Olivia was going out with you. So I hatched a plan."

"Why?" She was getting desperate for an answer to that question. Because they had been dancing around each other for a long time. And she didn't think there was any good reason for them to stop dancing around each other. For them to dance toward each other. Or whatever it would actually be.

She should tell him to go away. She should dump what remained of her beer in his lap and walk out of the bar.

But she didn't move. Instead, she sat there, staring at him. At the planes and angles of his handsome face, at the enticing curve of his mouth. The only part of him that didn't look sculpted, hard. No, it looked like it would mold right to hers. Or like it would mobilize easily to take control, to force her to conform to his shape.

She shivered.

And she knew without a doubt that he noticed that too.

He didn't miss anything. That was the scary thing about Wyatt Dodge. He played the part of cocky, easy-going cowboy. But there was an intensity to him that she could sense, vibrating beneath the surface. She wondered if anyone else did. She wondered if anyone knew what was beneath all of that laid-back, lazy cowboy charm he showed the world.

She had felt it the moment she had first seen him. In that second his eyes had first connected with hers.

Like she understood.

One person wrapped in a created shell to another.

They were different shells, that was for sure. But the reality of it remained the same.

Wyatt looked away from her, and she followed his gaze, to Bennett, who was standing at the edge of the table, holding drinks, and appraising them both with a speculative look on his face.

"Have a seat," Wyatt said, his tone hard.

"Sure," Bennett said, plunking down in the chair next to Wyatt. "Talking serious ranch and vineyard business?"

"Yes," Lindy said. "More about the grand opening."

The lie slipped smooth and easy through her lips. She didn't consider herself a liar by nature, but she was very good at keeping interaction smooth. She didn't like being caught off guard, and she didn't like it when someone else steered the interaction. Because of that, she had gotten very good at commanding subject changes, and giving easy, innocuous answers that would allow them to slide forward in the conversation without getting hung up on any metaphorical rocks.

"Yeah," Wyatt agreed. "Lindy has agreed to a karaoke competition. I'm going to sing 'I'm So Lonesome I Could Cry.' She's going to sing 'Shake It Off.'"

Lindy treated him to an evil glare. "We were not discussing any such thing," she said to Bennett. "Mostly because if I sang you really would be so lonesome you could cry, Wyatt, as all of the guests would leave."

"Music not your thing?"

She shook her head and laughed, picking up her beer bottle. "Not remotely."

"I'm sure you have other talents," Bennett said, his tone was completely innocent, but she and Wyatt looked at each other, and the heat in his eyes was anything but innocent.

"Sure," she said, taking another quick swallow of beer.

Somehow, she managed to extricate herself from the verbal triangle they had going and to loop in the rest of the table on the conversation so that she could manage to get some kind of relief from so much direct interaction with Wyatt. Except he was still sitting next to her with the heat of his body radiating onto hers.

He shifted, and his arm brushed against hers, a zing of attraction firing through her.

She spent the rest of the evening with sparks running through her blood. And she wished more than anything that it would just stop.

But she didn't move away from Wyatt either.

About an hour after the guys had joined them, Luke

and Olivia excused themselves. Olivia was tired, so she said, but Lindy had a feeling the actual reason was that Luke wanted to go have some alone time with his wife.

Either way, that shrunk the group. Bennett said his goodbyes after that, wanting to get back home to Kaylee—who had been on call that evening—and his son, Dallas.

That left Sabrina, Bea, Wyatt and Lindy.

The buffer had been reduced, and Lindy really didn't need that.

"I need to head back to Copper Ridge," Sabrina said. "Liam will probably already be asleep. Or about to be. And that makes him cranky."

"I can catch a ride with you," Bea said. "I have to be at the clinic early."

Was this a setup? Was she being set up by her friends? She was going to… Well… Nothing, because they were gathering their things and leaving and if she said something it was going to be obvious that she was really put out that they were leaving her.

"We were having so much fun," she said, grinning widely. *Fakely.*

"Yeah," Bea said. "But I'm tired."

"I can drive you…"

"I've got it," Sabrina said, far too cheerful.

Lindy doubted Bea had any idea what was going on, but Sabrina was orchestrating something. Sabrina was far from innocent.

Less than thirty seconds later she was sitting at the table. Alone. With Wyatt.

"I think you planned this too," she said.

"I swear I didn't," he responded.

"Really?"

"It's not my fault if everyone is invested in us hooking up."

"Everyone is not invested in that."

"My brother Grant is."

She rolled her eyes. "Really? Or are you just saying that because Grant has become a strange pawn in this thing."

"No," Wyatt said. "I'm not just saying that."

"He knows that we're not going to...actually have a relationship, right?" Just saying that felt like it had a cost to it, because it was acknowledging the fact that there was an attraction between them. And acknowledging that to herself was hard enough. Actually saying it to Wyatt was another thing entirely. It was much better to be annoyed with him.

Except... He had not only been sexy the other day on the trail ride, he had been downright... Well, not horrible. The things he had asked her. The subjects he had brought up. He had been interesting. He had seemed interested in her.

As more than simply a female body he would like to get up on.

She would never have expected such a thing of him. She had lumped him in with the rodeo guys. And, she had a feeling that assessment was somewhat fair. But there was more to him too. That depth again.

"Oh, I don't think Grant expects for one moment I'm going to magically transform into a relationship guy," Wyatt said, his tone dry. "But, he thinks that I'm wandering around being a surly asshole because I'm sexually frustrated."

"Really?"

Wyatt let out a long, slow sigh, and Lindy was suddenly conscious of the fact that they were still sitting right next to each other, even though now they didn't have to be.

She didn't move.

Neither did he.

"Cards on the table," he said. "I'm attracted to you."

If she'd grabbed hold of her hair and found it on fire she wouldn't have been shocked. Her whole head felt hot. "Well. I'm…female. And stuff. Men like you have a pretty low bar."

"*You're* attracted to me," he continued, as if she hadn't just insulted him.

Her throat tightened, a lump forming at the base of it. She felt like she'd swallowed a hedgehog. But what was she going to say to that? It was stupid to pretend she didn't find him attractive. Any woman would.

Denying it made it personal. Denying it made it bigger than *oh hey look at that hot guy*. She didn't want it to be bigger than that.

"So what?" She lifted a shoulder. "I'm attracted to brownies. I'm attracted to doughnuts. But, I still have to eat damn salad if I want to maintain my health."

"You can eat brownies sometimes."

She growled. "That's incredibly pragmatic and annoying. I'm trying to come up with metaphors on the fly with a beer coursing through my system."

"Stop talking in metaphor," he said. "Let's talk literally. *You want me*. Why don't you want to let yourself have me?"

"I'm not…" She clamped her mouth back shut when she realized she had literally been about to say she wasn't that kind of girl. "I'm still navigating what my life looks like post-divorce. I haven't figured out where all that stuff's at yet."

"Are you telling me you haven't been with anyone else since the divorce?"

Her face got hot. "I really don't think that's any of your business."

"We're having a conversation about sex," he said. "About the fact that I would like to pursue that with you. I think it's a fair enough question."

Her face was on fire. It had to be. That was the only way to explain the heat burning in her cheeks. "I'm going to go now," she said, standing up, her heart hammering, her blood running hot and reckless.

Again, she felt like she was trapped in some strange time parallel. Where she was both back in the past, and in the present.

Experiencing that intense, overwhelming sense of desire she had felt the first time she'd seen Wyatt, and the crushing regret that she knew would result from acting on it.

"Lindy…"

He reached out to grab her arm, but she pulled away from him and walked toward the bar, taking out money and putting three twenties on the counter, which she knew would be more than enough. Then, she clutched her purse tightly to her body, trying to hold herself together as she walked out the front door of the saloon.

"Lindy," came Wyatt's insistent voice from behind her. "Wait."

"Walk fast or get left behind, Dodge," she said, continuing on down the sidewalk.

The street had been crowded when she had arrived and she'd had to park at the end of Main Street. Walking alone at night in Gold Valley didn't scare her. In this town, the only ambushes that happened were unfortunate run-ins with people who wanted to add you to their yearly family Christmas card list.

"All right," he said, catching up to her easily. He was over six feet tall, there was no way he wasn't going to catch up with her. And easily. She sighed heavily, but continued to walk, stepping purposefully in the center of one of the pools of light on the sidewalk, cast there from one of the streetlamps.

"What's the worst that would happen?" he asked. "If you and I were to sleep together while we worked on this project."

She reached the end of the sidewalk, standing next to her little car. She turned away from it, looking at the large Victorian house that sat at the end of the block, a large house that had stood empty for years. There was a For Sale sign out front. "Look at that," she said. "That house is finally for sale. It's just been standing there forever. No one doing anything with it. What a waste."

"You're deflecting," he said. "But, as a matter of fact, that's exactly how I feel about you and me. About this thing between us. It's just been sitting there, unused for a long damn time. Seems a shame to waste something like that."

She looked over at him finally, their gazes colliding in the dark. His face looked even more chiseled right now, the only light coming from the streetlamp behind him. It forced those cheekbones, the hollows in his face into sharper relief. Somehow made his scars look deeper, more obvious.

"That isn't how I…do things." Except… She didn't have an answer about why. She had met Damien, she had fallen for Damien. She had married him. Because she had…loved him so much? Or she had loved everything that had come with him so much, anyway.

Sometimes she wondered if she was a gold digger. Or if part of her was. Not that she hadn't loved him. She had, really and truly. But, there had been something so enticing and attractive about this whole new life coming with a marriage. Not simply a husband, but all of that opportunity. She would be lying if she said she would have married a poor man just as quickly.

A man who could offer her nothing but more of the same life she had already lived.

In addition to that, she hadn't cried since the divorce. There had always been some distance between Damien and herself. There was distance between her and everyone.

She wondered what that said about her sometimes.

But, then she went back out to work on her land, and she decided she didn't care. She spent an awful lot of time worrying about who she was and why. What people thought.

Damien had cheated on her with a younger woman and walked around with his head held high. Hung out with the same friends, went to the same restaurants, with his new wife on his arm. He didn't worry. He wasn't ashamed.

Why did *she* worry?

Why was she still worried she'd never been worthy of him in the first place? That this was somehow her fault when she knew full well it wasn't.

"But what if you did?" he asked, taking a step closer to her, reaching out and cupping her chin, tilting her face upward.

She could take a step away from him. She should. He wasn't holding on to her tightly, he was simply holding her, the warmth from his touch spreading from where he was making contact with her, through the rest of her body.

"What's the worst that could happen?"

I could get hurt.

Except she didn't need anything from Wyatt. Nothing but his body, anyway. If, in theory, she were to give in to their attraction. He couldn't take anything from her. Not her house, not her land. And if she didn't love him he couldn't take her self-respect, he couldn't take her heart and he couldn't give her any pain.

Really, what was the point of going through the trauma of betrayal in a ten-year marriage if you didn't learn something from it? If she knew this was only going to be physical. Only temporary…

What was the worst that could happen?

"I…"

He leaned in, his face a whisper from hers. And oh… the way he smelled. Like sunshine and hay. Hard work and something that was unique to him. Only him.

She wondered if he would taste just the same.

She was about to find out, she knew. He was leaning in, so close now.

She wanted… She wanted to kiss him.

She wanted to kiss another man, finally. To take that step to move on. But more than that, she wanted to kiss Wyatt Dodge more than she wanted to breathe.

And bless him for taking the control. Something she never thought she would think, ever. But he was going to take the decision away from her, and she wasn't going to have to answer his questions, wasn't going to have to do a single thing other than stand there and be kissed.

She was ready.

He squeezed her chin gently, pressing his thumb down on her lower lip, and then he released his hold on her, taking a step back. "Think on it," he said.

"I... *What*?"

But he was already moving away from her. "Think on it, Lindy," he said, turning around and strolling away from her.

Leaving her standing between the real estate sign that had served as some kind of metaphor for their attraction, and her little car that served as a metaphor for her freedom.

All alone.

She looked around, incredulous. But the street was empty, and there was no one to shout her outrage to.

And damn that man, she still wanted him to kiss her.

CHAPTER NINE

You are cordially invited to my house to work on plans for the upcoming barbecue at Get Out of Dodge.

If you need a definition provided for the word *cordially*, it is as follows: I will groin punch you if you don't show up.

Bring all of the information you've collected so far, and your lovely attitude.

Warmest regards,

Lindy Parker

WYATT READ THE email and shook his head. Then he shoved his phone into his pocket and looked around the grounds.

The place was looking damned good. But, that was secondary now to the email he had received from Lindy.

Lindy, who apparently refused to call or text now that the issue of email had been made a Big Thing.

Fair enough. He admired her stubbornness.

And he admired his own restraint. Honestly, he thought he was a damn saint.

But for whatever reason, she was nervous. And he was not going to coerce her into a sexual relationship. Not when he knew that deep down inside she wanted to beg him for it.

He knew that he could get it there. And now, that was his personal goal.

He wasn't used to having to work to get a woman into his bed. It was a novelty. Like all the restraint he had shown with her over the past few years with her had been a novelty.

The fact that he had any.

Maybe that was growth.

Maybe.

Half of himself thought the other half was insane. Because he had wanted Lindy for longer than he had ever wanted another woman, and he had deferred pleasure already for a hell of a lot longer than he ever had before. So why he was continuing to do it now when last night she had looked up at him like she was daring him to kiss her, he didn't know. Except...

Except he kind of wanted her to beg. And when she did, it would be sweet.

To have all that resolve not only melted away, but to have it demolished completely. Enough that her reserve couldn't hold her ramrod straight anymore. Enough that she might just get down on her knees and ask him very nicely for dirty, dirty things.

Yeah. He liked *that* idea.

But a more simplistic part of him was still self-flagellating over the fact that he could have kissed her last night. Backed her up against her car and pressed his body against hers good and hard. That he probably could have finagled his way into her bed.

But then, she would have been full of regret this morning. She would have told him it couldn't happen again.

And he would be damned if he only got one time with Lindy Parker.

Hell no. A fantasy woman needed to have time spent on her. And she was his fantasy woman, for better or for worse. So one regret-filled night was not on the agenda.

Tormenting her until she was as mindless with want as he was? That would do.

And now she was summoning him by email.

He shook his head.

Then, he walked across the gravel lot toward the mess hall, where he knew lunch would be waiting for him.

Grant and Jamie were already there eating, soup that had been delivered earlier in the week from Mustard Seed.

"I hope you have a cook lined up," Jamie said. "Not that I don't like Lucinda's soup," she said quickly. "I do. It's just that we want to offer more than soup and burgers to our guests, don't we?"

"I do," he said.

He wanted someone who would put together a menu for guests that had the kinds of options people expected to see these days. From gluten-free to meat-free and everything else.

"Good," Jamie said.

"I've done a pretty awesome job with all this," Wyatt said, thinking of all he'd accomplished.

He had a damned binder. *A binder.* He hadn't had a binder when he was in school.

Which reminded him, he was going to have to bring that to Lindy's.

Lindy.

He gritted his teeth and pulled his phone out of his pocket, opening up a new message in the email app.

Thank you so much for your cordial invitation. I can be there at about 1:30. If that suits the lady of the manor.

I will bring the requested materials, the only question that remains is if there is a formal dress requirement.

Either way, I'm going to show up in boots.

He hit Send without signing his name. She knew who the hell it was from.

He stared at his phone, as if a response was going to come immediately.

"What are you doing?" Jamie asked.

"Email," he returned.

"You're emailing? From your phone?"

"Yes," he said, making his way over to the kitchen area and dishing himself a bowl of soup.

"That's weird," Jamie called.

"You're weird," he said back.

As comebacks went, it wasn't the best. But, quality wasn't the issue. Not when it came to siblings. They traded insults back and forth often enough that a filler insult was just fine sometimes.

The important thing was getting the last word.

He walked back out into the dining area and Jamie smirked. "So's your face."

"Ouch," he said, putting his hand over his heart. "That was incredibly wounding."

"Good," Jamie said. "I hope it was mortal."

"She's winning," Grant said.

"What is it? Take potshots at Wyatt week?"

"When have I taken a potshot at you?" Grant asked.

"Oh, I don't know, yesterday?" He was not supposed to bring this up. And he was definitely not supposed to get in Grant's face about it. But, here he was, bringing it up.

Way to go, Dodge.

As Lindy called him last night.

"What did I say yesterday?"

"Oh, just the stuff about me not giving a damn about anything." He was really doing this. The words seeming to burn through his lips like acid, whether he wanted them to come out or not.

"You know what I meant," Grant said. "It wasn't supposed to be an insult. From my point of view, a guy in the life I was in? Your life looks good. End of discussion."

"It's not the end of the discussion. You think that I went into the rodeo because I didn't care about you guys. Because I didn't care about the ranch. Do you know where my money went?"

"Wyatt…" Grant said, his tone placating.

Wyatt was not in the mood to be placated.

"No," he said. "I'm serious. Get Out of Dodge was in trouble about the time I went into the rodeo, and when I started to win, when I started to make bank, I sent my cash back here. You guys might have all been working your knuckles bloody, Luke might have been working his ass off, I don't dispute that. But I'm the one that ended up keeping it afloat. You can talk all damn today about how I didn't care, how I went off and didn't think about you guys. But it's not true."

Both of them were staring at him, agape.

"Dad didn't tell you, did he?" He knew their dad hadn't. And he knew why.

"No," Jamie said, muted. "I mean, I was a kid, so I kind of understand why he didn't talk to me… But…"

"Dad's a dick," Wyatt said. Except that he didn't mean it. His dad could be a dick, but then, so could Wyatt. That was in the genes, he supposed. And, at the time, his dad had had every reason to be pissed off at him. That was why Wyatt had left.

And then the atonement had begun.

And it never ended.

"You don't mean that," Jamie said.

"I do," Wyatt said. "He let you all think that I was just off doing my own thing while I was actually keeping the place afloat."

It wasn't his siblings' fault the entire situation with Louisa had been hushed up, that the reason Wyatt had left, the reason he had felt guilty and was sending his money back home in the first place, was something they had all agreed not to talk about. And it wasn't for his dad's protection. No. It was for Wyatt's.

Although, sometimes Wyatt wondered if perhaps his old man's pride had been involved in it as well.

Nobody wanted to admit that their fiancée had jumped into bed with their seventeen-year-old son, he supposed.

That Louisa had whispered all kinds of things in his ear, about his prowess and his stamina and how much she enjoyed his body. But most of all, about how much she needed him.

Not that he had repeated those things to his dad. Hell, in the end, it kind of killed him inside that it had happened at all. The whole thing was gross. Messed up. Twisted as hell.

He hadn't seen it that way at the time. There had just been…someone who had needed him. Him. Not his strong back to do the work, not his hands to help carry heavy things. To help raise his siblings. Someone who had *needed* him.

It had been intoxicating on a level that went beyond sex. Although, at seventeen, the sex had been a big part of it.

He had been a boy, trying so hard to be a man. A boy who'd been told to be a man, since the day his mother had died. When his father had called him into the living room and told him with a rough voice that he'd need help. That Wyatt would have to be strong.

That he had to be a man now.

But he'd been a boy. A boy who'd lost his mother, and who'd lost his father in a way too. He'd felt that. Deep down. No matter how hard he'd tried he'd felt empty. Bereft of something.

Until Louisa.

She'd made him feel like a man. Like he had someone to take care of who really, really needed him.

But then it had been discovered, and everything had fallen apart. And in the years since it had turned into a wound that they had simply covered up and left alone.

It wasn't that Quinn disowned him, or that he didn't speak to him. Hell, they interacted all the time. But it was never the same.

And it never would be.

"I cared," Wyatt said. "I still care. I have been putting my hard-earned money into this place since I was a teenager. And I did it for all those years. This is where my money went. This is where my investment is. It's the hill I'd die on. The hill I want to be buried under. So you might think you know who I am, Grant. You might think you get to talk about what I do and don't care about, but make sure you know what you're talking about before you start running your mouth." He stood up from the table. "I've got stuff to do."

"Wyatt…"

Wyatt turned and walked out of the mess hall, and he

felt like a coward walking away from Grant. But, that didn't change the direction of his footsteps.

"Wyatt," his brother said again, following him right out the door.

Wyatt turned around and faced Grant, crossing his arms over his chest. "What?"

"I'm sorry. I didn't mean what I said the way that you took it. I don't know how else to say it now. I look up to you. I always have. And yeah, I think I might have simplified your life a little bit when I built up your legend in my head. But I never had anything that wasn't grave and serious. I fell in love with Lindsay and I didn't want anyone else. And then she got sick."

Grant swallowed hard before he continued. "Watching someone you love go slowly is a terrible thing, and in my head sometimes I would imagine you out there under all those bright lights riding on the back of a bull. People cheering your name. Money, and women, and this life that I could never have. I wanted it to be perfect like I imagined it was, because one of us should damn well be having a good time." Grant closed his eyes, his throat working. "Making you into my hero gave me some measure of peace. I'm sorry that I wasn't able to express that. I would rather chew horseshoe nails than talk about my feelings. I don't want you to think that I don't respect you. And I don't want you to think that I meant you weren't out there doing something real. It was real to me. It meant something to me."

Grant's wife had been gone a long time now, but talking about it was still difficult. He did it sometimes. Unexpected times. Good memories mostly. But it was almost always followed by a drinking binge, though that was getting less and less frequent.

He couldn't imagine what Grant had gone through, and not just her loss. The fact that the relationship had garnered media attention, and his brother had been put on magazine covers that had celebrities on them, because he had been self-sacrificing enough to marry his dying high school sweetheart.

Fame. Something the Dodge family wasn't accustomed to having thrust on them.

Although, Wyatt supposed his success in the arena had garnered him a little bit of fame. But it was fame he had chosen. Fame over something good.

Fame the way that Grant had gotten it... That just sucked.

"I'm sorry," Wyatt said.

"I made my choices," Grant said. "I'd make them again. But I'm not a saint. It was never easy. And I... wanted out sometimes."

"I can understand that," Wyatt said. "But you know... sometimes I envied you."

"Me? Because I had the great joy of grieving the loss of the woman I loved?"

"No. Because you knew what you wanted. While I drifted from place to place, you found a job, you found a woman. You found a life."

"A temporary one," Grant said. "So now I'm on life number two."

"There might be a life number three yet," Wyatt said.

"I doubt it."

"I think for me this might be life number two as well. Though, not quite as much as yours. But this is me trying to care. You know, in a way that people can see. Trying to build something real."

Grant stared at him for a long moment. "Why now?"

Without bringing up Dad and the ultimatum, he didn't really know how to answer that question. So he gave the most honest answer he could.

"To prove that I can."

He pulled up his email program again, as Grant nodded and walked back toward the mess hall. Then, he started a new message.

On second thought, I think I'll head over now.

Wyatt had never been to the main house at Grassroots Winery. He didn't necessarily associate with Damien when they weren't on the road with the rodeo, and he had certainly never come to visit the guy at home. They had gone out drinking sometimes in Gold Valley, but that was it. And not very frequently.

The house was *impressive*. White siding and pink flowers climbing up the side, massive windows that overlooked the well-manicured grounds. It wasn't like the other more rustic buildings on the property.

It was much more ornate and sleek, old-fashioned charm combined with a modern luxury sensibility.

It made him smile a little, because it suited Lindy.

She was like that. A touch of luxury.

Definitely a different type of woman than the kind he normally gravitated toward.

But, he was past the point of questioning why she particularly appealed to him. He was embracing it.

He rang the doorbell and waited, feeling slightly ridiculous standing there with a binder in hand, waiting for a woman to come answer the door.

"I didn't expect you until one thirty," Lindy said, when she opened the door.

She was wearing a sleek little black dress that seemed to be made out of some kind of clingy, stretchy fabric with no seams anywhere in sight.

One of those dresses that a man would have to wrangle up over a woman's head, because there was no other exit point.

That was fine with him. He didn't mind working for it. And as it was, it was kind of a feat of engineering, tight in all the right places, skimming over her curves.

And she had them.

He was well acquainted, from a visual perspective, with the shape of her body.

But this gave him a little bit more than he usually got.

She had the most incredible breasts. Really, just damned incredible. Even with a dress like this with a high neck that reached over the top of her collarbone, his eyes were drawn right to them.

In fact, the little bit of prim this had to the style of dress only made him that much more of a letch when he was trying to get a good look.

It left a lot for a man to wonder about.

And he was very curious.

"I sent an email," he said, grinning.

"I got it." She narrowed her blue eyes.

"I sent a follow-up email," he said.

She frowned. "Well I was getting ready." She stepped to the side, and he looked down, noticing that her feet were bare.

Her toenails were painted red, and God knew why that was sexy, but it was. She also had on a little silver toe ring.

A little piece of jewelry that no one usually saw.

That...that said things about her. Things that he wanted to spend a good while thinking on.

But, not now.

"Come on in," she said, backing away from the door and walking ahead of him. It took a lot of willpower to look away from the gentle sway of her hips while she walked in front of him and take in any details of the house.

It was just as white as the outside. Clean and bright and open. The kind of place that a man like him didn't necessarily fit. He would sit on one of the white sofas and leave dust behind.

It was all...fussy. And impossible to live in, in his opinion. If you couldn't collapse on the couch after a long day of work and put your feet up anywhere, there was no point calling it a home.

That was what homes were for. Living.

This place was like a museum. A place that existed to show others. Not for you.

He couldn't wrap his head around living like that.

"Nice place," he said, following across the white tiled entryway.

It was true enough. It was nice. He thought it was impractical.

"Thank you," she said. "I've been doing redecorating."

He wasn't sure that white things on white things counted as decoration, but he wasn't an interior designer.

Also, he didn't care.

Lindy stepped into the living area, transitioning from the white tile to equally white carpet. Wyatt paused.

"Should I take my boots off?"

"You don't have to," she said.

But he could tell by the arch in her neck that he really did need to.

"I promise my feet don't stink," he said.

She choked out a laugh. "Wonderful."

He kicked his boots off, and his socks, and followed her deeper into the room. She sat down on a white chair that had wood framing, and gestured toward a matching couch.

He took his seat. He set his binder down on the coffee table that had a bowl on it filled with wicker orbs that served no discernible purpose that he could see. The room was littered with things like that. Tassels on curtain tiebacks. Throw pillows. Random-ass books that looked nice on the outside, but had gold edges—a sure sign that what was inside was probably boring, and had never been read.

But then, he supposed that was like her too. She seemed to like things that weren't always necessary. Things that existed simply to look nice, or to give pleasure. Which made it even more strange that she didn't seem to want anything to do with the relationship between the two of them that could bring them both pleasure.

But maybe her outlet was wicker balls and throw pillows, instead of sex.

He would go for sex. But, that was him.

"I want to get a comprehensive overview of where we're at," she said, leaning back in her chair and crossing her legs.

It was an incongruous picture. With the bare feet and red toenails. The toe ring.

She looked very much like a boss who had called him into her office. Except for that toe ring.

And, they were in her house. Not down in her office.

It was definitely an interesting move on her part, and not random, because Lindy Parker didn't do anything random. That much he knew. She liked her control. She certainly liked having him on her turf instead of the other way around.

But, if she thought that her fancy white house was going to put her in charge…

She really didn't know him that well.

Fine enough. He didn't need her to.

"I'm interested to see the accounting," he said, leaning back and putting his hands behind his head. He stretched his legs out in front of him, and he could tell that his relaxed posture put her on edge.

She leaned forward.

"Well, we'll start advertising soon. I've already arranged to have an ad put in the *Gold Valley Gazette*, *Copper Ridge Tribune* and in both of Tolowa's newspapers. Plus, I'm going to send Beatrix out on a poster mission."

"A poster mission?"

"I'm going to have her canvass the area. Physical advertising never goes amiss. But, I've also got everything set up to go on the community chalkboard online."

"I do appreciate all that," he said.

"It's my strength," she said. "And I think you having lodging that brings more people to the area benefits me in a huge way. Like I've said before, making Gold Valley more of a tourist destination is possible, and essential. So many small businesses here could benefit from that. We've been taking an overflow from Copper Ridge for a couple of years now, but I know it can be more. We can be the destination. We might not have the ocean, but we have mountains, lakes, and—" she gestured toward Wyatt "—fantastic dude ranches."

"True enough."

"So, let me know what you have lined up."

He opened his binder and gave her a rundown on the vendors that he had coming out to the property. Food stands and drinks, local stores bringing their wares—all arranged by Jamie, thanks to her connections to some of the storeowners on the main street from when she worked at the Gunslinger.

He'd done a hell of a lot of work, using his cachet as a formerly kind-of-famous bull rider, and his charm, to get a whole lot of people on board for the big party.

"It's going to be good," Lindy said, wringing her hands together. "I really think it will be."

"You seem nervous," he said.

"I just… It doesn't matter what people think about me. It doesn't. But anytime I do something that has kind of a high profile I think… I don't want it to fail. Because I know that the Leightons and a lot of people that move in their circle don't think I can actually handle any of this. They're waiting for me to crash and burn. To prove that I didn't deserve it. I'm just…trailer trash in over her head, I guess."

He leaned forward, covering her hands with his. And he tried to ignore the lightning bolt that zapped through his body. "People aren't trash," he said. "Anyone who thinks they are isn't someone I want to know."

He'd touched so many women. Casually. Sexually. He had spent years telling himself sex was nothing. A mutual good time to be had by consenting adults. A physical release. Like exercise.

Touching someone's hand shouldn't go beneath the skin. Shouldn't make his chest tight and his body hard.

But this was Lindy. He'd wanted her for longer than he'd ever wanted anyone else.

He'd been close to her last night, but they'd been in public. In a bar, on the street. There was no one here now. He wanted to kiss her. More than he wanted air.

But she needed to close the distance between them. He refused to beg her. And if he kissed her now, and she sent him away...he would end up begging.

"I know that," she said, the word muted. "But that doesn't stop other people from thinking it. And I know that I don't really have anything to prove, but..."

"But you want to be a part of reinvigorating Gold Valley. You want to have a stake in all of this. You want what you do to matter. And you want people to know it was you. That you are more than what you started out as."

She nodded, swallowing hard, slowly pulling her hands away from beneath his. But he didn't move away, his hands dropping to rest on her thigh.

"Yes. Exactly."

He nodded slowly. "I know a little something about that."

They both paused for a moment, and the heat from her body bled through to his palms. He wanted to do more than simply touch her like this.

He wanted more of her. All of her.

"I bet you're wondering why... I bet..." She cut herself off, and leaned forward, her lips pressing against his. It wasn't a deep kiss, or a long one. It was nervous and brief, and when she pulled away she was shaking, trembling beneath his touch.

"I thought about it," she said, her voice husky. "Like you asked me to."

And just like that, all his control was ground to dust.

CHAPTER TEN

SHE NEVER DID anything without a plan. That didn't mean it had to be a smart plan. But she didn't show up to anything unprepared.

She did have a plan. Of course, she'd had one since last night, and she had made her decision this morning when she had sent the email.

And now she was shaking. Now, she had no idea what she had been thinking. She wanted him. That was what she knew. Beyond that…it was a good idea, a stupid idea, one that was going to end up with her heart being ripped from her chest and stuck onto a pike, she didn't know.

But she knew when she looked at him her heart sped up, she knew when he had gotten so close to her last night, when she had imagined that he might kiss her, her entire body had lit up, come alive in a way that it never had before.

And she…

She had convinced herself that she owed her body this chance.

To get on the train that had gone by her all those years ago. There was nothing keeping her from climbing right on board now. Nothing except common sense.

She wasn't sure she cared about common sense right about now. Wasn't sure she cared about anything except for the deep, raging need that was threatening to swamp her utterly and completely.

She'd felt desire before. She'd been turned on before. She'd been married for ten years, after all.

This was…this was like nothing else. Like a totally separate feeling. Maybe she was a different woman. More confident. More certain of what she wanted.

Or maybe it was different because it was him.

Wyatt Dodge. The last man on earth she should sleep with.

The only man on earth she wanted.

No one had to know. It was just her and Wyatt. Her, Wyatt and the scathing feelings that they both had about love. About relationships.

She didn't know anything about Wyatt's love life, it was true. Beyond the fact that he had a love-them-and-leave-them kind of spirit. But a cynical soul could sense its own, and she had a feeling that he was no more a believer in love and happy endings than she was. His reasons were his own, and they could stay his own.

His body…she kind of wanted that to be hers.

He was staring at her, his dark eyes glittering. There was a sharpness to them she had never seen before. An intensity that she had barely caught a glimpse of last night when they were standing beneath those streetlights.

"I hope you're done thinking now," he said, his voice hard-edged and gravelly.

And then, she found herself being pulled down from the chair, his strong arm wrapped around her waist like an iron band. He took her across that distance between them, and brought her down on his lap, her legs on either side of his.

She opened her mouth to speak, but he silenced her, covering her mouth with his.

Fire had shot down her veins the moment their lips had connected, but this was like something else entirely. This was an explosion. The heat of Wyatt's body, his arms around her, the hard ridge of his arousal between her thighs, his mouth. His tongue.

She parted her lips easily for him, angling her head and letting him take it deep.

She had never been kissed like this before. By a man who acted like he was starving for her. And she had never felt like she was starving for a man before either.

She forked her fingers through his hair, pressing her body forward, her knees pushing up against the back of the couch, that hard evidence of his need for her pressing more intensely into that tender place between her legs.

He flexed his hips forward and she gasped, as lightning raced from her center and radiated outward.

She felt like he was going to consume her, completely. And she was going to let him.

No. This was more. It was deeper. She wasn't just letting him, she was devouring him right back.

She couldn't pretend this wasn't years in the making.

So many years when he was forbidden to her. Off-limits.

She had never thought about him in a sexual way while she was married. Nothing beyond that first, blinding incident when she had seen him and known that letting that man get too close to her would be a big, terrible mistake.

But after that…

In the time since, when they had started working together… It had been growing inside of her. Expanding.

Like molten rock building beneath the surface of a dormant volcano.

It was erupting now. All over the damn place. All over her. She was liquid. Fire and heat. Destructive.

He was right. It was going to burn the whole place down, and nothing would be left in its place except ash.

She still didn't want to stop.

Not ever.

Her heart was pounding so hard she thought it was going to burst through her chest, and then she pressed her palms up against his chest, and she felt he was doing the same thing.

But that was secondary to what else she noticed. How hard he was. How muscular.

She wanted to see him.

She wanted to lick him.

Without thinking, she dragged her fingers down his front, feeling the indent of each of his muscles beneath the thin fabric of his T-shirt as she did. Then she pressed her hands beneath the hem of that shirt and pushed it up. He released his hold on her, only for a moment. Only to grab the T-shirt with one hand and wrench it up over the top of his head, breaking the kiss for a moment as he did.

She whimpered when she saw him. She had never seen such a beautiful man in all her life. Not in a movie. Not on the internet. He was...

It was like he'd been created for her. A made-to-Lindy's-order man. Taut, lean muscle, covered by just the perfect amount of dark hair. She put her fingertips against his chest and watched as she dragged them down his torso. She bit her lip as she continued her erotic journey, her fingers gliding over hard-cut abs.

"Hey," he said, his voice rough. "That lip is mine."

Then he buried his fingers in her hair, pressed her mouth savagely against his. And bit her. Just like she'd done to herself a moment before.

But different. Oh, so very different.

She gasped, letting her head fall back, and he took advantage of the opportunity, angling his head and kissing a line down her neck, stopping at the high neck of her dress.

"This damned dress," he muttered. He reached down, pressing his hands to her thighs, shoving the dress up higher, and then pushing it up over her head, leaving her in nothing but a black lace bra and matching underwear.

She had prepared after all. She wasn't going to come to a seduction without matching underwear.

She had standards.

He kissed lower, all the way down to one curve of her breast, to the edge of her bra, before licking his way down the line of her cup. It delved slightly beneath, teasing one tightened nipple.

This was moving so fast. So fast and so intense.

She hadn't known what she had expected. He had played it so cool last night. He had made it her move.

She had kissed him. Her lips barely brushing his. And then she had moved away. She had expected for him to wait. For him to let her guide the rest. But he wasn't now.

She was being carried away on the current, in the rushing pleasure that was sweeping her away, pulling her under, his strong arms turning the tides, deciding what happened next.

It terrified her. And yet, that terror was firmly in the back seat for now. Hanging on for dear life. Because the rest of her…the part that was excited, full of need, full of desire like she had never felt before…that part of her was going in headfirst.

That part of her was powerless to do anything but let Wyatt control what was happening between them.

She had given it to him, to this undeniable attraction between them.

She was a woman who always had a plan, for better or for worse.

But this wasn't *her* plan anymore.

This was something else entirely. Something beyond thought and rationality.

And it felt so. Damn. Good.

Wyatt reached around behind her and unclipped her bra, the lace falling slack, sliding down her arms. She shimmied, getting rid of it entirely.

He ground out a harsh curse, letting his head fall back as he examined her.

Her heart was beating a thousand miles a minute, her entire body shaking. And she sat there, on his lap, letting him look. No man had ever looked at her like that. Ever. Like it was torture and bliss, like somehow her body contained heaven and hell, and he wanted it either way.

He gripped her hips, moving his hands up slowly, and she thought she might die of anticipation. Need gathered inside her, centering between her legs as those hands, calloused and rough from all the labor he did, made their way over her skin.

She'd never been touched by hands like this. Strong. Hard. Working man's hands.

He was the kind of guy she would have avoided back when she was younger. The kind of guy she would have thought led nowhere but back into the trailer park.

Maybe it was the kind of guy her body was always

destined to respond to. After all, her mother-in-law had been convinced that someday Lindy's bad blood would rise to the surface. And if that was what was happening here, if that was what was happening now, she didn't care. Because all that bad blood was heated to boiling because of those hands.

His thumbs skimmed the undersides of her breasts and she gasped, her breathing coming out in short, sharp bursts. He made slow, deliberate progress, his fingers curving around to cup her, his thumb lazily drawing circles back and forth, missing her nipple.

She was going to die. She was going to die right here on her couch because Wyatt Dodge would not touch her the way she needed him to.

It was an inglorious way to go.

Still, she had limited regrets.

But then he *did*. Then he was *there*, touching her, pinching her lightly. Her internal muscles tightened in response and she felt a wave of pleasure roll over her, a tremor before the big one.

He growled, wrapping his arm more tightly around her and turning, bringing her with him as he pressed her down to the couch and brought his body down over the top of hers. Her head was propped up slightly by the armrest, one leg draped over the edge of the couch, her bare foot on the floor. And Wyatt right there, pressed against that place where she was wet and needy for him.

He cupped her breasts in his big hands, squeezing gently, before sliding them down her midsection, those calloused thumbs scraping her skin on the way down, an erotic torture that she wasn't certain she could endure.

She arched her hips upward, gasping when she came

into contact with his hard length. Those flimsy panties of hers were no match for that most masculine part of him.

She didn't want them to be.

She just wanted him.

He hooked his finger into the waistband of her panties, drawing one side of them down, then the other, before grabbing them in the middle and yanking them off the rest of the way.

She forgot to be embarrassed. She couldn't be embarrassed when he was kissing her like he was, when he was touching her like he was. And when he pressed one hand down there between her legs…

He slid one finger through her folds, his breath hissing, harsh and raw through his teeth as he did. A curse on his lips.

He pushed a finger inside of her and she cried out, rocking against his hand, desperate for release. And he was a man who was clearly more than willing to oblige. He pressed the heel of his palm against that sensitive bundle of nerves there, worked his finger in and out of her body as he pressed hard against her, making a slow, rocking motion that built the need inside of her to unbearable proportions.

He was shirtless, but the blue jeans meant he still had on too many clothes. She skimmed her fingers down his back, glorying in that fine musculature she found there, stopping at the waistband of his jeans, letting her fingertips drift along that dip in his spine just before his ass. An ass she so desperately wanted to get her hands on.

She didn't think she had ever wanted to touch a man quite this much before.

No, she knew she hadn't.

She ached with it.

And not simply because he was touching her. But with the anticipation of touching him.

She brought her hands down around between them, working his belt buckle open, sliding his belt through the loops on his jeans and chucking it onto the floor.

He made a noise that fell halfway between a groan and a growl as she unsnapped his jeans and lowered his zipper slowly.

She reached inside, palming him over his boxer briefs. Desire, nerves, skittered through her. It had been a while, and he was a big boy.

He groaned, and she started to push his jeans down.

"Wait," he rasped, reaching behind him and tugging his wallet from his back pocket, setting it down above her left shoulder.

Then, she set to work pushing his jeans down, hooking her foot over the top of them when they got down to his knees and using her leg to shove them down the rest of the way. He kicked his feet free, and then made quick work of his underwear.

She could see him, all of him, just for a moment. And her throat went dry. Thank God, Wyatt Dodge lived up to the hype. Really and truly. She had wanted him for so long it would be a disappointment if he didn't.

Of course…something in her had always known he would. That same something that had been captive to him from the first moment she'd set eyes on him.

Like he'd reached inside her right then, in that bar, and taken a piece of her. Only a small one. But big enough that she had felt the loss of it.

Had felt that connection to him ever since.

There was no way he wouldn't be perfect for her in this way.

She curved her hand around his hard, impressive arousal, squeezing him and watching as that handsome face contorted with pleasure. He closed his eyes, a crease appearing between his brows. If she didn't know better, she would think he was in pain.

But she knew better.

She worked her hand up and down, watching him carefully as she did, reveling in this moment. This first moment where Wyatt was finally in her hands, right where she wanted him.

"We can go slower later," he rasped, taking hold of his wallet and tugging out a condom before flinging the leather article down onto the floor.

She wanted…more. Everything. She wasn't sure she wanted everything this quickly. But, she didn't want to stop either. Couldn't stop.

She needed him. Needed him like air.

There was no point holding her breath now to prove a point.

He tore open the condom and rolled it over his length. She mourned the fact that she didn't get as much time to look at him as she wanted.

She wanted a whole hour just to look at him. At that hard, honed body that she'd been fixated on for so long.

But she could do that later.

Later? Like you're going to do this again?

She pushed that voice aside. And then, she didn't even have to work that hard to keep thoughts from invading because everything in her mind was wiped clean as he positioned himself at her slick entrance and began to press forward.

She curled her fingers into his back as he filled her, slowly, thoroughly.

He was thick and perfect. Everything that she wanted. Everything she needed. She curved her legs around his thighs, clinging to his shoulders as he pressed forward slowly, slowly, much too slowly.

And then, he was filling her completely, all the way to the hilt, and withdrawing again, this time bringing himself back into her much more quickly, and with much less gentleness.

That was good. She didn't want gentle. She didn't want slow.

This had been building for years. And she needed to let it burn now. To let it ravage everything around them. To let it ravage her.

She needed this. She realized now, with him looking down at her, his brown eyes blazing, his cock filling her. She needed him. This was something important. Something essential.

Something she had known from the moment she had first seen him.

He wasn't a train she had missed, but one she had been destined to catch later. Something inside of her had clearly known that, even then, that somehow, for some reason, he was an essential stop on the route that was her life.

It made sense now. It felt right.

It felt...

Amazing.

The room closed in around them, until she could only see him, them. Her hands on his shoulders, those strong arms braced on either side of her. The cords in his neck standing out with all that tension and self-control it was taking for him to remain measured now. His square jaw held tight, though sculpted lips parted, his eyes closed.

She couldn't bear to close her eyes. She wanted to keep watching him. Watching this.

She had known that he had the potential to break her apart, to undo her. But right now…she could see that she had the potential to do the same thing to him. She had never considered that. That she might be able to destroy this big, hard man with her touch.

She had been afraid that letting go of her control with him would make her feel out of her depth. That she would feel like she had always done in situations where she was less experienced, less educated. But she didn't. Not with him. Never with him.

He wanted her.

That was enough.

Pleasure gathered tight in her midsection, spreading through her body, gripping her, holding her tight as Wyatt pushed them both closer to their release.

The only sound in the room was their breathing, their bodies moving together.

Pleasure built inside of her, a deep, endless well of need that she wasn't sure she could survive. She was going to keep falling, and never find the bottom. Never find the end. She had never felt anything like this before. Wound so impossibly tight like she was going to break, shatter completely. She dug her fingernails into his shoulders, not caring when she felt them sink in. She needed to hold on to him, with everything she had, or she was going to fall apart. Lose herself. Lose him.

She didn't know what scared her more.

His movements increased, his big body slamming into hers. And it wasn't enough. Not enough at all.

She whispered in his ear. Words of encouragement. Dirty words. Commands. Harder. Faster.

And then, simply his name. Wyatt.

Wyatt.

Wyatt.

Pleasure bloomed inside of her, suddenly. Brilliant and bright, suspending her free fall, catching her and holding her there until she was suspended in the stars, pops of light and fire going off all around her.

Wyatt grunted, lowering his head and burying his face in her neck as he thrust into her one last time, freezing as he pulsed inside of her, finding his own release. His body shook. That large, well-muscled body, so strong from years of labor. From riding giant, terrifying beasts that wanted nothing more than to kill him.

And yet, riding her had made him shake.

If her orgasm hadn't already undone her completely, she might have found herself falling apart again.

Instead, she lay there, holding him while his release shuddered through him, brushing her hands through his hair, down over his shoulders, down to his butt. It really was a very nice butt.

It occurred to her then that she had just had very dirty sex on her very white couch.

And she didn't even care.

She would put a thick velvet rope around this couch and make it a display. She'd buy a new one for people to sit on.

That the room was bright white, bathed in bands of gold from the sun filtering through the window, and lights from inside, caught up with her then.

She wasn't a prude. Not really. She liked sex a lot.

More now than she had ten minutes ago, to be perfectly honest.

But still…the fact of the matter was, she'd made love

with Wyatt Dodge on her couch in the middle of the day, and that was pushing the bounds of propriety. As much as she cared about those. And she was... She was so profoundly naked.

But then again, so was he.

Wyatt sat up, his muscles bunching and shifting as he did, the play of bronzed skin over all that hard definition made her mouth go dry, made her body hum with a little thrill of excitement that should be impossible considering how boneless he had rendered her.

She had never had an orgasm like that in her life. One that consumed her completely. That burned every thought from her mind like alcohol going up under a lit match.

He stood up and she gloried in the side view. That perfectly curved ass and his thick muscular thighs. She didn't really know she had a thing for men's thighs. But boy howdy, she had one now.

Reality was starting to try to crowd in to the moment. Trying to get her to acknowledge the fact that she had done something she couldn't undo. That she had unleashed a whole hell ton of demons and she wasn't going to be able to banish them again.

Whatever. She was post-orgasm and Wyatt was naked. If the mistake was made, she might as well enjoy it for a moment.

He said nothing, and made his way out of the room and she just...

Her warm fuzzy buzz felt dented. She hadn't expected him to do that. She didn't know what she'd expected.

Panic was like a haze over her vision, and it took her a moment to realize that while he'd left the room, he couldn't have left the house, only the room.

Right. He had protection practicalities to take care of, and he had to leave the room and find a trash for that.

She was being a drama queen. But in fairness to her she'd never had random sex with a random guy. She'd only ever had committed sex with a guy she was planning on marrying, and then of course sex with her husband.

Wyatt was...she wasn't even sure how much she liked him half the time. He irked her. He got under her skin and under her clothes. But he wasn't even really a friend. She didn't know what to do with what had happened between them, even though she'd been totally on board for it to happen.

And now she felt small. Silly and scared.

Insecure.

Wyatt reappeared a moment later and she turned away from him, trying to casually study the cord on her accordion blinds instead of his naked body. Then, much to her relief he turned slightly, moving back to the couch, obscuring the more explicit parts of his body.

She let out a breath.

"Lindy..."

Oh, no she wasn't going to let him talk first. She wasn't going to let him guide this.

She cleared her throat. "I have to take back everything I said before. About you bragging. Clearly...clearly it's somewhat deserved."

He turned to face her and her cheeks prickled, the pinpricks spreading outward, blooming into heat. Full frontal Wyatt was a whole lot to take in. No pun intended.

He was, after all, only the second man she had ever seen naked in the actual flesh.

Not to be drawing comparisons or anything, but it was difficult not to when there were only two men to compare, after all. It wasn't like she had a treasure trove of penises in her memory.

Now, Wyatt's penis was a treasure trove all its own.

"Only somewhat?" he asked, arching one brow.

"Only you," she said, frowning. "I'm paying you a compliment. Can't you just be nice?"

"No," he said. "And frankly—" he grinned "—you would be unhappy if I was."

Her frown deepened, and she wrinkled her nose. "I don't think that's true."

"I do," he said. "Because you like me to be shameless. If I wasn't shameless… This wouldn't have happened."

Lindy huffed out a laugh. "Really?"

She did not know why she was moving forward with this conversation. Naked.

It occurred to her then that she was still lying on her back, somewhat sprawled. And she imagined his view was…interesting at best.

She jackknifed into a sitting position and crossed her legs primly, folding her hands in her lap.

Yeah, she was still naked, but she was going to do what she could to reclaim some of her power.

"Really," he said, his eyes dropping down toward her breasts, making no effort to hide the fact that he was checking her out.

She sniffed. "Who invited you here? Because this wasn't your idea."

"I…" Whatever he'd been about to say died on his lips.

She sniffed. "Exactly."

"You…"

"I seduced you, Wyatt Dodge. Deal with it."

"I feel used."

"Good. You should. I used you good."

"That wasn't a complaint," he said. "I liked your style of using me pretty well."

"Well. So we're clear. It's not like you orchestrated this or anything."

"Right," he said. "I certainly didn't lay the groundwork for it last night."

She sputtered. "I… You…"

"You want me, baby. That's fine. But don't act like that isn't because of anything I did."

Her lips twitched. She was slightly hoisted by her own petard here. And by the fact that she had been unwilling to let him think that he had somehow manipulated this, when she was the one who had manipulated it. But then, the side effect of that was her confessing the fact that she wanted him.

Not that he wasn't fully aware of that, since he'd barely touched her and she'd gone up in flames.

Mostly, she had no idea why she was getting all arch and prickly now. Except she was starting to feel small and fragile, and he was standing there gloriously naked and completely unembarrassed. And she was… This wasn't like her. She felt completely like the inexperienced party now. It had been one thing when she'd been turned on. All easy and simple. But she didn't know how to play the sophisticate now.

She had waited to have sex with Damien until they were pretty committed to each other. Had held on to her virginity for a very long time.

She didn't know how to do casual sex. And she knew that Wyatt was a casual sex aficionado.

If you could be an aficionado of something casual. She wasn't really sure.

"Typical," she said. "Taking credit for a woman's seduction. Because you can't admit that I got the upper hand."

She screeched as Wyatt mobilized, grabbing hold of her wrists and laying her flat on the couch, his hot, naked body hard over hers.

"Who has the upper hand?" he asked.

"Me," she said, wiggling impotently against him, her wrists held fast above her head.

A wicked smile curved his lips upward. "Really?"

She parted her legs slightly, and that put his rapidly hardening arousal right into contact with her. "Maybe."

He closed his eyes, his breath hissing through his teeth. She flexed her hips upward and a spark of need shot through her body.

Wyatt groaned, tilting his head upward, a smile that bordered on pain crossing his face.

"Yeah," she said. "You seem very in control right about now."

"I think," he said, flexing forward and grinding himself over that sensitized bundle of nerves, "we have each other hostage."

"No," she said, gasping as the word escaped. "I'm not a hostage. I'm totally fine."

"Totally," he said, pressing against her again, "fine."

"I just had an orgasm. I'm good."

"That's aiming awfully low."

"I'm here with you. I never said I was aiming high."

He kept her wrists pinned with one hand, and used the other to skim over her curves, teasing her. "I'm wounded."

She wiggled beneath him again. "You don't *feel* wounded."

"I don't know," he said. "It hurts pretty bad. I bet you could kiss it and make it better."

Heat suffused her face, as she imagined doing just that.

She had her limits, though. There was no way they could... Again. Right now. Right after the first time. They were supposed to be working.

As if this isn't what you invited him over here for.

Still. There had to be boundaries.

"Open up your binder," she said.

"I don't know how much dating you've done, I know you were married for a long time, but that's not exactly dirty talk."

"I'm not trying to talk dirty to you, Dodge, sit up and get your binder."

He didn't comply. Instead, he lowered his head and he kissed her. Long, lingering. Slow. Like they had all the time in the world. Like he wasn't pressed up against the most vulnerable part of her, blazing with heat and obvious arousal. He didn't even move the lower half of his body, not at all. It was all lips. Except that they were touching, from chest all the way down to their toes. Completely naked, with nothing between them.

And shamefully, she was the one who started to move. The one who had to do something to try to quiet the intensity of the desire that was building inside of her.

And that was when he chose to sit up.

Bastard.

"What do I need my binder for?"

"Add a new page."

"You're demanding," he said, leaning over and grabbing his binder from the table.

"I am. I'm demanding, and I'm organized. I also like

to know exactly what I'm getting into before I get my-self into it."

She had made a decision, while laying on her back with Wyatt pressed against her. She wanted him. If she wanted him again after having him so recently, it was obvious that it was going to keep happening. As long as they were working together they were going to end up in bed together. Or on the couch together. Whatever.

There was no point fighting it. There was only mak-ing rules of engagement.

"Okay," he said.

"We need a new page."

"A new page," he repeated her blandly.

"Yes. We have a Get Out of Dodge/Grassroots events page. And we need a Wyatt/Lindy page."

"Right," he said slowly.

"Make a page," she repeated.

He sighed heavily, but took a pen out of his binder and flipped the page, making a new heading.

"All right."

"What does it say?"

"It has the information that I need," he said.

She scowled, and then leaned over. "I said to make it *Wyatt and Lindy*. Not *stupid sex rules Lindy made me write down.*"

"It's my binder. Use your binder, Lindy. I'll know what I'm talking about."

"Fine," she said. "I will."

She grabbed her own binder, making a page with the heading Wyatt/Lindy. "Okay," she said. "First rule. No-body knows about this."

"Why?" he asked, flinging his hands wide. "Everybody knows that we're attracted to each other. It was the worst kept secret ever."

"Even still. There is no reason for anyone to know. I want this event to go off without a hitch. And I don't want anyone thinking that I slept with you in order to make something run more smoothly."

"Lindy," he started.

She held up a hand. "Nonnegotiable," she said. "I'm already in a position where people think that about me, Wyatt," she said, her voice trembling, more emotion in the words than she wished was there. "Everybody thinks that I'm only where I'm at because of Damien. And the worst part is I can't even dispute that. Honestly, more or less, it's true. If it weren't for him, if I hadn't married him, I wouldn't know enough about business to be able to run Grassroots. And I sure as hell wouldn't have a property like this. What access would I ever have had to anything? The answer is that I would have no access at all. Now I'm partnering with you on something… If I was sleeping with you too… And everyone knew it…"

"Right," he said, "if that's what you need, that's fine."

But he clearly looked unsettled about it, and for the life of her she didn't know why.

"It bothers you," she said.

"I don't like being your dirty secret," he said.

"I would think you were used to that."

"Did it ever occur to you that maybe that's why I don't like it?"

There was a strange amount of heat and vehemence behind the words, not something she would have expected from a man like him. "No," she said. "It honestly didn't."

He shifted. "Do you know what I like? I like having sex with people who are adults. Who don't have an issue with it."

"Who treat it casually?"

"Yes," he responded.

"Well, I'm not that woman. I've been with one man, Wyatt. Now two. I don't take it casually. I can't. I don't want a relationship, don't worry about that. But still, I can't be blasé and running around like…oh, I just had him inside of me and now we're here having a droll conversation re—the saucy interlude we had in bed."

"You what?" He frowned, his brows knitting together.

"Damien was the only man I had ever slept with until fifteen minutes ago," she said. "So, I'm sorry if I'm not being a sophisticate about it, but I don't know how to be."

She let those awkward, uncomfortable words settle between them. They were like shards of glass, cutting down inside of her, exposing her. Making her feel like the exact thing she hated. Ignorant. Unsophisticated. All the things she had spent years battling when she and Damien had been married.

"I don't know what to say to that," he said.

"Don't say anything. But… You have to understand where I'm coming from. You can't expect me to see it the same way as some guy who slept with like a thousand women sees it."

"I have *not* slept with a thousand women."

"Whatever. You seem like the kind of guy who's used to making it casual. That's what Damien always said about you."

"He's not wrong. Look, I'm the kind of guy who's had a lot of access. And as long as everybody's there for a good time, I don't see why we can't have one."

"And that's great," she said. "I am here for that. But, without telling people."

"All right."

"Not because it's you." Because he had looked kind of stark and terrible, and maybe even wounded when he'd asked if he was her dirty secret, and she didn't like that at all. So, even though she thought he was kind of a big lug and she doubted he had finer feelings... Just in case, she wanted to make sure she was clear. "That's not the issue. It's me and my whole situation. And the fact that I... I want to process this without input from the million wonderful, caring, interfering people in my life. And without any thoughts from the judgmental assholes who hang out on the fringes."

"Okay," he said, but she still had a feeling there was an issue.

"Write it down," she said, and she wrote it down as the first item on her page.

"All right," he said, "what's the next item of business."

"It ends when we're through working together."

"Okay," he said, making a note of that. Apparently, that condition required much less discussion.

She found that vaguely wounding.

"Because... It's going to be neater that way," she said.

"I didn't argue," he said.

"No," she said, "you didn't. Just...providing information."

"I appreciate it."

"I don't think you do."

"I do. This entire thing is riveting. And exactly what I want to do while I'm sitting here naked with you."

She made an exasperated sound. "That's the other thing. We have to be able to get our work done."

"Got it," he said. "Prioritizing work."

"Right."

"So. Secret sex, time limit, work comes first."

"Sounds good to me," she proclaimed.

"I'm not sure we need a list."

"We do. To make sure that we're on the same page. Well, I guess we're using different pages, but they say the same thing. Except for your header, which is offensive."

"I'm going to be offensive," he said. "In fact, I'm going to write that down. Wyatt Dodge is an offensive asshole and will remain so for the duration."

Lindy bristled. "Fine." She wrote down exactly what he had said on her page. "And you can also add that Lindy Parker will be the timekeeper of such events as occur naked. As she feels most comfortable when she's in charge."

He laughed, and then suddenly, he tossed down his binder and leaned forward, ripping hers out of her hands.

"What…"

"That's not happening." He reached out, wrapped his arm around her waist, and literally threw her over his shoulder like she was a sack of potatoes.

"Hey," she said, letting her arms hang limp over his butt, trying to decide what to do next.

"You like it," he said.

She kicked her feet. "I don't."

And then, he slapped her on the bottom. She yelped, and much to her great shame, pleasure spread from where his hand had just made contact through the rest of her body.

"Rules are for later," he said. "For now, we have the afternoon, and an excuse for where we are. I say we take it."

Then he started to carry her up the stairs, and she was unable to argue.

CHAPTER ELEVEN

By LATE AFTERNOON Wyatt was in the most blissful state he had ever imagined he could be in while partly wrapped in a down-filled blanket. But, it wasn't the blanket that was responsible for the bliss. No, it was the woman who was also wrapped around him, laying there facing him, her face buried in his neck.

Lindy Parker was everything he'd fantasized about and more. And to have her…finally, like this, like he had wanted down to his soul from the moment he had laid eyes on her was…

It was more than intoxicating.

He ran his hands down the elegant line of her back, her skin so soft beneath his touch it was like cream.

He'd had no idea that delayed gratification could produce such a hard-core reward. But, now he was living testament to the fact that it could, that it did.

And he was the second man she'd ever been with. That had blown his mind.

He had sensed that she wasn't… *Experienced* was the wrong word. The woman had been married for a decade. She was experienced enough, but she didn't go out and have sex recreationally, and perhaps hadn't been exposed to a variety of sex.

He was more than happy to add some variety to her life.

She shifted, beginning to move away from him and he

tightened his hold on her, rolling over so that he was on his back and she was perched on top of him, her blond hair falling forward, messy and wrecked.

Like his insides.

"Where are you going?" he asked.

"It's four in the afternoon," she said. "I cannot stay in bed with you the entire day."

"Why not?" He treated her to his slowest, laziest smile.

"Because," she said.

He lifted his hand and brushed his thumb over her cheek, then arched upward, kissing her neck, up to her mouth, long and indulgent. Until she had begun to melt against him, all the tension in her muscles gone.

He'd had her three times to completion. *His* completion. Her own outnumbered his by quite a bit. And he was damned proud of that fact.

Of course, it was about more than pride. Her pleasure did something to him. He felt it. Echoing through him, almost as bright and real as his own.

"Wyatt," she said, scolding, but not meaning it.

"I'm a damned persistent bastard," he said.

"Yes, but this is not what you need to persist in. Persist in some *work*."

"Nevertheless…"

"Wyatt!" She grumped when he bit her earlobe.

But, she wasn't really all that grumpy.

He could tell, because her thighs were spread over him, and he could feel how much she wanted him again.

He was reluctant to leave this moment because right now, he had her and God knew if she was going to come to her senses thereafter. He'd rather make her come now.

He couldn't blame her if she did come to her senses. Even when it was good, they clashed. They laughed, but they clashed too. There were easier men she could play around with for a temporary fling.

The woman could hold a contest and idiots from all over would compete for the pleasure. Men who would let her have her way. Men who would let her be in charge.

Though, he didn't really think she wanted that. Didn't think she wanted someone she could manipulate or control.

If she did...

She wouldn't be here with him in the first place.

"Come to Get Out of Dodge with me," he said, not really thinking that through before the words exited his mouth.

"For what?"

"I'd like to show you some of the hiking trails." *Did he?* Honestly, it was amazing how much bull he could talk when he wanted to get his way.

She slithered away from his body, taking the duvet with her as she got up off the bed. Away from him. Stealing his warmth and his comfort in both forms.

"I really need to put in an appearance at the office. Sabrina is going to wonder what the hell is going on. Bea is probably going to be wondering where I am..."

"Bea is working at my brother's veterinary clinic today. Which, I think we both know."

"How do *you* know?" She treated him to a very skeptical expression.

"I pay attention," he said. "Damnedest thing."

"Well, whatever." She waved a hand, then grabbed hold of the blanket again, trying to keep it from sliding down. Too late. He saw a bit of lovely butt cheek, and he wasn't sad about that at all. "I really do need to get some work done."

He stood up, and he didn't miss the fact that the sight of him completely naked made her cheeks turn bright pink. "Okay," he said. "Tomorrow."

"I work tomorrow. I mean, I have to go to the tasting room in Copper Ridge. I'm not blowing you off."

Except, he had a feeling that she was. Not completely, but that she was trying to get a little bit of distance.

He should be singing hallelujah for that. He didn't do closeness. He didn't like it.

Historically.

Right about now he was wanting a bit more of it. And when the hell he had become that man he didn't know.

Or maybe it wasn't about the man he'd become, but the woman that he'd taken to his bed.

"Day after tomorrow," he said, pressing more, and wondering why in the hell his pride wasn't yelping like a wounded animal. But, it turned out he just didn't give a damn.

Funny that.

"Okay," she relented. "I will come over in two days and I will do that…hiking trail." The word hiking made her look pained.

"I really must be good in bed," he said.

"You are. Seriously. Otherwise I would not be…hiking." She twisted her lips to the side in a grimace.

"You're gonna need little boots."

Two glittering blue eyes narrowed, shooting metaphorical lasers at him. "I do not wear little boots."

"You have little feet," he pointed out.

She wrinkled her nose. "Stop it."

"Stop what?"

"Flirting with me," she said, wrapping the blanket

more tightly around her and turning away from him. "I have work to do."

"Yeah, well I have flirting to do."

"You're not a flirt, Wyatt Dodge," she said stiffly, marching over to her closet and disappearing inside.

"I'm not?"

"No," she called back from the depths of the large space. "You're a seducer of innocents."

"Oh honey," he said, chuckling, "there were no innocents here."

She sniffed loudly and then reappeared a moment later with a dress draped over her arm. "I was comparably innocent."

"Well, don't go using it in the past tense. We got a lot more ground to cover."

She blushed again. He really liked that.

"Anyway," she said, moving over to her dresser and digging until she found some underwear. "I have to go."

"I'm not leaving until the show is over."

"There is no show." She glared at him and then went back into the closet.

He laid back on the bed, his arms underneath his head, as he listened to her rustle around, covering up that gorgeous body of hers.

He couldn't remember the last time he had wanted a woman long enough to have built up fantasies about her.

Maybe never.

Usually, he just had sex.

He had wondered about Lindy. He had wanted Lindy. Needed her. He would have thought that no mortal woman could have ever lived up to all the things he had built up around her. But she had.

She more than had.

She emerged from the closet, looking prim, proper and a bit like an indignant owl. All stiff and straight, her eyes wide and blinking.

"You're still naked," she pointed out.

"Am I?" he asked, feigning shock.

Her lips twitched. "It seems so."

"You're the one who has somewhere to be," he said slowly, "not me." Then he grinned. "And my clothes are still downstairs."

"Right," she responded.

"I have to go get them."

She opened her mouth as if she was about to say something. Offer to get them maybe. But before she could get a word out, he stood up, making sure to move slow as he pleased as he made his way out of the room.

Lindy followed down the stairs behind him, high heels on her feet, and if he was not mistaken, her eyes on his ass.

"Lindy," he said, affecting a scolding tone. "Are you objectifying me?"

"You're asking for it," she shot back, sounding much more poised than she had a few moments earlier. But then, she had her armor back in place.

"I'm walking down the stairs to get my clothes."

He was gratified when she followed him into the living area and watched as he gathered his clothes and put them on slowly.

He was more than gratified when he pulled his shirt back over his head and caught a hint of disappointment in her expression as he covered the last bit of his skin.

"I will see you in a couple of days," he said, giving her his best level stare.

Congratulations

on becoming an
exclusive member of

Maisey's
Grassroots Crew!

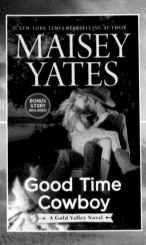

As a bonus member perk, you will receive
25% off any of Maisey Yates's titles that publish
between January 1, 2019 and June 30, 2019.
Go to Harlequin.com and use the coupon code
below in the shopping cart.

YATES19

Valid January 1, 2019 – June 30, 2019. May be used on multiple books.

INS-MY0818 08-96985

Welcome to Maisey's Grassroots Crew!

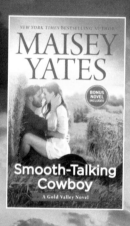

NEW YORK TIMES BESTSELLING AUTHOR

MAISEY YATES

BONUS NOVEL INCLUDED!

Smooth-Talking Cowboy

A Gold Valley Novel

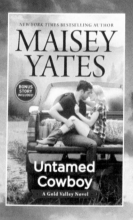

NEW YORK TIMES BESTSELLING AUTHOR

MAISEY YATES

BONUS STORY INCLUDED!

Untamed Cowboy

A Gold Valley Novel

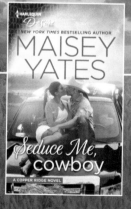

HARLEQUIN Desire

NEW YORK TIMES BESTSELLING AUTHOR

MAISEY YATES

Seduce Me, Cowboy

A COPPER RIDGE NOVEL

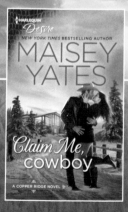

HARLEQUIN Desire

NEW YORK TIMES BESTSELLING AUTHOR

MAISEY YATES

Claim Me, Cowboy

A COPPER RIDGE NOVEL

"Yes," she responded, lifting her chin and giving him a haughty return glance. "See you then."

She turned like she was going to leave, and he took two strides across the room, hooking his arm around her waist and hauling her up against him, kissing her, deep and hard.

"No you don't, honey," he said.

"*No I don't* what?" she asked, breathless.

"No you don't go walking away from me like nothing happened. We are not working right now. And that means I get a kiss goodbye."

"Bye," she said, sliding her hand over her bun, as if she might find a stray piece of hair to brush away. But no. She wasn't disheveled anymore. Not like she had been when she'd been in bed with him.

She could put herself back together all she wanted. She wasn't the same as before. She couldn't be.

He wasn't.

She walked away from him like she was, though, and headed outside. He stood there for a moment, feeling stupidly out of place in the manicured room. He chuckled to himself when he remembered what they'd done in it, though.

He walked out of the house, into the sunshine.

The place was Lindy straight up. Brilliantly tamed wilderness. You could make a place like this look domestic, but it wasn't. The river rushed barely beyond the trees, the mountains stood tall beyond.

You could lay sod, keep it mowed, keep the flowers from overgrowing, but that didn't change what it was.

Yeah, she was a lot like that.

But in his arms she'd been wild.

He wanted more of that. He mused on that the rest of the way back to Get Out of Dodge.

He was halfway between the truck and the house when his phone rang. It was his dad. He stopped right there in the driveway, the gravel settling beneath his feet.

"What's up?" Wyatt asked, lifting the phone to his ear.

"Just checking in," Quinn said.

"Everything is going fine," Wyatt responded.

"I tried to call a couple of times earlier. You didn't answer."

And Wyatt hadn't checked his phone. Mostly because nothing had been as interesting as the woman he'd been with.

"I was busy," he said.

"I see. I wanted to make sure that…"

"Everything is going fine," Wyatt said, not bothering to modify his tone. He was exasperated. And he was tired of being treated like a prodigal son. The prodigal son had spent all his money. Wyatt had sent his home.

Wyatt had done all he could to do what his father wanted and it hadn't helped one bit.

"I'm hoping that I'll be able to come up for the barbecue."

"You know what? Don't tax yourself."

"Wyatt, I want to see what you're doing with the place."

"Why? So that you can give your stamp of approval and decide whether or not you're going to let me have what I've worked for my entire life? Be straight with me, Dad. Are you punishing me for my transgressions? Is that what this is?"

"You know that it isn't," Quinn said, his voice steady.

"No," Wyatt said. "I don't. If I did I wouldn't have

asked you, would I? So tell me straight. Are you punishing me because I stole your woman from you nineteen years ago?"

"Dammit, Wyatt, don't you know by now that I'm not angry at you for that? You said you wanted to leave, so I gave you my permission to go. I thought you needed it. I was never angry at you. I was angry at myself. I let a predator into my house. She seduced my son. You were a teenager. It was always her fault. Always. She took advantage of you."

"Right. I really hated that I got to screw a beautiful older woman whenever I wanted to."

"That isn't the point. You were a kid, she was an adult. End of story. You can put whatever spin on it you want, but she took advantage. Of me. Of you. That's how I feel. You wanted to know, so now you do."

Fire streaked through Wyatt, burning in his gut.

"I don't regret it," Wyatt ground out. "It was the best damn thing I had going for me back then. It was the only thing that was fun."

He was lying. He was being an ass. It hadn't been *fun*. It had been everything he'd needed, and then it had broken his heart when he'd lost the only love he'd felt for years. Broken his heart when he'd disappointed his father.

He didn't know why the hell he was doing this. Why he was pushing it. But he was so damned angry. Because whatever his father said he clearly did hold it against him. He clearly had his vision of Wyatt colored by it.

Ironic since he hadn't treated Wyatt like a child when he'd been one.

He wasn't a child. He never had been. His mother had died and his childhood had gone with her. His dad had made sure of it. And there was no getting around that. None at all.

Quinn Dodge with his latent overprotective nonsense didn't have any room in his life. Not now. Not when it was too late.

"If in the end you decide to take this from me when you know damn well it's mine," Wyatt ground out, "then don't you bother to call me again."

He hung up the phone and turned toward the house, to find Bennett standing there, about a foot away from him, his arms crossed, a frown turning the corners of his mouth down.

"What the hell are you doing here?" Wyatt asked.

"I was going to ask you the same thing. Well, not why you're here, but why you're standing outside yelling personal stuff into the wind."

"How much did you hear?"

"Enough to have some follow-up questions."

"Well, I'm not sure that I'm in the mood to answer any."

"That's not going to stop me from asking them," Bennett said, crossing his arms over his chest. A move that Wyatt knew well, because it was his. When he was feeling stubborn. When he was feeling like digging in.

"Bennett, honestly none of this concerns you. I mean, not as much as it concerns the others, and I haven't even talked to them about it yet.

"Why doesn't it concern me?" Bennett asked.

"Because," Wyatt said, "because you have another career. Because your whole everything isn't tied up in this ranch. You have a fiancée, you have a son. You have a veterinary practice. Jamie and Grant gave up everything to work this place with me. To invest in this place. And I..."

"You what?" Bennett asked.

Bennett had always been the good son. The one their father was the most proud of. Oh, Quinn Dodge would never say that, but Wyatt felt it. And why not? Bennett was the one who had gone to college. He was the one who had started a business independent of the ranch. Independent of anybody. He had taken that pioneer spirit that Quinn Dodge prized most and found a way to make a living off it. A good living.

He had even snuck in and given Quinn his first grandson, even if they had found out about him fifteen years after his birth.

Yeah, Bennett was the one who could do no wrong.

Bennett wouldn't understand this.

Which was maybe why Wyatt felt so compelled to fling it at him.

"Dad owns the ranch. Not me. He didn't sign it over to me."

"But you...you made it sound like he did. Like the place was yours."

"Yeah. I'm a liar. Because I didn't want you to know that Dad had me on probation."

"Say what now?"

"If I don't get this off the ground, if I don't have it solvent within the first six months, if I don't make it into the black in the first year, Dad is going to sell the ranch. To someone other than us."

"What? He can't do that. This is ours. It's Dodge land. It's been in our family for..."

"Yeah, since we were stagecoach robbers," Wyatt said. "Believe me. I know. And that's why I'm working my ass off to make sure that we don't lose the place. This is on me. I didn't want anyone else to worry about it."

"But it's our investment too."

"Sure," Wyatt said. "But nobody has a bigger investment in it than I do. I didn't want anyone else to be working under that kind of pressure. We can only do what we can do."

"That's BS, Wyatt. You're a good guy, don't get me wrong, but you're not that giving."

"Great. Why don't you go ahead and treat me to a litany of my many sins. I like hearing about those, and they seem to be all the rage lately. Grant. Dad. You."

"I'm not here to list your faults. I'm just saying, I don't believe you're doing this to spare us the stress. It's something else." Bennett narrowed his eyes. "What else were you and Dad talking about?"

"That," Wyatt said, "really is none of your damn business."

"Something happened, didn't it?" Wyatt started to walk away, the gravel crunching under his boots. "That's why you left back then."

He stopped, gritting his teeth. "It doesn't matter."

"I think it does. I think it's the source of all the problems now. At least, that phone call I overheard seems to indicate that."

"Bennett…"

"Look," Bennett said. "All my mistakes caught up with me, Wyatt. It didn't stay the secret I tried to keep to myself, did it?"

"Yeah, because your secret walks, talks and has fifty percent of your DNA."

"Sure," Bennett said. "But what I've learned from it

is that secrets don't stay secret. And when they do, they don't do anyone any good anyway."

"This one doesn't help anyone to come out."

"Try me."

"I slept with Dad's fiancée."

Bennett froze. His mouth opened, like he was going to say something. Then it closed again. He finally made a sound, something between a breath and a groan. Then he closed his eyes. "Freda?"

His confused expression was almost comical. Almost.

"No," Wyatt said. "Louisa."

Bennett blinked. "Louisa? I don't even… I don't know what to say to that."

"Why would you? It's messed up. If you had a ready response or a Hallmark card for it, I'd be surprised."

"You would have been…"

"Seventeen, if you're following along at home. That was when I left. Not a coincidence. You're right."

"But you…that was illegal. For her. Not for you."

"Sure. It doesn't matter, Bennett. I don't feel victimized," he said. "I was seventeen. I was a guy. I liked breasts. She had them."

"Now that really is bullshit, Wyatt. You didn't sleep with Dad's fiancée just because you liked breasts. You could get those anywhere. You've spent the past nineteen years proving that."

"Whatever. She was hot. She was older. She taught me some things. I liked it. Too bad it threw a big wrench into the family situation."

Wyatt gritted his teeth. He didn't like talking about Louisa. Not now. Not while he could still smell Lindy on his skin. It made it all feel sordid. And like maybe he was an asshole who didn't know how to keep it in his pants.

Except Lindy was different.

Yeah, you felt like Louisa was different.

Of course, he'd been a kid then. And that was half the problem. He had been starving for something. To feel good about himself.

She had played into that. Maybe that did make him a victim, but he sure as hell didn't like to think of it that way.

"And it still has the power to mess up my life. It only matters now because it's coming back to bite me in the ass," he continued. "Because Dad is still mad about it and whatever he says... I know that's what it's about."

"Wyatt, you have to tell Jamie and Grant."

"Right. I'm going to tell Jamie that I had a moment of temporary insanity and boned the same woman as Dad."

"Don't say it like that," Bennett said, his face contorting into an expression of horror. "Hell, maybe don't say that at all. But you need to tell them that this place is only ours on a probationary period."

"It doesn't make any difference," Wyatt said. "If we fail we would lose the place anyway."

"I don't think anyone's under the impression that our success or failure is on that razor-thin of a line. Leastwise I didn't think that. You're right. I have other stuff. I have more of other stuff than you do. That's a fact. I'm not as invested. How could I be? I'm not here as much, and mostly it's just my money going into the place, not my sweat. But dammit, Wyatt, let us help you. Let us work with you."

"You are."

"No. Not really. We're not partners. This is more of the same. You're my older brother, and I love you. I look the hell up to you, man. But you do this whole mysterious rodeo king thing. You don't let anyone in. You don't tell anyone what's going on with your life. Play like everything's great and easy. But I know it isn't. Hell, it obviously isn't. I had no idea that you… That all that happened between you and Dad. And you… Both of you have pretended that everything was fine and then I overhear you yelling at him on the phone. I've never heard you yell at Dad."

"In fairness, I haven't done much of it until recently. But, he's starting to get under my skin."

"Dad loves us."

"If Dad loved us half as much as you seem to think I don't figure he would be putting me on trial. He can justify it all he wants but I think he's gunning for me to prove that I can't do this. To prove that he can't count on me. I will be damned if I fail. Not again, Bennett. Not again."

"I believe you," Bennett said, in that way only younger brothers could. That real, deep belief that they seemed to be born with, that you didn't seem to have to earn or shake. "I believe that you can make this work. And I believe that you're going to do everything to make sure that we don't fail."

"I'm the only one that can do that, Bennett. If you feel like you have to talk to everybody else I can't stop you. But I don't have time to sit around having heart-to-hearts. I've got stuff to do."

Except, apparently he had all the time in the world to spend an afternoon in Lindy's bed. That had felt logical. Had felt right.

Hell, he wasn't going to feel bad about that. The rest of the stuff was just *stuff*. When he was with her…

At least he felt good.

There was so much he couldn't control. But at least with her there was some refuge. And he would take it.

He turned and walked away from Bennett, treating his brother to one last smile before he did.

Yeah, he was right. Wyatt had perfected a facade of not caring.

Sometimes he wasn't sure there was anything left underneath it.

CHAPTER TWELVE

SHE HAD PUT on hiking boots. Not because Wyatt had told her to, obviously, but because it made sense. She was hiking, after all.

She still couldn't quite believe that she was going *hiking*.

The whole day she had taken in between Wyatt sightings hadn't done a whole lot to clear her head in point of fact.

She had been distracted and moody, and Sabrina had called her out on it, which was annoying. Lindy had sidestepped the questioning in a rather feral fashion, which was exceedingly unlike her. She was never feral.

Though, it was undeniable she had done a fair amount of growling around since Wyatt had left her house the other day.

She knew what she had been thinking. She had been thinking of how amazing it would feel to touch him. How great it would be if she didn't have to hold back anymore. How wonderful it would be for just a moment to shed some of the exoskeleton that she kept so firmly in place. That she used to keep herself separate from the world.

She had done it.

It had been amazing.

Not only the time on the couch, but the times in her bed too. He was an *extremely* thorough lover. And he definitely seemed to get something out of her pleasure. He'd made a point of it, above his own.

The things that man could do with his hands…

The thought of it made her hot and bothered. She really needed to get her act together since she was about to face him.

She held her breath for the last five seconds between the highway and the driveway for Get Out of Dodge. She didn't know why she thought holding her breath might help. But something had to.

By the time she pulled in she was feeling no less flustered and a little bit dizzy.

And Wyatt was standing out there on the front porch waiting for her, arms crossed over that broad chest of his.

She knew how it looked without clothes now.

He had the perfect body. She wanted to see it again.

But whether or not this hiking trip fell under personal or business, she didn't know. And she had rules.

Maybe they needed to make office hours.

She parked her car next to his truck and got out. Unfortunately, as she approached him, he laughed at her. Which really didn't help with the flustered feeling.

"What?"

"You look like a catalog ad for one of those fussy outdoor stores," he said.

She wrinkled her nose and put her hands on her hips, looking down and examining her own appearance. Her olive green button-down shirt, her tan cargo style shorts and her boots. Plus the flannel tied around her waist.

"I do not," she protested.

"Yes. You do. You look like you asked for them to give you everything the model in the picture was wearing."

"I didn't," she said. "And anyway, I already owned this."

She reached back and flicked her braid around her shoulder. She had braided her hair, because it had seemed to go with the look. Apparently, her look was a little bit too put together in his estimation.

Not that she cared about his opinion on hiking fashion. It was practical. Plus, she looked cute.

He was dressed in battered old jeans and a white T-shirt. Which looked more delicious than they had a right to.

He should look *basic*.

But the fact of the matter was a man that was built like Wyatt Dodge didn't have to work hard to look good. He didn't have a fashionable bone in his body. She'd enjoyed that Damien had, in the beginning. Mostly because she'd never known a man to take pride in his appearance at all.

She preferred this now. Simple. Real.

A T-shirt and jeans was easy to peel off anyway.

A little zip of attraction worked its way through her body and she flexed her hips slightly, hoping that it wasn't too noticeable.

"You should be nice to me," she said, sniffing. "Since you have to spend the entire afternoon wandering around hiking trails with me. You never know what I might do to you. A body is basically half-hidden out here before you even start trying."

"Baby, you don't scare me."

"I don't?" She eyed him skeptically.

"There are bears out there."

"Believe me when I tell you, Wyatt Dodge, I can be scarier than any bear."

"I do believe that." He bent down and fetched a black

cowboy hat and a picnic basket from the bench by the door. When he put it on she nearly swooned.

She was a seriously sad case.

"A picnic basket?" She couldn't help but question it. It was so weird to see him—that epitome of simple, countrified masculinity—holding on to something so…well, frankly it was kind of frilly.

"Yes," he said. "I figured I'd pack us up some lunch."

"I figured you for a Yeti cooler kind of guy," she said, crossing her arms and treating him to what she hoped passed as a scathing look.

"Oh, don't you worry. Everything in here is insulated. And I'm definitely a cooler kind of guy normally. But, I *do* have a lady with me."

She huffed a laugh. "Does that nonsense normally work?"

"Yes," Wyatt said. "It works very well, *Melinda*. As I think you well know, since it worked on you no less than three times yesterday."

Her lips twitched, and she opened and closed her mouth like a guppy trying to get something out. Something fierce. Something sharp and snarky. Something that would fill his manly soul with terror the likes of which was typically only infused by bears, seeing as she had claimed to be more frightening than one of the great hairy beasts.

But, no such luck.

All she could do was think about the many ways in which his particular brand of hackle-raising charm had worked on her yesterday.

And it had been more than three.

He'd used his hands on her more than once to bring her to satisfaction. And then…talk about staying power.

He had it. And all that staying power had produced some very intense responses.

"Shall we?"

"You're going to carry a picnic basket the whole time?"

"No," he said, grabbing a utilitarian-looking camouflage backpack off a peg. Then, he carefully turned the picnic basket sideways and stuffed it into the pack before slinging it over his shoulder and clipping it around his waist.

"Okay," she said, fighting to hold back a laugh. "That seems much more *you* than a picnic basket."

"That way the bears don't know we have a picnic basket."

"I don't know," she said, squinting. "I think Yogi is a little bit better at sniffing out that kind of thing. He might just maul you and pull the pack off."

He shrugged his shoulders, straightening the pack before walking down the porch steps and leading the way down a finely barked path. "There is one thing you should know about me though, Melinda," he said, using her given name twice now in the same conversation.

He really *did* want to be mauled. For that reason alone, she decided to skip scolding him.

"And what one thing should I know?" she asked, following along behind him.

He turned to look at her for a moment, and then he winked. And it made her stomach flip over. Damn him. "I'm really not very good at following rules."

He continued to walk on ahead of her, the path blazing straight through a field before entering a copse of trees.

"Is that so?"

"It is," he responded. "A great tragedy in my life. In

fact, it might be said that the very idea of rules makes me want to break them."

She pushed her eyebrows down into a flat line. "Then why did we bother to make rules?"

"It was your idea." He pushed a tree branch out of the way, and held it for her like it was a door and he was playing the part of a gentleman. She tossed her head and walked past him.

"You were the one that outlined the rules. You were the one that brought binders into it. *Binders*, Lindy. Into sex. You had to know I was going to push back at that."

"I know no such thing," she said. "I'm used to civilized men."

He cleared his throat, and when he spoke, his tone had lost that light, bantering edge. "Here's the thing about me, I'm shameless, but I advertise that. It is no secret that I like to skirt the edges of what's acceptable. I'm not going to make apologies for that. And I'm not going to pretend it's not true. I'm going to make you this one promise, and because I'm up-front about what I am. So whatever I say to you, you can be sure it's true."

"Can I?"

"I have no reason to lie to you. I have no reputation to protect. It's become clear to me over the past few days that even my siblings think I'm kind of an ass. So yeah, I've got nothing to hide. And I have no reason to lie. But as long as you're with me, you're the only woman. Count on that."

That shouldn't make her feel anything. That was bare minimum, bottom of the barrel stuff. Except… Her husband had made that vow in front of God and everyone. And even though it had been for forever, and not until a barbecue, he had signed a paper. He had made it official. And he still hadn't stuck to it.

Wyatt was making that promise as easy as anything, with nothing but the trees for witness. But she had a feeling it counted for more.

"Okay," she said. "I promise I won't… I won't take any other lovers during this time either."

He drew his head back, his laugh like thunder, echoing in the relative silence of the forest. "Is that your fancy way of saying you won't bang anyone else?"

"Gross," she said. "That's a disgusting turn of phrase."

"Yeah, it is." He didn't sound bothered by that at all.

"I was being delicate."

"And I do appreciate your delicacy, honey."

He shook his head and walked a few paces in front of her. They lapsed into easy silence, their footsteps on the path the only sound. The bark had thinned out a few paces back, the trail natural, packed dirt now. It was an easy hike, relatively flat, winding through the trees, heading slowly and steadily up the side of a hill.

"Where does this go?"

"Well, the whole trail winds up to the top of Saddle Ridge. But, we won't go that far. There's something I want to show you once we get down farther."

"Are you going to put up signs for visitors?"

"I hadn't thought of it, but that is a good idea. That way they know which direction which attraction is at. I had some maps made, but I think signs might be good."

"Our partnership proves valuable yet again," she said lightly.

Wyatt stopped, turning to face her, his gaze intense. "It's been valuable. In a great many ways from the beginning. And I've certainly enjoyed it."

She didn't know why, but those words echoed through her. Made her feel…something.

Wyatt was impressed with her work. She didn't know why she realized that suddenly and sharply like she did. It had never been anything but obvious that he was. He didn't seem to care that she was from nothing. He didn't seem to care that she didn't have a degree.

He was… Well, he was exactly what he was. Exactly what he claimed to be. Shameless, an intentional pain in the ass. But he…

He seemed to think her ideas were good if they were good. And if he had an issue with one he would tell her so. But, it wasn't simply to oppose her or prove that he was smarter. It was never to make her feel small.

He had never once acted like she had made the winery a success because of Damien.

Because of her marriage.

Wyatt seemed to believe that she had earned it. He might even believe it more deeply than she did. It was…

It was enough to make her want to cry. She would rather gouge her own eye with a stick than do that in front of him. Or in front of anyone.

She shouldn't be so needy for something so simple. And yet, years of being made to feel small had done that.

Had made this easy respect that he gave her feel huge.

"Everything okay?" he asked.

He read her way too easily. She didn't like it.

"Fine. I was lost in the beauty of the wilderness." She waved a hand. "And things."

"You don't seem the type."

She frowned. "I used to be. You know… Growing up poor there's not much to do. Not much beyond wandering dirt roads, going to the store to buy forty-nine-cent candy bars and taking them down to the river so that you can swim. When you have nothing, you make entertainment out of what's already there. We were never going to drive to the city to go to a wave pool or waterslides, but Dane and I had a lot of fun jumping off rocks into a swimming hole. I haven't done that kind of thing in ages. You grow out of it, don't you?" She felt a heavy weight settle down over her chest. "Or maybe… Suddenly you have all the money that you want to make your world comfortable and you quit having to imagine ways to make it good. You quit seeing what's already there because you can just go out and get something new. I don't know."

"To a degree I think that's a hazard of growing up. Growing old. It's not enough to spend your days…whiling the hours away. You want to do something. Make something."

"That's what you're doing now."

"Yeah." He reached up and grabbed a tree branch, pulling it with him a few steps before he released his hold. "You know, I accomplished a lot as a bull rider. I mean, in that world. I went as far as you can go. I made a lot of money. I got a lot of glory. Endorsement deals. I was in a damned ad in a magazine for chewing tobacco. I don't even dip."

"How have I not seen that ad?" She was suddenly desperate to get her hands on it. Wyatt in one of those classic cowboy ads.

"None of it felt real. I did it. It's done. And there's nothing… It's not like if I had built a cabin with my bare hands. Then all that work I had done…it would be there. I could show someone. I could… I could take my dad over and I could say look, Dad, I built that. Not such a screwup, am I? But there's not a cabin. My life is a series of eight-second bursts. From the moment the gate opened, to the moment my boots hit the ground. Eight seconds I can barely remember because the adrenaline flows so hot and fast your brain is like a blank slate after. Eight seconds that built my bank account. My reputation. My life. And then they clean up the arena dirt, pack everything up and move on to the next town. There's nothing left."

She had seen him ride. Not often, but a few times. And she'd always held her breath. Her heart pounding in her throat, her hands shaking. She'd told herself it was because she'd met him, and that made it different. That he was Damien's friend, and it made her feel more.

She didn't let herself think it was because he was the most beautiful man on earth. That just looking at him in general made her shake, never mind watching him get on the back of a bull, risking all that vitality.

"That doesn't mean it didn't happen," she said softly.

"I know," he said. "But at my age… It just feels gone. The only thing it left behind was damned aching joints. I'm thirty-six, but flinging myself around on the back of an animal like that makes me feel a hell of a lot older. When I was starting out I didn't expect to be done by now, but it was time. It's a lot of things, you know. A lot of things that build up, and then sometimes…sometimes one more thing gets added and it makes a moment. A moment when you know you're done. You ever had that?"

She purposefully stepped on one rock in the path, feeling it dent into the sole of her shoe. Then she stepped on another. And another. "I was married to Damien for ten years and it wasn't perfect. There were a lot of things. Our marriage certainly didn't fall apart solely because he cheated on me. A marriage has to get bad in a lot of other ways before that can happen." She swallowed, blinking hard, staring at the sunlight filtering through the trees, blaming the light for her watering eyes. "I don't think I was a good wife, Wyatt. He was gone a lot, and I didn't mind. I enjoyed the free time. I started to enjoy the life he gave me more than I enjoyed his company. I loved him. Don't mistake me. But there were problems. I… I wanted a baby." Her voice became thick, husky. "I wanted a family. And he didn't want one. At least, not then. Never right then. There was always something. His career. The winery. Something. All that builds up. It became resentment. I wasn't happy. But the moment I knew it was over. The moment I knew I wasn't even going to try to save it anymore… It was the moment I found out he was sleeping with Sarabeth. When I caught them kissing each other in the wine cellar." She cleared her throat, her body crawling with revulsion even while she thought of it now. Not so much because it hurt her anymore, but because she could so easily remember how it had felt. "I'm not even sure if I was heartbroken. Or even all that wounded. I felt so…so *stupid*. And I'd had enough feeling stupid." She tried to breathe past the thickness in her chest. "What was your moment?"

There was a heavy silence between them.

"My dad called me," he said. "He said that he had to make a decision about Get Out of Dodge. That it was going to go to me and my siblings or he was going to sell it and give us the money. He said it was up to me. What I chose to do. Because I'm the oldest, and inheritance or some such. He said that it was now or never, and if I wasn't ready to give it a real try he would just as soon sell the place. Because he wasn't going to watch me half ass the commitment. And that was when it hit me, that no matter how much work I'd done, no matter how much success I'd achieved in the past near twenty years, it was going to seem half-assed to him. Because he doesn't understand the rodeo. He sure as hell doesn't understand posing for tobacco ads. He doesn't understand anything that isn't working the land, and then at the same time he doesn't even want us to do it. He doesn't think I can make it work. He expected to throw down that challenge and have me walk away from it. And knowing that is what made me pick it up. Is what made me want to do it. I knew I was coming to the end of my career. I'd already won the championship five years earlier. I wasn't going to be getting any better. It doesn't work like that in sports that break your body down. You get worse until you wish you had retired while you are on top. And I wasn't on top anymore, but I wasn't Michael Jordan playing baseball either."

She fought the urge to reach out and pat him. She didn't suppose men liked to be patted when they were talking about their mortality. "Well, I'm glad you were spared that particular indignity."

"Yeah, you've got to get out before it gets to that."

The path narrowed, the trail winding upward before it sloped back down. It was rockier here, less tamed. It pitched sharply downward and she found herself jogging slightly to keep up with Wyatt. She hopped from a rock down to the bottom of the hill, laughing as she did. Wyatt turned to her and smiled, his whole face lit up.

"You love this," she said, taking three strides to his every one, trying to keep up. "Don't you?"

"Yeah," he said, taking a sharp breath. "I do."

"So you're doing it to prove to your dad that you can.

But you want this too, don't you? Because if you didn't...
It's a pretty big commitment just to prove a point."

"It's not only to prove a point," he said. "Like I said,
I want to build something. To make something. To make
an impact that isn't...a bad one." He turned and grinned
sheepishly at that last part.

"I have a hard time believing you've ever made a bad
impact on anyone, Wyatt. You might be kind of a pain
in the butt, but you're really a good guy."

"Says the woman I gave six orgasms yesterday. Honestly, I think you're just feeling sweet on me because I'm
good in the sack."

"I'm not that easy," she said.

"True. You made me wait quite a while to have you."

"I made *myself* wait quite a while to have you," she
grumbled.

"Did you?" He sounded wholly interested in that.

"This doesn't need to be a whole discussion," she said,
shooting him a beady eye.

"I think it does. How long?"

"Stop it. I'm going to take back all the nice things I
said."

"And as wounding as that would be, now I want to
hear the rest of the story."

"I wanted you since before it was appropriate. How
about that?"

She shocked herself with the easy admission. With the
fact that she had gone ahead and copped to it.

"What does that mean?" he pressed.

"You know," she griped.

"*Melinda*," he said, stopping in the middle of the path.
"I'm going to need you to be more specific."

"And I'm going to need you to quit calling me Melinda."

"Why?"

She snorted and held her hand up. "One invasive question at a time."

"Okay. I want the answer to the first one. Because it's about me."

He was teasing, but she couldn't tease about this. It was too raw and still achingly real all these years later. It was a moment that had upended her life in small ways that no one else had ever seen. Something she'd never shared with anyone, because how could she?

"You have to know," she said softly, taking a step toward him, the forest seeming to close in around them, the silence almost oppressive.

"I don't," he said, his voice getting rough.

"Since I first saw you." She swallowed hard. "Maybe you don't remember the first time we—"

"I remember." He cut her off, his voice rough. "I remember the first time I saw you."

The air seemed to get thick between them. With tension. With meaning. The admission was shocking, and somehow not surprising at all. As if she had known.

"I'd never felt anything like it before," she said, reaching out and touching his cheek, his stubble scraping her fingertips as she dragged them down to the center of his chin, before pulling her hand away quickly. Like she had stuck it in a fire.

"Same goes, honey."

She cleared her throat. "So. Anyway."

"Lindy…"

She cleared her throat. "So, what were you going to show me?"

Wyatt shook his head, as if he had thought better about continuing on the current line of conversation. And she was just coward enough to be relieved.

"Right up ahead," he said.

She could hear the river again, and they were moving closer to it. The sound of water crashing on rocks grew louder with each step.

The path went down, then up again, winding through two massive boulders before opening up to a rushing river. There was a sheer rock wall across from them, trees seeming to grow from the side, reaching up toward the sky. She looked down the river, where the water made a sharp trip down a cliff, forming massive, white waterfalls.

"What is this?" she asked.

"Wishing Well Falls."

"I had no idea it was back here."

"It's on private property," he said. "Dodge property. And, other than the hikes for guests at the ranch years ago... I don't know how publicized it is. Do you think that this would be a good hike to take people on? We could serve up some Grassroots Wine and have a nice little picnic."

"Yes," she said, looking around. "It's perfect."

"I think so."

"Why is it called Wishing Well Falls?"

"Because of the wishing well," he said. "Down there."

She craned her neck to look past the waterfall, but all she saw was a surge of white-water mist rising up from below.

"Come on," he said, grabbing hold of her hand and leading her down a narrower part of the trail that went straight down alongside the river. Pebbles tumbled down past them, the dirt loose beneath their feet, but Wyatt held her fast, making sure that she didn't slip and fall.

"This is beautiful," she said, breathless, as soon as they reached the bottom. It was cooler down here, beneath the cover of surrounding pine trees, the earth around them soft and fragrant. Pine mingled with the sharp, fresh smell of cold water and the earthy scent of the dirt.

The swimming hole at the end of the waterfall was vast and deep. The water churned where the falls let in, but beyond that it was calm and clear, round rocks worn smooth covering the bottom.

"It does kind of look like a wishing well," she said.

"Yeah, I always thought it did."

"Have you made many wishes here?"

"Can't say as I have. But I don't want to go throwing any money into it. Still, I'm betting that I could appease the gods with an offer of a decent stone." He bent down and selected a flat, smooth rock from the shore. Then he closed his eyes, and she couldn't help but watch.

His strong profile, the set of his square jaw... He was an intensely beautiful man, though that wasn't the first thing that came to mind when she looked at him because he was so masculine, so very hard. Scarred and weathered from years of hard work and hard living.

In spite of it all, he was beautiful. Or maybe because of it.

He cocked back his wrist, and flung the rock down into the water, his lips moving slightly as he did.

"What did you wish for?" she asked.

"Can't tell you," he said, his face gravely serious. "You know that's not how wishes work."

"That's not fair," she huffed. "That's a tease."

"Maybe I'm a tease." He grinned. "I'll tell you what. Kiss me, and I might give you a hint."

She sighed, but then she stretched up on her toes, wrapped her arms around his neck and pressed a kiss to his mouth.

He took advantage. He angled his head and parted her lips with his tongue, stroking down her spine, down to her butt, while he held her tightly against his body. When they parted, they were both breathing hard.

How was it possible that she just…kissed him now sometimes?

It shouldn't be possible.

"Okay," she said, trying to disguise how affected she was. "What did you wish for?"

"I wished that you would kiss me," he said, that devil's grin curving his mouth upward. "I guess it worked."

She slapped his shoulder. "Wyatt Dodge."

He held his hands up. "Hey, sometimes I think we have to make our own wishes come true, don't you?"

"That is *not* how wishing wells work."

"I got my kiss either way, baby, I don't much care."

"You have no sense of magic." She waved a hand at him. "Or whimsy."

His dark brows shot upward. "You don't think I'm whimsical?"

"Not in the least."

He shook his head. "I would be happy to disabuse you of that notion. Why don't you come for a swim with me?"

"I don't… I don't have anything to swim in," she protested.

"You don't need anything to swim in. Skinny-dipping. How's that for being whimsical?"

"I am *not* skinny-dipping," she said, crossing her

arms and turning away from him slightly. "I know I have trailer park roots, but I do not skinny-dip."

"Did you ever?"

"No," she said crisply. "I never have. I never will."

"Suit yourself." Wyatt unclipped his backpack and deposited it on the ground, then stripped his shirt off, followed by his belt, shucking his jeans and underwear so quickly that Lindy didn't even have time to protest.

But then...why would she protest a man like him getting naked?

Even out here. Even where she wouldn't.

He turned away from her and headed toward the water, the muscles in his back flexing with each movement. Also, the muscles in his ass. Well. Indeed.

"I'm going to sit here with the sandwiches," she called out, scurrying to his backpack and retrieving the picnic basket.

"Good," he returned. "The sandwiches need your protection. Since you're meaner than a bear."

"If you pick a fight with me I will..."

"What? You said yourself, you're not coming in. So, I'm safe. I can say whatever I want." He turned around and slowly slid into the water, his breath hissing through his teeth.

"Cold?" she asked sweetly.

"I'm fine."

"I'm not sure about that." She retrieved a peanut butter sandwich from the basket and shook her head. Peanut butter. "I'm betting you're shrunken."

"Babe, I'm looking at you. *Nothing* is shrunken."

"That is the crassest compliment I have ever been paid," she said, around a mouthful of sandwich.

"That's me," he said, spreading his arms wide as he

kicked his feet and swam across the swimming hole. "Wyatt Dodge, giver of crass compliments."

She watched as he swam a circle, and she felt…she almost wished she *could.* But she couldn't imagine stripping off all her clothes in the broad light of day where anybody might walk up on them. Sure, it was private property, but Wyatt had a zillion siblings, and people were forever traipsing over the place. She just…couldn't.

The idea of being caught skinny-dipping…

She tugged her knees up to her chest and enjoyed her view, keeping her seat until Wyatt popped back up onto the shore.

He took his T-shirt and toweled himself off with it, and then pulled his underwear and pants back on.

She sighed heavily when he covered his body, but remained fairly pleased when he kept his shirt off. Then he sat down next to her and began to unpack lunch.

"I was thinking," he said.

"Oh no." She schooled her face into an expression of mock horror.

"Yeah, didn't you see the smoke coming from my ears?"

She laughed, taking a big bite of her sandwich. "Can't say that I did. But, that's because you're a very smart man. And I don't think that it's a trial for you to come up with ideas."

"I'm inventive when it comes to certain…physical activities that's for sure."

His tone left no room for speculation on what he meant by that. She blushed. "What have you been thinking about?"

"Well, I was thinking that maybe we should do a trial run for the barbecue."

"A trial run?"

"Yeah. You know, test the food and all that."

"I think…" She smiled. "I think it's a great idea. And good opportunity to give my staff a break from my manic craziness and give them something fun to do."

"Great," he said. "It will also give my people a chance to make sure we got this running smoothly."

"I'm all for that."

"I didn't expect you to agree so readily."

She frowned. "Why not? I'm very easygoing."

"You are. It's true. As long as all the decisions are yours."

She picked off a small piece of bread and flung it at him.

"Excuse me," he said, leaning forward and catching her wrist. "Do not waste bread."

She batted her eyes. "I'm feeding the birds."

He stared at her, his dark eyes glittering. She looked down and noticed a droplet of water sliding down his chest.

Without thinking she leaned forward, caught the drop with the tip of her tongue and licked him.

He shuddered, and when she looked back up at him he pulled her in, kissing her, deep and hard. She wrapped her arms around him, her hand skimming down his back. She let her sandwich drop to the ground as he angled his head and worked on devouring her instead of lunch.

"Wyatt," she gasped, letting her head fall back as he kissed down her neck. "We should…we should not."

"I think we should."

The intimacy of the moment was shattered. She felt one of those brick walls slam down between them. The distance returning.

She didn't want to be exposed like that. Not to him or to anyone. If they got caught people would know. If she dropped her control and simply let this happen...

"I'm not...skinny-dipping... And that means that I am damn well not...having sex with you out on some rocks."

"Okay," he said, moving back from her. "But the rocks are the only compelling part of that argument. Your maidenly modesty is not."

She shook her head. "You're shameless."

"Admit it," he said. "I wouldn't be half as much fun if I wasn't."

He wouldn't be. And she wouldn't be having half as much fun. She hardly knew who she was when she was with him. It was a strange and wonderful vacation from her regular life.

"Okay. When are we going to have this barbecue?"

"How about this weekend?"

"I'll be there," she said.

"You should spend the night in one of the cabins." A lopsided grin tipped his lips upward.

She hesitated. "Maybe."

"Maybe I'll come for a sleepover."

"You can't do that!" Her heart lurched, her stomach turning over. It wasn't that she didn't want it. She did. It was only that...

If it happened naturally then she could blame the heat of the moment. And if it happened when no one else was around, no one would have to know.

This was something else. Planned and dangerously intimate somehow. She was allergic to intimacy. Nothing with Wyatt should feel intimate at all. Ever. Sex wasn't supposed to be. At least, that was the plan.

"Just a quality check," he teased. "Turndown service."

"You'll get caught," she pointed out.

He shook his head. "No I won't."

"You think you're bulletproof, Wyatt Dodge," she said, exasperated.

She knew she wasn't. Fine for him to be cavalier.

"I wouldn't go that far," he responded, his voice rough.

She pressed her hand to his heart, felt it pounding beneath her fingertips. "You feel pretty sturdy to me. I'm betting nothing can touch that."

He didn't say anything. He simply looked at her, his dark eyes completely unreadable. "Why would you? When you could touch this," he said, smiling and grabbing hold of her wrist, making like he was going to drag her hands down to the front of his pants.

She laughed, not because it was funny, but because there was so much tension inside of her and she needed to do something to break it. Because laughing was what a woman who could do casual would do. He didn't put her hand over his arousal, though. Instead he lifted it to his lips and kissed her palm.

She would agree to the sleepover idea. And she wouldn't be stressed-out about it. Or scared. Because she could do casual.

"Ready to get back?"

"Yes," she said breathlessly.

"You better pick up your sandwich," he said, vaguely scolding.

"The animals will eat it."

"What if they have a peanut allergy?"

She rolled her eyes but bent down to get the sandwich. "You're ridiculous."

"Conscientious."

He put his shirt back on, then his hat, followed by his

pack. And then she stuffed the basket back inside. He turned and looked at her, an expression she still couldn't read. Something had changed. Between them. Inside of herself... She didn't know.

She felt...lighter and heavier at the same time. She wanted something. Maybe just to be different.

To be the person who would have skinny-dipped with him. Who would have made love to him by the river.

But she wasn't.

Her decision. No one else's.

She had a lot of time to ponder why she hated her decisions so very much on their walk back to the ranch.

CHAPTER THIRTEEN

"Beatrix bailed on me."

Wyatt shifted, pressing his phone more firmly against his ear and looking around his kitchen. Jamie was sitting at the table eating bacon, bacon that Wyatt had been very close to indulging in himself.

"On what?" he asked, careful to keep his tone neutral. Not too intimate. He didn't want Jamie asking questions. And his damn little sister was like a bloodhound when she caught the scent of something.

"The poster mission," Lindy clarified.

"Oh no," he said, "not the poster mission."

"I'm serious. I don't know how I'm going to get everything finished in time now. I mean, I understand. There was some kind of emergency at Bennett's clinic."

"Right," Wyatt said.

"Something to do with an orphaned bear cub. And until Fish and Wildlife come…"

"Well, what else would it be but an orphaned baby bear?" He had a sneaking suspicion that Lindy needed his help. He also sensed that she would rather pull all her own teeth out with a pair of pliers than ask for it.

"I'm stressed," she said.

"Did you need something, Lindy?"

There was a long pause at the other end of the phone. "I just have a lot to do."

"It wouldn't kill you to ask."

The silence seemed to sprout claws. She wanted him to offer without having to ask. He wasn't going to. That woman was stubborn as hell, and she needed to let go a little bit.

"Please," she said tightly. "Can you help me hang up posters, Wyatt?"

"Sure can," he responded in his most cheerful tone.

"You're terrible."

"But you need me." He forgot to modify his tone then, and he looked over at Jamie, who was staring at him now, far too keenly.

"In this instance, yes."

"Jamie and I will meet you at Sugar Cup," he said, referencing the coffee shop in town.

Now, Jamie looked slightly like a distressed guppy, seeing as he had co-opted her time without her permission. She'd live. He hung up the phone and that was when Jamie rounded on him.

"You did not ask me if I wanted to… What are we doing?"

"Hanging up posters. It won't take long. Not with all three of us."

"Who is the third?"

"Lindy," he said.

Jamie looked slightly gloating at that. "I thought it might be."

"Did you?"

"You had that tone."

"What tone?"

"That tone that you get when you think a woman is hot."

He chuckled. "I'm a little bit disturbed that you know that tone."

"Me too," she said. "But then, you're you."

He snagged a piece of bacon off the plate and took a bite. "Let's go."

A few minutes later he and Jamie were loaded up in his truck and on the road into town. Jamie had her elbow rested against the window, her attention turned to the scenery outside. Sometimes it hit him, and hard, that his younger sister wasn't a little girl anymore. And that made him wonder why she stayed. Why she did things like this. Going into town with him to hang up posters when she could have just told him where to stick it.

"Do you ever wish… Do you ever want to leave the ranch?" he asked.

She turned toward him, slowly, blinking. "What made you ask that?"

"You're twenty-four," he said. "I left home at seventeen. Made a lot of mistakes. Figured out what I liked. What I didn't like."

"Are you about to give me The Talk, Wyatt?" Jamie asked, her tone dry.

"Oh, hell no. Dad's remarried now. His wife can do it." He was joking. Surely Jamie didn't need… She was twenty-four. Though, he knew for a fact that she had been pretty damn sheltered. And that most of the men in Gold Valley would be terrified to lay a hand on her, since she had three older brothers that would cheerfully tear them limb from limb.

Plus, the place was populated by cowboys, and Jamie seemed pretty immune to that type. Early exposure to him, to Luke Hollister, and to a lesser extent Bennett and Grant had probably helped with that.

"Do you think I should want to leave?" Jamie asked.

"Not necessarily. I just… It occurred to me that you've stuck pretty close to home. I don't want you to miss out on anything. Not because of loyalty to me."

She looked away from him. "Would it be so bad if part of it was loyalty to you?"

"Why would you feel loyal to me?" He had left home when Jamie was so young, and had only been visiting after that. He couldn't imagine why she would feel... loyal to him.

"I know that you were the reason we were taken care of all that time. I know you were sending money to Dad. I saw the checks. And even before that... I don't know what it was like before Mom died. I never knew her. But I had my brothers. Wyatt, you always took care of me. Considering Mom died from complications after..."

"You don't blame yourself, Jamie. You can't. No one else does."

"I don't know about that. But either way, you're the reason we have the ranch, Wyatt. You're the reason that I'm strong. Because you are so strong. And I wanted to be exactly like you, always. So maybe some of it... Some of being here... Maybe some of that is loyalty. But is that such a bad thing? It feels pretty good to have someone to be loyal to."

Silence settled between them as they drove into the city limits.

"I'm done with the sincerity now," she said finally.

"Good," he said. "But, thank you."

"It'll be another twenty-four years before I say something that nice."

"That works for me."

He parked the truck in front of one of the old brick buildings, and when he got out, he felt a little bit lighter when he stood up. Which was impossible. What Jamie had said couldn't have made him feel lighter just by speaking it. But somehow... Somehow it did.

He pushed open the scarred black door, allowing

Jamie to go in before him. Lindy was already waiting, sitting at a table with three to-go cups in front of her, and a stack of posters.

"Caffeine," she said, gesturing to the cups.

She looked between him and Jamie, and he could tell that she felt slightly uncomfortable with the presence of his sister. He knew more than anything that she didn't like being thrown off, and this whole morning was throwing her off.

"I suppose we should split up," she said softly.

"I used to work at the Gunslinger," Jamie said. "I can start there. Canvass that side of the street. Everyone knows me."

"I appreciate that," Lindy said. She was being so funny and formal, and he knew that she acted that way a lot, but for some reason it was jarring now. Maybe because now he had seen her naked. Had had her beneath him and crying out his name.

"I can head to city hall, see if they have suggestions for places it might go. We can hit Mustard Seed."

"Okay," Lindy said. "That means I'll take the other side of the street."

"We can meet back here. Good to see you again, Lindy," Jamie said, taking the cup of coffee from the table and her posters and leaving.

Wyatt had a feeling that his sister was actually strategically giving him alone time with Lindy.

She was a dark horse, was Jamie Dodge.

"I guess I should…"

He looked around the room, and then reached out, taking hold of her hand. She paled. "It's okay."

She pulled away from him, nervously touching her hair. "I just don't… You know."

He did. And it shouldn't bother him. He didn't know

what the hell was wrong with him that it did. If he was in the market for a relationship that included feelings, it would make sense. But he wasn't. Been there. Done that. Had the emotional scarring to prove it.

"Why don't we see if they want to hang up a poster here?"

Without waiting for her response he walked up to the counter, and was greeted by a blonde girl with her hair in a bun, and the flattest expression he'd ever seen on someone manning a cash register.

"I was wondering if we could hang up a poster here," he said.

The girl tilted her head to the side. "I don't know. We have really strict rules about it. It has to be local."

"It is," Lindy said, stepping in quickly. "And in fact, we have some vendor opportunities available, if you might be interested in coming out and serving hot drinks."

"It's summer," the girl responded.

"But it cools off in the evening," Lindy pointed out.

She held out a poster, and the girl took it. "I'll talk to my manager."

"Thank you," Lindy said.

"Uh-huh."

Then, she turned away from both Lindy and Wyatt, busying herself with something else. Lindy and Wyatt exchanged a glance, but didn't say anything until they were out on the sidewalk.

"She wouldn't be my first choice to be the face of the coffee shop," Wyatt said.

"It is a very…unfriendly face."

Somehow, they ended up not splitting up. They went to several businesses together, as well as city hall. But, she still didn't touch him.

It was strange to hang out with her like that now that

they'd slept together. Now that they had spent some time together alone, and he had a much better idea of who she was beneath all her reserve.

But now he had to pretend there was nothing going on. But even still…he could feel it. As much as he could always sense her, he could feel it even more now.

When they were finished, they walked back toward Sugar Cup to meet Jamie, but he stopped her by the truck, just before they went in. The truck provided a small barrier between themselves and the road. A little bit of privacy.

"See? Asking for help wasn't so bad, was it?"

She let out a breath. "It's not that it's bad. I've never been able to depend on anyone in my life. Not anyone but myself. My mother raised us to never take anything from anyone. And when I married Damien… I never wanted to admit that I needed help. I didn't want to become a charity project."

"I don't see you as a charity project."

"Give the sad divorcée orgasms?"

"No," he said. "And you well know it. Getting help hanging up posters is not being a charity case. You organized this whole thing for me. And I've already told you how impressed I am with what you've done with Grassroots. I don't care what anyone else thinks, Lindy Parker. You're amazing. You've earned respect. That doesn't mean people will give it. But you've got mine. For all that it's worth."

Lindy didn't deserve to feel the way she did about herself. If anyone deserved to be proud, it was her. And needing help didn't have anything to do with pride. Shouldn't dent it at all.

"You know," he said slowly. "When I was a kid I would have given anything for someone to reach a hand out to me. My dad couldn't do it. He needed me to stand on my own. To be bulletproof," he said, echoing the words that she had said about him at the waterfall. "But we are just people, aren't we? Not any more bulletproof than we have to be. There's no harm in letting someone in." But even as he said that, he wasn't sure that he would be able to do it. But that was different. That was him.

He didn't deserve it. But she did.

"I'm not sure I know how."

"Well that's too bad," he said. "Because I sure as hell don't. I might be able to make proclamations, but I can't give any lessons."

She looked at him, her blue eyes pleading for something. Something he wasn't sure he knew how to give. And wasn't that a bitch? He wanted her to want more for herself, but he sure as hell couldn't be the one to give it.

No matter that the realization made his chest feel tight.

Jamie appeared on the sidewalk a moment later, looking at them both speculatively. Lindy took a step back from him.

"Are you ready to go?" she asked.

"Yeah," Wyatt said. "Lindy's busy."

Lindy nodded. "I am."

"And anyway, we have our small barbecue to organize," he said. "But if you need any more help…ask me."

She hesitated for a moment. "I will."

And dammit all, when he got in his truck, he felt even lighter.

CHAPTER FOURTEEN

WYATT'S WORDS WERE still echoing in Lindy's ears days later.

If you need more help, ask me.

He made it sound so easy to do this thing she'd avoided her entire life. And the thing was…she wanted to lean into it. Into him. And that scared her. She'd wanted the shelter of Damien's financial security. But not…him.

She did her best not to think about all of that while she got ready for the barbecue, and for the sleepover she'd promised Wyatt that night.

She was still working on being casual about all that, as agreed, but she didn't know how to do it when it felt like he was eroding those walls that had always stood between herself and the world.

Between herself and other people.

By the time Lindy, Sabrina and Bea arrived at Get Out of Dodge, the barbecue was in full swing. The mess hall was full of men in cowboy hats that Lindy had never met before. Apparently when Wyatt Dodge decided to throw an impromptu family and friends gathering, he could pack the place out.

Which was a good omen for the future of Get Out of Dodge, at least in Lindy's estimation.

Wyatt was standing in the corner, talking to a cute brunette who was staring up at him like he might offer her the secret to eternal happiness. Or like he might give her a thousand amazing orgasms.

A sharp pang hit her square in the stomach.

A little jealousy she had no right to feel. That she didn't want to feel at all.

Still, she gripped the bottle of wine she'd brought more tightly as she walked into the room. She scanned the hall, looking for more familiar faces. Trying not to stare at him. But then her eyes landed on him again, and this time, he saw her.

And he smiled.

There was something about that grin on his face that made the tightness in her chest ease, and that made her feel even sillier. Why was she worrying about anything? She had his attention now, for the time they'd agreed on. And after that it didn't matter. It didn't.

He tipped his hat in her direction, then stood up on one of the benches, putting him head and shoulders above the crowd. "Thank you all for coming to our family barbecue. If you're here, you're part of the Dodge family," he said, turning on that charm that she imagined had served him well on the rodeo circuit. Not only with women, but with the people he worked with endorsement deals on. She could see now why Damien had found him to be so valuable. Well, she had always been able to see that. A man with his kind of looks and charm was most definitely a force to be reckoned with.

"We're going to be eating outside, followed by some dessert, which we'll have around the campfire. We got a house band in residence, so if y'all want to dance you're welcome to. This is just a little precursor to our grand opening that's happening in a few weeks, and I wanted to make sure we all had a chance to party before we were working our knuckles bloody so that everyone else could have a good time. Most especially, I want to thank my siblings, Jamie, Grant and Bennett, for the work they've done out here. My nephew, Dallas, who does a lot of thankless work and makes sure that he grumbles loud enough that I know it, even though I pay his sorry ass."

That elicited a laugh from the crowd, and from Wyatt's nephew, Dallas, who waved as if this was a ringing endorsement of his character.

"I'd also like to send out a special thanks to the team at Grassroots Winery who has done so much work to help make the relaunching of Get Out of Dodge a success. Especially Lindy Parker. She's done a lot of work and she's had to put up with me. That's not an easy task." He grinned. "Thank you, Lindy."

Her face got hot and she shifted, holding on to the bottle of wine even tighter. She shrugged her shoulder, and smiled tightly.

"All right. Food will be ready soon. And give your honest feedback, because we have to put together a menu for our guests, and I want to make sure that it's something we'll all enjoy."

He hopped down off the bench and mixed back in with the crowd. Lindy didn't want to go and find him. Didn't want to cling to his side, even though it was her instinct to do so.

She didn't like that. She was starting to feel uneasy about all of it. About that premeditated hookup they were theoretically going to have tonight.

She had packed for it. Had brought sexy lingerie, for when he came to visit. And just thinking about it sent her whole body into overdrive. Made her hands shake.

She didn't know why she was letting it get to her like

this. She didn't know why she was letting him get to her like this.

Except there were all these things from the past week that were still making her feel a little bit crazy. That moment down by the water when she had felt almost wrenched into with her longing to be different. To do different. To be the kind of woman who could laugh easily, strip off her clothes and get into the water with him.

The kind of woman who could hold hands with a man in public and not worry what other people would say. What it would make her feel.

The kind of woman who wouldn't overthink this kind of stuff, because *he* didn't. It was all easy for him. This physical stuff. He could treat her like a friend and smile, tease her, and then strip her naked.

It made her feel like there was something wrong with her that she couldn't do that. That the idea made her feel like her skin didn't fit.

But this was new, and it made it all feel sharp and fresh in a way it hadn't in a long, long time. Maybe in a way it never had.

She *wanted* this. She wanted him. She had for years. But she didn't want…

She didn't want to feel jealous of the pretty girl that he had hired. She didn't want to feel insecure. She didn't want any of that.

It shouldn't matter if he liked the brunette, or if she was pretty. Because they were going to be done after the grand opening. They had made that agreement. She wanted to be like him. Wanted to smile easily afterward. Wanted to be able to go out for a beer as if they used to play one-on-one basketball together, instead of making love. She wanted to treat it like that.

She didn't want to be this weird, strung out creature all over what was just a casual adult relationship.

She didn't want that deep, hidden part of herself to suddenly start expecting more. That part of herself that would only be disappointed. She would only feel stupid in the end when it turned out that Wyatt Dodge was exactly what she knew him to be. Exactly what he claimed to be. And she could not get used to leaning on him, on that help he offered.

She was an idiot. No mistaking that.

An idiot who was currently standing in the middle of a party ruminating and holding on to a bottle of wine like it was her lifeline.

"What's going on?" Sabrina asked.

"Nothing," Lindy responded.

Just then, Sabrina's husband, Liam, walked over to where they were standing. She had driven Sabrina straight over to Get Out of Dodge from work, and Liam had been intending to come later, when he was done on his family ranch. He brought his whole family with him, and she knew they were milling around somewhere. His brothers Finn, Alex and Cain, and their wives Lane, Clara and Alison. Along with various babies, and Cain's teenage daughter, Violet.

Liam smiled when he saw his wife, and he curved an arm around her; the big muscular tattooed man looking so soft as he touched Sabrina made Lindy's chest feel like it was being crushed.

She didn't want what they had. She didn't. She was glad that her sister-in-law had found that kind of happiness. She really was. She just didn't think it was for her.

Anyway, she had plenty of things. And apparently, the capacity to have a no-strings physical relationship, even.

If she would never be a wife, if she would never be a mother… That was fine. She could adopt children, come to that. If she really wanted to have a family. There were a lot of options for single women.

She didn't need to be so rigid in her thinking. She needed to be more open, more creative. More flexible.

It was impossible to be flexible when she was wound too tight. She was trying to change. She really was.

Wyatt was the beginning of that. If she could only stop being moody about him.

"Hi," Liam said, addressing Lindy. "How's everything going?"

"Good," Lindy responded, stealing another look at Wyatt.

"Are you hungry?" Sabrina asked her husband.

"A bit," Liam responded.

"Why don't we go get in line for food? I bet you worked a full day."

That easy, casual concern for him, the fact that she was so in tune with what he felt, what he needed, was more affecting to watch than Lindy had anticipated.

Sometimes she missed being a half of a whole. Missed having that person that was an extension of herself. But she didn't think she and Damien had been that for a long time before the divorce.

They had started that way. But in the end, they'd just been two people who were legally connected on their tax returns.

Until they weren't.

And if it was that easy to separate…had they ever really been like this?

It was those walls again.

"I'll catch you later," Sabrina said, patting Liam on the chest. "Are you sure you're okay?"

"I'm fine," Lindy said. "Go feed your husband."

"Okay," Sabrina said, sliding her hand down Liam's arm and taking his hand, the two of them turning and walking back out of the mess hall.

Bea looked at Lindy. "Dane isn't coming, is he?"

"No," Lindy said. "He has a ride in Sisters. He should be back again before the grand opening."

Bea look slightly crestfallen. "Okay."

Lindy started to say something, then hesitated. There really was no point in lecturing Bea on her feelings for Dane. Lindy wished that she hid them better. It killed her to watch Bea being so vulnerable without even realizing it. The girl had never been hurt before. So she didn't understand. Not really.

"I'm going to say hi to Kaylee," Bea said. She turned and made her way toward Bennett, Kaylee and Dallas. At the appearance of Bea Dallas immediately brightened up, all of his teenage angst fading from his face.

Great, Lindy thought. Bea was mooning over Dane, who was too old and too experienced for her, and Dallas was mooning after Bea, who was far too old for him.

That was the way of the world. Nothing ever seemed to line up.

The world was a jackass.

She looked back over at Wyatt, the man that she was currently mooning over. No. She would not moon. She needed to…

It was like anything else. Coming from the trailer park to the Grassroots Winery world. She had to fake it until it felt real. Until it felt possible. She could have a physical-only relationship with him. She didn't need to have feelings. She didn't need to be possessive. All of that was ridiculous, and it wasn't what she wanted, anyway. Not really. It was an old habit, that's what it was. She didn't know how to have sex without commitment. Because she'd never done it. She was learning. That was all.

It was a good thing that they were going to meet up tonight, actually, her reticence aside.

It would take some of the intensity away from that first time they were together.

There was no way the sex was actually as good as she remembered anyway. He was a mortal man, after all, not a god.

Until that afternoon at her house it had been a couple of years since she'd had sex, and that wasn't natural. So, the…orgasmicness of it all had been amplified.

Plus, Wyatt had been the object of her guilty lust for long enough that it had felt big. She had to make it…normal. Common. And she realized that she needed to get back under him as soon as possible. Because that was the only thing that was going to help her deal with these ridiculous feelings that she had inside of her.

She continued to mill around the crowd, circulating in the mess hall before going outside and went and said her hellos to all of the Donnellys.

There was a tall, handsome cowboy standing near the table laden with food waiting to be served. He looked familiar, but she couldn't quite figure out why.

He looked to be around Wyatt's age, brutally handsome and made only more so by that slight weathered look about him. He had a dimple in one cheek, and a decent-size scar next to his eye on the other side of his face. It seemed an intentional counterbalance. One that made him look both more approachable than he should, and about as dangerous as he ought to.

He looked at her, a small smile on his lips, then he took a couple of steps, closing the distance between them. "Are you Lindy Leighton?"

"Lindy Parker," she said. "I'm no longer married to Damien." Those words were a relief.

He nodded slowly. "Probably a good thing. That guy is kind of an ass." Not one of the riders Damien had worked with, then. Or at least not one who'd parted ways with him amicably.

She laughed. "No argument from me. Do we know each other?"

"I've seen you around," he said. "Gabe Dalton. I know your brother."

"Obviously not well if you hadn't heard about my divorce."

"I ride saddle bronc. I see him around sometimes, but we're not at all the same events. My family has a ranch in Gold Valley."

"Oh, I didn't realize."

"Well, you didn't recognize me, so why would you realize where my family lived?"

"Good question."

"I'm friends with Wyatt," he said by way of explanation. "I was in the area, so he asked me to stop by. I'm not going to be here during the official grand opening."

"I see."

It hit her then, that this guy was flirting with her. It made her wonder if she could make a career out of casual relationships with handsome cowboys. After all, her relationship with Wyatt would be over soon enough.

And apparently, she wasn't completely unappealing to other men.

"Howdy, Gabe," Wyatt said, walking up to the two of them. "I didn't see you get here."

"Far be it for me to pass up a free meal, Dodge," Gabe returned. "I was just saying hey to Lindy. I remember seeing her around sometimes years ago."

"Yeah. She doesn't hang out on the circuit anymore."

"She told me," Gabe said, crossing his arms, like he was ready to challenge Wyatt.

Oh good grief.

And then, even more startling than the fact that Gabe had been flirting with her at all, was the realization that Wyatt was being territorial. She did not know what to make of that. Not at all.

"Interesting," Wyatt said, his tone indicating he didn't find any of this interesting. "Well, it was real good to run into you, Gabe. Glad we got a chance to chat. If you'll excuse me, I have to show Lindy something. Feel free to grab an extra steak."

He hooked his hand underneath Lindy's elbow and guided her away from Gabe.

"Bye," Lindy said, waving at Gabe to exasperate Wyatt. "It was nice to see you again." She added a sparkling smile to that farewell.

"Excuse me," she said to Wyatt when they were out of earshot. "What was that?"

"I wanted to ask you how you were finding things," he said. "I wanted to find out if you had been to see your cabin yet."

"You did not. You were…intercepting me."

"I wasn't."

"You were. Were you jealous that I was talking to Gabe?"

She wanted to marinate in this delicious irony. Because she had been wrestling with her jealousy only moments ago, and it seemed like Wyatt had a few issues of his own. She felt vindicated.

She'd been so sure the jealousy thing was all her glitch, but no. Mr. Call For a Good Time could be possessive too.

"Not at all," he said. "But, you should know that he's a total manwhore."

"Different from you how?" she asked.

"Not different than me at all," Wyatt said. "Except he's a sissy who rides saddle bronc."

"Wow. So I'm supposed to avoid him because he's like you."

"Hell yeah," Wyatt said. "You know how I am. I'm shameless."

"You are," Lindy said, "it's true. But I agreed that I wouldn't sleep with other men while we were together," she said archly. "If I want to scout for what's next, what business is it of yours?"

"No scouting on my land," he said, his voice getting hard. "That's a big no."

"I don't recall signing up to let you tell me what to do, Wyatt Dodge," she said.

"Oh, you sure as hell did."

"My body is not your business," she said crisply.

He leaned in, lowering his voice. "You made your body my business the minute you let me inside."

"I… This is supposed to be casual." That was for her benefit as much as his.

"It is casual," he said, smiling, but even she could

tell it was forced. "But that doesn't mean I want another man to touch you. And it doesn't mean I want to watch you flirt."

"I didn't flirt," she protested.

"Like I said, Gabe Dalton is shameless, and I wouldn't let him near any woman I liked."

"You invited him to your friends and family barbecue." He had to see how ridiculous he was being.

"Because he's a friend. But I'm realistic about how he is." He huffed out a laugh. "If I ever saw him even look at my sister I'd kill him."

Lindy rolled her eyes. "Well, I'm a good ten years older than your sister. And I think I can handle myself. And now I'm done arguing with you. I'm hungry and I want to eat."

"Get a plate of food then," he responded.

"Am I dismissed?" she asked.

"I'll grab a plate too."

"Oh joy. You're such wonderful company right now, I can think of nothing better."

Her sarcasm didn't deter him. She wasn't sure she'd wanted it to.

The two of them walked back over to the table of food, and began to fill their plates. Bread, steak and corn on the cob were the first things that Lindy grabbed, followed by a green salad, pasta salad and she managed to wedge a partial scoop of potato salad on there for good measure.

Then, she and Wyatt wandered down to the outdoor dining area. There were long wooden tables with bench seats, shaded by pine trees, overlooking the rushing river down below.

There were free spaces at the Dodge family table. There was an open seat next to Jamie, which ended up occupied by Wyatt, and Lindy sat across from him, and next to Kaylee Capshaw, Bennett's fiancée.

"How's it going?" Wyatt asked Jamie.

"Great," Jamie said. "The chef you hired is a genius," she said, taking the last bite of steak from her plate. "You should *marry* her."

"Marriage isn't in my future, kiddo. I've got a ranch to run." That seemed pointed at Lindy, and it annoyed her. She didn't want to marry him. He could calm the hell down.

Jamie laughed. "Haven't you heard? A great many ranchers manage to find wives. Running a ranch hardly precludes getting married."

"All right," he returned. "When are you getting hitched?"

"When pigs fly over a frozen hellscape."

"I figured as much," he said. "So maybe stop trying to marry me off."

"You know," Bennett said from the other side of Kaylee. "Marriage isn't all that bad."

"How would you know?" Jamie asked. "You're only engaged."

"We might as well be married," Bennett said, putting his arm around Kaylee.

"It's true," Kaylee said. "We live together, work together and already have a kid."

"I'm not a kid," Dallas said, with full-scale teenage indignation. "I'm a young adult."

"I doubt that," Bennett said.

"There's an entire book genre that supports my claim," Dallas pointed out.

"Speaking of guests," Bennett said, not speaking of

them at all, and obviously just purposefully shutting his son's attitude down. "How are the reservations going?"

"We're full up for the first couple of weeks," Wyatt responded without missing a beat.

"Good," Bennett said. "That is good."

There was a strange kind of tension between the two of them, and Lindy couldn't quite pinpoint why or what it was.

She knew that she shouldn't even be curious, but having dinner with his family was not going to go very far in helping her figure out how to have a detached relationship.

She ate quickly, and then went and found other people to socialize with, until the sunlight began to dwindle and big bonfires were lit. There were four separate fire pits stationed at the center of the cabins. Little benches surrounding each one. Lindy took a seat next to Bea, and the supplies for s'mores started getting passed around. There were also bananas in tinfoil with chocolate chips, to make banana boats, roasted on grates over the flames.

Lindy opted to go with a classic, taking hold of a stick and marshmallow, putting it over the fire.

She and Bea spent the next while building s'mores and eating them, and Lindy suddenly felt awash in a kind of nostalgia she had never felt before.

It reminded her of her childhood. More shocking than that…it wasn't terrible.

Suddenly, she wished that Dane were here too. She had turned away from this kind of thing. Eating steak outside on benches, sitting in front of a fire and eating camp food.

Like she had to be altered or nothing. This polished, fancy version of herself, or the trailer park her.

And maybe, these fragmented pieces that seemed like they didn't belong were just all her. Maybe the fact that she was pretending it wasn't was part of why her skin didn't fit quite right.

Quite a revelation to be having over a s'more, but, she seemed to be having it either way.

She wondered, for a moment, what her life would have been like if she had never met Damien. If she would have been the kind of woman who would have skinny-dipped with Wyatt the other day. Who wouldn't have worried so much about appearances, who wouldn't have felt so married to the image that she layered on.

Like her outfit that looked like it came from a page in a catalog, as Wyatt had put it.

Was that what she was so afraid of? That she would undo her hair, and take off her clothes and become something different? Undo all the work she had put in to becoming someone who fit in with that world she had married into?

Did she even want to be in that world anymore? Or did she think she had to be in order to run the winery?

Had she ever even wanted to fit into that world? Or had she just not wanted to feel stupid?

Was she her own woman, or was she simply a woman created by the life her ex-husband had wanted to live?

"You look very serious," came a husky voice from behind her.

She turned and saw Wyatt, who slid onto the bench right next to her, his denim-clad thigh resting against hers. It shouldn't get her all excited. But it did.

"I'm pondering the mysteries of the universe over marshmallows." She waved her s'more in his direction.

That was true, but he would never believe it.

"One Minute" Survey

You get **TWO books** <u>and</u> TWO Mystery Gifts...

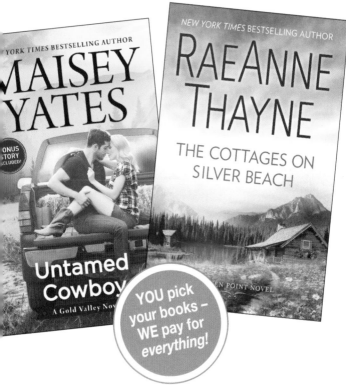

YOU pick your books –
WE pay for everything.
You get TWO new books and TWO Mystery Gifts…
absolutely FREE!
Total retail value: Over $20!

Dear Reader,

Your opinions are important to us. So if you'll participate in our fast and free "One Minute" Survey, **YOU** can pick two wonderful books that **WE** pay for!

As a leading publisher of women's fiction, we'd love to hear from you. That's why we promise to reward you for completing our survey.

IMPORTANT: Please complete the survey and return it. We'll send your Free Books and Free Mystery Gifts right away. **And we pay for shipping and handling too!**

Thank you again for participating in our "One Minute" Survey. It really takes just a minute (or less) to complete the survey… and your free books and gifts will be well worth it!

↖ We pay
EVERY!

Sincerely,

Pam Powers

Pam Powers
for Reader Service

"One Minute" Survey

GET YOUR FREE BOOKS AND FREE GIFTS!

✓ Complete this Survey   ✓ Return this survey

1 Do you try to find time to read every day?
☐ YES   ☐ NO

2 Do you prefer books which reflect Christian values?
☐ YES   ☐ NO

3 Do you enjoy having books delivered to your home?
☐ YES   ☐ NO

4 Do you find a Larger Print size easier on your eyes?
☐ YES   ☐ NO

YES! I have completed the above "One Minute" Survey. Please send me my Two Free Books and Two Free Mystery Gifts (worth over $20 retail). I understand that I am under no obligation to buy anything, as explained on the back of this card.

194/394 MDL GM32

FIRST NAME

LAST NAME

ADDRESS

APT.#

CITY

STATE/PROV.

ZIP/POSTAL CODE

◀ DETACH AND MAIL CARD TODAY! ▶

READER SERVICE—Here's how it works:

Accepting your 2 free Romance books and 2 free gifts (gifts valued at approximately $10.00 retail) places you under no obligation to buy anything. You may keep the books and gifts and return the shipping statement marked "cancel." If you do not cancel, about a month later we'll send you 4 additional books and bill you just $6.74 each in the U.S. or $7.24 each in Canada. That is a savings of at least 16% off the cover price. It's quite a bargain! Shipping and handling is just 50¢ per book in the U.S. and 75¢ per book in Canada*. You may cancel at any time, but if you choose to continue, every month we'll send you 4 more books, which you may either purchase at the discount price plus shipping and handling or return to us and cancel your subscription. *Terms and prices subject to change without notice. Prices do not include applicable taxes. Sales tax applicable in N.Y. Canadian residents will be charged applicable taxes. Offer not valid in Quebec. Books received may not be as shown. All orders subject to approval. Credit or debit balances in a customer's account(s) may be offset by any other outstanding balance owed by or to the customer. Please allow 4 to 6 weeks for delivery. Offer available while quantities last.

◄ If offer card is missing write to: Reader Service, P.O. Box 1341, Buffalo, NY 14240-8531 or visit www.ReaderService.com ▼

NO POSTAGE
NECESSARY
IF MAILED
IN THE
UNITED STATES

BUSINESS REPLY MAIL

FIRST-CLASS MAIL   PERMIT NO. 717   BUFFALO, NY

POSTAGE WILL BE PAID BY ADDRESSEE

READER SERVICE
PO BOX 1341
BUFFALO NY 14240-8571

"That sounds dangerous."

"I don't recommend it. I do recommend the marsh-mallows." He leaned in and took a bite off her s'more.

Her stomach sank and she did a frantic sweep of the people around them to see if anyone had noticed. It didn't seem like anyone was paying attention to them, not even Bea, who had started up a conversation with Jamie.

"What?" he asked, looking innocent.

"You just *do* things like that," she said. "And you don't seem to care about the consequences."

"What consequences? Other people knowing about us?"

"Yes," she said. "That."

"What does it matter?"

"We've been through this before. It's what they'll... think of me."

"Your family is not going to think anything different of you. Mine certainly won't care."

"That's not... That's not the point."

"I think it is. Actually, I think the real issue is what you think about yourself. You're afraid of something, Lindy, and God knows what."

"I don't think of sex as a handshake," she said. "I'm trying to be more casual... But it's never going to be... that to me."

"No see, to me, sex is the easy part."

"I know," she said.

She stared at him for a moment, and she was reminded of what they had talked about down at the river. When she had put her hand on his chest and said that he was bulletproof.

Wyatt liked everybody. It hit her then with the force of a brick. He liked everyone, and everyone liked him.

But she wondered if he *felt* much of any of it. All this stuff, all these interactions, they were easy for him. He didn't struggle like she did. He didn't worry. But she… She felt things. Deep. She sometimes wondered if he felt anything at all. He wasn't grumpy, he wasn't hard, and that made it easy to think that he was just happy. But she didn't think he was. The only way all this stuff could be so easy was if he didn't care much at all.

Except about the ranch. He cared about that.

"It's a good thing this is temporary," she said slowly.

"Why is that?" he asked, his voice getting sharper.

"We really don't go together," she said.

"No argument there," he responded. "We're compatible in the only way that matters," he said, his voice husky.

They sat next to each other in front of the fire, and she really wanted to lean into him. Into his strength, into his body. Even now after they'd been fighting. But she didn't.

The evening washed over her, the campfire and the sound of laughter, the strains of country music filtering out over a speaker somewhere, filling her.

This was simple. A simple life. But it was happy. Maybe that was the real reason she had run so hard and so fast from her own childhood. It had never felt like this. She had never felt safe. Not the way she did with Wyatt's heat and hardness, all of his strength, right next to her. Like he was the rock wall she would be able to lean against if everything started to crumble.

And so she did scoot a little bit closer to him. And then he put his hand over hers, the hard press of his touch doing something to her that she didn't want to think about.

"We never went camping," she said suddenly.

"Never?"

"No. My mom never did anything with us."

"My mom died when I was eleven."

Her heart twisted. Hard. She stared at the fire, resisting the urge to look at him. "I'm sorry."

"Me too," he said. "It changed everything. It changed us. You can't go through a loss like that and not feel it. I had to be the man of the house. I had to help my dad. I couldn't fall apart. Not when he needed someone to take over while he did."

"You were a boy."

"And you were a girl whose mother didn't take her camping. Life is hard."

She shook her head. "Not going camping isn't a struggle."

"I know," he said. "I'm a good listener. And I'd say that I heard a lot more behind those words than what you actually said."

She didn't like that. Didn't like how easily he read her. It was all great for sex. Less so in these quiet moments they kept on falling into.

She hadn't been able to force moments of emotional intimacy with Damien. With Wyatt, they were like potholes, and she didn't seem to be able to avoid them.

"Your sister must have been a baby," she said, changing the subject back to him.

"She was. Dad had to look out for her. And somewhere in between all that I had to figure out how to look out for Grant and Bennett. How to look out for Get Out of Dodge. They weren't good times. That's how the place ended up falling into disrepair. How we ended up in dire straits financially. Anyway, I left when I was seventeen. I went to the rodeo. I sent money back."

"That's a lot." She didn't know what else to say. She

knew that he was leaving things out, and part of her wanted to press for more.

Another part of her, a self-protecting part, wanted to forget he'd told her any of this.

The way they had taken care of each other was... She had no idea how to even process that. She loved Dane. And he loved her. But he had taken off when he was a teenager, had taken care of his own self. He hadn't wanted her to do anything for him. He was fiercely independent and he had wanted to make a better life his way. Lindy had met Damien. And in many ways, she had done the same.

It was funny, in the end, how both she and Dane had found their way out in such different ways. It was how they'd been raised.

But Wyatt had *given*. Given to his siblings, to his father.

She had thought only moments ago that he didn't care at all about anything. Now she wondered if he cared so much there were reasons he pushed it down deep.

That thought was more terrifying than the realization that he might be a wasteland of emotion. Because that man... The one he was describing now, the one who had given so much to be there for his father, for his siblings, that man was one she could have feelings for.

And she wanted feelings about like she wanted the plague. In fact, they amounted to about the same thing in her world.

Wyatt cleared his throat. "I better keep making the rounds."

She didn't want him to go. But she almost needed him to.

Sex. She had to remember why they were talking at all. She had to get it back to that.

Regain her control.

"Right," she said. "I'm in cabin six. If you didn't know."

He looked at her, his expression half shadow in the firelight, his eyes intense. "I know."

Then he stood and walked away, and she had a feeling it had nothing to do with the fact that he needed to check on anything. He was just walking away from her. From that moment.

And it was good that he had.

She didn't want to have deep conversations with him about what made him human, and what made him something other than that cocky bull rider that she had written him off as the first time she had met him.

He was supposed to be her fantasy. The last thing she needed was for him to become a man.

BY THE TIME everything had wound down Wyatt was getting antsy. Hell, he was somewhere past antsy. It had taken all of his strength not to haul Lindy away from the fire and take her straight to bed. It was for that reason alone he had decided that he needed to wait. She was right. They weren't compatible. Not in any damned way. Except the physical.

He liked irritating her, sure. But, that was not the same as getting along. Not in the least.

He hadn't meant to tell her all that about his past. Not the other day, and certainly not now.

None of that mattered. She was so prickly that it was his inclination to try to put her at ease with conversation, but it was one thing when that was all easy banter, and quite another when it became a whole discussion about feelings and things like that.

The problem was, he liked talking to her.

That meant he couldn't do his usual. It wasn't just sex and nothing else. It was getting tangled.

But tonight, it was about to get a lot more simple again. Tonight was going to be all about the physical. And that was what he knew.

He looked around the darkened lot, heading toward cabin six not wanting to have to stop and chat with anyone. Thankfully, it seemed like everyone had either gone home or gone to bed in one of the cabins.

He walked up the front porch and knocked. And waited.

If she was messing with him, he was going to be pissed off. This had to end. This weird dancing around each other. Talking by campfires and bringing up his mother. That wasn't him.

Hell no.

And if she was trying to manipulate him, trying to play like she was in charge, she was going to be sadly disappointed.

But then the door opened, and there she was, wearing exactly what she had been wearing during the barbecue, looking pale-faced and a little bit concerned.

"Howdy," he said, knowing the casual greeting would put her on her back foot.

"Howdy," she returned, her tone dry.

"Can I come in?"

She shrugged. "I suppose."

She moved out of the way and allowed him entry into the tiny cabin. They had been remodeled over the past few months, and were looking the good kind of rustic, rather than the kind that meant no one had touched them in a couple of decades. There was a small kitchenette, a little seating area with wood-framed couches and, most important, a big bed at the back of the room.

"I put you in this one on purpose," he said, tugging his shirt up over his head. "So you know."

"We're doing this already?" She looked a little bit nervous.

"That's what I'm here for," he said.

If she wanted more of what had happened earlier, she was out of luck. They had a physical-only arrangement. Beginning and end of story. And some of the things that had happened between them the past couple of times they'd been together had put that arrangement in a strange space.

He didn't do strange spaces. He did hot spaces. Fun spaces. But not strange ones.

"Well…"

He approached her, wrapping his arm around her waist and pulling her into his arms. "Has anyone ever told you that you talk too much?"

"No," she said. "I'm surprised no one has ever said it to you."

"I didn't say they hadn't."

"Well. Pot. Kettle."

"I'm not here to talk," he said. "We've done a lot of damn talking over the last couple of days. We haven't got a lot of time. Whatever game you were playing making me wait…"

"*You* could've instigated sex with me if you wanted it. You could have called."

He ignored the truth in that. "It's good for you to have to make the move," he said. "You're so uptight," he said.

"So worried about what everybody else thinks. What would happen if you just didn't care for a while? I think what would happen is what happened in your house the other day. On your couch. I think you're a lot wilder than you want people to think you are, Melinda."

"Call me that one more time, and I'll show you how wild I can be."

He reached down, sliding his finger along the edge of her jaw, stopping at the tip of her chin, tilting her face upward. "Little girl, do not make empty promises. Because when I call them in, your pretty ass will be in a world of trouble."

"It's not an empty promise." She pressed her fingertips against his chest. "Keep pushing me, Dodge, you'll give me a chance to test my bulletproof theory."

He captured her wrist, holding her fast as he bent his head to take her in a searing kiss.

If she wanted a fight, he was good with a fight. He knew how to fight with her. And he liked it. The other stuff... He didn't need that. Didn't want it.

He sure as hell hadn't asked her for it.

This was what he wanted. This was all it was. It was all it ever was with him. He didn't do that feelings stuff. Not anymore. Feelings were just black holes. They took from you. They ate away at you until you became something that you didn't recognize. Until you forgot who you were for long enough that you became the kind of man who would be part and party to destroying his own father's one bit of happiness since the death of his mother.

He didn't want to think about that. Not now. Not while he had Lindy in his arms. He didn't want to think about it ever.

He shouldn't be thinking about it, because there was

nothing in this that he didn't want. Nothing he hadn't chosen.

He was in control. Not this woman who had been with one other man. Who could hardly take her clothes off with the lights on without blushing.

He wasn't a boy easily manipulated by those weaknesses he hadn't yet managed to harden over into callouses. No. He was a man. And he knew this game. Damn Lindy Parker for making him feel like it might be a different game when it wasn't.

Anger poured through his veins as he grabbed the hem of her top and jerked it up over her head. She gasped, but he didn't stop.

Their first time... He'd been so wrapped up in the fact that it was her. The fact that he had wanted her for all that time and was finally having her. Well, he'd had her. It didn't matter. It was only hot sex. That was all it was. He grabbed hold of the straps on her bra and wrenched them down her arms, exposing her breasts. Then he bent down and sucked one nipple deep into his mouth, which tightened like a ripe berry on his tongue. This was what he knew. This was what he wanted.

Raw. Dirty. Sex.

He propelled her back against the wall, working the front of her jeans, getting them pushed partway down her hips. Then he unhooked her bra and dealt with it completely, before pressing his hand between her thighs and sliding his fingers through her slick folds, discovering her more than ready for his touch.

This was honest. There were no words for this. And there didn't need to be. This was all he wanted. All he needed.

This was what he was good at.

He shoved her pants and underwear down all the way to the floor, dropping to his knees along with them before holding her hips steady, pressing her against the wall even firmer as he examined her.

"Wyatt…"

"What did I tell you about talking?"

"You can't…"

He chuckled, leaning forward and letting his tongue between her thighs, the same trail his fingers had just wandered down.

He tasted her, deep and long, luxuriating in the feel of her, the taste of her, until she started to shake, until she started to whimper. But it wasn't enough. He wanted more. He moved his hands down her legs, forcing them apart, spreading her wider for him. He moved one hand up to cup her, sliding it back and pushing a finger inside of her while he continued to lap at her with his tongue. She held on to his shoulders, her nails sinking into his skin, her cries becoming harsher, more broken.

But as he felt her pleasure coating his lips, he couldn't forget who he was with. He couldn't make it not matter. It was Lindy. Lindy Parker, the woman he had wanted for the past five years. And he was tasting her. She was coming apart at the seams because of him.

And he *wanted* it to matter.

He damn well needed it to, and he hated that.

It reminded him of the boy he'd been at seventeen. Wanting so desperately for someone to care about him. For someone to see him. Touch him. For his touch to affect someone else.

No. This was nothing like that. He was nothing like that. It didn't matter. Except that it was a triumph. And every man was allowed a moment to glory in the triumph. In getting what he wanted. After so damn long.

He needed her mindless. He needed to take control here. Of her. Of himself.

He shifted again, grabbing hold of one knee, draping it over his shoulder, before lifting her other leg up off the ground, pressing her against the wall and holding her fast, his hands braced on her hips as he took advantage of her even more open position to continue devouring her. That was when she broke. Shattered underneath him, crying out his name. And he tried not to care. Tried not to care that she said his name over and over again. Not anyone else's. Not a generic cry, and not even a blasphemy. No. It was his name.

Him.

He was the one she was thinking of.

He gritted his teeth, setting her back down on the floor before rising up and capturing her lips with his, showing her exactly how far she had fallen. Letting her taste her own arousal on his lips.

"See?" he asked, his voice rough. "You're not that buttoned-up woman you pretend to be. This is who you are. You don't have to be this when you're out running that winery, but don't pretend this isn't you."

He didn't know why he cared. That was what he kept coming back to. Why had he taken her out to that damned waterfall? Why had he wanted her to strip off her clothes and get in the water with him? Yeah, so he could see her naked, but there had been more to it. And he didn't know why in hell there was. It wasn't right, it wasn't reasonable. It shouldn't matter.

It did.

He shook his head and kissed her again before she

had a chance to ask why. She wasn't part of that fight he was having with himself, and he didn't want her to be. She started to grab feebly at his belt buckle, trying to get his clothes off.

"In a minute, babe," he said, lifting her up and wrapping her legs around his waist, and carrying her back toward that bed. He deposited her on the edge of it, her legs draped over the side, and then he began to take care of his jeans and underwear.

He started to bend down to get his wallet, to grab a condom, and she stopped him.

"Wait," she said.

"I'm past the point of waiting, sweetheart."

"Well I'm not." She leaned forward and kissed his hip bone. "Maybe you're right," she said softly. "Maybe I don't know who I am. But maybe you do."

She was playing sweet and demure now, and he just didn't believe it. Not for a moment. And when she wrapped her hand around his cock and leaned in, parting her lips and sliding her tongue over the head of him, he knew that he had been right. She was trading him. Trying to make it so that what he had done to her, the fact that he had reduced her to something mindless and needy and more than a little bit out of control, was less somehow.

He reached back, forking his fingers into her hair, trying to grab hold of her. Trying to find the strength to pull her back.

"We're not trading," he said through gritted teeth as she swallowed him down, her tongue tracing an erotic pattern over his length.

She pulled back. "Who's trading?"

"You," he gritted out. "You, dammit. And I'm not playing games."

"Neither am I."

"Like hell." But then, he lost the will to have this fight. Lost the will to have this conversation, because she took him in again, her hands and mouth playing havoc with him, making it so he couldn't breathe. Couldn't speak. Couldn't think at all.

She played him with extreme expertise, and he found himself bucking his hips against her mouth, completely lost in the experience. In the slow, wet glide of her tongue, the firm grip of her hand. And the fact that it was Lindy. Lindy who had him in her mouth.

She was trying to take him over the edge. She was trying to trade. One for one. He got down on his knees in front of her, so she was doing it for him.

That was what pulled him back from the brink. Only that.

He gripped her hair more tightly, drawing her head back, pulling himself away. "No," he ground out. "Not like that."

"Why not? You did it to me."

He growled, lifting her up and hauling her back onto the bed, coming down over the top of her. "You got yours and now I get mine, is that the game you think you're playing? Are you just trying to stay in control, honey?"

She blinked her eyes, slow, trying to look innocent, he assumed. "I'm not trying to do anything."

"You damn well are. And that's not how this goes. You don't get to stay in control, baby. Not with me. I want you like you were the first time. I want you panting and breathless and screaming out my name. You understand? I want you to beg."

"I don't beg," she said simply.

"You should know better than to challenge me."

"Oh, baby," she said. "Don't make empty promises to me."

He growled, putting his hand between her legs, stroking her, finding her slippery with her need for him. Then he kissed her, deep and hard, toying with that most sensitive part of her while he did. He brought her up to the edge, moving his thumb over her clit in a circle, and then drew back. Pumping two fingers inside of her until he could feel her beginning to pulse beneath him. And then he pulled away. He did that. Over and over again. Until he thought he would lose his mind, until she sounded like she had damn sure lost hers.

She was tossing her head back and forth on the pillow, and then she wrapped her hands around his wrist, like she was trying to get him to stop, or trying to hold him there, she didn't know.

"I make good on every threat, you remember that," he said, his voice low, his lips brushing against hers with each word he spoke. "You can't play me."

Except he had a feeling that she could. That if the situations were reversed he would be as helpless as she was now.

But he wouldn't allow that. He sure as hell would not.

Her hips bucked up off the bed, desperately seeking more, and he left his hand still, two fingers deep inside of her as she feebly attempted to give herself some satisfaction.

"What is it, honey?" he taunted. "What is it you want?"

"For you to go to hell and die," she bit out.

"I think I'd have to die before going to hell, at least, if my understanding of things is correct. Granted, I paid terrible attention in church."

"Wyatt Dodge…"

"Beg. Me."

"Go. To. Hell."

But she kept on wiggling her hips, and he could tell she was getting closer. And so he teased her. Just one more pass of his thumb over her clit. She let out a wretched-sounding growl, her head tilting back.

"What do you want, Lindy?"

"Nothing."

"Yes you do." He reached down, wrapping his hand firmly around his cock, pumping it a couple of times so she could see. "I think you want this."

"I've got a vibrator."

He chuckled. "Did you bring it with you? I don't think you did."

"You can't do this," she panted. "It's cruel."

"I've got a price. And you know what it is." What was cruel was the fact that he could barely see straight. He was so hard he could hardly stand it. What was cruel was that he had never wanted a woman like he wanted her, and he thought this woman might kill him.

What was cruel was that this game was ready to defeat him. No way around it. If she didn't beg, he would be the one begging soon. And that was a fact.

"Wyatt," she whispered. "Please."

"What was that?" he asked, trying to keep his voice steady.

"You heard me. Please. I need you. I need you inside me."

She did not have to ask again. He reached down to grab hold of his wallet, tearing open the condom, sheathing himself as quickly as possible. Then he pressed himself against her entrance, and when he went in, he went slow. He savored her. The feel of that tight, wet heat clos-ing around him, overtaking him, inch by delicious inch.

The sounds she made when he was in her. The deep, raw satisfaction. And then, they were both out of con-trol. He couldn't tease, not anymore. But in the end, they were both mindless. They found their release together, and she sure as hell cried out his name.

But then, he cried out hers.

And it was clear that what they'd been fighting for wasn't a release. It was something bigger than that. More than that.

He had a feeling that they'd both lost.

And Wyatt Dodge didn't like to lose.

CHAPTER FIFTEEN

SHE WAS ALONE in bed.

That was Lindy's first thought when she woke up. Her second thought was wondering why she had woken up. It wasn't because of the empty bed. Wyatt had left as soon as they had finished making love.

Having *sex*.

He had made it abundantly clear that was all he was there for last night. She was fine with that. She needed that, in fact. So why it bothered her at all, she didn't know.

It wasn't why she had woken up, though. The little cabin was comfortable, and quiet, and for a moment she just lay there, puzzled by the faint background noise that was coming from...

Her phone was buzzing.

She scrambled to the edge of the bed, and grabbed the phone off her nightstand, where she had left it right before she had fallen into a fitful, lonely sleep in the unfamiliar bed.

She didn't recognize the phone number.

She answered. "Hello?"

"Melinda Parker?"

"This is she."

"This is Three Sisters Regional Medical Center. We're

calling because you're on your brother's list of emergency contacts."

"What happened?" Immediately, she was up, her heart hammering sickly in her throat. "Is he okay?"

No, no, no. She started scrambling around the room, looking for her clothes, trying to make sense of what this call actually was.

"He had an accident tonight."

"Car or bull?" she asked, fumbling with her bra.

"Uh...bull. And I apologize that it's taken so long to call you, but the doctors have been working to get him stabilized, and he wasn't able to talk to us."

"To get him stabilized? Does that mean he's... He's not stable?"

"He is for now. He was intubated. He is not breathing on his own, and he isn't conscious. He's had some significant swelling around the brain, and other injuries..."

"I'm coming. Right now."

"We can give you more information upon your arrival."

"Thank you," she said, hanging up the phone, sitting there feeling numb. Had she really just thanked someone for calling her and telling her that her brother was... Unconscious? In an accident? She knew that was a possibility. She always knew. That was the nature of playing at such a dangerous sport. But nothing had ever happened. Not until now. All this time and nothing had ever happened. He had always been safe. He had swelling on his brain. He wasn't conscious.

"Oh... *God*." She pressed her hand to her chest and sobbed the word. It wasn't a blasphemy. It was a prayer. It was all she could think of. She said it, over and over again, because she didn't know what else to say, all while she was getting dressed. And when her numb feet carried her to the front door of the main house, she wasn't sure quite why.

Except that Wyatt knew Dane. And Wyatt was a bull rider. So Wyatt knew. He understood. Whatever the real reason, that was the one that she gave herself.

It was the one that worked.

She knocked, knocked until her knuckles were numb, until she heard footsteps coming toward the door. It was wrenched open a moment later, and Wyatt was standing there, shirtless and looking disheveled.

"What the hell?" he asked, looking and sounding dazed.

"It's Dane," she said. "He got hurt tonight in a ride, and I don't know all the details, because I had to hang up the phone. Because I have to go. I have to go to Three Sisters Regional Hospital, wherever the hell that is, and I'm not exactly sure. But I have to start driving now."

She wasn't in control now. Wasn't holding it together at all. She was shaking. She was about to come apart.

"The hell you're driving," Wyatt said, gruffly. "Come inside."

"Okay," she said, too shocked to argue. All she could do was what he said. There was nothing else to do.

"Just a second," he said, disappearing from the room for a moment. He returned later with a T-shirt in his hand. He sniffed it and then gave her an apologetic look. "Grabbed it from the laundry. I'm making sure it's not beyond redemption." He pulled the T-shirt over his head and grabbed a jacket off the peg by the door. "Let's go."

"I have to… I have to tell Sabrina and Bea."

"It can wait until morning," he said.

"No it can't. What if he dies? It can't wait until morning. I can't tell Bea that he's dead." She realized that she had moved closer to him, that she had grabbed hold of the edge of his jacket. She was losing her mind. No doubt about it. But she didn't know how to hang on to her mind, not while her brother was lying in a hospital.

"Do you want me to drive your car?" he asked.

She nodded. And then, wondered why she was letting him do this in the first place. Sabrina would drive her. Or Liam could. She didn't need Wyatt to do it. Except, she wanted him to. She needed him to.

She picked up her cell phone and dialed Sabrina, while she walked toward Bea's cabin. She needed everyone to know. As quickly as possible.

Sabrina answered the phone. "Hello?"

"This is Lindy," she said, uselessly, because of course Sabrina knew who was calling her cell phone. "Dane was in an accident."

"Lindy! Oh no. What can I do?"

"Nothing," Lindy said. "I had to tell you." She hung up, knowing she was going to have to offer more of an explanation and soon. But she was right at the front of Bea's cabin. She knocked on the door. "Bea!" she shouted.

The door opened and Bea appeared, looking rumpled, wearing baggy pajamas. "Lindy," she said, looking immediately worried. "What's going on?"

"Dane was in an accident," she said, reaching out and grabbing Bea's hand. And she realized then that she hadn't just needed to tell Sabrina and Bea because they cared about Dane, but because they were her sisters. They were her family. It didn't matter what their blood relation was, didn't matter what the end of her marriage meant in terms of legal connection. They were her sisters. She needed them to know.

She *needed* them.

"Dane?" Bea looked faint.

"They said he's unconscious," Lindy said. "And I have to go to him. I have to go…"

"No," Bea said, a tear falling down her cheek, making Lindy conscious of the fact that she hadn't cried yet at all. "He…he's going to be okay." Bea was trembling, and Lindy didn't have it in her to offer comfort.

"I hope so."

"No… I can't…" Bea gulped. "No."

"I'm going to go to the hospital," Lindy said.

"I will too," Bea said.

"I'm going with Wyatt," Lindy said, and Bea paused, giving Lindy a strange look.

She couldn't have Bea in the car with her. She wanted her support, but she needed… Someone who wasn't more of an emotional mess than she was, and she wasn't entirely sure why she hadn't realized it was going to be like that.

"Bea," Lindy said. "I know you love him. He's my brother. And I just need…"

"I'll drive," Bea said.

"No," Lindy said. "Please don't drive yourself."

"He's not really my brother," Bea said, blinking hard. "I can drive."

"Beatrix," Lindy said. "I *know* you love him." She repeated it, making the words more meaningful.

Bea looked away, blinking hard. "There's nothing… It's nothing."

"Right now it's not nothing. See if Sabrina and Liam will drive you."

She turned and saw that Liam and Sabrina were already headed toward her. Liam was still doing up his shirt, and Sabrina was wobbling like she was in a daze.

"How far is the hospital?" Sabrina asked.

"I don't know yet."

Wyatt appeared then, his phone in his hand. "Two and half hours. We'll be there around four."

"Wyatt…" She looked around, "I'm sorry. You don't have to…"

"Yeah," he said. "I do. Don't worry about it, sweetheart. I'll drive you."

She didn't even think about the fact that everyone was there, she moved beside him and grabbed hold of his arm, took his hand. "Thank you," she said.

No one said anything. Instead, Sabrina and Liam focused on collecting Bea, Lindy gently suggesting that she get dressed. Bea went back inside the cabin and Lindy stood there.

"Why don't you and Wyatt go," Sabrina said. "I'll make sure that Bea gets there okay."

"She… I don't know if she's going to be okay," Lindy said.

"She's going to be fine. You need to get to him. You need to make sure that you're okay."

She nodded mutely, and Wyatt led her over to her car. She handed him her keys, and they headed off.

If you need help…ask me.

His words echoed in her now. And she needed him. She did. She didn't care if Sabrina saw it, or Liam. She had no idea what that meant. She just knew…

Wyatt Dodge had changed her.

She wanted to lean against him. Wanted for there to be nothing between them. No walls. No emotional boundaries. Life was…too damn short to hold back and even though she wasn't sure she even knew how, she wanted to hold on to him.

"You really don't have to do this for me," she said as they made their way onto the main highway.

"I want to," he said gruffly. "Hell, but for the grace of God go I, and stuff."

"I want to know what happened. I… I wish I knew… what happened. How. I wish someone could tell me."

"I'm sure we'll find out what we can once we get to the hospital. And he'll tell you everything once he wakes up."

"What if he doesn't wake up? She said his brain was swollen. What if he isn't the same again?" Lindy asked, feeling desperate and frantic.

"I don't know," Wyatt said, his voice rough. "But I know you can survive it."

She shook her head. "I might not be able to."

"Listen to me," he said. "You will. Because you don't have another choice. My mother died. I lived through it. It sucked. But I lived through it. You're going to live through this."

"He's the only person who knows me," she said. "The only person who knows where I came from. Who knows who I am now. There's not another person on this earth that knows all that, Wyatt. Not really. Not the way he does. He's always been there for me. And it's not… I wasn't as good of an older sister as you are a brother. That's for damn sure. I didn't take care of him. I should've told him to quit riding. I should've told him to just take all the money that I had. Why was he even still doing that? He didn't need to."

"Maybe he wanted to."

Somewhere, deep down she knew that was true. That Dane making his own way was something essential to him.

Right now, the fact she had no fault was hard to take on board. She was upset, and she wanted to blame something and someone. It seemed easiest to blame herself. All the shortcomings she was afraid that she had.

Wyatt put on music, they stopped once to get coffee, but otherwise had a silent drive. Lindy felt the weight of everything pressing down on her. Dane's injuries. The way her feelings were shifting for Wyatt.

Everything.

They got there before Sabrina, Liam and Bea, and made their way from reception to the emergency room.

They met a doctor who sat them down and explained the extent of Dane's injuries. He had been trampled. His head was not the only thing that was injured, though his scalp had been cut from his forehead on to the back of his skull, and his leg was broken. Completely mangled by the raging animal. But it was the brain injury that was causing the most concern.

"At the moment we're going to keep him in a medically induced coma," the doctor explained. "Depending on how things look. The best way to minimize damage in situations like this."

Lindy nodded as if she had any idea what that meant. "Can I see him?" she asked.

"Yes," the doctor said. "Though I feel like I should warn you that he's in rough shape."

Lindy nodded. "That's okay."

It wasn't okay. It wasn't okay at all that her younger brother was lying in a hospital bed *in rough shape*. But she didn't know what other response to have to that. She had to make it seem like it would be okay, so that she could see him. Because if she didn't see him she wasn't sure she would ever believe he was actually alive. She went back to his room, and Wyatt followed behind. At the doorway, she squeezed his hand. "Can you let me... By myself."

She didn't want him to see her break down. Of all the things, she didn't think she could handle that. Didn't think she could handle herself if Wyatt was standing there being a strong wall for her to lean on. She had never wanted quite so badly to lean on another person. If he was there to hold her up, then she feared she wouldn't be able to stand on her own after.

Wyatt seemed to root deeper to the hall floor, crossing his arms. "I'm going to be right here," he said, his expression grim.

She wanted to move closer to him. To kiss him. So she didn't. Instead, she walked into the hospital room alone.

Her heart slammed against her breastbone. She hadn't been prepared for this. Not really.

He was lying there, hooked up to so many things. The gash going down the front of his head was horrifying. The stitches only made it look worse. Like he was Frankenstein's cowboy, all sewn back together. It didn't look anything but grizzly.

His leg was elevated and completely encased in some massive brace, but she could see stitches coming out the top and the bottom.

And there was a tube down his throat. His mouth was open... The tubes.

He looked dead.

And that was when she started crying. Crying for the first time in her memory. All the tears she hadn't shed for every pain she'd endured for the last decade suddenly spilled out and down her cheeks.

She cried in great, gasping sobs that she didn't think

would ever end. Her knees went weak and she slid down to the floor.

A nurse came in and grabbed hold of her shoulders. Or maybe the nurse had already been in the room. She didn't know. "Do you feel faint? Are you okay?"

Lindy couldn't say anything. She shook her head.

And then, it wasn't a nurse holding on to her anymore. It was stronger arms. Familiar arms.

Wyatt was watching her cry. She should be horrified. But she wasn't. He was the one she wanted to hold her when she cried. And it stunned her to realize it wasn't embarrassing. She felt safe. She felt protected.

As she soaked the front of his T-shirt with tears, it felt like release.

One that had been coming for years. Maybe all of her life. She was being lifted now, brought up off the ground and still held, safe and close.

Wyatt held her tightly, leading her from the room, back out into the area where there were chairs for family. "He's not awake," Wyatt said gravely. "You don't need to be in there."

"I should be," she said, feeling miserable. Feeling weak and so terribly inadequate.

"You don't need to be," he said firmly. "Don't be a martyr."

Bea, Sabrina and Liam came into the waiting room a moment later. Bea's eyes went wide, her face going pale. "Is he…"

"He's unconscious," Wyatt said, sitting Lindy down, and taking a seat beside her, wrapping his arm around her shoulders. "He looks a bit of a mess. You might not want to go in and see him."

Bea looked determined. "I'm going to see him."

"Family only right now," Wyatt said.

"I'll tell them I'm his sister," Bea said, smiling slightly. "It's what he would say." Bea went in and she didn't return for a while, and Lindy wondered what that made her, that she couldn't handle it, and Bea could.

Bea returned about a half hour later with a doctor behind her. "We're going to take him in for surgery. He needs reconstruction of his femur, and he needs pins placed in his knee."

Lindy nodded, as if they'd been waiting for her agreement. She knew they weren't. None of this was up to her. She couldn't fix it or make it better.

They couldn't get out of this one on their own.

She and Dane had always gotten through. But she didn't see how her whip-smart, funny younger brother was going to get himself out of this.

Not even he could charm away a head injury.

They sat in the waiting room until the sun rose. Wyatt sat there with them. No one asked Lindy why Wyatt had come. Sabrina didn't tease, and Bea didn't look speculative. Liam, for his part, was stoic, because that's what he was good at.

At around 7:00 a.m., Damien walked in.

"I called him," Sabrina said, her tone apologetic. "I just thought…"

Damien and Dane had been close once upon a time, and even though Dane had taken it as a personal affront when their marriage had dissolved, they had been like brothers once. Lindy only nodded.

"Thanks for coming," she said.

She didn't get up.

"How is he?" Damien's eyes went to Wyatt, who was

sitting next to Lindy, his expression questioning. She didn't have any answers for him. She didn't owe him any.

And that was that.

"Good," Wyatt responded, his posture going stiff, energy radiating from his body. "He got out of surgery a few hours ago. He's still unconscious, but they said they're going to go ahead and keep him that way for a few days. Until the swelling in his brain goes down."

Wyatt said that like he knew it would all go that way. According to plan. He said it with such confidence that Lindy was tempted to just blindly believe him.

It would be so nice to just believe him.

Then Wyatt put his hand over hers. She looked at him, and he was looking at Damien, his expression a subtle challenge.

She had stopped him from doing this in town when they'd hung up flyers. Had flinched when he'd been less than discreet by the campfire. And suddenly...suddenly she was grateful for his touch. Here, in public. In front of her friends. In front of Damien.

Not because she thought it might make him jealous. Because it felt good to have someone be there for her, in her corner.

Conversation was odd and stilted after that, but she was grateful at least that Damien hadn't brought Sarabeth with him. Not that she couldn't have handled it. Right now... Damien's presence just made it slightly uncomfortable. It wasn't painful. Nothing was painful in comparison to Dane being so badly injured he might never wake up. To Dane being in actual, physical pain.

"Have you talked to your mother?" That question came, suddenly from Damien.

"I... No," she said, frowning.

It hadn't even occurred to her to call their mother. She was a terrible daughter, but then, she knew that already. Wasn't anything her mom hadn't said to her many times before. Too good for them. Above herself.

Whore.

That was a good one her mother liked to use.

"I should," she said, frowning.

"I could call her," Damien offered.

Everything in her rebelled at that. She didn't need his help. Of course he knew that she had a difficult relationship with her mom, but it wasn't his job to try to help with anything right now.

"No, don't worry about it."

Wyatt tightened his hold on her, a show of possession, she had a feeling. She was okay with that.

It occurred to her then, why it was so different to take help from Wyatt, than it had been to accept it from Damien. If Wyatt saw that she needed something, he was there to fill the gap. He was a good man. It was who he was.

Damien would have used it against her. He had. She'd come into their marriage guarded. And the subtle ways he'd talked down to her over the years had trained her to strengthen her armor even more.

To build the walls higher.

To never look like she needed anything.

She looked between the two men. And again, she was stunned by how…little she felt for her ex-husband. There was no pang of longing. No feeling of nostalgia. If she saw him walking down the street these days, she wouldn't even notice him. He was still handsome, but… not in the same way that Wyatt was. Wyatt affected her on a deep, visceral level. He scared her as much as he enticed her, and she couldn't ignore him.

Damien was like white noise. Nothing of interest to her at all.

She placed her hand over Wyatt's, rubbing it for a second before getting up and making her way into the hall. She dialed her mother's number, and got an automated message telling her it had been disconnected.

She groaned. That was all she needed. To have to go and pay her mother a visit.

But she would have to. She couldn't not tell her mother, no matter how frustrating she found the woman. Dane was her son. She had to know.

"Her number's disconnected," she said when she came back in. "I'm going to have to... I'm going to have to go and see her."

"I can stay," Bea said. "Everybody needs to take a trip home and grab their things, I can stay."

"I'll stay with you," Damien said.

Lindy didn't know why the small show of decency surprised her so much. Bea was his sister, and she looked...pale and determined, but like she might break at any moment. Damien would have to be heartless not to notice that. And no matter how much she felt like he lacked common decency when it came to her, he wasn't completely terrible.

The fact of the matter was, he had been a decent man for most of the years she had been married to him. And she had loved him, in the way she could. She hadn't married him for his things, whatever niggled at her sometimes now in the evenings when she couldn't remember why in hell she had fallen for him in the first place, and the only answer she could come up with was his money.

No, he *had been* a good man. He maybe even still was. Not to her. And not so good that she would ever want to be with him again, even if that option were on the table. What he had done to her was terrible. But he hadn't always been. And it wasn't…the beginning and end of who he was.

He was Bea's older brother. Sabrina's too. He could see that his younger sister was upset, and he cared about that. He even still cared about Dane.

Maybe, in some weird corner of his heart, he cared about Lindy too. It didn't matter either way. She was ready. Ready for it to be over and done.

Ready to quit hiding behind this particular wall.

"Can I talk to you for a second?" she asked.

Damien's brows shot up. "Okay."

Wyatt squeezed her hand, but released it, and she went out to the hall with Damien by her side.

"Thank you for coming," she said.

"He's like a brother to me," he said simply.

"I know. But thank you for not letting me keep you away. That was decent of you."

"Thanks for not kicking me out." He looked boyish when he said that. And it made her think of the boy he'd been when she'd met him. The boy she'd first fallen for.

Oh, that boy just wasn't for her now. It was such a freeing thing to realize.

"We're never going to be friends," Lindy said. "I don't want to be. I like being divorced. I like mostly not seeing you. I'm not going to pretend otherwise. You hurt me. And… I got to hurt you back when I took the winery. I'm not sorry about that. At all. But I don't hate you. Not anymore. And I… I'm glad that part of the man I did love is still in you. He came here today. And I appreciate that."

His jaw went tense, his eyes cool. "I didn't come here to have a discussion about us."

"Yeah. But you came. So… We never did have a discussion about us. And I think I'm due this moment. So you have to live with it. We had a lifetime together. Ten years is a long damn time, Damien. It really is. And I can't look back on all of them with bitterness. Even though I'm tempted to. I wish so much that you hadn't done to us what you did. I know that we weren't happy, but we might have been able to fix it." She closed her eyes. "But I'm glad we didn't. Now. When all is said and done. I don't feel like I owe you a debt of gratitude, and I don't think it absolves you, but I'm happy we're not together."

"I have no idea how I'm supposed to take that," he said.

"Good. Be confused for a little while. I've been confused for the last couple of years. But I think I'm finally not."

"You're with Wyatt Dodge now?" he asked.

She shook her head. "Not really. I mean…you know. There's something. But we're not together. You know."

He looked extremely annoyed by that, and she felt gratified. Gratified in a few ways, because he had shown that he had some decency in him by coming here, but it didn't make her ache. And he was doing a good job of demonstrating now why she found him to be such a pain in the ass. Why she didn't actually want to be with him at all.

"It's a stretch to say I'm happy for you," she said. "But I'm not mad at you."

"I'm not mad at you either. For the winery. I can't

speak for my folks. But I don't care. Not anymore. I don't want it."

"Thanks," she said. But she didn't mean it. Because she didn't need him to not be mad at her about it. She didn't really care if he was.

"You care about it more than I do," he said. "God knows you'll do a better job."

"I do. And I will." She wasn't going to give him an out, wasn't going to waste any time placating him. He didn't deserve it.

"I'm glad it worked out like that. In the end."

"Me too."

She got the winery, but not the husband. And that had never been the goal. For some reason, all that had been clarified for her just now. Things had gotten tangled up in all of her anger. And there was something about letting that go, about clearing that all out that had brought a sense of real clarity to her. She had married him for the right reasons. She had divorced him for the right ones too. And everything else... It was just life. She didn't need to prove herself. Not to anyone. Now that she knew...she felt different.

She had doubted herself, that was the problem. Had gotten lost underneath who she was versus what she wanted to be. Had bought desperately into the lie that who she was beneath her polished exterior wasn't enough.

That wasn't true, though.

And now that absolutely no part of her at all cared about spiting this man in front of her... It all seemed a hell of a lot clearer. She was finally ready to let him go. Oh, the love feelings she had let go of a long time ago. But the anger... Yeah, she was ready to let go of that too.

"I hope he gets better," Damien said.

"Me too. Thanks for staying with Bea. It means a lot. She and Sabrina love you, you know. I mean, they love me too. And they've been angry at you. But they do love you."

He nodded. "Nice to know they haven't written me off completely, I guess."

"Here's the thing, Damien. It's too late for us. And that's fine. But they're your sisters. And it's not too late with them. So keep doing stuff like this. Keep being there for them. Really, be there for Bea right now. Because…"

He nodded. "I know."

"Great. I'll see you around."

"See you around," he said.

She went back into the waiting room, leaving Damien behind her. "I'm ready to go," she said to Wyatt.

Wyatt nodded. "I'll take you wherever you need to go."

CHAPTER SIXTEEN

HE ENDED UP driving Lindy back to her house. He waited downstairs, half dozing while she went up to shower and get dressed. She returned a few moments later with a little bag packed, and a determined look on her face.

"I'm ready," she said.

She sounded like she was riding into battle, not going home for a visit.

"Okay," he said.

They drove slowly away from Grassroots Winery, down the winding two-lane road lined with pines that led into Gold Valley. Through the main street with its vintage brick buildings, where the lunch traffic was starting to appear, the little parking lot of Mustard Seed packed full as people went to get their burgers. The curb in front of Belissima packed out as well, the restaurant full, people chatting over their lunch, visible through the windows.

It was amazing what a normal day it was, when nothing else was normal.

And somehow… In all of it… Lindy had decided to lean on him.

Him.

The man that all of his siblings would say was apparently a bad bet.

This wasn't sex. This was something else. And yet… here he was.

He had no idea what in the hell he was doing.

But he drove, all through the main street of town until they exited out the other side, past the winding hillside drives that led to the mountaintop homes that overlooked the entire valley with million-dollar views and matching price tags.

"Turn here," Lindy said, directing him the opposite direction of those fancy houses.

They took a narrow, pothole-filled road, down in a flat spot, surrounded by fields. Eventually, it grew more and more unkempt, sections of fence downed, ripped up barbed wire everywhere.

There was a sign, beat up and peeling, that said Boulder City.

He knew what Boulder City was, but he hadn't realized Lindy was from there.

The trailer park was little more than a shantytown, the place barely habitable. And *trailer park* was a stretch as a descriptor. There were no neat rows of mobile homes, no kept-up lawns—Astroturf or otherwise.

The collection of dwellings was haphazard at best, half of them covered in bright blue tarp, to cover up holes and keep moisture out, he imagined. The porch on the first house was collapsed, the step up to the front door treacherous. They continued on the gravel road, and Lindy didn't say anything.

"I didn't know this is where you were from," he said.

"I told you I was trailer trash," she said, turning to him and forcing a smile. "I wasn't kidding."

"I wish you wouldn't say that," he said.

"Well, I wish it hadn't been said to me."

"I guess if you say it enough times yourself…"

"In theory it quits hurting," she said. "But… I'm still testing that out."

She blinked, and for the first time since he had pulled her out of Dane's room earlier, he saw tears in her eyes.

"Right here," she said, her voice scratchy.

They pulled up to the front of a dilapidated blue structure, with peeling metal siding, a strange yellow substance exposed beneath. It looked like someone had tried to use expanding foam to hold the place together and it hadn't worked.

"I hope she's here," Lindy said.

He couldn't tell if she meant that or not. He had a feeling that she would be relieved if her mother wasn't here, if she had tried, but hadn't succeeded.

He didn't know what call he had to make that kind of judgment. He only knew he was pretty certain he was right.

He didn't ask if she wanted him to come with her or not. If she hadn't wanted him here, she could have driven herself. He was going to go ahead and assume that he was welcome all across the board. Because why in hell not.

He had a feeling that his rationale wouldn't go over well with her, so he didn't bother to give it to her. Didn't bother to ask. He followed her, up the depressed front steps and to the door.

"Okay," she said. She looked at him like she was thinking about offering an explanation, and then didn't. Instead, she raised her fist and knocked.

The door opened almost immediately, and Wyatt was struck by the similarities between Lindy and the woman standing there in the doorway. She wore her years on her skin, hard and cut deep, grooves around her mouth that indicated years spent smoking cigarettes. She was wearing an oversize sweatshirt and loose-fitting pants, but even so, he could see the resemblance between her and Lindy. Her blond hair was graying, pulled back in a bun almost exactly the way Lindy wore it. And they had the same blue eyes. Wary. Reserved.

"Why are you here, Melinda?" Lindy's mom asked without preamble.

The way she said Lindy's name brought a few things into startling clarity for Wyatt.

"Your phone is turned off."

"I changed my number," her mom said. "Rick took off with the phone," she added. "I was not going to give that bastard the satisfaction of having me pay for a red cent. I cut off the service. Got a new number."

"I have the same number I've always had," Lindy said, her tone faintly accusing. "You could have called me and let me know."

"That happened two years ago, Melinda. If you're just now noticing that I have a new number I'm not sure you have a leg to stand on when it comes to being angry with me."

Lindy rubbed her forehead. "No. But then… I never do."

"You came here for something." She looked at Wyatt. "Are you getting married again?"

"No," Lindy exploded with the response. Wyatt, for his part, tried not to look surprised by the question. He tried not to have any reaction at all.

"This is just…a friend."

"I know about your friends, Melinda," her mom said, the words clipped. "He looks exactly like the kind of friend I would expect you to have."

"We're not having this particular discussion, Mom. I need to come inside for a minute."

Lindy's mom shrugged and stepped away from the entry, allowing both Lindy and Wyatt in.

"Why don't you sit down?"

For the first time, Lindy's mom showed a flash of serious concern. "You're not sick, are you?"

"No," Lindy said. "Dane is in the hospital. He had an accident yesterday during a ride."

Wyatt didn't miss the flash of horror that streaked through her mother's eyes. The instant paling of her complexion, the way her lips went waxen. But then, she recovered. Her expression held tight and firm. "I never did like him riding those animals. Is he going to be okay?"

"They don't know. He's not conscious. Right now, he's in a medically induced coma. They don't want him to wake up, because his brain is swollen. If he woke up now… Anyway. He's really bad. I couldn't call you to tell you. But I thought you needed to know."

"He's not awake?"

"No," Lindy said.

"So there's not much…not much point in going to see him."

"I can give you a ride, Mom. If you don't have a car that can make it that far. He's a couple of hours away."

Lindy's mom shook her head. "No. I wouldn't want… If he's not awake anyway…"

"Mom, if you want to go, I'll pay for your lodging. I'll get you there. You don't even have to ride with me. I'll rent you a car."

"I don't need you to hand me money, Melinda. Just because you have some, doesn't make you the lady of the manor."

This wasn't the first time they'd had this conversation. Wyatt might not be the most insightful or emotionally intelligent guy, but he knew enough to realize that. That this was an old wound, not a new one.

"I was never trying to be the lady of the manor, Mom," Lindy said. "Maybe I wanted you to not have to live in a trash heap if you didn't want to."

"What I have, I earned," her mom shot back. "I don't take handouts. I taught you better than to take them too."

"Well, if what you said about me is true, Mom, that I work for what I have too. Just not in a profession that you approve of."

Wyatt knew he was in the middle of a hell of a lot of hard feelings. And he wasn't sure quite what to do about them. In the Dodge family, you stuffed those feelings down deep. You certainly didn't end up yelling at each other in a small living room, with an audience.

Hell, if you were a real good Dodge you didn't even use yourself as an audience for your bad feelings. You simply had another drink.

"If you were wondering, Wyatt," Lindy said, her neck arched. "My mother thinks I'm a whore because I married a man with money. Who couldn't possibly love me."

"He left you, didn't he?" The words were sharp as knives. Wyatt felt them cut.

"That he did. And I got his money. So… I'm a smart whore at least."

"Lindy…" Her mom started to speak, but Lindy held up her hand.

"No. That's what you think I am. Because why would anyone love me otherwise? I was trading it for money. But at least I had the good sense to take money when it was there. Unlike you. You'll just die miserable and alone in this horrible house because you won't take help from anyone. Because you won't let your boyfriends help you, you won't let your kids help you. You can tell me how that's better, Mom. I'll listen."

"I didn't say it was better. But I have pride."

"So much pride you won't let me take you to see your son that's laying in the hospital? That's how much pride you have? What's the point of that. It doesn't keep you warm. It keeps you away from the people that love you."

"Because people leave," her mom said. "Pride is all you have at the end of the day. You're not here. Dane hasn't been by to see me in God knows how long, Rick left. Your father left. What I have is mine. Don't ask me to feel guilty about that, Melinda Parker. I will not. What you have… That's not yours."

"No. It is mine. My name is on it. And you know what? Maybe if you acted like you wanted someone to stay they would. Dad would have stayed if you would have… Dammit, Mom, you let us live in poverty rather than let him support his own children."

"How long would that have lasted if I had let him in? Then we would have gotten dependent on him, and he would have left. I wasn't going to change my life around just to suit him or even you kids. You left too."

"That is what people do when they grow up. They go make their own way," Lindy said, her tone stiff.

"Is that what you think you did? Made your own way? There's not a lick of truth to that. You married rich, and you took his money. If the judgment had gone another way, it could've been taken from you. This…" her mom said, gesturing to the dilapidated building around them "…this is mine. Nobody, not the government, not a man, can take this from me. I don't live a life that can be taken from me."

"Dane could be taken from you. He could die. Mom, he could die. And your pride would have kept you from seeing him one more time. Your pride can take a hell of a lot from you. It already took me away from you. But this… This is serious. This might be it. And if you can't set it all aside for a bit… If you can't just put it all away so that you can see your son while he's injured like that… I don't know."

"I'll find a way to get to see him. I have some money in savings. I can borrow a truck from a friend if need be."

"But you can't borrow my car? You can't take a ride from me?"

"It's different," her mom said.

"It's not," Lindy said, her tone rising, her shoulders shifting back and forth in an agitated motion. "You're just stubborn for the sake of it. And you hang on to baggage you don't need to hang on to so that you don't ever have to admit you were wrong. You can make it about money, and about security if you want, Mom, but I actually think that it would make you break in half if you had to admit you needed someone. That you love someone. That it hurts you to know that Dane is injured. He's your son."

"Of course I'm upset that he's injured," her mom shot back, her voice hard. "Whatever you think about me, I'm not a villain in a movie. But how does falling apart help anyone? It doesn't. It doesn't get anything done."

"Neither does this. You have my phone number if you decide you want my help. Chances are, I'm going to be at the hospital. But I will help you if you want to get there. All you have to do is ask. That's all you ever had to do."

Lindy turned and walked toward the door. "Come on, Wyatt."

Wyatt was experiencing some kind of strange, out-of-body experience. Where he almost identified with the wooden, angry-faced woman sitting on the couch in front of him. Wanting to handle it all. Wanting to be an island. But in this instance, it was ridiculous. Flat-out ridiculous.

"I'm a friend of Dane's from the rodeo," Wyatt said. "And I know how much it sucks to ask for help. But sometimes you have to. Sometimes even I need help. Lindy has been helping me with my ranch. Because she's good at business. She's smart. However she got the winery that she has now, she's running it better than her ex-husband ever could have. Even he admitted it. She helped me figure out how to get my business off the ground in a way that I couldn't have done without her. She's the one with the head for this, not me. And if I hadn't taken her help when it was there on offer, I would have been a damned fool. I would probably be losing my ranch about now. There's no shame in needing help. But there is shame in stiff-necked stupidity. And I've had my share of that, but not this time."

Lindy walked out of the trailer, not waiting for him. That was fine. But he wasn't done.

"Call me," Wyatt said, scribbling his number down on an old business card in his wallet. "If you decide you want to get over to the hospital. And if you don't want to accept help for you, do it because it will help Dane. Because it will matter to Lindy. This? This brand of independence is nothing but pure selfishness, whether you can see it or not."

He turned and walked out of the trailer, not waiting

for a response from Lindy's mom. Not waiting to see if she tore up the offered number, or kept it.

"You didn't need to get in the middle of that," she said, marching to the car and getting into the passenger side.

He got in beside her, starting the engine. "Right. I didn't need to help?"

"Shut up," she said.

"She's definitely your mother."

"What the hell is that supposed to mean?" Lindy asked, practically growling.

"I think you know."

"She wouldn't let me help her," Lindy said. "When I got married to Damien, he offered a bunch of money to help get my mom out of the park. He's an ass, there's no denying that. But, he had his moments. I wanted her to take it. To take the money. To have a better life. She wouldn't do it. That was when she… When she said I was a prostitute. Because I was sleeping with him, and getting money. And she sure as hell was never going to be a man's prostitute. She's always done that. Kept everything separate. She never married our father. She never took a damn thing from him. He would come by and visit sometimes until he stopped coming at all… Dane… Dane was crushed. We lived a harder life because of her stubbornness. And I reached a point where I couldn't deal with it anymore. And what the hell is wrong with a woman who doesn't think a man can love her daughter unless it's a transaction?"

"I don't know," Wyatt said.

He heard her draw in a sharp breath, a shocked, pained sound. "Well, she never really did. She loves herself more. Her sense of security. All that stiff-necked pride she talked about. So no. I don't suppose I ever did. She was never happy for us. Never gloried in our achievements. She was…distant. Like that. All the time. For one second I thought… It looked like she cared. Like she was going to go right to his side. But she shuts it down. She doesn't let herself have it. She doesn't love her own children all that much. So no, I don't suppose I ever thought my husband loved me all that much either. And then… He didn't, did he? That's actually the worst thing about him. He's not awful. He's not a mustache-twirling villain. He's not a completely morally bankrupt human being. He didn't love me enough."

Wyatt put his hand on her shoulder. "It's his loss, Lindy. It always was."

She smiled, small and a little sad. "I think I actually, finally believe that."

"Are you ready to drive back over to the hospital?"

She paused for a moment, and then sighed heavily. "I think I'd rather go back to Get Out of Dodge. For just a couple of hours."

"Okay," he said, not quite sure what to make of that.

"Yes," she said, sounding determined. "I need to… I want to go back to Wishing Well Falls."

CHAPTER SEVENTEEN

LINDY'S MIND WAS RACING. Her heart was thundering hard. She'd gone back to the place she'd avoided for years and found something of herself there. That something she didn't like. That she saw every time she stared down into her mother's blue eyes. Those blue eyes that were so similar to her own.

She was angry at her mother, but it was so very difficult to stand up on her high horse when realizing she was essentially looking in a mirror. Oh, Lindy had found ways to make it seem like she was normal. Well-adjusted. She had convinced herself that because she had a good relationship with Dane, because she had gotten married, that she was poles apart from the woman her mother was.

But the fact that she had stayed away with rare exception for the past decade over an argument...

The fact that she hadn't wanted to go to her mother for sympathy, for help, after her divorce.

The fact that she had never, ever wanted to have a moment in front of Damien, or his friends, where she didn't know what she was doing.

It was hard to deny that she wasn't her mother's daughter. So damned hard. She didn't give anyone anything. Not honesty. Not really.

It hurt her to realize her own mother hadn't thought Damien could ever actually love her. But the fact was, she hadn't ever believed it either. But she wasn't entirely sure she had loved him with all of herself either. Because there were always parts she kept back. She was always trying to be the right thing, to do the right thing. To avoid feeling stupid. To avoid being rejected.

When she had cut ties with her mother, she had burned it all to the ground, because that was safe. Easy. Her decision.

Distance was easy.

When she had sensed Damien begin to withdraw from her, she had withdrawn herself from him. They hadn't worked on it. It was easy to blame the fact that he wasn't home, but she hadn't put herself out there. Not ever.

She had never made herself vulnerable, not once.

And it was why she was alone.

It was why she was always going to be alone if she didn't figure out how to just… Be. Her. Without those walls and separations between herself and the world. Herself and other people.

"Yes. I want to go to the waterfall."

She wanted to fix it. To reclaim a moment she should have taken weeks ago, but didn't. To reclaim herself.

Or maybe, find herself for the first time.

The girl she was back then, the woman she was now. All those things were her. All of them.

"You don't have your little hiking shoes," Wyatt pointed out.

She shook her head. "I don't care."

Wyatt parked his truck outside the house, and he and Lindy walked in silence through the rows of cabins, back to the path that led to the falls.

Lindy watched the way that Wyatt moved through the landscape, so confident, broad-shouldered and strong.

He was a part of this. A man at ease in his own skin, and while she knew there were plenty of demons inside of him, plenty of things that didn't sit well at all, he was at ease with his body.

With who he was.

He was Wyatt Dodge. He was a former bull rider. He was a cowboy. The scenery around him seemed to move in his wake, tree branches bending with ease to accommodate him. That was how he was in every social situation she'd ever seen him in. It wasn't about pride or holding himself back, standing stiff-necked and refusing to stand out. He stood out easily. Happily. And other people wanted a taste of it.

God knew she did.

She thought back to that day she had seen him for the first time in the bar. The way that light seemed to shine down on him. Like no other man she had ever met. He was easy, and he was hard all at once. Someone you couldn't look away from. Someone who demanded focus and attention.

It was the kind of thing that would have horrified her. And yet... It was the same. She was who she was. Lindy, from Boulder City, who wasn't born into money, who had never set foot on a college campus. Who had tried so desperately to pretend that she fit in so that she wouldn't be rejected. So that she wouldn't be too much work. So that she wouldn't have to show all of her rough, unpolished places and have those real, insecure, wounded spaces rejected. No. Far better to keep those things hidden and never experience real rejection.

So, so much better.

Seeing Wyatt for the first time had been like a lightning strike. And lightning struck what stood out. What stood taller than everything else around them. The feelings that had erupted between them had been bigger than anything else in that bar. They couldn't blend, not in that moment.

And maybe that moment had been necessary. Because…she didn't know if she would want to change if it weren't for him. She didn't know if she would know she needed it. Her mother was a mess, and it was easy to make her the cause of that early pain. Damien had wronged her, and it was easy to blame him for everything.

Easy to ignore her own issues, when he'd dropped such a destructive bomb into the middle of everything. For all the platitudes she'd given about the dissolution of a marriage being the responsibility of both parties, she'd still been able to walk around knowing she was the most wronged.

As long as she clung to that, she didn't have to figure out what was wrong with her.

But there was something about being with Wyatt that made her want to…

He had brought about a peace with herself. She wanted more of that. To take those pieces of herself she'd let fragment and splinter and join them together. Find Lindy, the way she wanted to be. And not Lindy, the way the world expected her to be.

And she wanted the woman she'd found, the woman she was, the real woman, to get beneath that easy grace of his, because for all that he could accomplish about a thousand things she couldn't—that ease with himself, that casual ability to look silly, to be wrong, to be dirty or forward—there was also something deep and hidden in him. Maybe even deeper than the things she kept hidden inside of herself.

She felt like it was the key to herself. Getting rid of all that space that was between them. Wyatt was everything, and if she wanted that everything, she would have to give everything in return.

She realized that with clarity as they walked down the steep part of the trail, heading down to the bottom of the falls.

When she had first set eyes on him he had seen her. In a way no one else had. She was sure it was the same with her too. She had been married, and she would never have violated her marriage vows. She knew Wyatt well enough to know that he wouldn't have asked her to. They had both ignored that moment. That lightning strike. Had both gotten up and gone on with things as they had always been.

But they didn't have to now.

She stood there, on the banks of that swimming hole, and she let that realization wash over her.

Things didn't have to stay the same.

She didn't have to stay the same.

"I've changed a lot," she said, to herself more than to him. "So many times. I imagined that if I could somehow be this perfect wife for Damien he'd love me forever. And when that didn't work I clung tighter to all my changes. New hair, new clothes. New money. I was a new woman. A strong one. But I haven't changed at all. I'm just like my mother, Wyatt. I don't let anyone close to me, and I call that pride. I call it being independent. But it's just protecting yourself. Because you don't think anyone can love you. It's pride. And it pushes people back."

She swallowed hard before continuing on, "I never let

him see me cry, Wyatt. Ten years I was married to that man and I didn't let him see me cry. I didn't let him see me cry when I caught him kissing another woman. Not in court after. Never. Not when he came into the winery with her when she was pregnant. I never let him see me cry. I never let him know how much he hurt me."

"You let me see you cry," he said, his voice rough.

She nodded. "It was easy to give you that, to let you see it. Now. It wouldn't have been, not before. But something changed. You changed something in me."

"I couldn't have."

She turned to face him. "If I had been a single woman the night we met in the bar I still could never have followed through on that attraction. It was so real and intense. The most raw thing I've ever experienced in my whole life, and it was just a look. I would've run away from it even if I hadn't had a ring on my finger. It was too strong, and I didn't want that. Not really. You don't let me hide, Wyatt. And I would've hated that then. I think I've hated it all this time. Because something in me always knew that you saw me. Melinda. From the trailer park. You call me that. And no one else does."

"I don't..." He cleared his throat. "I don't call you that because I look at you and see somebody from a trailer park. I call you that because it irritates you. I call you that because no one else does."

"I know, but still. That's what it feels like. And that was the thing that scared me most. Because I would rather be rejected for this thing that I'm not, this part of me that isn't real, than to be rejected for my real weaknesses. For my real shortcomings. It's easier to not let people see them."

She was trembling inside, but she had to keep talking. She couldn't go back now. "I didn't want people to know about us because… There's something real in it. And I can't control it. I didn't want anyone to see… I feel exposed when I look at you. When you look at me. How can people not see everything between us when they see us together? But you can't really love people if you have walls between you. And I am so tired of my walls." With shaking fingers she took her hair down, and then she unbuttoned the shirt she had on slowly, methodically.

After that, she threw her bra down onto the rocks before shimmying out of the tight pair of black pants she was wearing and kicking her shoes off by the wayside. And before she knew it, she was naked. Naked in the sunlight, in front of Wyatt Dodge.

Like she had been that first time he'd seen her.

Oh, she had been dressed, it had been night and they hadn't been alone. But she had felt, even then, that he had *seen* her. Really and truly seen her.

In him, she had seen the possibility of who she could be. And finally, five years later, she was taking a chance on it.

Getting on the train wasn't just hopping into bed with him. No. Getting on the train was this. This moment. It was deeper than touch, deeper than skin.

"I don't know how to do this. How to be…exposed and unprotected. This is the best I can do. This is all I am. Everything else… Clothes… Makeup. A big winery. My mother is right about that. All that can be taken away. But I don't think the solution to that is building up taller walls around myself. I think it's about opening myself up. Because this…" She took a step toward him, and pressed her hand to his clothed chest. She could feel his heart thundering beneath the layers of shirt, his skin. She could feel his heart.

Even with his clothes on, he was naked too.

"This is what can't be taken away. This thing between us is real. There was nothing that I could put up that could hide it. There was no defense against it. It was undeniable. Then and now. And we had a choice not to act on it, and we didn't. Because then it was the right thing to do. But it was still there. Wyatt, it's always been there. There was nothing and no one that could take it."

She stretched up on her toes and pressed a kiss to his lips. "I think I'm ready to skinny-dip with you now."

"But what will people think?" he asked, his voice gruff, the words light, spoken with humor, but she sensed so much more underneath them. And she wanted to know everything that was there. She wanted to dig beneath those words, to explore the context. To explore the meaning.

But after. Right now, she just wanted to explore the feeling. The one she had been running from for so long. The one she was ready to feel.

Finally.

And she knew that tangled up in all this was the way her emotions were running because of Dane. She knew that. But hell, this was the kind of thing that brought perspective, after all.

The fact of the matter was there were no guarantees. And maybe her brother would never wake up. And she would never have told him all that he meant to her. And if it were her lying in that hospital bed, then she would have lost her life without ever really living it.

A business was easy. You could love it. You could

pour all of your energy into it. But it didn't ask for your secrets. It didn't ask for your heart.

She had loved Damien, but it hit her then that they had never been *in love*. It was impossible for them to have been. He didn't know her. Not really. And she hadn't really known him.

If they had felt distant, it was because they were. Because they'd had a marriage without sharing and sex without intimacy.

She didn't want to die without that. She wanted to live. She could go to the end without experiencing real devastation. Could keep on giving all she had to project after project, to expanding the winery. She could live a good life, and never be hurt.

But she couldn't live a *real* life without pain.

And if that pain came through Wyatt, then that was all the better. She was ready. Ready to let him destroy her. Because he was worth it.

And so was she.

He stripped off his clothes, slowly and methodically, stood out there in the sun naked right along with her. And he was beautiful. The most beautiful man she had ever seen. And she felt it. All the way down.

Not only her body, but her soul.

Wyatt swept her up off the ground and started to carry them both into the water. It was cold, so cold it almost burned her skin. But she didn't mind because it mirrored what was happening inside of her. Those untouched places opening themselves, the feeling almost too intense to fully take in.

The first time they had been together they had been desperate, hungry for each other, and it wasn't that she didn't feel that now. That intense, irrepressible appetite for his body. She did. She wasn't sure if there was anything in the world that would ever make that go away. That would ever ease it.

But it didn't feel frantic. Not right now. It was deep, down all the way into her bones, but she felt like they had time. She pressed her hands to his chest, lifted her chin and kissed him on the edge of his jaw. He hadn't shaved today. He had spent most of the night at the hospital, and then when they had come back, he hadn't seen to any of his own needs. Instead, he had spent all of today dealing with her.

She loved that. Loved the evidence of that. But he had neglected himself for her, she couldn't remember the last time anyone had ever done that.

If anyone ever had.

"Wyatt," she whispered his name, as she kissed him again. Then again. Along that stubble-lined cheek, all the way to his mouth. She clung to him as he held her there in the water, suspended, warmed now by his touch, unconcerned with the temperature of the water.

The way he looked at her, like it was all he wanted to do…it was magic. That kind that had only ever existed with him.

His arms were strong around her. Steady. She slid her hands down his chest, down beneath the surface of the water, across the rippling ab muscles there, all the way down to his arousal, which defied the temperature of the swimming hole.

She didn't linger there though, instead, she traced a path back up, curving one hand around his neck before sliding her fingers through his hair. Then she took both hands, pressed them against his face, touched the lines by his eyes, the grooves by his mouth.

Had they been that deep when they had first met? Had he had that scar above his eyebrow? The one that nicked his chin? She couldn't remember. She wished she could have explored his face then so that she could appreciate the changes.

She wished that she could explore it again in five years and mark the changes that take place between this moment and that.

But she wouldn't think about the futility of that. The ways in which that desire would never come to pass.

It felt like they had time, but she knew that they didn't.

Right now, she was trying not to care. Trying not to let that affect her. Because this was about her. Her heart. Protected and sheltered for all of this time. Like a bird in a cage whose wingspan had been thwarted by being kept in such tight confines. She wanted to stretch them out. She wanted to be set free.

And whatever happened after...

She would simply have to survive it. But, God in heaven, how she wanted to fly first.

If she was going to hit the ground either way, she wanted to soar to blistering heights. There would be no preventing the fall, so why not make it a long, blissful ride. It would leave her changed. Broken, maybe, but she would heal.

She would because she had been created for this. For him. For this moment. And so she had to trust that she would be strong enough to endure whatever it brought.

She learned him with her fingertips, every inch, every line. Every scar. Smooth, beautiful acres of skin, and some covered by rough hair. All of him.

She traced figure eights down his back, down to that glorious ass, and then around the front again, gripping his hard length in her hand, holding all that vitality and just letting herself glory in the beauty of it.

The beauty of him.

He could be everything if she let him. And she had never let anyone be everything. Not even once.

For now, in this moment, she wanted him to be.

He groaned, letting his head fall back as she continued to explore him. And all she could do was stare. At that strong column of his throat, the way his jaw flexed as her fingers continued to explore his body. The way he fought for his control, the way that he wanted, and the way that she brought him to the edge yet again.

"I wanted this," she murmured. "I wanted this for so long. Since the beginning."

He captured her wrist, turned her hand toward him and kissed her palm. "I knew you liked me pulling your pigtails."

"Of course I did," she whispered, looking down. "Because I never actually hated you. I was just scared of what you made me feel."

She had been so lost in exploring his body she hadn't seen the way he was looking at her, his eyes now blazing down into hers. There was fire in them. Heat like she had never seen before. It was so deep and dark and terrifying that she wanted to turn away from it. But she couldn't. She had promised herself she wouldn't.

"I've been so afraid," she said. "Even of myself. Mostly of myself."

And it wasn't that there was nothing to fear. There was. All the flying, the falling, and the pain that would result. Yes, she knew exactly what she had to fear. It wasn't so much about not being afraid. It was deciding that the journey was worth the risk. That finding a way to open herself up, to be loved, to be known, would be far better than being safe.

Damien had been a man who had allowed her to keep her secrets. Who had allowed her to keep her heart protected.

Wyatt was a man she could love.

With all of herself. With every beat of her heart.

Not a gentle, steady rhythm, but an intense drumbeat that she knew would leave her bruised, ragged. But that was what a heart was for. And if she knew what it was beating for, it would be all the better.

It was him.

Tears stung her eyes as the revelation thundered over her like the falls thundered into the water behind them.

She loved him. Not the picture that being with him painted in her mind, not the security he represented—because there was no security at all—not the physical pleasure he gave her. No. She loved him. This wild, untamable man who had rocked what she believed about herself and the world down to its core. This man who she knew beyond a shadow of a doubt could paint her life with deep, bold strokes that would go far beyond what anyone else could do. If only he would open himself up to it.

She had sensed it, that night by the fire. That this man could *love*. That he cared on a level that surpassed anything most people could understand. That he covered it up with that ease of his. She used a tight bun and buttons, and he used a devil-may-care smile. But the result was all the same. It was hiding.

It was just that Wyatt liked to do his hiding in plain sight.

But he had made her free, and she wanted him to join

her. Because she was the one who could love him like he was. Who could love everything in him. No matter what. If he would only be the one who loved everything in her.

She said nothing. Instead, she kissed him. She kissed him until she couldn't breathe. Until they were both gasping for air. She kissed him until she couldn't think straight. Until the world was spinning and the sound of pounding water was the only thing in her ears.

Then, he carried her out of the swimming hole, and he laid her down on a patch of sun-warmed grass a few paces from the water.

"I need you," he said, his voice rough.

And that didn't scare her. She wanted to be needed. By him.

"I need you," she said, and that didn't scare her either.

She had never needed anyone before. She had never let herself.

Pride prevented a hell of a lot of things.

She didn't think anyone had ever needed her before either. But here they were. Gasping for air because of that need.

She felt like something that had been broken inside of her for all this time was fixed. Or maybe it was being held together, by Wyatt Dodge's strong hands. And if he could hold on long enough, then maybe all those pieces would stay together. Would heal on their own. But until then, she needed him to hold on. She had only just started to sift through that wreckage in her soul, had only just found all those little fragments inside of her. She hadn't even known they were there, let alone how badly they needed fixing. But she did now.

"I don't think I have…"

"I'm on the pill," she said, her heart thundering hard. "I trust you."

He nodded slowly, gravely, and she felt something weighty stretch between them. Something real and deep. He cradled her face as he slowly filled her, bare, nothing between them.

Nothing at all.

She squeezed her eyes shut, trying not to cry. Trying not to make this feel bigger than it was.

Then she opened her eyes again, and her gaze collided with his.

It was like deciding to let go of the edge of a cliff. Like deciding to fall. But she did. She stopped holding back. She stopped trying not to feel. As he thrust deep inside of her, she felt it in her heart. Everything, her physical need, her desire, her emotions, rushed to the surface. Her chest felt so full she thought she might burst with it.

This was it. The full burst of that moment she had first laid eyes on Wyatt Dodge. It hadn't been love at first sight. But it had been the promise of love. The taste of it. And now, she was immersed in it, like a baptism. In fire, in heat and desire. An unending, all-consuming love.

This was the moment she had known she would have. The fulfillment of that destiny that had been promised the moment she had walked into that bar. And if anyone had told her that there was such a thing as meant to be, as the one, she would have laughed at them. If years ago she had been told that she was running toward a fated moment, one she couldn't avoid, no matter what, she would've called them a fool.

But this right here, this moment and Wyatt Dodge's arms. This was that moment.

She hadn't missed the train that night in the bar. She

had simply seen the one she was already on. Had caught a glimpse of that destination she was headed for. Nothing she could do about it.

All she needed to do was say yes to it. Open herself up, and embrace it.

She loved Wyatt Dodge. She *loved* him.

A tear slid down her cheek and she pressed one hand between his shoulder blades, clinging tightly to him, the other wrapped around his neck, their fingers laced through his hair. He pounded into her, beating a steady rhythm along with the waterfall, driving them both higher, higher. To the ultimate peak. But she had reached it already. She loved him.

His eyes met hers and another tear fell down her cheek. She loved this man.

His control slipped, his jaw going slack, his thrusts growing erratic. And then he froze above her, groaning out his pleasure as he spilled himself into her. And then she was lost. Pleasure breaking over her like a wave, but more than that, love. That certainty. Feeling every corner of her body. With nothing held back. Nothing reserved. Nothing protected.

She loved him.

And she would never, ever be the same again.

CHAPTER EIGHTEEN

WYATT COULDN'T MOVE. He was frozen above her, his heart pounding hard against his ribs, a dull pain he wished to hell would stop. Except that would mean he'd stopped breathing.

Hell, maybe he had stopped and his heart was trying to get it going again.

Something had happened. Something big. Something transformative. And he had no idea if it had come from the waterfall, from around them, or if it had come from straight inside Lindy.

She had changed. Not into someone different, but it was like she had become the woman he had always sensed was there. Right before his eyes. Bare in the sunlight, her pale skin glorious, her pink-tipped breasts more beautiful out here somehow, bathed in the glow of the sun.

Naked. Unprotected. For him.

And when he had slid inside of her… It wasn't sex. Not like he knew it.

With her, it never had been. Had never been that handshake he had always joked about sex being. No. It had always been more. Deeper. Better.

But this had been something new. His skin felt too sensitive.

He couldn't…breathe. Couldn't think. Couldn't move. Didn't want to.

He wanted to stay inside of her forever. Nothing between them at all.

He'd never, ever been with a woman without a condom before. It had felt… It wasn't so much the difference between latex and skin, not physically. It was the fact that there had been no barriers at all. Nothing between them. He *felt* it.

Not down where their bodies were joined, but in his heart.

And he had no idea what the hell he was supposed to do with that.

"Lindy…"

He had nothing else to say. Just her name. And it echoed inside of him.

It may very well have been echoing in him for the past five years.

She reached up, those blue eyes clear and focused. Not clouded like he imagined his own eyes were. He had no clarity, no focus, nothing but her name.

And a deep, wrenching pain started at the center of his chest and moving outward, spreading like an ugly, dark oil spill he couldn't contain.

He didn't know what was happening to him. To them. Only that it was. And he couldn't stop it.

"Wyatt," she whispered. "I think you could love me."

He stiffened, moving away from her, his heart lurching. "What?"

"I… I think you could love me. And I've never really thought anyone could. But I think you could. All of me. Not the parts I show the world. Or even myself. Stuff that only comes out with you. This… I would have never said this was me. But with you it is. Maybe it always was. But it took you to bring it out. You."

Everything in him recoiled at that. Screamed inside of him for release. For escape. She had no idea what she was talking about. No idea at all.

She didn't know him.

She was talking about him like he was some white knight who had showed her the right path. Instead of just a marauding cowboy who knew how to make her come. He couldn't save anyone. He couldn't love anyone.

"Lindy," he said, his voice steady. "What I can and can't do has nothing to do with you."

She looked at him, her eyes large, luminous. Different. Something had changed in her, it had changed in them, over the past few hours. Or maybe it hadn't. Maybe it was all coming to the surface. Because of her. Because whatever was true about the two of them, something had changed in her. Something big and scary, something he wasn't ready to face. Something he couldn't confront in himself or with her.

She stood, her eyes meeting his, level and cool. "I don't understand what that means."

"I think… I think you've been going through some things. And, I am damned glad that you're… Whatever this is. I am. But it's not me. Whatever you feel like is changing you, whatever you feel like is fixed, honey, it isn't because of me. I don't have anything to do with that."

"Yes," she said. "You do. Wyatt, you have everything to do with it."

"Lindy, I didn't change you."

"Yes. You did."

"If Damien couldn't make you see the worth in yourself in ten years, I don't see how I'm supposed to have been responsible for it after a few orgasms."

The air between them cooled, and he felt like an ass. But not enough of one to stop, not now.

"I didn't love him," she insisted.

He felt like he had been stabbed through the heart. "Yes, you did."

"I did," she said, amending quickly. "You're right. But it wasn't the same. I didn't give him everything. It wasn't... It wasn't being in love. The amount of time doesn't change that. Because it was stagnant. I was stagnant. So was he. He was a convenient shelter, Wyatt. And every traveler loves a shelter when they're trying to escape a storm. But that shelter isn't a choice when you're in a desperate place. I'm not trying to hide anymore. I'm not hiding right now. I don't need a shelter. I need a partner. I made a life secure enough that I didn't need anyone. I'm like my mother in that way. So now it's not about needing someone for survival. It's about wanting somebody. Because you know my heart. I think you might know it better than I do."

"I don't think that can possibly be true," he said, shaking his head. "Lindy, why do you think... Why do you think I can give you something that your husband of ten years couldn't give you?"

"Because you're a better man," she said. "And you make me want to..."

He took a step back, his heart hammering. "I'm not a better man. That's the problem. You think I'm a better man because I haven't made you any promises. And because I haven't made any promises I haven't broken them. Because you spent a few weeks in my company, you think I'm a better man. Because you don't know the things I've done, you think I'm a better man."

"That isn't true. I've seen the way you are. With your family. With this ranch. Your determination to prove to your father that you can do it. You're stubborn, you're like me. I think we recognize that in each other. I think we respect it in each other. It's one reason we partnered up, I think. But all that attitude you carry around, all that acting like you don't care, I know that you do. And I understand that losing your mother was hard for you, I understand why you hold people and things at a distance, but that's not all that you are. It's not all that you're capable of."

Nausea flooded him, and he took a step back. "That's real sweet, honey, that you think you can be my armchair psychiatrist because you know a couple of things about me. You think that's the beginning and end of what I am. Lindy, I don't know how many women I've slept with. I've lost count. I doubt even Damien could say that for himself. I don't… I don't treat it with respect. I haven't. I've been responsible about it. I didn't make vows to any of those women. I didn't have unprotected sex with them. But how is that being a better man? That is doing whatever the hell you want. That's what I've done for the past twenty years of my life. Whatever the hell I want. I'm not the kind of man you should be looking for promises from. I'm not the kind of man you should be hanging these revelations on. You are someone that deserves love. Of course you are. But dammit, don't put that on me. I've never loved anyone more than I love myself."

"That isn't true," she said, insistently, "you do. Every day. You love this ranch more than you love yourself."

"It's penance," he said, the words sliding up his throat

like broken glass, shredding him up on the way out. "Do you know what that is? That's not love. That's just crawling across broken glass until you're cut up enough that maybe you've come close to experiencing the amount of suffering you've caused other people."

"I don't understand," she said, shaking her head slowly.

They were still naked, and he felt like that was fair enough. Because if she wanted to know him, if she wanted to see him, if that was what it was going to take for her to understand, then he would damn well be naked. He would show her. What he was. Really.

"I am as selfish a bastard as I look like I am," he said. "If you count on one thing, you can count on that. When I was eleven years old my mother died, and you know what that worked itself into over the years? Anger. Anger because when I lost my mother I lost my father too. Because he poured all of his emotions into everyone else. Everyone and everything. My baby sister. My younger brothers. But I had to be a man. I had to be strong. But I was still... I still had to be home when he said. I still had to do what he said. But he didn't give me a damn thing. Nothing but work, responsibilities, because he thought that would keep my head on straight. I rebelled against that. And then..."

Wyatt shook his head. "Then he started dating again. When I was seventeen he brought a woman home. Louisa. Said they were going to get married. And he was going to give us a mother. Give Jamie a mother." He swallowed hard, battling against his anger now. Because he had never told this story before. Not to anyone. Not even in his own mind. He'd never laid out all the events from start to finish like this. He was angry. And he didn't realize how much. At his father. At himself. At her.

At every damn person who had been involved.

"I can see how that would have been hard…"

He laughed. There was nothing else to do but laugh. She couldn't even imagine. Because it would never occur to her.

"Yeah. It was. But you know, she was really nice. She paid attention to me. She said that I was special. Strong. And yeah, I was. I was strong. I'd been carrying the weight of everything for a long time. And no one had noticed. But Louisa noticed. I was lonely. I had been doing so much to hold things together. She didn't just *tell* me that I needed to be a man. She treated me like one. She said I'd been doing the work of one all that time. And then she started telling me about her life. The abusive husband she was with before she was with my dad. How she needed someone to make her feel safe." Wyatt firmed up his jaw, stood straight and met Lindy's eyes. "She said I made her feel safe. And she made me feel like I was the most important person in the world."

He started collecting his clothes, because it turned out he couldn't tell the story naked. He threw her clothes toward her because…he couldn't look at her.

And he couldn't have her looking at his body while he talked about what happened next. Because it made it all feel sordid. As if he could look and see Louisa's handprints on him. He felt sick with the shame of it. And he hated that too. He hated everything about it.

"I lost my virginity to her," he continued.

Lindy looked like she'd been hit in the face with a two-by-four. One that Wyatt had been wielding. And that made him feel even worse. He tugged his shirt on, covering himself completely. "I was in love with her. Plain and simple. At least, that was what I thought at the time. She wanted me. She needed me. She said I was the only person who made her feel safe. Who really listened to her. My dad was distracted by his other responsibilities. His kids. But not me. I was a real man. I died... I ate that up, Lindy. My ego... I felt like a king. My dad didn't pay any attention to me. And then he brought home this woman and she treated me like I was the most important thing in her world. She was broken and weak and she needed me. She let me be there for her. She let me play at being a man. She made me one."

"Wyatt, you were seventeen."

"Yes. And there's laws that make that illegal, I know that. But that's all BS anyway. People used to get married younger than that. They were sure as hell having sex and babies by then. That's all just numbers. It doesn't mean that it was actually abuse."

"It's not your age that makes it abuse, Wyatt. Your dad trusted her with you. She was in a position of authority, because you were seventeen years old and you would have seen a woman her age as being in authority. She played on your weaknesses. On the things she saw in you that she knew she could manipulate. That's what makes it abuse."

"I was a seventeen-year-old boy desperate to get laid. That's not abuse."

"It doesn't sound like you were desperate for sex. It sounds like you were desperate for someone to show you that they cared."

Those words hurt more than any condemnation could have.

"It doesn't matter now. It was wrong. And I jumped in with both feet. That's what matters. That's who I am."

"Is that why you left?" Lindy asked. "Is that why you

had to leave your home and join the rodeo? Because of her? Because I would argue that that proves that it wasn't okay."

"I'm not telling you this story to make you feel sorry for me. It was a situation. I handled it."

"Did you? You left. And then you… You sent money back home. That's why you gave your dad money. Because you were trying to fix it."

"The ranch needed it. If I could help, I was going to help. Though, I'm not going to pretend that I wasn't trying to make up for what I did. My dad had one chance at being happy, all these years of grief, and I was so lost in my own that I couldn't… I didn't care about anyone but myself." He shook his head. "That's who I am. Deep down. If I want something… I can move everything else out of the way to justify having it. You tell me how that's different than Damien."

She looked up at him, her chin jutting out, her eyes flickering like a blue flame. "I'll tell you how it's different. Damien had a wife. He had parents who loved him. He did what he wanted to do and he found a million ways to justify that. So that he could please himself. You were a boy. You were lonely, and your father hurt you. And maybe you did give in partly because it would hurt him. But you were *drowning*, Wyatt. I can hear it in the way that you talk about it. You were drowning and she was there."

He hated that. Hated that she saw him as a victim. Because that was too kind. He'd made his choice. And if she knew why he'd done it…well she wouldn't have any sympathy for him at all.

He didn't deserve it. He didn't want it. He'd wanted what had happened between Louisa and himself. She made him feel strong. She was there for him in a way his father hadn't been.

And best of all…

Best of all…he'd taken her away from his father. Had taken away what he'd used to distract himself. The person he'd clung to instead of Wyatt.

He felt guilty about it. About what it said about him. And sometimes…

Justified. Justified as hell.

"Maybe he felt like he was drowning. And she was there," Wyatt said, meaning Damien and Sarabeth, and he knew that Lindy realized that.

"No," Lindy said simply.

"I'm just saying, if I can justify this… What else can I justify? I'm not a better man. I'm just another man who gets led around by his private parts."

"So you think that you would cheat on me? Is that what you're saying?"

He shook his head. "No. I don't think that. But I… I wouldn't make that promise to you. I wouldn't. There's a reason we have a time limit, Lindy, and it's because I know myself. In that, maybe I am a better man, but that's as far as it goes. I have this ranch to run. I have to meet my father's obligations. I have to prove that I can do this. I can't take on anything else."

"Maybe you could if you would let someone in."

"I don't know what that means."

"It's the same as me. You were hurting, and you've never told anyone, have you? You've never told your dad how he hurt you." She paused for a moment. "Did your father ask you to leave, or did you leave on your own?"

"I left on my own," he said. "I needed to go figure myself out."

"Right. Without letting anyone in."

He shrugged. "I wasn't exactly going to sit around and talk to my dad about all the sex I had with his fiancée."

"That's not what you would have talked about, and you know it. Did you ever talk to one of your brothers?"

"No. Bennett knows now. But… He only just found out." Wyatt shook his head. "And it wasn't my intention for him to know."

"Wyatt, you hold everyone at a distance. Because you don't… I don't know what. You don't want to admit that you're not bulletproof? Is that it?"

He grabbed hold of her hand and held it steady, let it hover right above his chest. "You're the one that said I was bulletproof, Lindy. You saw it. Maybe in the same way that I saw you. You should trust that."

She shook her head. "No. I think you've done your best to make the world think you're bulletproof. To make yourself think you're bulletproof. But underneath that… Honey, I think you're a mess."

Honey was what he called her. He'd called her that dozens of times. But he didn't mean it. He was being flippant. Her words felt serious. Real. He didn't want serious and real. Because it made him feel other things, made him want other things. And he couldn't… He couldn't.

"Lindy," he said. "We have until the barbecue. Let's not do this."

"Wyatt," she said, looking at him square on, and he knew, better than he knew anything else in the entire world, that she was about to ask him a question he didn't want to answer. "What happened when your mother died? You were eleven. I know you have to remember. Remember how things changed."

His back went stiff, his entire body freezing up. Memories crowded in like a cloud, things he didn't think about ever. There was no point, because there was no fixing it. No bringing her back. No restoring their family to what it had been.

"I don't remember," he said.

"Yes, you do," she said softly.

"I don't remember," he said, the words ground out. "Why don't we talk more about the day your mother called you a whore? Or the day you found your husband kissing some other woman? How about that?"

"Okay," she shot back. "I remember those things. Do you want to hear about it? I walked into the wine cellar, at the winery that I had worked so damned hard on, that I had been spending all of my time on, and found my husband with his tongue down another woman's throat. Backed up against the wall. And you know what? I'm a coward. Because I never asked him how many other women. I let myself think it was just her, but I'm sure there were more. It wasn't the one he got caught with… That wasn't the first one. That was when he got careless. And I didn't see what I didn't want to see. I didn't want my shelter to be taken away from me. But once I saw, I had to deal with it. Except… I didn't. Not until today. I didn't deal with all of the reasons that I protect myself. It's going to take years to sort it all out. But that's okay. It's not the end of the world if it takes time. I found a reason to do that work. It's you."

He shook his head. "Don't you dare make me the reason. *You* be the reason, Lindy. You. Be enough all on your own. Don't you put this on me. I can't have it. I have enough, dammit. I don't need you to…to make you my responsibility. Because that is just like Louisa."

"Don't," she said. "Don't do that to me. It's not the

same. And you know it. Don't use it now that you've told me just to hurt me. That's not fair."

"I can't," he said. There was nothing else that he could even say. Because there was a rising tide inside of him that he couldn't stop. That he couldn't roll back. Memories. The ones he didn't let himself have.

The one that made him who he was.

"We need to go. Your brother is literally laying in a hospital bed unconscious. I think we should deal with all of that before we deal with this."

"Not me," Lindy said. "I want to deal with you. Because you matter that much. Don't make this all about me. This is about you too."

He took in a breath, but it was sharp, and it cut him, all the way down, the jagged edges of the air painful in his lungs. Maybe it wasn't the air. Maybe it was her. Breathing her in like this. Looking at her. And the way she looked at him. Like he damn well might be something, when he knew that he wasn't.

He couldn't ask for love. For help. Not again. Not ever.

"I'll walk you back," he said.

"Don't bother," she said. "Not unless you want to talk the whole way. And when I say talk, I mean really talk. Not about the weather or how much you like my ass. You have to talk to me."

"I don't want to fucking talk," he said. "I made that clear."

"I don't care what you want. You getting your way, me getting mine, that's how we've stayed this messed up for this long. Have you ever thought of that?"

He reached out, and he grabbed her arms, drawing her forward. "Maybe I like it like this. Maybe it's the way I keep going."

She looked at him. "But what's the point? What's the point of walking forward when you're headed toward nothing?"

"I have my ranch."

"And I have my winery. I pour a hell of a lot into it, but it doesn't pour anything into me. I'm standing here, and I'm telling you that I would give you everything. Everything I am. Everything I have. All the parts of myself that I kept protected for all that time. When I got naked for you that first day in the living room… It was more than just my body. And today it really was everything. My heart. My soul. That's all. I'll give it to you, everything I am. Wyatt, please."

And he was frozen. Couldn't move. Couldn't breathe. Because he was lost. In another time. More than twenty years ago.

Dad, please.

Into that moment that he did his best to never remember. When he'd been down in the dirt, crying. When he felt like he couldn't stand up, never would again.

Every time he hit the dirt in the arena and he stood back up he defied that moment. That boy. That weakness.

All that anger.

He'd spent years defying that moment. And now he felt like that little boy all over again. Crying like he'd lost his mother. Because he had.

With no one there to give him a hand. To help him back up.

So he'd learned to pick himself up. And he'd done it ever since.

You have to be a man now, Wyatt. No more crying. You have to be a man.

"I'll drive you back to Dane if you need me to," he said, letting go of her and taking a step back.

"I don't," she said, dressing slowly now. Finally.

"Lindy…"

"Don't." She held up a hand. "But I want you to realize something, Wyatt Dodge. You're alone because you choose to be. You're alone because you won't reach a hand out."

She finished dressing and she turned and began to walk away from him, heading up the path.

Showed what she knew. He'd done it. He'd reached out. And he'd learned he had to stand on his own.

He wasn't going to go back now.

CHAPTER NINETEEN

SHE HAD BEEN DIVORCED. She had gone through the dissolution of a ten-year marriage. She was literally sitting in a hospital waiting room, where her brother was in a coma in the next room. And she was…disintegrating inside. Over Wyatt Dodge.

He didn't love her. He didn't want to love her. And she just now thought that maybe he should. And she didn't have any time to marinate on that desire. Because the dream was already over. She felt like a tragic song from the nineties.

She was supposed to somehow still do this barbecue thing. She wondered if she could get Sabrina or Bea, or even Olivia to act as her envoy.

They were supposed to be able to deal, like grown-ups. That had been the agreement. She was the one who had broken it, and she knew that. But she couldn't help it. She had changed, and it was his fault. And because she had changed she wanted to fight for what she felt like they both deserved.

But apparently, Wyatt was going to keep pretending that everything was just what they had agreed on in the beginning. Easy. Physical. Sex.

It wasn't that. It wasn't, and it never had been. She knew that. She felt it. Believed that in her soul.

And she should probably think about Dane, who was

still in a precarious state right now. And not think about her broken heart.

"Are you okay?" Sabrina asked quietly.

"No," Lindy said, honestly.

"You didn't miss anything while you were gone. I mean, there wasn't any change. Damien left a couple of hours ago. But he did stay for a long time."

"I'm surprised," Lindy said.

"I am too. But I'm glad."

"Is Bea sitting in his room?"

"I think she is," Sabrina said. "She came out for a while but she… Mostly she's been with him."

Lindy's heart hurt. For herself. But for Bea too. Because in so many ways the situation with Dane was impossible. But she knew that Bea felt it all keenly. It didn't make it less real.

"I'm sorry that your mother didn't want to come," Sabrina said. "I know that… I know that that's a really hard relationship."

"I seem to be replete with hard relationships," Lindy said. "It's my lot in life. But then, I guess I'm kind of a hard person."

"No you're not," Sabrina said, standing up from the pink seat she was sitting in and moving to the light blue one next to Lindy. "You're a wonderful person. And more of a sister to me than Damien has ever been a brother. Our family is difficult. You know that. My dad disowned me for the better part of a decade. Wouldn't speak to me over Christmas dinner. We might be fixing things now, and it might be better, but it's still…weird. You've always just loved me. No strings attached. You have no idea how much of a revelation that was, Lindy."

"I might," Lindy said. "Because it's probably pretty close to knowing what you and Bea have done for me."

"Is something else wrong?" Sabrina asked, a little bit too insightful for Lindy's liking.

"Wyatt," she said.

"Oh no," Sabrina groaned. "God spare us all from pigheaded cowboys."

"Yeah, I know you went a few rounds with one yourself."

"True. But I ended up engaged to mine. And that made all of the stuff we went through worth it."

Lindy laughed softly. It was either that or cry. "I don't think that's going to happen for Wyatt and me."

"I didn't think you wanted it to," Sabrina pointed out. "I thought that you were strictly anti-relationships. Sisters doing it for themselves and all of that."

"I was. Until I fell in love with him. The idiot."

"He made you fall in love with him?"

"Yes. With his incredible bedroom skills and his fantastic personality, and his ability to help me see the value in myself."

"That bastard," Sabrina said.

"I know, right?" Lindy huffed out a laugh. "I don't know. I just wish that… I don't want him to be different. I love him like he is. But I wish that he could let me. I wish that whatever it is that causes him so much pain… I wish he could let it go. I don't want him to be different. I just want him to love me."

"I…might understand that a little bit. Liam had…a hard childhood. And it was difficult for him to let go of that. It was difficult for him to let someone in. And we didn't come together easily. But we did. I think as long as you don't give up completely, as long as you don't shove him out of your heart altogether… There's always hope."

"But what if…what if it doesn't work? It worked for you and Liam eventually but that's not how it is for most people. And it scares me. Because I'm trying this thing where I…where I let people in. I don't know if you know this about me, Sabrina, but it's hard for me. To connect with people."

"Lindy, I don't know what you think about yourself, but you're not cold. And you certainly don't push people away. It takes a little bit of work to get to know you, but you're worth it. And I've always thought you were. I don't know absolutely everything about you, but I know what kind of person you are. I know that you're a good friend. A good sister. And you were definitely a better wife than my brother deserved. Don't second-guess that now. We all have things that we can work on, but that doesn't mean that you've given nothing or done nothing in the lives of the people you love for the past ten years. You have. You were there for me when I was going through stuff with Liam. You're the one who bailed me out after he took my virginity and left me without a car. You were there for Olivia when everything was going down with Luke. You've never made Bea feel silly for harboring this intense crush on Dane for all these years. You… You took care of us. You cared for us. Maybe it's hard for you to sit down and talk, to share, but it's not hard for you to love. And you've done that. Truly, deeply. For as long as I've known you. When no one else was there for me, you were. I love you for that. Forever."

Lindy's heart felt like it was expanding. "Thank you. You have no idea how much that means to me."

Bea appeared in the waiting room, looking between Sabrina and Lindy. "Did you get bad news?"

"No," Lindy said, shaking her head.

"You both look sad."

"We're contemplative," Sabrina responded.

"Okay," Bea said. "They said the swelling in his brain went down enough that they didn't need to keep him under anymore. He's been off the ventilator for about an hour."

"Oh," Lindy said, scrambling to her feet.

"I thought you might want to sit with him, instead of me. He would rather see you when he wakes up."

Bea in her practicality, even through that fierce love that she felt for Dane, touched Lindy's heart, and it made it feel like it might break a little bit more.

"Okay," Lindy said. "I'll go."

She rubbed her hands on her legs, trying to infuse her limbs with some feeling, trying to drag the horrific pain away from her heart, and then walked back slowly, taking her position by Dane's bed.

The nurses explained the process to Lindy, how they had eased him off the barbiturate drip a few hours earlier, that he'd been breathing on his own since the effects had begun to wear off. She nodded, like she understood, but she wasn't sure that she did. It didn't matter. Either way, they were going to do what they had to. And she just had to trust that. As difficult as it was.

"Oh, Dane," she said, reaching out and touching his hand. It was the first time she had touched him since she'd seen him in that hospital bed. The first time she'd touched him in a while.

"We're such a mess. The two of us. Except, I think I

might be a little more broken than you are right about now."

She inhaled sharply, the scent of hospital antiseptic and stale air filling her lungs.

"I love you," she said, sliding her thumb over his hand. "And I think you know that. At least, I hope you do. You are amazing. What you did with your life. On your own terms. I'm so proud of you. I also think you're an idiot and I'm going to punch you in the face when you wake up. But I also think you're incredible. And I just hope that… I hope you realize that. And it better not be too late for me to tell you. You better wake up, and you better know who I am. If this is a *50 First Dates* situation I'm not going to be walking you through your life every morning. Because I love you, but I'm also very busy. I don't have time to walk you through the steps of daily life every darn day."

There was a rusty chuckle, followed by a groan, and Dane moved beneath her touch.

"Dane," she said, leaning forward and touching his face. "Can you hear me? Do you know who I am?"

"Shit," he croaked. "Where the hell… *Lindy*?"

"You do know who I am," she said.

"What are you doing here?" he asked, his words slurred.

"You're in the hospital. Where else would I be?"

He made a noise that sounded like a question. She couldn't be sure.

"You had an accident." She hit the button to call the nurse, because she was sure that Dane being conscious, at least, mostly, was something they needed to attend to.

"Shit," he said again. Apparently the part of his brain

that controlled his cowboy vocabulary was intact. "Did...
someone else win then?"

"*You* sure as hell didn't win," she said, incredulous
that *that* was his concern. "You got trampled."

"I do feel like I got trampled," he said, groaning again.
"I wanted to win Pendleton."

"You weren't in Pendleton," she pointed out.

"I wasn't?"

"No," she said. "You were in Sisters."

"No," he said. "Sisters is in June."

"It's June," she said.

"Huh?"

Worry sliced through her, because she wasn't sure
what year he was even remembering. Or if he was just
jumbled up in general.

But, they would have time to sort all that out later,
and whatever he did or didn't remember they would sort
out too.

The door to the hospital room opened, but it wasn't a
nurse who walked in. It was their mother.

"I figured out how to get here," she said.

"Mom," Dane said, his voice croaky.

"You really got yourself in a tangle," she said, looking at him, holding herself stiff, her pale blue eyes filling slightly.

Lindy was not used to her mother showing emotion.
And just that little bit of it about undid her. "Your sister
was right," she said. "You do look bad."

"Thanks," Dane returned.

"Thank you for coming," Lindy said.

"He told me to call him if I needed a ride."

"He?" Lindy asked.

"Your man," she said.

Lindy's heart slammed against her breastbone. "Wyatt brought you?"

"He left already."

"How did he get you to…come?"

Her mom frowned. "He told me it was selfish not to. I never thought of pride that way."

Lindy looked down at her hands. "I don't know what hurt you, Mom. Not the first time. But I am sorry. I'm sorry that I was part of it. That I had too much pride to come back and talk to you after we fought. That I wanted to protect myself more than I wanted to fix us."

"No, Melinda. I'm your mother. I was supposed to be the adult. And I never could be. I just wanted to be safe. Loving people doesn't let you be safe. Just wait until you have kids. You'll see how dangerous that feels." She looked over at Dane. "They grow up and leave you. And then this happens."

"I'm okay," Dane mumbled, but then his eyes drifted closed. The monitors showed his heart beating strong still, and that at least was a comfort, in spite of how rough he looked.

"I want you to be happy," her mom said. "I really do. I'm sorry that my own issues kept you from that."

I'm sorry wasn't going to erase so many years of pain. So many years of hardship. But, it was a start to fixing what was between them. It was a start to moving on. After all of this, all Lindy wanted was to move on.

"We can start over, Mom. And whatever you need… I'm going to try to give it to you. And try not to give you more than you want. But if I offer you something…try not to be offended."

"I'll try," she said.

But Lindy knew that she had already changed. And

she also knew that she had to figure out what that meant for the future. What that meant for Wyatt. What that meant for herself.

Wyatt had brought her mother here. Whatever he said…it didn't matter. What he did told her just what kind of man he was. She had no idea what to do about it.

She supposed she had until the barbecue to figure that out. And now that she knew Dane was going to be okay, at least she could focus on that.

More time to reflect on her broken heart. Lucky her.

CHAPTER TWENTY

WYATT HATED EVERYTHING.

Everything.

His ranch. The sun, which shone in spite of the fact that everything was terrible, the dumb-ass cows that had broken his fence earlier today.

He hated himself most of all. He was an idiot. And he was an asshole. And he had to get this place in perfect condition by the time the big barbecue happened, or they were probably going to end up looking like a two-bit, rinky-dink operation that wasn't worth sending customers to. That wasn't worth booking. And then he was going to have failed absolutely everyone. From Lindy on down to Jamie.

His dad would win, and Wyatt would lose.

And Wyatt did not fucking lose.

Except he already felt like he had.

And for the life of him, he couldn't figure out why.

He couldn't have the kind of relationship she wanted. He didn't want a relationship like that. He didn't. So he didn't know why it tore him up now that he had told her so. She was the one that had gone back on their agreement. She was the one that had changed things. He hadn't changed anything. He was exactly what he had said he was. A man who wanted a sex-only relationship.

She was the one that had gone and made it about feelings. She was the one that had gone and made it...

"Dammit," he swore, as he brought his hammer down on his thumb. "Damn cows," he shouted. "I'm going to make you into steak. No. Steak is too good for you. I'm going to grind you up and make you into burgers. I will enjoy every bite of your damned hide."

"Do you feel better?" Wyatt turned and saw his father standing there—of all people—hands in his pockets, his cowboy hat pulled down low over his face.

"Don't push me right now," Wyatt said, shaking his hammer at his father. "I hit my damn thumb."

"Which would drive even the most sane of men to cussing at bovines. I suppose."

"Whether or not I'm sane is currently up for debate," Wyatt growled, turning back to the fence. "Unless you wanted something specific, I'm busy."

"What crawled up your ass and died?" That was his dad, exhibiting the Dodge charm. And butting in when he wasn't wanted. Rather than being around when he was needed.

He tightened his grip on the hammer, anger and pain swamping him. "What the hell are you doing here, Dad?"

"I'm here for the barbecue," Quinn said.

"The barbecue is in four days." Wyatt slammed his hammer down on the fencepost, doing nothing in particular but hitting the thing. "You have no call to be here now. You checking up on me?"

"Do I need to be?" he asked.

"Does it matter?" Wyatt shot back.

"You're spoiling for a fight, boy, and I'm not about to give it to you."

"Oh, bull, Dad. You've never paid enough attention to me to give me a fight. Why would you start now?"

Silence fell between them, hard and heavy. And Wyatt was just...sick of this. Of all the things that were left unsaid between them. Of all the things that had gone unshouted for the past twenty years.

Lindy had asked him about the day his mother had died, and he had shoved that aside. He didn't like to think about it, and he and his dad had sure as hell never talked about it. But maybe that was part of the problem. They didn't talk about a damn thing. His dad acted like he wasn't there half the time.

"Why the hell are you doing this to me?" Wyatt asked. "Why don't you just punch me out? Why don't you just yell at me? Tell me what you really think of me. None of this passive-aggressive bull. Putting these impossible standards out in front of me so you can watch me fail. You know you're setting Grant and Jamie and Bennett up too. And I thought for sure that you cared a little bit about them."

"What the hell is the matter with you, boy?" his dad asked.

"The same thing that's been the matter with me from the beginning. You don't care. Not about me."

"I only spent all those years raising you for the hell of it? What do you mean I don't care about you?"

"Did you raise me? You let me work your ranch, you walked by me, you ignored me. From the day Mom died. When you let me cry in the dirt by myself. You walked right by me."

"Wyatt..."

"No," Wyatt said. "You came out here to talk, I assume. So let's talk. Let's really talk. I've been spoiling for this fight for the better part of my life. Let's have it. And if you take the ranch away after... I don't care. But I'm not going to do this anymore. I can't do it anymore. I needed you, and you weren't there for me. I want to know what the hell is wrong with me."

"Nothing," his dad said, his voice rough. "Nothing is wrong with you."

"You sure as hell could've fooled me. I tried to get your attention. I tried. I did everything you asked me to do. Be a man, that's what you told me. Be a man for Jamie, for Bennett and Grant. You asked me to do that when I was eleven years old. But who was a man for me, Dad?"

Quinn looked like Wyatt had hauled off and decked him. But Wyatt wasn't in the mood to pull punches, verbal or otherwise. "You didn't...didn't give me a damn thing. After she died it was like you were just looking through me. I needed you. I needed you to tell me it was all right. Dad, I saw her after she died. And you never talked to me about it. You could barely look at me after. We were close and then I lost her, and I damn well lost you too.

"And then you brought her home. Louisa. At least she saw me." Louisa with her dark hair and eyes, who had touched him. Just casually at first. His shoulder. His hand.

He hadn't been touched in years at that point. He was just doing his best to please a father who looked through him, working the ranch, taking care of his siblings.

He'd felt guilty when he'd started feeling something other than comfort from that touch. She had been so pretty. In her late thirties, but there was a vulnerability to her that called to something starving in him. He had needed attention from her, but there had been something intoxicating in her needing him too.

She'd come to him vulnerable, and had made him feel like he could be the protector. Like he could find some new strength in himself.

And for the first time since his dad had told him he had to be a man, he'd felt like a man.

He'd been torn, with the desire to please his dad, to get back what he'd lost…and his desire for her. In the end, his desire for Louisa had won out. She'd come to his room one night, and said she needed him.

He hadn't had it in him to turn her away. He'd needed her too. It had been more than sex, though at seventeen, sex had mattered on its own. But it had been deeper.

The only time he'd ever let it be deeper.

He'd been consumed with her. With someone caring so much, needing him so much.

And then it had all gotten blown to hell. They'd gotten caught by his father and Louisa had left. Quinn had taken the most important thing Wyatt had. The relationship Wyatt wouldn't have needed if his dad had been there in the first place.

One that would never have started if Quinn had been paying attention to his oldest son at all.

"Do you know what?" Wyatt asked. "I loved her. I loved her more than I loved you. You brought her home, giving her all that attention, and love and care that you never gave me. Using her to heal your grief. What about mine? You told me to be a man. Dust myself off. Pick myself up. But I didn't feel like one. Until her. She treated me like a man. And I loved her. I loved her. It killed me, you know. To betray you like that. But I felt good for the first time in so damn long and I just couldn't…" He swallowed hard. "And then it was only worse after. You found out. Sent her away. It destroyed the one good thing I had, and you got worse after. You couldn't even make eye contact with me."

"Whatever you think, I'm not punishing you for it, Wyatt. I'm not. And I never have been. You were seventeen. You didn't know what you were doing. You were a boy."

"A boy you told to be a man. Don't you dare absolve me like I didn't know what I was doing. Don't treat me like a boy now when you wouldn't let me be one then. I can't be both, Dad. I can't be a grown man expected to carry on with his head held high, not feeling anything, not talking about anything, and also be a boy who can't be held responsible for what he did."

"Wyatt…"

"No," Wyatt said. "If I was a boy, if I was innocent, then you should've been treating me like your son and not your ranch hand. And if I was a man you should've punched me out. But you didn't do either. You just shut me out even more." Wyatt tightened his jaw, tilting his chin up. "You couldn't shut out the money I sent though, could you? You took that. You spent it. You had to acknowledge me then."

"You think you were invisible?" Quinn Dodge closed the gap between them, and he shocked Wyatt by grabbing hold of the collar of his shirt and dragging him forward, surprising Wyatt with the strength that he had left in his body. "You think I didn't care? I didn't know what the hell to do with you." He released his hold on Wyatt, and Wyatt stumbled back. "I know I didn't deal well with losing your mother. And then I tried… I tried to fix things by bringing Louisa around. But she didn't help you. I let you get hurt. I didn't know what to say to you. I didn't know how to talk to you about what had happened. I wasn't angry. Not at you. I was so damn angry at myself, Wyatt. Because I could see that what I'd done…it hurt you, the way I handled you, the way I didn't handle you…"

"Why couldn't you handle me? You can handle everyone else?"

"Because you were the one who saw it," Quinn said. "And I didn't… Wyatt, you have to understand… I'm no good with feelings."

"No kidding," Wyatt said.

He threw his hammer down on the ground, the clawback sticking into the dirt. "I lost both of you," Wyatt said. "I lost both of you when Mom died. And I wanted… I needed something."

"She took advantage of that…"

"I loved her," Wyatt said. "She was the first thing I loved for a long time. And then I lost her too. And you didn't…step in. You didn't try to fix what was broken. You weren't paying attention to what had been going on under your nose for months, and then when you did find out you didn't check to see if I was okay. You didn't check to see if I was broken. And so I learned. I learned not to need again. When Mom died, I lost the two people I needed most. Then I let myself need, just one more time. Just one more. Not again. Never again."

"I'm trying. I've tried in the past few years, Wyatt, I have. I've had more than twenty years to figure this out. But it was only just… When I called you and said I was going to sell if you didn't want it… All of that was when I started realizing some things. I have Freda to thank for that. She cleared some stuff up inside me that had been jumbled for a long time. You saw me break. You saw that moment… I didn't know how to face you after that. When every time I looked at you all I could see was you coming to tell me that your mother wouldn't wake up. When I knew that you had seen me on the floor like that, completely undone. It wasn't your fault. It was mine. We were like survivors of the war. And every time I looked at you I flashed back to it. Not just to what happened to her… But to what I failed to do for you. And so I tried to give you freedom. I tried to give you work to do. Anything that was going to let me off the hook. It was never you."

"And you're still playing these games with the ranch…"

"What I said to you is true. I don't want you trapped here. I don't want you in over your head like I was for so long. I spent so many years barely keeping my head above water. Drowning in grief, drowning in debt. Don't you think it pains me that you… The son that I felt most… That you are the one that bailed me out? I didn't deserve that. Not from you. And I wanted to be able to keep an eye on things here and bail you out if it was going wrong."

"You can't have it both ways, Dad. Pick one. Am I a boy or a man?"

Quinn stepped forward. "You're my boy," he said. "And whether or not you're a man now, it doesn't matter. You're still my boy. And I'm going to protect you. I should never have put all that on you back then, but I was trying to…to find a way to make it hurt less for both of us."

"It's too late for that."

"Why?" Quinn asked.

"Because I'm screwed," Wyatt said. "I wanted to love you. I tried. You didn't give it to me. So I found someone else to love. And then you killed that too. And now I… I got a woman I think I could love. But I don't know what to do. I don't know how to go forward. You've already messed me up. You don't get to come in and apologize for it now. Everything I can't have is because of you. Mom died, and she couldn't help it. You… You just pulled away."

"Listen to me," Quinn said, his voice low. "I loved your mother. I loved her more than anything. I never wanted to love another person in the whole world. She was my compass. She guided me. And when I lost her… I lost my way. I'm sorry. I'm sorry that I hurt you, Wyatt. It was my fault," Quinn said. "I messed up. I wasn't a good father to you. I didn't know how to be. I was too lost in my own pain. I couldn't see yours. And that is a terrible thing to do when you're a parent. There. Does that help you?"

No. It didn't. It damn well didn't. He had shouted it all now. His triumph over having stolen her from him. Over having hurt him when he had caused Wyatt so much pain. And his father had admitted his mistakes.

But the ache in his chest wasn't gone. Knowing he was right, that he had a right to be angry… It didn't fix anything.

"I want the ranch," Wyatt said.

"Will that fix it?"

"Yes," Wyatt said, his voice gruff.

"Then you can have it."

It didn't feel like a win. Not at all.

"I'm still pissed off at you," Wyatt said.

"What do you want me to do? You want me to crawl

over broken glass? You want to punch me. Because you can punch me."

He took a good look at his father, who looked the same as he always had. But old. Wyatt's height, his dark brown hair faded into a gray.

Somehow, over the passage of time, his father had aged. Wyatt supposed that was how things went, when the world turned on as it should. And that man that he had been so angry with as an eleven-year-old boy. And then as a seventeen-year-old... He was gone. And in his place was this old man in front of him. Not an old man, not really. But not the same one. And Wyatt couldn't go back and yell at the father he'd been. Sure, he could punch the father he was now. His dad had offered it up. But it wouldn't take them back. None of this would restore time that was already gone. None of it was going to fix the thing that hurt now.

And then there was Lindy.

He could have Lindy now. If he just... If he just found a way to let go.

"I've spent my whole life trying not to care. Because it hurt too much to want something from you I didn't get. I didn't want to need someone, not again."

"I'm sorry," Quinn said. "I know it's too little too late. But that doesn't mean I'm not sorry all the same. I've always loved you, though. I was just too mired in my own pain to figure out how to show it."

It was on the tip of Wyatt's tongue to shout again. To be angry again. But then he thought of Lindy. Of the way she looked at him. The way she'd asked for him to love her.

He already did. That was the thing.

Perhaps he had from the moment she had walked into

that bar. Like a moment of faith. One he wouldn't ever fully understand. Like he had seen her and known something, deep in his bones. Like he had looked into a crystal ball. And still, when she had spoken those words… He hadn't been able to tell her what she wanted him to.

He hadn't been able to tell her what he wanted to.

"I think I understand that," Wyatt said, surprising both of them with those words. "I… I spent so long feeling like I couldn't have love. That on some level I must not deserve it. And I thought I at least gave you a reason to hate me when I took up with her. That was what I wanted. To make it something other than a flaw within me that made you hate me…"

"I never hated you. I hated myself. I couldn't reach out to you because of it."

"That has to stop," Wyatt said.

He didn't know much, but he knew that.

"I agree," Quinn said, his voice gruff. "Freda has helped me a lot. Loving someone has helped me a lot."

There were other things that needed saying. More that needed to be talked about. But right now Wyatt needed to know one thing. The most important thing. "How did you let yourself love her? After everything. After the way you shut yourself down, how did you open yourself back up?"

Quinn shook his head. "You don't choose to get hit by lightning."

Wyatt thought it was the damnedest description, because he knew exactly what his father meant. Because he'd been hit by that same lightning five years ago.

"I don't suppose. But, you still have a choice of what you do after. How did you choose her instead of being alone?"

"I failed at a lot of things with you, Wyatt. I'm going to do my best not to fail you here. If you have someone who loves you, don't turn them away. Because it doesn't matter whether you might get hurt in the end. Fear is the enemy. That's what destroys things, don't you see? I didn't think I could love you right, so I just didn't try at all. I tried to protect myself, and look what happened. Love only adds to you. It doesn't take away. You gotta trust it. You gotta believe it. If you found a woman who loves you… It's the best gift. The best in the world. It's not about deserving a damn thing. If you've got it, hold on tight with both your hands."

It occurred to him right then, that the real problem was his arms were too full of a whole bunch of stuff that couldn't be fixed. Not now. So he just had to set it all down. He had to be willing to do that, so he could step into something new. So he could have something better. He tried yelling. He tried anger. It hadn't given him anything. A small amount of satisfaction, maybe. But only for a moment. He couldn't go back. He could only go forward.

He was just going to have to decide to do it. Because his mom was gone. And so were all those years he spent being mad at his father. But right now, his father was here. And Lindy… Lindy might still want him too. And hell, if she could open herself up to him after all she'd been through…if she could be so brave, how could he not do the same.

"I love you, Dad," Wyatt said, the words slow and deliberate. "I always have. Even when things got twisted up in me, and I betrayed you like I did…"

"Don't you apologize to me," Quinn said, his voice rough. He reached out and grabbed hold of Wyatt, draw-

ing him in for a hug. The first hug they'd shared since
Wyatt was eleven years old. "I'm sorry. I'm sorry I wasn't
a good father to you. I'm sorry I didn't love you like I
should have. Didn't protect you like I should have. And
that I tried to meddle when I had no call to. I'm sorry
I tried to protect you when it was a day late and a dol-
lar short. I want to do better and be different. I'm real
sorry I messed up." He clapped Wyatt on the back and
pulled away.

"The ranch is yours if you want," his dad said. "If
that's what you want to pour yourself into, then you deserve the chance to do it. I'm not going to stand in your
way. Not anymore. I trust you," Quinn said.

Wyatt hadn't realized how badly he needed to hear
those words. How much he needed to know that that trust
so willfully destroyed between them all those years ago
could be fixed.

"Why don't you show me around your place?" his
dad said.

"Thanks, Dad," Wyatt said. "I'd like that."

Quinn walked ahead of him for a moment, and Wyatt
closed his eyes, and he felt something like a release wash
through him. A weight that he had been carrying around
for most of his life easing away.

He needed her. Plain and simple. Need was something he'd avoided for a long damned time. He'd made
it his mission to stand on his own, to be self-contained.
And that had been rocked, shaken the first moment he'd
seen Lindy Parker.

Need.

It had haunted him, filled him, ever since. And it had
changed, deepened.

He had come back home to make something permanent. He had thought all this time that it was the ranch. But a ranch could burn away. People could be taken too, he knew that. But there was only one thing that endured. That lasted. That lived on even after people died.

It was love.

And of all the temporary, vain things in the world, it was the only thing that would stand tall in the end. It was the only thing that was worth the fight.

And Wyatt Dodge was going to go down swinging.

CHAPTER TWENTY-ONE

LINDY WAS MORE than a little bit impressed by the way the barbecue had turned out. If only looking around Get Out of Dodge didn't make her chest ache in unspeakable and horrible ways. She had decided, in the end, that she needed to come. Because she was not a coward, even though she kind of wished she could be one. Kind of wish that she could hide away and nurse her broken heart.

But she was going to make Wyatt face her. And she was going to face him.

And however she reacted… It didn't matter. Maybe she would cry. Maybe she would make a fool of herself in front of everyone. Maybe she would jump up on a stage and declare her love for him. She couldn't guarantee she wouldn't. But the idea of making a fool of herself didn't scare her anymore. It didn't matter what anyone else thought if she had no pride left. The only thing that mattered was that she loved him. She didn't know quite yet what she was going to do with that. But she still loved him. Even though he was stubborn. Even though he was a mess.

She sighed heavily, walking through the booths that were set up in the open field. There was a band up on a stage, surrounded by bales of hay and people dancing to country music covers out in the field.

She saw Jamie Dodge standing off to the side, her hair

in a neat, practical braid. She was gathering people up because she was about to do a short trail ride around the property. But she saw Lindy, and she waved.

Lindy waved back, hoping that Jamie wouldn't come over and try to have a chat. And was gratified when she didn't.

Then she looked up, and she saw Wyatt. He was standing there, wearing a black T-shirt, a pair of jeans and a cowboy hat. Her heart tried to leap through her throat. She thought maybe he would stay where he was. That maybe he wouldn't come over to her. But then he did.

She felt like she had that first moment she'd seen him. Rooted to the spot. As if she'd been struck by lightning. The unique brand of Wyatt Dodge lightning.

"I didn't know you were going to come," he said.

"I couldn't miss it." She could hardly breathe looking at him. "Not after all the work we put in."

He rubbed the back of his neck and her heart ached. "How's Dane?"

"Awake," Lindy said. "He's going to be in the hospital for a while. At first he was really disoriented. He didn't remember what time of year it was, or what event he'd been at. He's starting to kind of piece it all together. But his leg is useless right now and they're going to keep monitoring him."

"I'm glad to hear it. I mean, not that his leg is a mess, but that he's awake."

"Thank you. And… My mom came. Thank you for what you said to her too."

The strains of a fiddle wound their way around them, the sounds of people talking and laughing. They'd planned this together, and she'd been looking forward to it. Now she just felt hollow. This goal that had consumed her simply didn't anymore. She was full of Wyatt, and her love for him, and she didn't know how to act like she was okay.

"I can't do this." His words were harsh and abrupt, and could have easily come from inside her. Because she didn't think she could do it either.

"What?" She wanted clarification because for all she knew he meant he couldn't do the country line dance they'd just started out in front of the stage.

"I can't stand here and talk to you like we just met." His eyes turned intense, the kind of intensity she'd glimpsed before, but that he'd covered quickly. He wasn't covering it now, not at all. And it burned her all the way down. "I can't stand here and act like I haven't been inside you before."

"Wyatt," she said, her heart slamming against her breastbone. "Don't..."

"No," he said. "I need you to understand that that matters. Because I've been with a lot of women, Lindy. And I could stand there and shoot the breeze with any one of them. Because they didn't matter. I can't do that with you. I can't just stand here and talk like we haven't been skin to skin. You're different, I'm different. Together we're something else."

Her heart slammed hard against her breast and she took a step back. "Great. Is this torture Lindy hour? Because that is not why I came. And I will leave."

He reached out and grabbed hold of her arm. "It's not torture Lindy hour. I need to... Come with me."

"I don't think I want to."

"Then you're about to have a very intimate conversation in public."

She looked around, at the many people enjoying themselves, and she was tempted to tell him to go right ahead and speak his piece right there in front of everyone.

He took her hand and led her away from the booths, from all the people down away from the places that had been landscaped and polished, to an old barn on the property that she had never seen before. It was red, like a classic barn from an old painting, the trim no longer crisp and white but faded and peeling.

He opened a small door, and wrapped his warm fingers around hers, drawing her inside.

She wanted to lean into his strength. She wanted... She just wanted. But part of her was afraid. Still. Because she had been hurt, and badly. So many times. She didn't want to be hurt again. But, she wasn't going to cut him off either. She wasn't going to hide. Not now. "What?"

He didn't speak, but she could see that he was breathing hard, his chest rising and falling like he'd been running a marathon.

"I need you," he said. And then he wrapped his arms around her and pulled her in, kissing her, deep and hard. "I need you. And that is the scariest damn thing I have said in a very long time. I worked so hard not to need anyone, Lindy. Because I was sure that it would only lead to more pain. More rejection. I've had too much of it. But I had the talk with my father that I needed to have for the past twenty years. There's a lot of hard feelings. Mostly mine. And I realize that one conversation isn't going to clear that up. Not in the least. But I have a choice. I can hang on to it all... Or I can let the past go. Baby, watching you let all that go by the waterfall was the most beautiful thing I've ever seen. You're the bravest person I know." He cupped her cheek, slid his thumb over her skin. She closed her eyes and savored it. Wyatt's touch.

"You rode bulls for a living," she said, feeling shaky. "So that can't be true."

"Yeah. I did. You know why I did it? When my mom died… I was there. I came into the room and I saw her there. Laying on the floor. Jamie was in her bassinet crying. I knew it was too late. I knew she was already gone. I just… I knew. And after the paramedics had come… After my father had come running in from the field… I don't know if I tripped and fell, if I passed out or what. But I fell on the ground, and I ended up with a mouthful of dirt. I called out to my dad to pick me up. But he didn't. He just walked on by. He was too mired in his own pain to deal with mine."

"Oh, Wyatt…" She reached up and held his face, held his gaze.

"He and I have to work that out. We will. But it…after that, I decided that the next time I fell down into the dirt I'd just pick myself up. And that's what I've been doing all these years. Riding bulls, falling in the dirt, picking myself up. But that wasn't me being brave. It's not brave to live a life by yourself. No responsibilities. No ties to anything. It's easy. I didn't want to need anyone. Not again. I let myself need Louisa, and I lost her too. And yeah, all that was messed up, but it was real to me. And I've been walking around with no connections ever since. But I don't want to do that anymore. I can't. I think that moment in the bar… You know when people die for a minute, and they go to heaven. That's what that was like. When you walked into that bar I died for a minute, and I saw heaven. And it was you. It was a promise. A taste of something that was coming. Like everything… Everything cleared away. All the pain we had ever been through, whatever we were living in in that moment.

That's what it was like. A taste of what we could have. Of what we could be. And it's this. It's love. I can't… We can't be done. Not us. I think we might be the real thing." He cupped her chin. "No I know we are. I knew it then. I wanted to hide from it. Run from it. But at the same time… I never could help myself when it came to flinging myself into danger. There were a lot of ways I could have gone off and made money. But…"

"You decided to become a bull rider."

"Sure as hell. So I flirted with you. And I teased you. And you know what? I thought I was going to escape unscathed. But I didn't. And now… I don't want to. Not anymore. I've spent a long time being worried that there was something wrong with me. That I wasn't worthy of love. And I'm still not sure that I'm worthy of yours. I'm not sure that I'm a better man than Damien. But I love you more. I'd die for you. I'd make myself bleed for you. I'm willing to stand here and face my biggest fear. I'm willing to be terrified, admit that I'm terrified, for you. Just you. You're right, Lindy. I could love you. And I do. I don't know what all that's worth. But I'll turn myself inside out for you."

"Wyatt," she said, closing the distance between them and flinging her arms around his neck, clinging to him. Kissing him. "I love you, Wyatt Dodge," she said. "I love you with every corner of myself. You are the most wonderful man I've ever known. You're fearless."

"I feel pretty damn scared right about now," he said. "I'm damn near shaking."

"But you're here. Isn't that bravery? Being afraid, but saddling up and riding anyway?"

"I don't know. After all this… You and me, I'm starting to think that bravery is loving even when you know how hard it can be. Lindy, I've never been married. I loved, and I've lost. I've made mistakes. I've done bad things out of anger. I don't know how to be a husband. But I promise that I'm going to spend the rest of my life learning how to love you just right. And if I make mistakes, I'm going to stay around and fix it. No running. No hiding. If you start to feel like you've lost touch with me, you tell me. I swear I'll tell you. My world changed the minute that I saw you the first time. And I swear I'm not going to forget that. I'm going to stay changed. You struck me like lightning, baby. You changed me.

"I love you," he said. "You. Not who you pretended to be. But who you are with me. You're who I want. Forever. I want to have babies with you, and live with you. I want to marry you. And I never thought I would say those words."

Lindy was trembling, her hands shaking, tears filling her eyes. "I want to marry you too. And I really, really never thought I would be saying those words. Not ever again."

"Good. Then let's get married."

Her eyes went wide. "Now?"

"I don't see any reason to wait."

"Don't you want…a wedding?"

"I don't care. I just want you. I want you to be my wife. As soon as possible."

"Well… Wyatt, where are we going to live?" They both lived on the properties they ran their businesses on. Not that it was necessary but they were both pretty connected to their home bases.

"Where do you want to live?" he asked. "We don't

have to live here. We don't have to live at Grassroots even. It could be anywhere."

She loved that. The meaning behind that offer. She'd gotten married before, and she'd stepped from one place she hadn't chosen into another. A foreign world where she'd felt like she had to bend and change. And he was offering her the chance to choose her world. One she wanted, one she fit.

"Here," she said, without thought. "We worked on this together. And I love Grassroots. I'll always spend a lot of time there. But I don't need to stay there anymore. That house was just a reminder of what I thought I needed to be, and I don't need to be that anymore. I don't need to be the perfect woman. I just want to be your woman."

"That's all I want, Lindy," he said, his voice rough.

She leaned in and kissed him. "Call me Melinda," she whispered against his lips. "You're the only man who ever has."

"Melinda," he whispered. "I love you." He stopped, his face looking serious, and he grabbed hold of her chin, holding her face still. "I remember thinking Damien had to be the dumbest man on the planet. I couldn't imagine wanting another woman if I had you. I still can't. You're the dream I didn't let myself have, didn't think I could have."

"So are you," she said, her voice getting quiet. "Wyatt… I never thought… I never thought there was a man who could love me like this. Who could love *me*."

"Baby," he said. "I couldn't not love you. I've never put any stock in things like fate… But I think you might be mine."

She stretched up on her toes and pressed a kiss to his lips. "I know you're mine."

Lindy Parker had hated the rodeo for a long time. And if there was one thing she hated more than the rodeo itself, it had been the bull riders.

Cocky. Arrogant. Jerks.

She had classified Wyatt Dodge as the cockiest, most arrogant of all. But oh how things changed. She couldn't hate the rodeo, not now. Not when, in the end, it was the reason she'd found this man.

Oh, this man. She loved him most of all.

And the very best thing was, he loved her back.

EPILOGUE

THE DAY DANE got out of the hospital they did their best to limit the fanfare. He still wasn't feeling great, and the long road of recovery ahead wasn't helping matters.

Lindy wrapped her arms around Dane's shoulders and hugged him, once they got him inside the house.

"On the bright side, you get all of the main house at Grassroots to yourself," Lindy pointed out, sounding overly cheerful,

She'd been doing that a lot. And he could tell it left Dane bemused.

Wyatt knew exactly what his brother-in-law was thinking. That it was a damn poor trade for a leg that worked. Dane wasn't even on crutches yet. He had a halo around his thigh, and he was rooted to a wheelchair. It was temporary, but Wyatt knew it was difficult.

"Well, the downstairs," Dane said, his tone dry.

"For now," Lindy said, putting her hand on Dane's shoulder. "You'll be going up the stairs in no time."

"Honestly, right now, that's not even appealing," he groaned. "It makes me hurt thinking about it." He looked between Lindy and Wyatt. "I can't believe you just… got married."

"It was a long time coming," Wyatt said.

"You guys just started dating," Dane pointed out.

"No," Lindy said, her eyes meeting Wyatt's. "It really was a long time coming."

When Lindy was satisfied that Dane was settled in the house, they headed for home. For Get Out of Dodge. The ranch was booked up to full capacity, and it would be for the next several months. Everything had been more successful than he'd possibly imagined.

But that didn't even matter. Not now.

He parked the car, and took Lindy's hand and the two of them walked up the front porch together. He turned to look out at the place, the dark sky dusted with stars, the mountains like fat black brushstrokes against the midnight blue.

This place meant the world to him. He'd learned about loss here. He'd taught himself not to need here. And then Lindy had breezed into his life and shown him that while he could stand on his own, it was so much better to stand with her by his side.

It was true that Wyatt Dodge didn't lose. But he'd had absolutely no idea it was possible to win this big.

* * * * *

Return to Gold Valley, Oregon,
where the cowboys are tough to tame, until they
meet the women who can lasso their hearts.
Look for Grant's book,
A Tall, Dark Christmas Cowboy,
from Maisey Yates and HQN Books!
Read on for an exclusive sneak peek...

CHAPTER ONE

GRANT DODGE WAS ALONE. And that was how he liked it.

He had spent the entire day out in the cold mountain air conducting roping demonstrations and leading trail rides. Not that he minded any of those things in isolation. It was the addition of *people* that made them somewhat challenging.

Worse than having to deal with people in a general sense was dealing with people who recognized him.

Not the typical small-town recognition—he was used to that. Though, he could live without getting sad widower face from people he barely knew in the grocery store, but even then, at least it was all people who knew him because he'd lived in Gold Valley all his life.

What *really* got to him was the people who recognized him from the news stories.

Eight years hadn't done anything to make those moments less weird. People often couldn't place where they knew him from, but they knew they did. And they would press, and press, until he told them.

The woman who had recognized him today had been a grandmother. A great-grandmother, even. Sweet and gray-haired and looking at him with sympathetic eyes that made him want to jump off the nearest bridge.

It always seemed worse around the holidays. Perhaps

because of the sentimentality people seemed to feel that time of year. And tried to inflict on him.

He didn't really know.

Whatever the reason, he seemed to have an uptick in well-meaning-but-irritating interactions.

Maybe that was why he always wanted to drink more this time of year, too.

He shook his head and settled down into his chair, looking around the small, cozy cabin that he called home. And then he looked into the full, inviting whiskey glass he called salvation.

He didn't have a problem or anything. He was functional. He considered that the benchmark. Low though it might be.

He was functional enough that his family mostly *joked* about his drinking, which meant it was probably fine.

But the one thing he didn't want to do was get in bed at night stone-cold sober. Sometimes he could. When the long, hard day of work came inside with him, resting on aching shoulders and in the lower back that was getting touchier with each passing year—because age. Not that thirty-four was exceptionally aged, not at all. But, physical labor had a way of speeding all that up.

But then, the alternative had been to spend the rest of his life working at the damned power company, living in a little house on a quiet street in a neighborhood tucked back behind the main street of Copper Ridge. Living the life of a man lost in suburban bliss, without any of the trappings that generally made it blissful.

No children.

No wife.

Not anymore.

He never had the children, but there had been a time when he and Lindsay had hoped for them. Even though...

That had always been a pipe dream, he supposed.

But for a while, he and Lindsay had lived in a world of dreams. Reality had been too harsh. And sometimes sitting around and making plans for a future you knew wouldn't be there was all you could do.

He took a long swallow of whiskey and leaned back in his chair. This was why he didn't go to bed sober.

Because it was these quiet moments, the still ones—particularly this time of year—that had a way of crushing in on him, growing louder and louder in the silence of the room.

Solitude was often as welcome as it was terrifying. Sometimes it had teeth. And he did his best not to get savaged by them.

He took another swallow of whiskey and leaned back further in the chair before setting the glass on the table with a decisive click. Then he let his head fall back.

He must've dozed off, because when he opened his eyes again the hands on the clock hanging on the wall had made a more pronounced journey that it would have if it had only been the few minutes it felt like.

He stretched, groaning as his joints popped. He stood, making his way over to the window and looking out into the darkness.

At least, he *should* have been looking out into the darkness.

Instead, he saw a dim light cutting through the trees.

They did have guests staying on the property, but none out in the woods behind Grant's cabin.

Grant lived well out of the way, on the opposite end of Dodge land from the guest cabins. And if there was anyone out there right now, they were not where they were supposed to be.

He opened up the drawer in the kitchen and took a small flashlight out, and then shoved on his boots before heading outside. He supposed, if he were thinking clearly he would have called his brother Wyatt. But then, he was half-asleep and a little bit drunk, so he wasn't thinking all that clearly. And instead, he made his own way out through the trees and toward the single light that was glowing in the woods.

When he was halfway between his house and the light it occurred to him what he was probably about to walk in on.

The back of his neck went hot, tension rising inside of him.

Odds were, anyone out in the middle of nowhere at this hour was up to one thing. And he didn't especially want to walk in and find two people having sex in a cabin in the middle of the woods, interrupting his drinking and sleeping time. The teeth on that would be just a little bit too sharp to bear.

But then, if he wasn't getting any, nobody else should either.

Especially not right next to his house.

That only increased his irritation as he continued on toward the light, the wind whipping through the trees, the bitter cold biting through the flannel shirt he was wearing. He should've put a jacket on, but he hadn't thought of it.

He swore, and then he swore again as he approached the light.

He frowned. Right. There was a cabin back here, but it was dilapidated. One of the original buildings on the property, from back in the late 1800s. One that hadn't been inhabited in a long time. At least, not by humans. He had a feeling there had been several raccoons, and about ten thousand spiders. But not humans.

But raccoons did not light lanterns. So he could safely assume this was not a raccoon.

He was on the verge of storming in—because why the

hell not?—but something stopped him. Instead, he soft-ened his footsteps and walked up to the window.

It was not what he'd been expecting.

It *was* a person, but not people. And nobody was hav-ing sex.

Instead, there was a small woman, curled up beneath a threadbare blanket. She looked like she was asleep, but the camping lantern next to her head was turned on, a thin yellow beam of light stretching across what he could see of her face.

She was not one of the guests, at least, he was reason-ably certain. He didn't make a practice of memorizing what they all looked like.

Mostly because he didn't care.

It was also difficult to identify her positively, because she was curled up in a ball, the blanket halfway up over her head. He shifted his position, looking to see that there was a duffel bag in the corner of the room. But nothing else.

He frowned, looking at her again, and he saw that there were shoes on her feet, which were sticking out just past the edge of the blanket.

He dragged his hand over his face.

She could be a criminal. A fugitive from the law. But then, most likely she was a woman running from a dif-ficult situation. Possibly from a man.

If she needed help, it was something not even Grant could turn away from.

Hard Riding Cowboy

CHAPTER ONE

LAUREN BISHOP TOOK her cup of coffee from the pickup counter at Sugar Cup and collapsed at the nearest table. She set the coffee and her planner down in front of her, staring morosely at both. There was so much left to do. And right now, she resented that cheerful, pink-and-white planner more than she could remember resenting anything.

Including her late husband.

Maybe she should just spill her cup of coffee on the thing. Hope that the dark liquid bled into all the pages, made them stick together. Made the ink run and made everything unreadable. And then she would have a good excuse for why she hadn't gotten everything done. Her entire life was contained in that book.

Doctor appointments, orthodontist appointments—both of which required that she arrive early to fill out new patient paperwork—client information, phone calls with banks, a meeting with the school district...

Moving was hard. The last time she'd done it alone she had been nineteen years old, stupid, in love and with nothing more than what she'd been able to stuff into a knapsack. Everything else was expendable, at least in her idiotic teenage head. She'd felt like an adventurous sojourner and not an empty-headed child who was headed for disaster.

Now, she wasn't moving alone, but she was the only adult. If it weren't for her parents, she would have lost it completely.

But at least Ava and Grace were taken care of. They were angry at her, resentful that she was making them leave, but time spent with their grandparents was helping at least.

None of that took care of the long list of projects Lauren had set out before her to make their new house habitable. To make everything official. They had signed an agreement with the previous owners to be able to do repairs in the house before closing, and with paperwork still unsigned Lauren was holding her breath hoping that nothing fell apart.

If so, she was just out... So much money. And so much time.

And probably living in her parents' house for the next several years. Possibly until Ava went to college.

Assuming she would even be able to afford to send Ava to college.

She had come to the coffeehouse not just to get a hit of caffeine, but to sit in silence and make some phone calls, go over the work that she had to do. It just didn't seem at all appealing.

She sighed and leaned back in her chair, looking around the room. Looking anywhere instead of at that horrendous little book that told her what she should do and where she should be at all times.

It had come with stickers. As if putting daisies on it would make it less overwhelming. She'd tried that for about two seconds, and had then decided it was just one more stupid thing she had to keep track of. Not only did women have to be organized, they had to be fancy while doing it?

That was a big *hell no* from her.

The little coffee shop was full of people sitting at tables, with groups or by themselves. Most of them with shiny silver laptops in front of them. Drinking coffee, talking, on the phone or to someone else. It was definitely the unofficial office space of everyone who worked for themselves in Gold Valley.

She tried to see if she recognized anyone. She wasn't sure if she was hoping she did, or hoping she didn't. On the one hand, having a conversation with someone she hadn't seen in years would give her an excuse to delay in her responsibilities. On the other hand, then she would have to talk to someone about her life.

That fell so low on her list of things to do it wouldn't even make the planner.

The door swung open and she turned her attention there, grateful for yet another distraction. But distraction didn't even begin to cover it.

The man who walked in was…

Unreal.

From his cowboy boots, to the way his jeans conformed to all the very masculine places on his body, to that tight black T-shirt that showed off his flat, solid-looking midsection, muscular chest and broad shoulders, to his black cowboy hat settled on his head.

All that, and his face was good, too. A chiseled jaw with a bit of a five o'clock shadow. Lips that made her own tingle in response.

It had been more than three years since she had been kissed by a man.

That thought came out of nowhere, and was one she

honestly hadn't had any interest in over the last three years. She was too overwhelmed by Mount Planner. Too underwhelmed by what the reality of love and marriage had been. And far too involved in the parenting of her daughters to have those kinds of fantasies.

But she was having one right now. Big-time.

The man moved deeper into the coffeehouse, moving up to the counter and giving her a solid view of his broad back and very compelling ass. She would have said she didn't spend a whole lot of time looking at men's asses. But right now, this particular ass seemed about the most important thing in the world.

Certainly more important than the pink-and-white planner.

She did her best to look away from him enough times that anyone casually observing her in the coffee shop might not think she was totally checking him out. But whatever. He wasn't looking at her. He wouldn't know. And anyway, she had already established that she didn't know anyone in here. So why not?

She was a thirty-five-year-old woman with two children, who had been married unhappily, widowed and left on her own to deal with all the fallout. If she wanted to check out a guy, she was going to do it. And she wasn't going to feel embarrassed about it.

He turned around and she looked away quickly. Not embarrassed, sure, but she had pride.

She looked back up, and her eyes connected with his perfect blue ones. The color of unwashed denim. She had only ever seen eyes that color in one family.

But there was no way...

"Lauren Bishop." And then he smiled. That mischievous grin that she'd seen once on a dirty-faced little boy.

But he was not a little boy now. Oh no. This man standing before her was… Well, he was all man. "I haven't seen you in… Too long."

Oh. No.

No. No no no no.

That was wrong. So…so wrong.

Calder Reid.

Ew. No. *No.*

Of all the men she could have possibly checked out, it had to be the one she used to babysit.

She couldn't remember how much younger he was than her. Maybe five, six years. Probably nothing in the grand scheme of things. Except she had *babysat him.* And now, she had looked at his ass.

"It has been a while," she said, keeping her voice measured.

Seventeen years, actually.

Which didn't make her any less appalled she had gawked at his butt.

His name was called by the barista, and Calder grabbed his cup of coffee from the counter before moving closer to her table. He pulled out the vacant chair across from her, taking a seat without asking. She wrapped her hands over the top of her planner and pulled it across the table, closer to herself. As if she could use it as some kind of shield.

"Are you visiting?" he asked.

"No," she said.

"You moved back?"

"Yes." She had no idea how much Calder knew about her life. She didn't think her mom was in contact with anyone who would send direct gossip down to his family.

She had no idea what was going on with his family,

which was probably a pretty good metric for how much he knew about her. She had no idea if he'd ever gotten married, though judging by the bare left hand, he wasn't married now. Or, maybe he was. There were plenty of ranchers who didn't wear rings for safety reasons. And, she assumed he was a rancher based on what he was wearing.

"Well, welcome back," he said, leaning back in his chair, his large hands circling the coffee cup in front of him. They were very, very large hands. It was easy to imagine them against her skin. Rough and calloused and… She was insane.

She blinked, trying to get a hold of herself. "Thank you."

"Are you working here?"

"Here?" she said, gesturing around them.

"Not in the coffeehouse. In town."

"Kind of," she said. "I'm a freelance web designer. So, I can work anywhere."

"That sounds nice," he said.

"Yes," she said. "I make my own hours, no dress code. I can live wherever I want…"

"A lot like being a rancher, then," he said. "That's what I do. I work the family ranch now. I have my own place on the property. I'm not living in the house or anything. But, of course, animals and the sunrise make my hours, I have to live on the damned ranch and, while there is no official dress code, it's the kind of work that makes it pretty important for you to keep things strapped in. You don't want to lose any parts."

Her face got hot. Was she blushing? She did not blush. But also, she didn't usually think about what were essentially a stranger's parts while she was sitting across from him thinking about how attractive he was. He'd always been a bold kid, brash. On a preteen it had been funny to moderately irritating. On a man it was…oh boy. "Yeah," she said, looking away. "I can see how that would be…a consideration."

"Definitely," he said. His lips quirked upward into a smile and he leaned in, shifting his hands so that they were practically stroking the coffee cup. And it was killing her. Because there was no way she could stop herself from thinking about those hands stroking her. "Since you're new to town again I imagine you haven't made a lot of new friends. Maybe I could take you out tonight?"

Was he hitting on her? Little Calder Reid was hitting on her.

Of course, Little Calder Reid was also not little at all. He was clearly over six foot and muscular enough to wrestle a steer down to the ground. But nonetheless, in her memory, he was Little Calder Reid.

"I…" She lifted up her hand. "I have to stop you there."

"Do you?"

"Yes. I am busy tonight."

"Tomorrow night?"

His eyes collided with hers again, and she felt it. Like an electric shock. Where everything inside you froze for one moment. Her blood. Her heart. Her breath. And she knew beyond a shadow of a doubt that he felt it, too. This insane, instant chemistry. There was attraction, there was checking out a hot guy, and then there was this. She wasn't sure she had ever experienced this. It was the stuff of romantic comedies and romance novels. Stuff that happened in fiction. Something she had never thought might happen in reality.

"No," she said softly, gritting her teeth to keep any

more words from following. She'd said no. And that really should be enough.

Her heart kicked back into gear, going over the appropriate speed. The sad thing was it didn't feel like enough, because she wanted to throw out all of her justifications, all of everything and say yes to whatever it was he had in mind.

"Breakfast. I draw the line at brunch. I'm not really a brunch guy."

"No," she said. "I'm… I have kids, Calder." She waited for him to respond to that, but his handsome—Lord it was handsome—face was unreadable. "And, I have a feeling that…that isn't all that you're asking about."

He leaned back, and then in again. "Are you married?"

Another piece of baggage to chuck on the pile. He would run the other way. "Widowed."

"I'm sorry," he said. He genuinely sounded it.

She never knew how to respond to that. She was very sorry that Robert was dead. He was the father of her children, and nothing could ever change that. But she was angry with him, too. Angry that she had been right about where his behavior was going to end up. He had been irresponsible, always. And what she had found exciting and fun when she had been a teenager had become stressful, worrisome and painful as a woman.

"Thank you," she said. He didn't want her life story. And anyway, she didn't want to give it to him. "I'm actually here because I'm in the process of closing on a house, but there are some repairs that need to be made first, and I'm in kind of a precarious arrangement with all of it. There's home-improvement stuff to do, so that the bank will agree to the loan and… It could all fall through, and I'm pouring time and money into it."

"What needs to be done?"

"A lot of things. There's one room that only has sub-floor. I need steps built up to the back door…"

"I can do that."

"I don't… Calder. That's very nice of you, but I don't have a lot of money to pay you. I'm just going to look up YouTube videos. I can figure it out."

"No," he said, his voice firm. "I don't want your money. I want to help you out. It sounds like you're in a tough spot, and all of that would be easy for me."

"I just… I can't…"

"I'll come over tonight."

"I really…"

"I can bring food."

She frowned. "You want to fix my house and you're going to bring me food?"

He shrugged. "Yes. Consider it a welcome back to Gold Valley."

"I'm not in a position to…" She didn't know what to say. And she didn't know how to say it. Not without sounding full of herself. And not without sounding hopeful.

"No charge," he said, his voice steady. "I mean that. No expectation. You need help. I have time and the skills. It's a good thing we ran into each other. Though if I'm going to help, I'll need your number."

She could decline. But she needed help. And wanting help from him had nothing to do with how darn pretty he was. Nothing at all.

Anyway there was something… Well, it was flatter-ing. None of her old friends were waiting in line to help her. She'd left town so long ago it wasn't like she expected it. Still, this unexpected…kindness. Attention. Whichever. It felt good.

It felt better than sitting here filling in planner pages.

"Okay. Give me your phone." She took it from him and called herself from it. "There. Now I'm in your call log."

"Perfect." He stood up, tapped the table, then picked up his coffee cup. And then, he tipped his hat. By the time he turned around and left, her head was spinning.

And she couldn't help but think that it *was* a very good thing she had run into him. Except…

Except she felt kind of dizzy. And she didn't think it was just because of how fast all that had happened.

He wants to help you. And you need help a hell of a lot more than you need a kiss… Or anything else.

It was true.

And anyway, she had taken care of Calder when he'd been a little boy. Now he was taking care of her.

There. That should kill any and all ridiculous attraction she felt.

It should. But it didn't.

But, ridiculous attraction or not, suddenly the list of things in the planner seemed a whole lot less insurmountable.

And she was just going to take that as a win.

CHAPTER TWO

LAUREN BISHOP WAS back in town.

There had been a lot of women in his life between that moment when she had walked into his family home when he was twelve years old, his new babysitter and also the most beautiful creature he'd ever seen in his life, and now.

But she was still the ultimate fantasy. She always had been.

Of course, he'd been a kid and had felt every inch the twelve-year-old standing next to the tall, beautiful seventeen-year-old she'd been.

But now, he was much taller than she was, and he definitely didn't feel like a kid around her.

She had kids. She was a *widow*.

He supposed that was something he was going to have to think on. When he thought of Lauren Bishop—and God help him, late at night sometimes he did, because she'd been the very first object of desire he'd ever had— he thought of them as equals.

But they weren't. And that was a helluva thing. She'd done more living than him. Had more baggage.

That easy, fun hookup he'd fantasized about... Well, that was looking unlikely.

But for now... He was consumed with the fact that he wanted to help her. He wasn't exactly the most altruistic son of a bitch in general. In fact, usually, when helping a woman he would have an ulterior motive.

Well, if he were honest it wasn't that he didn't have one now. It was just that… He had meant what he said. He didn't want payment. Not in the form of sex. If she wanted to have sex, fine. He was all for putting to bed one of the oldest fantasies he possessed. Literally, if the opportunity presented itself.

But there was something about her. About the way she had looked sitting there, and hell, the way she had been checking him out. And, she *had* been checking him out, there was no doubt about that.

He took a deep breath and looked around him, at the mountains, standing sentry all around the fields, which rolled forward in a lush green spread toward the fence line of the Reid family ranch. This place hadn't changed a lick in the last couple of decades, and given that, he supposed he shouldn't be very surprised that the way Lauren Bishop made him feel hadn't changed much either.

Of course, the big difference was that now he knew exactly what feelings like that meant. He knew exactly what to do with a woman now.

The idea made desire pool low and hot and heavy in his gut.

"You got plans for tonight?"

He turned and saw his brother Tanner standing there, looking at him speculatively.

"Yes," he returned. "Why?"

"Savannah and Jackson were planning a dinner to plan a dinner. It's almost Lily's birthday."

"Oh." He frowned. "Well, I'll make sure I'm around for the squirt's birthday but I might skip the planning stage. I promised a lady I would come help fix some things in her house."

Tanner arched a brow. "Is that a euphemism for a booty call?"

He shrugged. But, for the first time since Lauren had set him so firmly on his ass, he felt a little bit more balanced. Because the fact of the matter was, it was *not* a booty call. He actually wanted to help.

Mostly.

He felt a little bit superior to Tanner in that moment. Mostly because he doubted Tanner could say that he had ever helped a woman for the sake of it.

"I'm just helping out," Calder said.

She needed something, and he could give it. His whole damned family was so stunted in that area. His father going from marriage to marriage, ignoring his boys. Treating them more like ranch hands than sons half the time.

Calder had always wanted to help. To try to make an impact. His father hadn't let him. Granted, fixing floors and throwing some paint on the wall wasn't an emotional fix, but it was what Lauren needed, and he was happy to give it.

"Is that so?" Tanner looked completely skeptical.

"It *is* so. Is that so hard to believe?"

Tanner snorted. "Hell yes."

"You remember Lauren Bishop? She used to baby-sit me."

"Oh yeah," he said. "Pretty. Blonde. You used to drool on her when she walked in the door."

He frowned. "I never drooled on her."

"I think you did."

"That was just because I had braces and it was impossible not to drool sometimes, you asshole." Tanner looked amused, and Calder made a deliberate effort to calm down because his brother didn't get to make him that mad. Not about bullshit from seventeen years ago. "But anyway," Calder continued. "She's back in town."

"And you can't honestly tell me that you are hoping to do something other than satisfy your *hot for babysitter* issues?"

"*Hoping to* and *planning on* are two different things. She's trying to fix up a house. She's a single mom."

"Oh," Tanner said, frowning.

"What's that for?"

"It's just… I know you're not going to take it there now."

"Do you?"

"Yeah. That's not your thing."

"I don't… What's not my thing?"

"Single moms you have to be careful with. Single moms are either supertemporary or very permanent. But if it was the supertemporary thing, you would already know that sex was happening."

"You know this from experience?"

Tanner arched a brow. "I'm not a monk."

"Yeah, you're not me either. So it's not like you have a hell of a lot more experience." That was just a fact. Tanner was… He was the oldest. As a result he was a little bit more… Measured in his activities. Jackson had been the real manwhore in the trio of brothers, but that had all come home to roost in the form of a baby he hadn't realized one of his one-night stands had given birth to. Until the woman had dropped her off on Jackson's doorstep and fled. Leaving him holding the baby.

He had been in over his head for a while, trying to

adjust to fatherhood, until he had hired Savannah Sturm to be his nanny. Savannah was now his wife, the baby was about to turn a year old, and Calder had never seen Jackson happier.

Which really was something to think about.

"Still," Tanner said. "I get around. I just do it with a little less of a show than you two."

"Why is that? So you can avoid Chloe stamping around and passing comment on your behavior?"

Their younger stepsister lived on the property, and it was pretty obvious to Calder that she had a bit of a crush on Tanner. Inappropriate as that was. Tanner didn't seem any the wiser, though, and seemed to regard Chloe as little more than a gnat buzzing in his ear.

"Chloe passes judgment on what I do no matter what," Tanner said. "But we're not talking about me."

"I'm just helping her out," Calder said. "Her husband died, Tanner."

He didn't know how long ago. He didn't know what the story was. It hadn't been pure sadness on her face when she had said she was widowed.

There was something else.

She had looked fragile, but angry. And he had wanted to dig, had wanted to find out what exactly had gone on. That was uncharacteristic. He had watched his father live out a series of relationship dramas. There had been many wives, many stepmothers. A whole lot of angry fights. Calder had never really had the desire to enter into the institution of matrimony. He figured the Reid men collectively had exceeded their personal allotment of marriages, anyway.

Also, having never seen it last... He'd been cynical about it from the get-go.

Granted, Calder's father had been married to Chloe's mother until the old man had died. But, he had half wondered if his father simply hadn't had the energy to cycle through wives anymore at that point. Calder had always liked his relationships easy. And nothing about Lauren Bishop would be easy.

"I'm sorry to hear that," Tanner said. "Must be rough. And really rough for her poor kids."

Calder's stomach twisted. He might not know about losing a parent when he was a kid, but he knew what it was like to have one walk away. It was tough. There was no way you can go through that and not feel loss. Anger. Abandonment.

He thought back to the anger on Lauren's face, and he wondered if she felt something of the same, even though she had lost her husband to death. He wondered if her kids felt the same, too.

"I'm really not going to mess around with her," Calder said.

"Good," Tanner responded. "I can come with you if you want. Lend a helping hammer."

Calder bristled at the thought. All right, maybe he wasn't holding out hope that anything would happen between himself and Lauren, but being alone would certainly raise the odds. And anyway, he wasn't sure he wanted to share the glory of helping with Tanner.

He possessed only so much altruism in his body. If he wasn't going to get laid, he would be the knight in shining armor. If it was going to be courtly love, then he would be the only knight at the round table.

"I got it," he said.

Tanner shook his head. "You can't help yourself, can you?"

"What?"

"You're hoping. You might not be actively trying to get something going, but you're sure as hell not closing the door."

"Hey," he said. "If the woman wants to have a no-strings fling at any point while I'm helping her out, I'm not going to say no. I'm not going to instigate either, but I'm not going to say no."

"Just so we're clear."

Tanner just laughed. "Well, enjoy swinging a hammer tonight."

He watched his brother turn and walk away, and he let the previous conversation roll over him.

Lauren had kids. She had lost her husband.

All of it should make him want to run the other direction and not pursue anything. Not the potential of no-strings sex, not even nailing a picture frame to the wall. Because hell, for all he knew, she might be looking for a replacement husband. And he certainly wasn't going to fit the bill.

Of course, she was the one who had tried to chase him off with the mention of the kids earlier. So, her looking for a husband was unlikely.

Even still, he knew plenty of men who would run the other direction for fear that she was on the prowl for something permanent.

He didn't feel compelled to run. In fact, he found himself looking forward to doing repair work more than he ever had in his life.

CHAPTER THREE

LAUREN DIDN'T KNOW what to do with herself, not just because her house didn't contain any furniture. Though that didn't help at all.

It was empty, and she had nowhere to sit but the floor. There was a blanket laid out there on the carpet, because Calder had said he was going to bring food. But that meant the two of them were going to be engaged in some kind of weird indoor picnic. And it was going to make her protestations from earlier seem awfully hollow.

Because there was no way that didn't look like she was hitting on him.

Was she hitting on him?

She was not the kind of girl who hooked up just because she saw a man and thought he was hot. And sure, most of that was related to having been married for thirteen years, but regardless, because of circumstances, she hadn't really experienced anything like that. And she couldn't say that she was that eager to either.

But Calder made her feel eager to. Unbidden, she had a flash in her mind of what it would be like. To experience all that strength pounding into her.

She bit the inside of her cheek and closed her eyes. She never thought about things in those terms. She hadn't had a fantasy that graphic when she was married. Of course, then, sex had been pretty casual. Easily accessible.

Her husband had always been up for it, more or less. The question was always whether or not she was in the mood after spending two days being ignored, or if he came home with beer on his breath. How able she was to ignore the fact that he had probably been driving.

Robert had never been cruel. At least, not intentionally. He had just never aged past eighteen, when the height of a good time to him was going out, getting drunk and riding on the dunes with his buddies. Disappearing for a few days to go on a hunt. To go camping. He thought nothing of making big purchases without checking with her. Thought nothing of going out drinking every night and coming home late, totally missing family dinners.

Didn't see why he should be expected to show at the kids' birthday parties, because they were boring. He could never get it through his head that she didn't really think they were fun but she threw them anyway. Because love was about giving. Not taking.

He'd never understood that.

The fact of the matter was he had been a terrible husband. And that would have been almost forgivable if he hadn't been such a neglectful father. He had loved the girls, in a strange, hands-off kind of way.

He had showed off their pictures to anyone who came into his garage. Had talked about them like his world revolved around them, but his actions had never once matched up with that. He wasn't the one driving them to sports and lessons. He wasn't the one sitting through recitals. The money he made working for the body shop paid for all that stuff, and in his mind, that had been enough. Except, there was a certain point where she had been making as much as he was, and then later more with her home business, and he had never quite realized that.

That it saved them when he went out and did dumb-ass shit like buying a toy trailer without asking. Without checking to see what they owed on their taxes.

Those thoughts made her feel guilty because she couldn't think about anything without remembering the frustration she had felt toward him at the end.

Couldn't think about the way she had felt about him in the beginning. Couldn't think about the fact that that first time they'd had sex had been really nice.

Fun.

He had been fun. In the beginning.

And more than that, he'd been her choice. So everything that followed…it was her consequence and she had to own it.

Sometimes she could remember why she'd made that choice.

How he felt like a chance to escape her somewhat sedate and restrictive upbringing. Something wild.

But as their family had grown, as their list of responsibilities had grown, fun hadn't been enough for her anymore. And he had never been able to understand that. He had always said that she was the one who had changed. And he wasn't wrong. She had changed and he hadn't. But considering they had gotten together when they were still teenagers, he should have changed. For their children if not for her.

Instead, he was dead. He was dead because he drank too many beers and had thought doing a round on the dunes in his four-wheeler was a good idea.

It damn well hadn't been.

There was a knock at the door and she stood, grateful for the interruption of her thoughts. The *Robert rabbit trail of thought* was unhappy. No matter how she looked at it. Even down to the fact that she wasn't able to mourn him the way that she wished she could.

Because he hadn't been the husband and father she wished he had been.

She sighed and walked over to the door, her chest tightening a bit when she saw the vague impression of Calder through the mottled glass.

She could see that he was carrying a large brown paper bag. The food, she presumed.

She pulled the door open.

"Hi," she said, the word starting strong, then fading to a whisper as she took in the sight of him. Damn he was hot. Really, really hot. He was wearing that same black T-shirt and black cowboy hat he had on earlier, and he was carrying food. Which frankly, just made him all the more attractive.

"Burgers," he said. "I forgot to check if you were like a vegetarian or something."

"Not," she said.

He nodded and came in without waiting for her to invite him. His eyes fell to the blanket on the floor and she shifted uncomfortably.

"I don't have any furniture in here yet. Technically, the house isn't mine. But the owners agreed to let me have a key, and let me do all this work. My real estate agent is opposed to it, because the bank could still ultimately decline the loan."

"Why are you doing it?"

"It's a short sale. And it's a killer deal. And it's kind of an endless circle, because the bank won't give me the loan unless these repairs are done, but the owners can't afford to do the repairs. So, I'm going to do them so that it passes inspection. And I might lose all my money. And my whole investment."

"Not if I have anything to do with it."

"I really do appreciate your offer to help," she said.

He walked farther into the room, setting the bag down on the blanket, and sitting himself down, as well.

"Thank you," she said.

"Honestly—" he waved a hand "—it's no problem."

"Well, it was a big problem to me. So, you can't minimize it. It's everything to me."

He began to get the food out of the bag, burgers and fries. Identical as far as she could tell. And two cans of Coke. It made her smile that he'd brought soda. Soda and not beer. Like he was giving her a callback to an innocent, simpler time.

Too bad sitting near him like this didn't feel simple or innocent.

"Where are your kids?" he asked, the question doing something to break the weird sex haze she was in.

"They're with my parents."

"Boys? Girls? How old?" he pressed.

She blinked. "Are you really interested?"

"I am. I don't know anything about your life after you left town."

"Well, I don't know anything about yours either."

He seemed to take that as an offer to trade. "My dad passed a year ago or so. I'm running the ranch with Tanner and Jackson. Jackson has a daughter. He's married. Tanner is still single."

She hadn't known the Reid family well, but she vaguely remembered Calder's dad. A big, serious man who always wore a Stetson, no matter the occasion. "I'm sorry to hear about your dad."

"Yeah. We're all sorry. But, I've never been married. No kids. Just a rancher like my old man."

"There's no *just* about being a rancher," she said. "You and I both know that being a rancher is hard work."

"I suppose. But you know what they say about idle hands. I've always figured as badly as I behave while doing hard work I better never let my hands grow idle."

His blue eyes clashed with hers, the spark there undeniable. He was trying to make her think dirty things. And it was such a basic line. She should not let something like that affect her. Thrill her. And yet it did.

She swallowed hard, trying to do something to minimize the chain of heat moving through her body.

"Well. I guess it's good to know your strengths. And your weaknesses."

The corner of his mouth tipped up. "I never said I had weaknesses."

She cleared her throat. "Girls. I have girls." There, that would get her back on solid ground. "My oldest is fourteen. Ava. And Grace is twelve."

His eyebrows shot up. "Wow," he said. "I guess I didn't imagine…"

"Were you thinking I had babies?"

"I guess so. I know you're older than me, Lauren, but with time, the age gap seems pretty small."

"You were doing better before you mentioned my age," she said, narrowing her eyes.

He lifted his hands. "I didn't mean it like that. I was just saying… I don't have kids. Like I said. So, it just kinda blows my mind to imagine someone I consider close in age to me having…teenagers."

She hopped out a laugh. "Yeah, it blows my mind, too, sometimes. When it's not terrifying me to my soul."

"How long has your husband been gone?"

She looked up sharply, meeting his gaze, then grabbing hold of the paper bag, digging around inside for the food.

"I'm sorry," he said. "You don't have to answer that if you don't want to."

"No," she said. "It's just... Most people dance around it. Most people don't just ask."

"I figure as people we can get a lot more accomplished if we would just ask. I don't see the point in dancing around things. Of course, I don't really see the point in dancing."

She picked a french fry up out of the bag and crunched it. "Really?"

"Nope. Dancing is just a prelude to what people really want to do. I don't do pretense."

She nearly choked on the fry. "Then why are you here?"

It felt bold to say that. Like she was applying motive that might not be there. And she might well embarrass herself by doing that. Assuming that this...younger... hotter guy wanted her.

That was the thing. She was a mom. A mom in her midthirties. She had stretch marks and dimples on her thighs and stuff. And he was like...

Well, he was fantasy material.

The true hilarity was the age difference had worked to his disadvantage years ago. He had been a kid. And now... Now she just felt ridiculous lusting after him, really.

Assuming that it wasn't one-sided.

But, hell. She was going for it. Because she felt like

there was a vibe, and she was just going to assume there was. "Isn't this a pretense?"

He looked her over, slow and lazy, and she felt it like a touch. "No," he said. "I want to help you. Now… Would I say no if you tried to kiss me? I sure as hell would not. But I swear to God I'm not manipulating you. I'm not pretending anything."

"You're not?"

"Hell no. I'd fuck you right now if you were into it."

Her internal muscles clenched. Hard. That should have been impertinent, and not at all hot.

But she felt very, very hot.

"Well…"

"See? No pretense."

"Not really sure how we got from my dead husband to you being willing to *fuck me*."

"When you put it like that it does seem odd. But it seemed natural in the moment."

She tilted her head to the side. "You don't embarrass easily, do you?"

He shrugged. "I don't think I embarrass at all."

She sighed heavily. She didn't know what the hell kind of conversation they were having. Covering everything from his dad's death to her children, and his total willingness to do it with her on the floor. So she might as well keep on making it weird. "Three years. He—my husband, Robert—has been gone for three years."

Calder nodded slowly. "I do know what it's like to lose someone like that. I'm sorry. I mean, my dad died, but your parents do tend to die before you. That's the order of things. And when you're an adult. Not when you're a kid like it was for your girls. I'm really sorry about that."

"I'm sorry they lost him, too," she said.

He didn't say anything, but a flicker of understanding ignited in his blue eyes.

"I think it would be best if I just took help with the flooring," she said slowly.

"Probably," he agreed.

"Just…so we're clear."

"Perfectly clear," he said. "No pretense, like I said."

"Then let's finish eating and I'll show you where the work is."

CALDER COULDN'T FIGURE out whether or not he'd made a misstep by making it so clear that he was into Lauren. But then, like Tanner had said earlier, a woman in her position was going to be interested in only two things.

Something purely physical, or something permanent.

He was attracted to her, and the attraction had only intensified when he had walked in tonight and seen her.

He loved everything about the changes the years had sculpted into her body. Her hips were wider, her breasts larger, her cheekbones a bit more sculpted. There was a world-weariness to her eyes that he didn't like, but there was also something else. A depth. It intrigued him. Called to him. And that had nothing at all to do with sex. So he didn't know what the hell to do with it.

He was pretty deep into the flooring job, and all that physical labor hadn't done anything to dampen his libido, so he supposed he could take comfort in the fact that even if sex wasn't the only thing on his mind when he looked at Lauren, it was on his mind.

Three years. Her husband had been gone three years. Which meant her girls would have been eleven and nine when that happened. And she was having to go through raising a preteen and a teenager all alone.

He knew sweet fuck all about raising kids. He certainly wouldn't be of any help to her.

She didn't ask, asshole.

Well, he wasn't even thinking about offering. Not at all. He hammered harder at the flooring, bringing the gap between the two wooden slats to a close. It was pretty easy work, as it went. There was just no making it go faster than it could.

While he was doing that, she was painting in the other room. Not necessary, she said, but she preferred to get it done before the floor was in for ease. And, he had a feeling that she was avoiding him. Which, after the way he had run his mouth, he couldn't blame her.

Except, he knew that she wasn't completely turned off by the idea of sleeping with him either. No, not completely.

He had seen the interest there. Seeing that little spark in those lovely brown eyes.

She wanted him. That was obvious.

But there was a hesitance to it, and he wasn't quite sure what it was. Unless it was the same hesitancy he was feeling. Knowing that there couldn't be a middle ground.

He didn't particularly want middle ground. Not at the moment. He'd have her on the ground. That would work.

Shit. He really needed to get himself together. Yeah, she was a fantasy, always had been. But, she was also a complication. And there were any number of women in town who wouldn't be complicated. Why was he fascinated by the one who would be? One who had just come back into town?

It was all a holdover from old adolescent feelings. That was all. It was all it could be.

They hadn't exchanged very many words. She couldn't

actually be unique, or special. Not really. Not so quickly. He was too damned old to be getting tied up like this by his hormones.

Twenty-nine and with a lot of experience under his belt. But no matter how many times he repeated that simple truth to himself he still felt... Way the hell too much.

"Would you mind...?"

He turned around and saw her standing in the doorway. She hesitated, tucked a strand of blond hair behind her ear. "Would you mind helping me reach something?"

He looked down at his project, dropped his hammer onto the subfloor and stood up.

"Not at all," he said, his gut tightening.

No pretense. There was no pretense between the two of them. Not at all. Which meant that if the woman wanted sex, she would say so. And if she wanted him to reach something for her, she would say that. So that was it. That was all. And still, heat flooded him.

He followed her into a bedroom, which was clearly an addition, since the ceilings were a hell of a lot taller than any of the other rooms. The slab foundation was exposed, and he imagined this was the next floor-length project.

"I need to get tape around the light fixtures, and I just can't get myself into a position where I can reach them," she said, gesturing to the ladder. "Nothing really works."

"Lucky for you, I'm a bit taller."

"True."

"I've got it." He grabbed a roll of blue tape and began to climb the ladder, applying tape around the perimeter of the first recessed lighting can, before moving to the other.

"My daughters are mad at me," she said.

"Really?"

He was surprised she volunteered that bit of information.

"Yes," she said. "They didn't want to move. They liked living in Hillsboro. Being closer to Portland. There was so much more to do. They had friends there. It's one reason I took so long to come back. They were settled into their schools and… They had friends. But Grace is starting seventh grade, and at that age girls change a lot and have friend drama sometimes anyway. Ava is going into high school. I figured with Ava changing schools, that was the best time, if it was going to happen. And really, I know there's no good time. But I couldn't stay there anymore. There was nothing for me. My parents are here. Gold Valley is my home. I was tired of being in the place I was because of… Because of him. I didn't move there for me. I moved there because he liked living there. And I was just tired of that. Plus, I couldn't afford any houses in the area. So I was just going to be stuck in the rental, and I didn't want that anymore either. I wanted to come home. I wanted to be somewhere that felt like me. The town and the house. And they both think that I've ruined their lives."

He nodded slowly, climbing down the ladder and shifting it so that it was by the next light fixture. "It's my understanding that teenagers and preteens are supposed to feel like you ruined their lives."

"Yeah. I guess so. I remember feeling that way. And then I left home at nineteen and married the first asshole that I fell in love with. So, I was kind of hoping to avoid that sort of thing with my own kids."

"He couldn't have been an asshole that whole time," he said, realizing it wasn't exactly his place to push on this. But she was talking. And he was… He was interested.

"He wasn't. You're right. And actually... He would never have been an asshole if he wasn't in his thirties. If he wasn't a husband and father. He would have been a fun guy. A nice guy, even if he drank a little bit too much. But that kind of stuff isn't attractive on a man that age. Not when you're depending on him."

"I get that."

Really, he understood exactly where she was coming from. There was a reason he hadn't gotten married and had kids. He hadn't been sure he could handle that yet. His life had been serious. Far too serious. All manner of relationship drama with his dad, who had not been ready to get married and settle down. He had been a stable man in many ways, working the ranch his entire life. But he had been a bad husband. He had been a decently involved father, but Calder couldn't help but wonder if part of that was due to the fact that he had sons who had been willing to work the place with him. What would have happened if he had daughters? He had been decent to Chloe, but she had been older, as had their father, when he had married her mother.

If he had been a young man with daughters who had required something other than him to act as foreman more than father, he wasn't sure how that would have gone. And in the end, the fact of the matter was their father had been more their boss than their dad. And that was a difficult thing. Calder had never wanted that for himself. And so he had avoided it. He didn't have a hell of a lot of respect for a man who didn't know himself well enough to know what he should or shouldn't get into.

"He should have stepped up," Calder said.

He shouldn't have said that anymore than he should've

started questioning her about her late husband, but he found he couldn't help himself.

"That simple?" she asked.

He could feel her eyes on him. Not just looking at him, but checking him out. He'd never felt a woman's gaze like that. Like a physical touch.

Damn. He was fighting a hard-on and trying to keep on task and not making it about sex between them. But the problem was her. That she wanted him, too, even if she couldn't admit it.

"Hell yes, I think it's that simple," he said. "If a man has responsibilities he should rise to them. If not, I'm not sure that he's a man."

He climbed down the ladder, stood in front of her and looked at her. Really looked. At the sadness in her eyes, that vulnerability. He wanted to fix that, too. But hell, he knew it wouldn't be as easy as fixing a wooden floor.

"You know, part of me always felt like it was, too," she said, the words soft and choked. "And I have spent years making excuses for him. I did it while he was alive, and even though I've been angry at him in death, I've done it since he died, too. But I... Sometimes I think it would have been so easy. He just needed to grow up. He just needed to quit being selfish. I did it, Calder, why couldn't he? I was young, too. But I took care of the girls, and I worked hard, and I didn't hang out with friends every time I wanted to. And I didn't buy things every time I wanted them. And I quit drinking so much, and I quit staying up late. And I just don't understand why he couldn't. He thought I wasn't fun. He thought I was the one who changed. But I was just being... I was just being the adult. Half the time I felt like I had three children, and I didn't like one of them very much."

She was breathing hard when she finished her rant, her shoulders rising and falling with each labored breath. "And then he went and got himself killed. I can't even grieve him, not really. I was so angry at the pain that he caused. Me, my daughters. More angry than I am sad. Because he was the one who chose to get drunk before he got on the quad. He was the one who was still acting like he was eighteen when we were parents. It's his own fault. It was avoidable." She pounded her hand against her chest, punctuating her words. "And that's a terrible thing to say, I know it. But sometimes I'm just so damn tired of trying to be the mature one. He's not even alive anymore and that's what I'm doing. Making excuses. Trying to cover it. I have to. I can't say anything bad about him in front of the girls… He's gone. And he's their father. And…"

She stopped talking, her brown eyes colliding with his. "I'm tired. I'm tired of doing the right thing. I'm tired of being predictable and organized and mature. I'm tired of my planner."

The air got thick between them, and everything inside Calder went tight. "Maybe I want to do something wrong," she said, the look in her eyes changing, growing more intent.

There was a breath, one moment, where he knew exactly what she was about to do next before she did it. And in that moment he decided a couple of things.

The first was that he was 100 percent here for this.

The second was that he wasn't just going to be her mistake. Wasn't going to be her little rebellion. She was a woman who had given everything to a man who didn't deserve it. She had given him children. She had given him years of hard work and faithfulness, and a hell of a lot more forgiveness and credit than he deserved from the sounds of things.

And Calder didn't want to just be a moment of escape for her.

They could start there. But what he knew in that moment was that he wanted to give her everything her husband hadn't.

Why he knew that with such absolute certainty, he couldn't say.

But he knew it wasn't just lust. He knew it with a kind of baseline certainty he couldn't begin to comprehend.

But Calder was a man who dealt in certainty. And for a hell of a lot of years he had been certain that he didn't want the responsibility of a wife and children. And as the feelings of certainty surrounding Lauren clicked into place, those other truths about himself shifted on its axis. And it didn't even scare him.

That was when she kissed him. It was like an explosion of heat and fire. Like nothing he had ever experienced before. And he had experienced quite a lot.

Then, he let everything else fade into the background. Because the rest would take care of itself. But for now, he was kissing Lauren Bishop.

And he was going to go ahead and glory in that.

CHAPTER FOUR

LAUREN FELT LIKE she was losing her mind. But, she also didn't want to stop.

She had never felt anything like this before. She felt reckless and crazy and wrong, and she wasn't going to do anything to fight against it.

Because Little Calder Reid was *not* little anymore, not at all.

He was all man.

Hot and hard and fixing things in her house.

Telling her all the things she had needed to hear for so long. Things she hadn't known she needed to hear. And he was here. He was here and he wanted her. He'd said that he did. In no uncertain terms, crude and explicit and somehow hot.

Robert had used words like that, and it hadn't felt the same. It felt thoughtless. Like he couldn't be bothered to say something softer, more romantic. Like he couldn't be bothered to seduce her.

When Calder said it, it was like a promise.

A filthy, explicit promise of pleasure.

Like he had used cruder terms because he couldn't help himself. Because he had been driven to it by his desire for her. And maybe that was all her projecting what she needed, but it didn't really matter.

Because this was about feeling. About need.

So she wasn't going to rationalize it. She couldn't. Not even if she wanted to. She grabbed hold of his face, pushing her fingers around through his hair and holding on to him, kissing him deeper. He growled, reversing their positions and backing her against the wall, his hand, large and rough on her face as he angled and took the kiss deeper. Sliding his tongue deep inside her mouth, the friction so hot and wet that it made her tremble.

He braced his other hand on her hip, dragging his thumb slowly back and forth across her rib cage. Her T-shirt was between his touch and her skin, and still, that slow movement of his thumb made her shiver. Made her tremble.

She felt it. Everywhere. She didn't even know how that worked.

This was crazy. She didn't do things like this. Ever. But hell, she was now. Why not? There was no one here. It was like an insane, ridiculous fantasy, except it couldn't be.

Because he was too hot, hard and pushing her into the drywall to be a fantasy.

She wouldn't be surprised if there was a little Lauren print left behind. At least he hadn't backed her up against the wall she had recently painted. Because that would be hard to explain. Showing up at her parents' house later tonight with a paint splotch in her hair.

But of course he hadn't done that. His every movement was too smooth. Too practiced.

Except it didn't feel like it. It felt raw and real and just for her. And she needed that.

She needed something to be about her.

Because the bottom line was every single one of those things in her planner was something she had to do. They didn't make her feel good. They just had to be done. She didn't want to be painting at eight thirty at night.

She just was.

But this was more than a box she had to check off. *She* needed to get done. She wanted to do this. With him.

And dammit, she was going to.

Because she didn't want to be a widow. She didn't want to be a single mom. It had never been the plan.

So why couldn't she have this? In the long line of shit she hadn't signed up for, why couldn't this be one of the things? Having a moment of wild, uncontrolled lust with Calder Reid.

It was a hell of a lot better than any of the other random surprises life had thrown at her.

At least this one had a nice ass.

There was no more thinking after that, because he pushed his hand beneath the hem of her shirt, and that calloused skin made contact with the sensitive flesh there, and suddenly, she couldn't speak, let alone think. She was melting. Her center completely liquid with her desire for him.

It was all going so fast, and thank God, honestly. Because if he went slower she might start thinking. She didn't want to think. She wanted this. She had never been this insane. Ever. His hands were electric, skating over her skin and leaving a trail of sparks behind. He pushed her shirt up, dragged it over her head, and she had a moment of insecurity.

Her stomach wasn't flat.

But those hot blue eyes didn't go to her stomach, but to her breasts. And what she saw there was pure male appreciation. The kind she hadn't seen in...

Well, she had been celibate since her husband's death.

And before that, it had been the two of them together for more than a decade. He might have been turned on by her, in the way that men were turned on by women. But he didn't…appreciate her body. Not like that. Calder's eyes said more with a hot look than her husband had said with about a thousand words.

And maybe she shouldn't compare the two men. But, it was unavoidable to an extent. She hadn't been with anyone other than Robert in a very long time. And it was difficult not to revel in the differences.

He groaned, unbuttoning her jeans, and drawing the zipper down slowly.

Giddy satisfaction went through her when he shoved his hand down between her legs, into her panties, his fingers insistent and quick, finding that sensitized bundle of nerves between her slick folds with unerring accuracy.

He stroked her.

Made her shake.

Made her cry out.

He was good. So, so good. There was a wealth of experience and knowledge in that touch. With each roll of his wrist. That man knew just what he was doing. Just how to touch her. All she could do was hang on to those broad shoulders as he coaxed a response from her that she wasn't sure she'd known her body was capable of. He moved his thumb over her, then pressed two fingers deep inside her. She gasped at the invasion. It had been a while. But it was good. So good. He moved his hand in a steady rhythm, drawing his fingers in and out of her body, making her feel more. Better.

Making her feel like she might break apart into a thousand pieces if he didn't make good on the climax he was promising.

She looked up, her eyes colliding with his, and she broke. The sound that escaped her lips would have been humiliating if she weren't so completely lost in the shattering pleasure overtaking her.

She was shaking, and not entirely in control of her actions when she reached out and grabbed hold of his T-shirt, ripping it over his head. She needed to see him. Needed to touch him. The intense climax had done nothing to dampen her desire. If anything, it made her a crazy woman. She wanted more. She wanted everything.

She ran her hands over his muscles, over all that hot, hard skin. The chest hair there. Lord. He was just so much a man. She had never touched a man who looked like this. Had never even known to fantasize about it.

Women aren't visual.

She'd lost track of the amount of times her mother had said that when she had cautioned her on the clothing that she wore. Women aren't visual. Men are. That was why women had to be careful. About what they wore, and how they acted.

Well.

She felt pretty damn visual right now. And tactile. And desperate for sex. Raw, hard sex. She needed his cock inside her. She needed it more than she needed to breathe.

She didn't recognize this creature he had transformed her into. She didn't care. She loved it. She felt wanton and wild and utterly out of control.

She hadn't put this in the damn planner.

And it felt glorious. She moved her fingers over his washboard stomach. And she didn't care if she wasn't perfect. He was. And he was all for her. He pushed her jeans down her legs, dragged her panties down with them. And she didn't feel self-conscious anymore. How could she? Especially when she reached out and covered his denim-clad legs with her hand, taking the evidence of his desire for her in hand. He was so big. So hard. For her. How could she feel anything but accomplished right now?

She unbuckled his jeans, and his arousal sprang free. She wrapped her fingers around him, felt that hot, hard length in her hands.

He was everything she hadn't realized she was missing.

She pumped his erection, once, twice. He groaned, his beautiful head falling back, his lips going slack.

She needed him inside her. Now. More than she needed to breathe.

She needed...

A sinking feeling hollowed out her stomach. "Condoms."

"I have them," he said. He reached down, grabbed hold of his jeans and produced his wallet, pulling out a plastic packet. "I promise they weren't for you."

She laughed. "Ordinarily that would be offensive."

"Oh, I know. But I wanted to make sure that you knew I wasn't plotting this."

"Just part of your average cowboy survival kit."

"Yes'm. I've always got a Swiss Army knife because you never know when you might need to repair something. And condoms, because you never know when a nice lady might need a good orgasm."

She couldn't even be mad. She was glad. Glad that he was kind of a slut. Glad that he had brought protection. Glad that he knew what the hell he was doing. When he tore the packet open, and wrapped his hand around himself as he smoothed the latex over his length, she gloried in everything about him. Every last inch.

He pressed her up against the wall then, kissing her hard, grabbing her wrists and drawing her arms above her head, pinning them hard against the drywall as he positioned himself between her legs. "I figure the floor's a little hard," he said, using his free hand to grip her hip, then sliding it down her thigh, lifting it up so that she was open to him. He arched his hips forward, pressing the head of his arousal into her slick entrance. "This will do just fine."

He thrust up inside her, and she gasped. He was big. So, so big.

She loved it. Because she felt him everywhere. Fully possessed.

And as he began to pound inside her, as the pleasure began to build in her again, she lost herself completely. There were no worries. There were no more appointments. There was nothing but this. She was just a woman. And he was just a man. She was all feeling. That heavy length pounding hard and deep. Fingernails dug into his skin. Slick sweat and desire.

He shuddered out his release, slamming into her one last time, and she broke, her internal muscles pulsing around him as she came harder than she could ever remember coming before.

She felt like she was outside her body. Outside herself. Because good, sensible Lauren Bishop would never screw a guy up against the wall that she didn't even know.

Knowing him seventeen years ago did not count.

And yet, as he stared deep into her eyes, still buried inside her, she couldn't escape the feeling that he might know her better than she knew herself.

That he might know her in ways no one else ever had.

He released his hold on her, slowly, withdrawing from her.

"I don't even know what to say," he said.

"Don't say anything," she said. "I'm… I'm sorry," she said, a rush of regret filling her.

What had she just done? She had just acted like a giant hormone. That wasn't her. It felt perfect for a minute. Liberating and everything. And now it just felt… humiliating.

"That was a mistake."

He looked at her, lifted a brow. "I haven't even taken the condom off yet and you're telling me it was a mistake?"

Her skin flushed, her face going hot. He was right about that. He was standing in front of her, still totally naked, with all of the evidence of what had just occurred…right there.

"I just… That isn't me. I'm responsible. I'm…"

"What about that was irresponsible?"

"It just is," she insisted. "How would I ever explain behavior like that to my children?"

"The way I see it, Lauren, you're an adult and you don't owe your kids an explanation for things like that."

"My mother would be disappointed in me."

"You don't owe your mother an explanation either. What we do in the privacy of…your almost home is our business."

"I…"

It wasn't that she hadn't disappointed her parents before. Running off and marrying Robert hadn't exactly been a popular decision. They had accepted it, sure. There were no other options at the end of the day. What had been done had been done. And when he had died, her parents had been very supportive of her. They had spent a lot of time at her house. They had stayed there for weeks at a time helping her get affairs in order, helping her take care of the girls. It wasn't that their love had ever been conditional. But all the things inside her that had been unspoken, all the anger at him… She knew that they had felt the same—that Robert had brought it on himself. And that Lauren was grieving because she had made a bad decision when she was nineteen years old. That all that pain had really been self-inflicted in many ways. Because she should have chosen more wisely from the start. She should have gone to college. She should have done something with her life that wasn't just running off and being impetuous for love. A love that she had clearly felt more strongly than her husband ever had because if he had loved her even half as much as she had loved him he would have changed. For her. For the girls.

And the fact that all of that was tied up in this stolen moment made her angry in a lot of ways. But it was also unavoidable.

"I can't just do things like this."

"Why? You need the house fixed. And that was fun. Why can't we do both?"

"Because I can't… There's no room in my life for this. There's no room in my life for… I can't play around with man children. Okay?"

"Man children?"

"Yes. You're… What are you?"

"Twenty-nine," he said.

"Exactly. Twenty-nine. I'm thirty-five years old, Calder, I have children. I have responsibilities. I can't just… I can't just screw around with some guy because he's hot."

"Why? Why the hell can't you? You're not just a mother. You're a woman. And you don't live for your parents, and you can't live just for your children."

"That's where you're wrong. Somebody has to live for those girls, Calder. God knows my husband never did."

"Are they taken care of right now?"

"Yes… But…"

"But nothing. Look, Lauren, if that wasn't good for you and you don't want to do it again, fine. But if this is just a bunch of excuses… I'm going to call you out."

"It was good. You know that."

"Then I don't see what the problem is."

"You don't understand because you don't have any real responsibilities to anyone but yourself. And that's what I mean by *man children*."

"That's not fair. Just because I've never had that kind of responsibility doesn't mean I couldn't handle it if I did. It doesn't mean I'm too terminally selfish to try to understand your situation."

"My experience indicates that it doesn't happen that way."

"Your experience is limited. And unfortunate. I'm really sorry that you had a bad experience in your marriage. But that's not every man. And it sure as hell isn't me. I'm attracted to you," he said. "That's obvious."

That declaration sent a wave of desire rolling over her. And it shouldn't have. Because she should be taken care of. She hadn't had an orgasm like that in… Ever, maybe. And every orgasm she had in the past few years had been self-induced.

So she should honestly be set for the next little while,

but already, she wanted more. He was naked, they were both naked, and they were yelling at each other. It was weird. She was upset. She felt unsettled. And she still felt turned on. She didn't know what to make of any of it.

And it was very hard to argue against Calder right now. Because he was beautiful. Because he wanted her. Because he made her feel good. Like a woman. And not like... Well, a walking to-do list.

"My time is so... Stretched. I work, I work on this house, I keep appointments for myself, for my children. And then with every moment I have I try to spend it with them. I don't have a whole bunch of moments to trade around. To devote to... This. So when I say there's no point... Everything in my life has a point."

"What about you?" he asked. "What about *you* feeling good? What about you having a little bit of fun?"

"I can't be like him. They can't have another parent who only thinks about their own pleasure. They just can't."

"There is middle ground, Lauren. There is. There's more than just devoting every spare moment to other people, and thinking of no one but yourself. Your kids deserve to have a happy mother. And you deserve to be happy."

"And you think that a little bit of sex with you is going to make me happy?"

That was bitchy. And completely uncalled for.

But, the corner of his mouth lifted upward, and he looked her over. "Yeah. I think I could do a pretty damn good job of making you happy, Lauren Bishop."

"I'm sorry. You're going to have to find another sad, lonely woman to devote your time and abs to."

He tilted his head to the side, frowning slightly. "My abs, huh? I assumed my dick was the star of the show."

Her lips twitched. Well. She'd never think of him as *Little* Calder Reid ever again. That was for sure. "All men do. Don't get me wrong. It's a really good one."

"Oh, I'm aware of that."

She laughed. And she didn't feel like laughing at all. At least, she hadn't a second ago. She didn't know how she could be angry, turned on and amused all at the same time.

Something thick and hot stretched between them. Need. Oh, she wanted him. She wished she could have him. But there was…no point.

"I just can't," she said, finally. "I'm sorry."

"Don't apologize to me. Apologize to yourself."

He began to get dressed, and she felt like an idiot standing there naked. But, she wasn't sure she could bend over and move around to get dressed in front of him either. Things bunched up and rolled when she did that. She would rather stand there in more prime positioning naked.

Conversely, while Calder moved around, nothing jiggled, or rolled. Muscles shifted and bunched, smooth golden skin moving over that tight physique.

And damn, that man's ass.

It was a thing of beauty.

The man was like a sculpture that had been brought to life.

She wished she had touched his butt more. Wished that she had looked at him longer. She wished they'd had a bed.

Sex against the wall was all well and good. But there

was so much they hadn't… Done. So much they wouldn't get to do because she was being practical.

It was like finding the world's best playground and only going on the swing. And only swinging once.

It was depressing.

Completely dressed, Calder straightened and treated her to a grin. "I'm going to go finish that floor."

She blinked. "What?"

"I'm going to finish the floor. And then tomorrow I'll do the flooring here."

"But I just… I just said we weren't having sex anymore."

"You also told me how stressed you are. And explained this whole situation. I'm going to help you, Lauren. I already said I was doing it for nothing. I didn't have sex with you as payment. I wanted to have sex with you. I'd do it again. But if you don't want to, that's fine. You better understand this about me. If I say I'm going to do something, I will damn well do it. I'm not playing games with you. If I start a job, I finish it." It was the conviction in his voice that shocked her. The absolute certainty. He held her gaze. Unflinching. "I started this. I'm finishing it."

He moved toward the door, then paused. He reached out, gripping her chin, and tilted her face up toward him. Then he dipped his head low and kissed her, firm and hard on the mouth. He lifted his head, those blue eyes boring into hers. "You know my feelings. If you change your mind, you can count on the fact they won't have changed."

"You don't know that," she whispered.

"I do. Yes, I'm twenty-nine. I'm younger than you.

I've never been married. I don't have kids. But I know my damned mind."

Then he walked out of the room, and a few minutes later, she heard the sound of him pounding boards together.

And she honestly felt like the pages of her planner had been torn out and scattered all over the place. Like she had no idea what her world was anymore.

Or what she wanted.

And the strangest part about all of it was that she wasn't even that sad about it.

CHAPTER FIVE

WHEN LAUREN GOT up the next morning she had half a mind to try to avoid her mother. But, it was impossible. As soon as she got up, she saw her mother in the kitchen. Her daughter Ava was already up, sitting at the table with a mug of hot chocolate and a piece of buttered toast.

"Good morning," Lauren said.

Ava looked up at her, then back down at her breakfast. The stony, teenage silence was getting old. It had been all she had gotten from her daughter since they'd moved back to Gold Valley.

"Nice to see you, too, Ava," she said, determinedly overbright. "It's a beautiful day outside. I hope you do something other than lie on your bed and morosely text."

"There's nothing to do here," she said.

"If you're bored," Lauren's mother put in, "you can always pick up a few extra chores."

Ava made a growling sound in the back of her throat and picked up her toast, devoting all of her focus to it.

"Don't growl at your grandmother," Lauren said.

Her mother gave Lauren a sympathetic look but didn't make any comments to Ava. Delores Bishop would not have held her peace at all, had Lauren growled at her when she was a teenager.

But, her parents had definitely mellowed a little bit as grandparents. She supposed that was the way of the world. It stuck in her craw sometimes, though. Because she certainly hadn't been allowed to have moods and attitudes.

And really, if her mother had chastised Ava, Lauren would have probably resented her stepping in and co-opting her role as parent. So there was that.

"What's your plan today?" her mom asked.

"I have to go back over to the house. There's flooring to finish. And once that's done, we can actually schedule the inspection. Then, hopefully we'll get a close date and... All of our things can come out of storage."

"You did the right thing moving back," her mom said. And, Lauren supposed that made up for her ease on Ava.

"I know," Lauren said.

Unbidden, flashes of last night burst into her head. All the wrong things she had done with Calder Reid.

Her mother would *not* be in support of that.

But it didn't matter because Lauren wasn't going to be doing that again. No, she was not.

"I'll take the girls downtown," her mom said. "Maybe we can do some school shopping."

Lauren imagined that Ava would have a lot of opinions about school anywhere other than Portland. But she was going to have to deal with it.

"Thank you," Lauren said. "For helping out. If I had to do all of this by myself, I don't think I'd be able to."

Ava got up, saying nothing as she shuffled out of the room.

"Hopefully, someday my kids won't hate me," Lauren said.

Her mom sighed. "*Someday*, they won't. But, you didn't think that I knew what was best for you either."

Ouch. That stuck hard in Lauren's ribs. Even harder

because in many ways, Robert had been the wrong choice, and her mother had been right. But if she hadn't married him, she wouldn't have Ava and Grace, and she didn't regret that part of her life one bit. Which made it all… Complicated.

Which, she supposed, was actually a decent thing to realize.

That sometimes her kids would do something she didn't approve of.

That they might even be bad choices, or not the ideal choices. And there would be good in that anyway.

Her mom and dad, to their credit, hadn't cut her off for what she did. They'd come to her wedding. They'd dealt with Robert's hard-drinking friends and relatives who'd felt that was required at a wedding.

Once they'd realized her mind was made up, they'd supported her.

"I loved him," Lauren said. "I mean, I wasn't just rebelling against you. Just so you know."

Her mom, turned to her, hugged her quickly. "I know that. I mean, I didn't know that for the first couple of years. But when you actually married him, had the first baby…"

"I would've stayed with him," Lauren said quickly.

I know," her mom said. "And you would have been unhappy."

She thought of last night again. Of Calder. Not of the sex, but the way he'd worked on the house. The way he'd promised to finish what he'd started. He was so different from her late husband. "Not with everything," she protested. "Not with the girls."

"You deserve better than that."

"Why?" Lauren asked, going over to the coffeemaker.

"I didn't make the right choices. I didn't choose the right man. I chose the exact kind of man you warned me about. So, I'm not exactly sure why I deserve happiness now. Don't you reap what you sow?"

"Yes," her mom said. "I believe that you do. But I also believe that you don't deserve to be miserable for your entire life. Should you suffer forever?"

"I thought I was going to have to."

Her mom shook her head. "I was strict with you because I worried about you. And some of my fears for you did come true. And I very much didn't want you to lose your husband. I especially didn't want the girls to lose their father. He was…"

"He wasn't quite bad enough to spit on his grave," Lauren said. "But… Now I realize that things are easier without him. And I feel bad. I feel guilty. I'm glad that I got back here. Glad that I'm not with him. I don't think I would've been brave enough to leave ever. Because it's not like he was abusive. He was just…"

"You didn't love him."

Lauren shook her head. "Not anymore."

"No matter how it happened, that part of your life is over now. Don't you deserve something better? Something different?"

She couldn't take those words on board. Not now.

The sad truth was, as she stood there in her mother's kitchen, all she could really think was that she deserved to be exactly where she was standing. Really, she deserved to be married to Robert still, while he lived. To have to live with her choices for the rest of her life.

This was actually a little bit of deliverance that hadn't required any action, bravery or thought on her part.

If she was a little bit lonely, if her girls were angry at her...

Well, those were the seeds she had planted.

It was all fine and good for her mother to say she wanted Lauren to feel differently now, but she hadn't raised her to feel differently. She had raised her to think deeply about her choices, and to understand that what she did in the moment was going to impact her future.

And Lauren hadn't listened. Because it had been inconvenient. Because it had been prescriptive, and unfair. And Lauren had been convinced that she knew better.

And still, standing there in the kitchen she could get back inside the head of that eighteen-year-old girl who had basically run away from home to marry that charming redneck she'd met on the beach. The one who'd stolen her heart and her virginity in very short order. Of course it had felt unfair when her parents had told her she was being crazy. That she needed to think about her future. That her future might not be the easiest with a man like him.

But she had felt like they were Romeo and Juliet. Destined and doomed all at the same time, and she had felt like she had no choice but to follow her heart. She'd had such pure conviction, even now she could feel it echoing inside her.

Wasn't it right to fight for love?

But she had been wrong. Catastrophically.

Even three years on the other side of it she was still sorting through what all of that meant.

Well, she had decided what it meant. That she couldn't just follow her heart. That she needed to make plans and follow those instead. That she needed to think.

That she needed to think about other people, and a

whole lot less about what she felt she deserved. What she felt she knew.

"I better go," she said.

"Do you want your dad to come over and help?"

Right. And explain the giant, burly cowboy working in the house.

"You know he can't get down there onto the flooring. He'll never get back up again. We already discussed this." That was true.

"Yes," her mom said. "Although, he would never admit it."

"No. Which is why it's just better if I let him have his pride and enlist you guys to watch the girls."

"Yes, you're right about that. But I worry about you."

"I've got it handled," she said.

But as she gathered her things, and headed out toward her car, she wondered if she had anything handled at all.

BY THE TIME Lauren showed up, Calder had been waiting in the driveway with doughnuts and coffee for twenty minutes.

She pulled up and stepped out of the car, her blond hair blowing over her face, her expression cautious when she saw him. And his stomach felt like it had been kicked by a horse.

"I brought breakfast," he said.

"That was… Really nice of you but I already…" She shook her head. "I guess I didn't. I had coffee. But I wasn't really feeling hungry." She eyed the doughnuts. "I'm feeling a little bit hungrier now."

So was he. Starving. But, not for doughnuts. For her. He really, really didn't want for things to be finished between them. Once wasn't enough. He didn't think there would be an *enough*, not with her.

Of course, he had to sort out what that meant. Because it wasn't just her.

Though, here it felt like it.

It was tempting to believe he was making a place here just for the two of them.

He waited for that idea to terrify him. But it didn't.

He wondered if his dad had felt confident every time he'd found a woman he wanted to marry. And his father had done it more than once. He wondered if his father had ever once questioned his own authority or motivations. His own judgment. He doubted the old man ever had.

And he should have.

It made Calder wonder if he should question himself a bit more right now than he was.

"Let's go inside," he said. "I think doughnuts and coffee are best had on a blanket."

"Why are you being so nice to me?" she asked, cautiously reaching out and taking the cup of coffee from his hand. Their fingertips connected, and desire stirred in his stomach.

"I like you," he said. "And I haven't said that to a girl since seventh grade."

"Hey," she said as they walked toward the house, their shoulders bumping together. "I thought you liked *me* when you were in seventh grade."

"I did," he responded. "But you were a little bit out of my league. I figured I would aim for an easier target."

She shook her head. "Then you say things like that, and you sound a lot more like a regular old guy."

"Yeah, I am."

They paused in the doorway, looking at each other.

He was just a regular old guy. Not actually any better than her late husband, not in a measurable sense. It wasn't like he had ever been put to the test. Wasn't like he'd ever been asked to give up anything he enjoyed in order to be a better partner.

He'd never been in a real, long-term relationship.

In the abstract, he didn't see the appeal in it.

Lauren Bishop wasn't abstract.

"I think the world is full of regular guys who try to do just a little bit better when they meet a woman who's extraordinary," he said. He wasn't sure who the hell had put those words in his mouth, because he wasn't any kind of poet. But they were true enough.

She gave a little half role to her eyes, then looked down, as the two of them took their seats on the blanket, and she opened up the box of doughnuts, purely as a distraction method, he was sure. "And what makes you think I'm extraordinary?"

"This house is a pretty good indicator. The way you're working on it. The way you're working for your kids. You know, I love my dad, Lauren. I really did. I do. But I don't think he was going to win any father of the year awards. What he did he did for the ranch. He didn't do it for us. As far as the women he married… He did that for himself. What he found with Chloe's mother… That was something else. It was something special. It just so happened that she was an extraordinary woman. But make no mistake, as someone who lived through being abandoned by his real mother, someone who lived with a father who was distant at best… I see that what you're doing here is extraordinary. For your kids. And just from the little bit you told me about what you've been through…"

"So your attraction to me is still... A caregiver thing?" She wrinkled her nose.

He laughed. "No. Although, I guess you couldn't prove different."

"Thank you. For everything. You're being astonishingly nice."

"It makes me pretty damned sad that the act of me bringing you coffee and a couple doughnuts seems extraordinarily nice. You deserve better than that."

"There's been a lot of talk today about what I deserve."

"Oh yeah? It's pretty early in the morning for there to have been a lot of talk at all."

"My mother. She thinks... That I need to forgive myself."

"Do you?" He met her gaze and she looked away.

"I don't know. Though, I'm not sure that I'm punishing myself so much as... Just trying to make sure I don't make the same mistakes twice."

He thought of everything she'd told him about her husband. And he turned his next words over carefully. Because she wasn't a woman he could play with, and he didn't want to. He wanted...

His life had been fine until she had shown up. Totally fine.

And now it felt empty. And the only moment he felt like there was something real, something full, was when he was sitting with her.

"The thing is, at any point your husband could have changed. He could have fixed those problems. You did what you could. You make it sound like you were the only adult, the only person, involved in that relationship. And that just isn't true. He could have done better for you. He could have done better for Ava and for Grace. Those are not your mistakes. They're his."

Her daughters whom he hadn't even met. And why should he have met them? He'd been in her life for two days. And they might have had sex, but that didn't mean anything. In his world, historically it hadn't meant anything at all.

So why did it now?

He couldn't exactly say why. He wasn't sure he cared about the *why* right now. All that mattered was Lauren.

"I mean, you're right. He could have changed. But he didn't. And, as a result, my daughters…"

"You have your daughters," he said. "And it sounds to me like you've done your very best to give them the best life you can. You're a good mom."

She huffed out a laugh. "You've never even see me with them."

"It doesn't matter. I bet you lose your temper with them a lot. I bet that sometimes it's frustrating, and sometimes it's fun. But…you handle it."

"How can you possibly know that?"

"Because here you are," he said. "Handling all this."

Silence fell between them and she picked up a doughnut, taking a bite out of it and chewing slowly. He was transfixed. By the way her pale pink lips closed around the soft treatment. By the way she chewed. He wanted her. Bad.

But he also wanted her to know that this was different. Not just another fling. Not just another *anything*.

She looked up at him, caught him watching her. And he smiled.

She looked away, color bleeding into her cheeks. He didn't know what the hell was going on with him.

She was blushing, and his chest felt tight watching for more signs that she might be affected by what was happening between them.

There was a little crumb of doughnut on her lower lip. He reached out, brushing it off with his thumb. She ducked her head, and his cock started to feel heavy. Her skin was so soft beneath his. He wanted to keep touching her, but he didn't want to push it either. He lifted his thumb to his own lips, licked the crumb away.

"Calder…"

But then, she seemed to think better of thinking. Instead, she started to lean forward, her lips achingly close to his.

She jumped, a buzzing sound cutting through the moment.

"I need to get this," she said, pulling her phone out of her purse. She looked at the caller ID and frowned, then slid her finger across the screen. "Hello?"

She listened, strange, daunting horror going over her expression. "When? When was the last time you saw her? Did she take her phone? She's not answering?"

Calder stood, ready to spring into action, because he knew exactly what it sounded like, and he was ready to fix it.

"I can track it. As long as she didn't turn it off or something. I'll handle it." She sighed heavily, her hand on her forehead. "Just let me try this. Stay with Grace." She hung up the phone. Her hands were shaking, her face pale. "Ava is gone."

"That's the fourteen-year-old?" he asked.

"Yes. She's gone. She ran away. At least, that's what we assume." She stood up and put her bag over her shoulder. "Hopefully she didn't run away with a man she met on the internet, but what do I even know? She ran away. I guess I don't know her very well at all."

"You said you could track her phone."

"Yes," she said, already heading for the door.

"I'll drive."

"You don't have to…"

"Lauren," he said, his voice stern. "You use your phone to track hers, see if you can find out where she is. I'm going to drive you *wherever* that is. If we can't find it, I'm going to drive you to the police. We're going to look until we find her."

"You don't have to do this," she said.

"I fucking want to," he said, the words hard and definitive in the space.

He thought she might argue, but she didn't. Instead her lips firmed into a grim line and she looked down at her phone.

They walked out to his truck, and he opened the door for her. She was swiping at her cell screen, doing something to track the phone he assumed. He wasn't really up on all that kind of stuff. It wasn't like he and his brothers had a shared family plan.

Mostly, his use of phones was limited to swiping right.

"It's not coming up," she said, her tone flat and shaking. He could tell she was trying her best to say calm but was about one second away from losing it completely.

He pulled out of the driveway, indecisive about where to turn.

"What does it say?" he asked.

"It just says that her phone is offline. But I can't believe that she'd keep it offline. She texts her friends all the time. I'm not really totally sure she knows that I can track her with it. She's fourteen. She's not a mastermind.

I know that I've used this feature to find it for her when she misplaced it…"

"It could just be spotty service," he said. "Out here it's not always great."

"What if she's hitchhiking? What if she got in a car with someone? What if she was meeting someone?"

"We'll handle all that if we find out it's the case. Right now, we don't know anything. And you need to breathe."

"Don't tell me to be calm," she snapped.

"I won't tell you to be calm, Lauren," he said, reaching his hand out and pressing it over her thigh. "I just told you to breathe. You have to keep breathing, okay?"

"Oh, there it is," she said, holding her phone up to her face. "I can see it. On that…" She was zooming in frantically on the screen, and he stole it from her. He zoomed back out. "Highway 62," he said, keeping one hand and one eye on the wheel while he glanced at the phone. "Past…" He zoomed in slightly. "Past Get Out of Dodge. So, that's up the road apiece. It doesn't look like she's driving."

"She's just walking on the side of the road?"

"There are some woods to walk in. She might be just off the road. But, we can find her."

"Thank you," she said. "I'm not safe to drive."

"Of course you aren't." He turned left. "We'll find her soon. I promise. She's not far away."

"I can't believe she would do this. I don't know what she's thinking. I knew that she was mad at me, but I thought she understood. It's not… It's not a democracy. This is a dictatorship. I'm not going to… Not going to be dictated to by a fourteen-year-old who doesn't understand…" There were tears in her voice, the words growing thick. "Who doesn't understand that I was going to go crazy if I stayed there. I couldn't live that life anymore."

He didn't know jack about kids. But he knew what it was like to grow up in a house where parents made mystifying decisions. He knew what it was like to feel helpless. Like you couldn't fix the damage happening around you. "Maybe you should talk to her about that."

"All she has left of her father are memories of him. I can't ruin them."

"The fact that you would ruin his memory by telling the truth is his own fault. That's called a legacy." His chest tightened, awareness filtering through him that what he was saying applied to him in many ways, too. "People shouldn't have to behave themselves talking about you after you die. You should do enough good things that they have good things to say."

"He's her father."

"And I bet she remembers the reality of the situation. She was what... Eleven when he died? I'm sure she saw some of it."

Lauren sighed heavily, her eyes fixed on the trees outside the window. "I know you're probably right. That kills me. It kills me because I did love him. In the beginning. It kills me because I wanted a better father for my girls. And... It would be really nice if we could just rewrite it. He's not here. What's the harm?"

"The harm is to you, and even though you keep acting like that doesn't mean anything, it does, baby. It does. *You* matter."

She swallowed hard, her breath stuttering as she sucked in deep.

"Can you refresh her location?" he asked.

"Are we close?"

"Yes. We're getting pretty close."

She studied her phone carefully. "It hasn't moved much."

He nodded, going slowly. "That means that she's definitely walking." He looked into the trees, keeping an eye out for something. Anything.

And then he saw it. A figure in a bright white jacket, blond head bent low, loose strands of hair blowing in the breeze. A pink knit hat on her head. Her arms were crossed, and she was wearing a backpack.

"There she is," he said, pulling off the road quickly. And Lauren was out of the truck like a shot.

"Ava!" She stumbled toward the woods. "Ava Marie."

But once she reached her, she didn't yell. Instead she grabbed hold of her daughter and pulled her up against her chest, crying, broken and miserable, and he didn't feel like he had a right to witness the moment, but there he was all the same. And that was when it clicked into place. Every bit of it made sense. Because he didn't feel like he was standing on the outside of this, even if he should have.

This was *his*. This whole situation.

And this was why—this unfiltered display of who she was down to her soul—this was why Lauren was special.

She *loved*.

And he wanted some of that. Just a bit. For himself.

He wanted to fix this. And he wanted her to love him.

How many times had he wanted the same in his own life? His father had looked for a quick fix in marriages, and long hours worked on the ranch. He had never looked to Calder. Calder wanted to fix this. He could. He cared enough to.

"I was scared to death," Lauren said, holding Ava's

shoulders and looking into her eyes. "What were you thinking?"

"I don't want to be here," Ava said, her tone full of anger and the kind of fear that he recognized. That fear teenagers carried when they realized too late the kinds of consequences their actions might have had. When you can only stand back in awe and terror at what you had done, because your brain had finally caught up with your emotions.

"Where were you going?" Lauren asked.

"Back to my friend's house. I figured when I got close enough I'd call Sarah's mom and have her come get me."

"And Sarah's mom would have just sent you back."

"I know," Ava said, angry tears in her voice now. "I know that. But I thought maybe... I just..."

"I can't go back," Lauren said. "I'm sorry if you don't understand that. But that's not my home."

"Well, it's mine," Ava returned, defiant.

"I know that it has been. I promise that we're going to go back and visit. I do. But I needed to be with my parents. You need to be with me. We've lost enough, Ava. And I couldn't live in that place where we had that other life. I couldn't deal with the reminders. I have to move on. I have to get away from my sadness. From my anger."

"Anger?" Ava asked. "What are you mad about?"

He watched, as Lauren took a fortifying breath. Making the decision. "I'm so angry at your dad, honey. I'm angry at him for being irresponsible. I'm angry at him for not being there for us more when he was alive. And I'm angry at him because no matter how much I thought he could've done better, I still miss him. Mostly for you. Mostly for Grace. But it would be better if he's here, and he isn't. I just couldn't take all that anymore."

Ava said nothing, her head bent low. Then she took a breath, her shoulders shaking.

"Do you know what the worst thing is?" Ava asked, her voice small. "It's that… As long as we were still there in the house in Hillsboro… It wasn't that different with him gone. Because he was never home anyway. And he never did anything with us. So… As long as we were in that house it seemed like he might still walk in. And I kind of wanted him to. Even though… I know he didn't come to school plays and things. But he was my dad."

"I know," Lauren said. "I know he was. And he will always have a special place in my heart for that reason." She cleared her throat. "I think it's better, though, if we don't live thinking that he might walk in."

"I miss everyone," Ava said, her tone full of misery.

"I know. We'll make friends here. And if you don't… If you don't we'll go back."

"But you just said you can't live there."

Lauren nodded. "I know. But if you are miserable, I'll be able to find a way to move back. We'll find a different house. We'll make it different enough." She sighed heavily. "You have to talk to me. Don't just go taking off. You *scared* me. I'm just thankful we found you as quickly as we did."

"I was just angry," she said. "I didn't think."

"Why don't we get in the truck?" Calder asked, conscious of the fact that he was witnessing this and he maybe shouldn't be.

Suddenly, it was as if Ava saw him for the first time.

"Who's that?" she asked.

"This is Calder Reid," Lauren said. "I used to babysit him."

Ava looked him up and down. "Really? He doesn't look younger than you."

"I am," he confirmed. "As a matter of fact."

"He's been helping get the house ready," Lauren said, overexplaining in his estimation. He doubted Ava really cared.

"Oh," Ava said.

"It's very nice of him. There's a lot of work to do."

"Yeah," Ava agreed. "That is really nice."

They got into his truck, the three of them, Lauren right next to him, her leg brushing against his. He wanted to touch her, offer comfort, but he had a feeling that with Ava in the car that would be extremely unwelcome.

"I'll drop you back off at your car," he said. "And, I'll go inside and start working."

"You don't have to," she said.

"I'm going to, though," he said, making sure his tone offered no chance to argue.

She said nothing for a moment. Probably because she was trying to figure out a way to argue with him.

"Thank you," she finally managed.

They took the rest of the drive in silence, and when they arrived at the house, Ava and Lauren got into Lauren's car. Calder went into the house, surveying all the work that needed to be done. He could do this. Do this for her.

This was different.

She was different. And he felt different with her.

He had a feeling that was the last thing in the world she'd want to hear.

So he was just going to have to keep on showing her.

CHAPTER SIX

LAUREN WAS EXHAUSTED by the time she was finished talking with Ava.

Ava tearfully promised not to do anything like that again. And Lauren, for her part, had tried to be honest with her daughter, trying to explain why she had needed a fresh start so badly.

She and Ava had cried together, and then she'd asked Grace to come and talk with them. They'd shared memories about Robert. Good and bad. Lauren had been careful, but she did try to come up with a way to honestly express why the situation with their father was complicated.

The fact of the matter was Robert had died driving his four-wheeler while under the influence. The death was preventable.

She needed to address that responsibility and choices mattered. She couldn't just protect him and not use that to teach them. She had also tried to impress upon them that whatever they felt, it was okay. She was angry, but she also loved him. He was their father, and he would always be that. No one and nothing could change it.

She'd talked to her mother after, and cried more. She didn't have time to be in the middle of an emotional meltdown but she also couldn't ignore it all anymore either.

If this was going to be a fresh start, then it needed to be new. Open.

She also needed to go to her house and deal with Calder and all of the work still to be done. The sooner they could be in their house, the sooner everything would be fixed. Maybe.

It was so tempting to believe that. So tempting to believe that this one conversation might be the end.

Her rational self knew that wasn't true. Her rational self knew that this was just one conversation of many that they would need to have. A part of her wanted to believe that for now things were settled.

She thought about that all the way back to the house.

Calder's truck was still there. She honestly couldn't believe it. He had said he was going to stay and work, but... It had been hours. She was sure he would've left. She didn't understand this unwavering devotion he seemed to have to fixing everything.

It was alien to her. This kind of caring.

If he wanted sex, surely there were easier ways to get it. With a younger, more beautiful woman who wasn't carrying her amount of baggage.

Women would line up to lick those abs.

God knew she would.

She didn't deserve to think about that. Not now. Not when there was too much...

She sighed heavily and turned the engine off. She went inside and heard the sound of a hammer going. Walking into the bedroom, she saw that it was absolutely and completely done. She didn't even know where he was working.

She followed the sound down the hall toward Ava's

room. There he was, putting up trim around the windows. "What are you doing?"

"There's a lot more that needs to be done, beyond what needs to be done to satisfy the bank, I mean. Thought I would help."

"Calder," she said. "I mean, there's no guarantee at all this is going to…"

"I wanted to help. And I figure, maybe, if Ava sees that she has a place that's hers…"

"Calder, this is just scratching the surface on my life right now. I don't know what else I'm going to be facing in the next few years with her. With Grace. Right now, Grace still feels like a kid, so I don't have the same issues with her that I do with Ava. But Ava is… I mean God only knows what's going to happen next, and then Grace is going to be a teenager. It's going to be…two times that. It's going to be ongoing like *this*. You're twenty-nine years old. I don't think you actually want to step in the middle of all this."

He nodded, his blue eyes appraising her. He set the hammer down gently on the window box and began to walk toward her. He cupped her chin, holding her gaze.

"I don't like to be told what to do," he said. "Any more than I like to be told what I want."

His touch made her tremble. The way he looked at her… It wasn't fair.

"Why are you here?" she asked. "My life isn't going to bars and having fun. It's not…no-strings sex and getting to be naked in any room of the house. I have to be responsible and go to school functions, and any relationship I decide to have in the future will have to be contained to beds and bedrooms and possibly soundproof spaces so that I don't scar my children for life."

"You think I need it to be that? Sex in weird rooms and nights out at bars? Because I don't. I don't need that." He slid his hand up to cup her cheek and she turned her head away, taking a step back.

"I wish I could have it," she said. "I wanted to run away from home, too. That's what I was trying to do coming back to Gold Valley. But it didn't work. I thought maybe I could leave that life behind. Could leave trouble behind. But I can't. I can't."

"Maybe you can have a life that's not all or nothing. Did you ever think of that?"

"Only people who don't have kids think that." She shook her head. "She ran away. She was walking on the highway. Anything could have happened to her. She's a fourteen-year-old girl. What if… What if some creep had been driving by and…"

"I would have hunted him down and killed him with my bare hands," Calder said, his tone suddenly intense, fierce. "You wouldn't have been alone. You're borrowing trouble, babe. You shouldn't do that either. Because everything was fine. But if ever there was a time when everything wasn't fine, Lauren, I would be there for that, too. I swear it. I wouldn't let you go through that alone."

"Calder…"

"What do you need?" he asked. "Right now, what do *you* need?"

He was the only one who ever asked that. And she wanted to tell him.

She *knew* what she wanted. She wanted to be with this man, skin to skin. Feel his body against hers, in hers, again. She just wanted.

Wanted to feel like a woman, and not a rung-out husk like she felt now.

She wanted all these things she couldn't have.

Desperately. Intensely.

Outside this house, outside this moment, she wouldn't be able to. But maybe just for now. Just for tonight.

"I want you," she whispered.

It didn't matter if it made sense. It didn't matter if it should work. Or shouldn't work. She just wanted this.

She didn't have to ask twice.

He held her against his body, kissing her hard, kissing her like he was desperate, a man starving for air.

His tongue was slick against hers, and his lips were so firm, fierce and decisive.

He was her whole world right in that moment.

The only thing that mattered.

The way those firm, masculine hands gripped her, the way they moved over her body.

She needed this man. Needed.

She couldn't remember ever *needing* a man before, and that terrified her.

Sex had always been nice, but it hadn't been this. This had sharp edges. It wasn't just comfort. It was a challenge. It demanded as much as it gave, but she found she wanted it all the same. Maybe even more because of that.

She found that she kissed him back like he might be her oxygen, too.

In this moment, he damn well felt like it.

He lifted her up, cradled her in his arms and carried her out to the living room, where the blanket was laid out on the carpeted floor. He set her down, stretching out beside her, his blue eyes intense as he looked her over.

"Beautiful," he said.

"Calder…"

"Listen to me," he said. "You are the most beautiful woman that I have ever seen. I've always thought so."

"You're a beautiful man," she responded. "I know that maybe men don't want to be called *beautiful*, but you are."

"Baby, you can call me whatever you want, as long as you keep looking at me like that."

He stripped her shirt from her body, her pants, her underwear and bra and everything else. Then he began to work on his own clothes, slowly revealing that delicious body to her gaze.

All those muscles.

Every inch of him. She was desperate to touch, taste, to explore every dip, every ridge, every beautiful place on that masculine body that she hadn't been able to before.

She knew exactly where she wanted to start.

She rose up on her knee, pressing her palm against his abs and kissing him right in the center of his chest. He groaned, and she continued her exploration, moving down his body, taking her time over those gorgeous abs. She darted her tongue out, tasting, taking a slow, leisurely tour of every inch of him.

His head fell back, breath harsh as his hands moved to grab hold of her hair, tugging, but she kept on tasting, her tongue swirling over him like he was a particularly sweet lollipop.

"Shit," he said, his hips bucking upward as he thrust deep inside her mouth.

Arousal kicked her, and she couldn't remember ever being so turned on by this act before. Usually it was a gift. And if anyone deserved a gift, it was Calder. But she found that it was more than just that. It turned her the hell on.

His surrender. His enjoyment.

His flavor.

Everything.

She tormented him and teased him until he was shaking, until he forced her away from him, words on his lips that she couldn't quite understand.

"My turn," he said, growling at her as he pushed her back onto the blanket and lowered his head, taking one nipple into his mouth and stroking the other one, then trailing down her stomach, tracing a circle around her belly button before going lower.

Lower.

His broad shoulders forced her legs apart, and he looked at her. The open, carnal appreciation on his face sent a wave of desire through her. He wrapped his arms around her hips, pulling her toward his mouth, lowering his head and taking a deep, long taste that nearly had her coming with the first stroke.

She gasped, crying out. He didn't stop. He kept going. Fingers joining in with his lips and tongue. He thrust deep inside her, her orgasm swift and shocking, crashing over her like a sneaker wave. But he didn't stop there. He didn't stop until she came again. Until she was shaking and sobbing, until she had lost sense of everything. Everything except who he was. Who she was. Who they were together. In this world that contained nothing but the two of them.

Where nothing but her next climax mattered at all.

He collected a condom, then moved so that he was positioned over her, thrusting inside her in one easy stroke. She gasped at the invasion. So welcome, so intense. She felt like they were one body. Like she would never again be quite certain of where he began and she ended again.

She wasn't sure she wanted to know.

And she had a hard time imagining what life would be without this. How had one man come to mean so much to her so quickly? It had nothing to do with a fixed floor, and nothing to do with anything half so simple as an orgasm. It had everything to do with this feeling of completion that she felt very deep inside her.

And each stroke, each thrust of his body brought that truth back home harder. Deeper.

She needed him. She needed this. Everything he had to offer. Everywhere. Every part of her. She loved him.

It was as true as it was impossible. As unwanted as it was all-consuming.

Her face was wet with tears.

She couldn't love another person. She didn't have the room. She didn't have the strength inside her to love one more person, and yet here was Calder Reid. Inside her body. Inside her heart.

As he came, the sound feral and low, reverberating inside her, she found her own release, wiping away everything but that moment. While they lay there together, tangled on the floor, their naked bodies resting against each other, it seemed like maybe it was possible.

She held her breath. In that space, in that moment, it seemed like this was real. Like it was her life.

She was going to hang on to that moment for as long as she could because she knew that when her breathing became normal again, and when her heart rate settled, she would remember all the reasons that it wasn't.

She rested her hand over his heart and felt the steady beat against her palm.

And pretended it was the only thing in the whole world.

CHAPTER SEVEN

THE NEXT MORNING, when Lauren woke up, she wished that Calder was there. And that was a dangerous thing.

She had left him late last night, after they'd started painting Grace's room. He had been shirtless. She had ended up putting a stripe across his broad, bare chest and then laughing as he pushed her into the shower and made her help him clean up.

It was not a task that she minded. But she'd found herself distracted with other places on his body. And then she'd been distracted because he was blessedly, wonderfully inside her again.

Those moments with him felt simple. Good. She couldn't remember a time when she had felt that...

Carefree.

Happy.

Whole.

But it was all gone this morning. Vanished completely.

Because she was back to wanting something that she didn't have. Wishing that she had something she couldn't.

She pushed last night's revelations to the side. All of those inconvenient feelings. She didn't need to deal with that. She didn't want to.

That morning, her parents and the girls decided that they wanted to go see the progress on the house. Lauren could think of no good reason why they shouldn't.

Dammit.

So, the group of them caravanned over to the house after breakfast. And when Lauren pulled in the driveway and saw that Calder's truck was there, her heart sank to her toes.

"Who's here?" her mother asked.

Oh dammit *all*.

"You remember Calder Reid?" Lauren was opting for being direct, because the fact of the matter was her mother would never make assumptions about her relationship with someone she used to babysit.

She hurried them all out of the car, her nerves trembling as she did.

"Oh, of course I do," her mother said. "Such a nice boy."

Lauren could think of several things he had done to her last night that did not go under the header of "nice boy."

"He's been helping you out?" her father asked. Sadly, Mark Bishop was no fool, and Lauren suspected that her father had more of an idea about the potential ulterior motives of a man assisting a woman with this kind of thing.

"Yes." She attempted to affect an expression that would hit right at the crossroads of casual and innocent. It was not easy. "We ran into each other at the coffeehouse a week ago. He offered to help me with some of the projects I had to do on the house."

He studied her closely, and Lauren kept her face purposefully blank. "Awfully nice of him."

"Yes," Lauren agreed. "It is."

Ava and Grace, for their part, seemed oblivious to the situation entirely. They were walking around, taking stock of the house, which they hadn't seen since the first time they had all come to Gold Valley as a family and looked at it a couple of months ago, right before they'd made their offer.

"It looks completely different inside now," Lauren said, trying to sound bright.

"Well, I would hope so," Ava said, clearly not as contrite as she had felt yesterday.

"Let's see it," her mother said.

Lauren walked up to the front porch and pushed the door open, praying that Calder wasn't in there naked or something.

She should have texted him the minute she pulled in. She hadn't been thinking. She had been too busy being thrown off by the fact that he was here.

"Here it is," she said loudly, hoping that he would hear and understand quickly that she wasn't alone.

"Very nice," her mother said. Lauren said a private prayer of thanks for her mother voicing her admiration loudly.

Calder appeared from the back bedroom, paint streaking his forearms. He was wiping his hands on a rag, and he was—thank God—fully dressed.

"Howdy," he said, smiling at her family, looking for all the world as if this was completely normal.

"Howdy," her father returned, extending his hand. "I was sorry to hear about your dad, son."

"Thanks," Calder said. "We were all sorry."

"I hear you've been helping out around the place."

"Just a bit," Calder said. "Nothing too tricky. Finishing up painting right now. And then, I think everything should be good to go." He looked around. "This place should pass inspection with flying colors."

"That's great," her father said. "I was pretty worried when she bought this place, and did that deal…"

"It's worth the risk," Lauren said. "And anyway, like Calder said, everything has turned out great."

"Looks like it has," her father said.

Calder looked so perfectly at ease it was only making her jumpy. That lazy confidence of his was…well, it was sexy. There was no denying it. But it also gave the impression he was somehow operating off his own plan at all times. And she had no plan. Not when it came to him.

She did not trust his plan.

"Hey," Calder said. "We are all having a barbecue at my place tonight. I was wondering if you wanted to come out."

"Oh," Lauren said quickly. "I'm not sure if…"

"I live on a ranch," Calder said, directing that at Grace. "We have horses. I bet my stepsister would love to take you out for a ride." He looked back up at her. "If that's okay with your mom."

Grace looked completely unapologetically rapt. Ava had that sense of teenage reserve about her, but Lauren could see excitement sparkling behind her eyes.

"Horses?" Grace asked.

"Like I said, if it's okay with your mom." He looked up at her, his blue eyes twinkling just a bit damn much.

She didn't know what she'd expected him to do when he met both the girls but it wasn't this. He was…at ease. And he was clearly more than willing to get right in there and connect with them. Which she hadn't expected at all.

"Well," Lauren's mom said. "We have our cribbage game tonight, or we would love to come. But, Lauren, you should go."

Lauren blinked. "Should I?"

"Yes," her mother said. "You've been working so hard on this. I think the girls would really enjoy time at the ranch."

Lauren fought to keep from rolling her eyes. Because obviously her mother had thought sincerely that she needed to consult with her on whether or not she should go to a barbecue at Calder's place.

A barbecue that Lauren wasn't entirely convinced was even real.

Well, you'll be having one now. But she didn't quite know what he was doing.

She also had no reason to reject that kind of hospitality.

"I'd love to come," she said. "We would. Thank you."

After that, she showed them around the place, and when the girls and her parents were wandering around the backyard, Lauren took the chance to question Calder.

"A barbecue?"

"It's my niece's birthday," he said. "Anyway, I want you to come out and see the place."

"I have seen the place. When I used to babysit you."

His lips curved upward. He was clearly amused but totally unabashed. "Yeah, well, I would like you to see it now."

"You know I can't..."

"You can come to a barbecue at my house. The fact of the matter is we're going to be neighbors. There's nothing wrong with a little bit of hospitality."

"Sure," she said "except, I'm not entirely convinced that's what you're doing here."

"I care about you," he said. "I would like you to come out and meet my family. I... It means something to me to meet your daughters."

"I don't think I can have it mean anything to me," she said, her heart twisting a little bit.

"Just come to the barbecue. Please."

The way he was looking at her… Hopeful. Like her answer would change something for him. It was different from having someone demand something. It was mattering to someone. Not just to her kids. Not because the person depended on her for basic survival. But…it was about her. And it felt too large for her to carry, but too important for her to turn away from.

"Okay," she said. "I'll go to the barbecue."

"Good," he said.

Lauren had a feeling she'd somehow agreed to a whole lot more than just a barbecue. And she wasn't sure how she felt about that.

She only knew there was no going back now.

CHAPTER EIGHT

"YOU INVITED A stranger to my baby's birthday party?" His sister-in-law was looking at him like he was insane.

"She's not a stranger," he said. "She used to baby-sit me."

Tanner was standing in the living room doorway, and his head whipped around sharp, his gaze connecting with Calder's. "So, that's how you know her? That's what you're going with?"

"Yes," he said.

"Really?" Calder was about ready to punch his brother in the face. "So, that's why you're inviting her to the barbecue? A little bit of nostalgia about when she used to babysit you?"

"She's new back in town. I figured a little bit of a social gathering might be welcome. And I thought it would be nice if Chloe could show them the horses."

"Them?" Tanner asked.

"Her girls," Calder said.

"Girls?" His stepsister, Chloe, looked up from where she was sitting across from their other brother, Jackson.

"Lauren has two daughters," he said. "And she's having a little bit of a hard time with one of them. Ava ran away from home yesterday. I'm trying to help her out. I thought that she might enjoy coming here and seeing the horses. And judging by her reaction when I mentioned it, I was right."

"I don't mind taking them out riding," Chloe said. "Although, it might have been nice if you would've asked first. I have a life, you know."

Tanner snorted, pushing away from the wall and moving over to where Chloe sat. "No you don't."

"Tanner, don't be such a relentless ass," Chloe said.

"Yeah," Jackson agreed. "It is tiresome. And relentless."

"If you're going to have a fistfight, please don't do it in front of Lily. It's her birthday. I would hate for one of her early formative memories to be her father and her uncle punching each other out."

"She's a Reid," Tanner said. "I can't promise that she won't experience it at some point in her life."

Savannah rolled her eyes. "Sure. What was I thinking? That you guys might get civilized at some point."

"Never," Jackson said, grinning broadly.

"Maybe you can behave yourselves long enough to show Lauren and Ava and Grace a decent time," Calder said.

"What exactly is going on with you and Lauren?" Jackson asked. "Because you don't normally care about stability. Or, random women's children."

"I've been helping her get her house in order. What she's been through… I can't be neutral about it. I feel for her," he said. "Her husband died a few years ago, and her daughters are having trouble adjusting to this move. I've been helping her out."

"And you care about her," Chloe said, looking at him intently.

It made him want to snap back at her that he knew

full well she cared a hell of a lot more about Tanner than anyone in this room cared to acknowledge. But he wasn't going to. He wasn't going to let her make him petty.

"Yeah," he said. "Is that so hard to believe? That I might be a decent guy some of the time?"

"Kind of," Chloe said.

He looked over at his sister-in-law. "Do you think that, too?"

She looked at Lily, carefully avoiding his gaze. "Savannah," he said. "You, too?"

"Well, I can honestly say that I haven't seen you do all that much out of the goodness of your heart. Not that you aren't decently good. I just mean… It's not like you go around rampantly doing good works."

"Well, thank you very much. Anyway. My guests are going to arrive soon," he said. "So if you could all behave…"

He heard a knock at the door, and his stomach twisted.

He shot a look at Tanner, who was surveying him far too sharply. He ignored him and went to the door. Lauren was looking up at him with trepidation on her face, and Grace and Ava gazed at him shyly. He took his hat off and pressed it to his chest. "Ava," he said. "It's nice to see you again." He looked down at Grace. "How are you, Grace?"

"Good," she said, her expression serious. "I'm in sixth grade, but about to be in seventh."

He nodded slowly. Grades were a very important thing when you were that age, if he remembered right. It was basically your whole identity. "Middle school, huh?"

"Yes," she said.

"Are you excited to start a new school?"

"No," she responded, not elaborating at all.

He laughed. "Fair enough. Why don't you come in?"

The three of them traipsed inside, and Chloe stood up immediately. "Hi, I'm Chloe, Calder's stepsister. I heard that you girls might want to come and see some horses?"

"Yes," Grace said.

"Sure," Ava responded.

Chloe looked up at Lauren. "Is it okay with you?"

Lauren nodded. "It's okay with me."

With great excitement, the three of them hustled out of the house, heading toward the barn.

"She's good with kids," Calder said. "And even better with horses. They're in good hands."

Lauren smiled slightly. "You know, it didn't occur to me that they wouldn't be. I knew that if you were okay with that it was fine."

He pressed his hand to his chest, mystified by the feeling of pressure there. "Good."

"Hi," Tanner said, extending his hand. "I'm Tanner. I'm not sure if we've ever formally met."

"I don't know either," Lauren said. "But I've heard a lot about you."

Jackson lifted a hand. "Jackson."

"I'm Savannah," Savannah said, taking a step forward. "Jackson's wife. And this is our daughter, Lily."

"The birthday girl," Lauren said, smiling.

"Yes," Savannah said. "She is."

"Thank you for letting me come to the party," Lauren said. "I hope we haven't crashed anything."

"No," Tanner said. "We're happy to have you."

Lauren looked right standing there in his family home. Of course, if he were to marry her...

Yeah, that was about what he was thinking. Her and him, Ava and Grace. In the house that she had chosen.

His chest burned with a sense of rightness, a sense of conviction.

"I hope you're hungry," he said. "Because we have a whole bunch of burgers about to be finished."

"Should I get the girls?"

"No," he said. "Let them have fun. When they're ready to eat I'll fix them a plate. Take care of yourself first."

Calder decided to assist Chloe in helping the girls ride. She paired up with Grace, while he stuck close to Ava, the horses plodding in an easy circle around the arena.

He'd been wanting to say something to Ava and he suspected it might be out of line, because Lauren certainly hadn't said she wanted him around on a permanent basis. But something about Ava had made him think of himself as a kid.

And yes, she had a mother doing her best, which Calder hadn't had. But still.

"You know," he said, looking up as he watched her guide the horse gently. "You don't have to fix your mom's problems."

She looked down at him. "I've never tried to do that."

"I just wondered... I wondered if you wanted to run away because it felt a little heavy. And you didn't know what to do. But you don't have to do anything. You can just be a kid. Adults have their issues, and they have to work them out. You can't do it for them. And your mom just loves you, she doesn't...she doesn't need anything from you, not like that."

It was something he wished someone could have said to him. Something he wished could have been true.

Lauren loved her kids with everything. Their happiness was important to her.

His dad...

He didn't think his dad had much cared about happiness.

"She's not happy, though," Ava said.

"I think time is the only thing that will fix that."

"I thought maybe if she didn't have to worry about me…"

"No, Ava. You're not a burden, trust me. If I've learned one thing about your mom, you're not a burden. You're her world."

Ava smiled, not a wide one. But something small and hopeful.

And Calder thought that just maybe he might have actually fixed something.

DINNER WAS WONDERFUL. Calder and his family were wonderful. Her girls had an amazing time with Chloe on the horses, and they were barely able to calm down enough to eat before they were begging to go outside again. Lauren hadn't seen them that happy in… She couldn't even remember.

She couldn't remember the last time she'd met someone she felt an instant friendship connection with, but Savannah was warm and funny. Easy to talk to. It made Lauren so very aware of the deficit of friends in her life over the past few years.

Being a single mom had made her shrink her life down to necessities, and she'd unintentionally cut out a lot of people who cared for her. Moving somewhere new certainly hadn't helped.

She'd found the very idea of meeting friends daunting. But this wasn't daunting. And really, the whole barbecue had been wonderful.

Calder had been great with the girls, handling everything with cheerful ease. She appreciated it, even though she shouldn't. He'd helped Chloe teach the girls to ride, and he was so...

The involvement he'd given tonight was more than Robert had given ever as a father. And it twisted her in knots. Because she wasn't supposed to want Calder for any of that.

But seeing him with the girls it was hard not to.

When they were finished, she joined in with Savannah, clearing the table and getting things prepared for the big birthday cake moment.

"You don't have to help," Savannah said.

"It's fine," Lauren said. "I don't mind. I actually like cooking. I've been displaced for so long now I haven't gotten a chance to do anything."

"I like cooking, too," she said. "And I love being here. Throwing this birthday party is... I couldn't imagine that I would be here eight months ago."

"What do you mean?" She could sense the intensity of the emotion radiating off the other woman, but she didn't know why. She racked her brain to think if Calder had told her anything about his sister-in-law.

"Did Calder not tell you? Jackson and I are only newly married. Lily isn't my biological daughter. Jackson hired me to be his nanny. And... It was just kind of..."

"Perfect," she said.

She didn't know why that word occurred to her. Except the way that Savannah looked right now echoed something inside her. The feeling of a key turning in a lock. Putting everything into place. Securing it.

"Yes." Savannah smiled. "I came out of a pretty rough divorce. Wanted to start a new life here."

Savannah's story was going a little bit too close to Lauren's own personal scar tissue.

"And you did," Lauren said.

"I did. And I got more than I bargained for. But, in a good way."

Lauren swallowed hard. "I'm not sure how you balance out…"

She stopped talking. The woman was about to serve cake for her daughter's first birthday party. She didn't need to offer Lauren a counseling session. Anyway, it wasn't like they even knew each other. But then, Lauren didn't really have any friends, not here.

"How did I balance out what?" Savannah asked, her tone kind.

"Your need to be safe and not make the same mistake again, with… You know how it is. You meet somebody new and you have… Feelings. And you've been down that road before. Where you had feelings. More feelings than sense."

"I think…" Savannah began slowly. "I think you just have to trust that everything you've been through has taught you something. That you can never look at life, a friend, a man the same way that you would have years ago. Because you weren't the same person."

Lauren nodded slowly. "Part of me wants to believe that… That things could be different."

"Calder?"

Lauren tried to force a smile. "He's great," she said. "He's really great."

"Then what's the problem?"

"I'm worried that *I* am," she said. "That the girls and I might be. I mean, for him. He's so young and I just don't know why he'd ever want to take all this on long term."

Savannah looked at her. "Why don't you ask him how he feels about that? I think his take on it will be more important than mine could be."

"I'm worried he'll say one thing but it won't actually be what he wants." She sighed. She felt like such an ass saying that. Like Calder didn't know his mind. She was sure in many ways he did. She was also sure men didn't always know what they actually wanted.

"Why is that?"

"I have some experience with men thinking they're up to a certain amount of responsibility but actually wanting nothing to do with it," she said, perturbed by the bitter edge in her voice.

"I have some experience with that, too. At a certain point, you have to trust yourself. More than that... You have to learn to trust another person again."

Well, that was impossible. It was just impossible. There was no way in hell she could do that.

The vehemence and certainty of her own internal response shocked her.

But what she knew was that she'd made choices. Flawed ones. That her judgment had been bad and if she was in a bad situation now, well...

She ruminated on that through the whole dessert. She tried not to fixate on how happy Grace and Ava looked at the table, cooing over baby Lily, enjoying their cake.

Chloe was their brand-new hero, a woman who was great with horses and had a fantastic sense of humor. Ava kept looking at Calder like he was a superhero. Captain America and Thor rolled into one.

It wounded Lauren a little bit that she couldn't be their hero, but she also understood the attraction to Chloe. She was young, and pretty, and a badass.

And Lauren didn't feel like any of those things.

When Calder looked at her, she did. He made her feel… Well, he made her feel a little bit too much.

When the birthday party was over, he walked her back to the truck, and he took her hand as they walked behind the girls.

She almost pulled away, but he stopped her with that steady hold and level gaze of his.

"Tonight was good," he said.

"It was."

"I'd love to have you out again," he said.

Those words made her ache everywhere.

"The house is getting inspected tomorrow," she said, moving to interrupt him, because it seemed easier than actually talking to him. Than getting into any kind of talk of the future.

"I'm glad to hear that," he said. "Do you want me to come out?"

She shook her head. "It should be fine. Depending on how long it takes to get all the paperwork submitted… Well, we should have a close date."

"Congratulations," he said.

The girls turned, and he dropped her hand. It made her feel good to know that he realized that she wasn't ready for them to see. She might not ever be.

"I'm proud of you," he said.

She tried to laugh that off. "That's a weird thing to say."

"Maybe. But I didn't know if anyone had said it to you for a while. And they should. They should, Lauren, because you're doing a hell of a job here. You really are. You're doing a hell of a job with these girls. With your life."

She ducked her head. "Thank you."

She noticed Ava watching her, and she took a step away from him.

"I'll call you tomorrow and let you know how everything goes."

"Good," he said.

"I'm not ever going to be able to repay you for this," she said.

"I don't want you to repay me," he said. "I just want you to be happy."

"I was really happy tonight."

"That's all I needed to hear."

She wanted to kiss him, but she knew that would be stupid. So she didn't. She kept her distance and simply stuffed her hands in her pockets, nodding and walking backward to the truck.

When she got in and started the engine, Ava turned to her. "Is he your boyfriend?"

Lauren stiffened. "I... No," she said.

"Do you like him?"

She flashed back to their naked, sweaty moments from the night before. She cleared her throat. "Of course I like him. He's been helping out a lot..."

"She means do you *like* him," Grace said.

She didn't know what to say. She was all for this new talking-and-being-honest thing, except she didn't know what to tell them about this. That sometimes you could like a man—a whole lot—and there was still just no way to work it out. Anyway, she had no idea what they would think about something like that. She was their mom, not a woman. Besides, even if they did acknowledge that she was a woman, they probably wouldn't realize that women as old as her still had crushes and got fluttery and wanted a boy to like them back.

"I don't think there's any room in my life to *like* someone," Lauren said as she turned out onto the highway.

"Why not?" Ava asked.

Her daughter's question surprised her. "Wouldn't it bother you if I did?"

Ava said nothing for a moment. "Their ranch is really nice."

"It is," Lauren agreed.

"And he's nice. He helped you work on the house. I don't remember Dad—" She looked away. Then she took a shuddering breath and looked back at Lauren. "I don't remember Dad ever helping you with anything. Not housework, nothing. He seems to like to help you."

"He likes helping," she said. "It's who he is."

"Well, if you were going to be with someone it would have to be someone like that. It would have to be someone who made you happy."

"Would that make him our stepdad?"

"No," Ava said, matter-of-factly. "Only if she married him."

"That wouldn't bother you?" Lauren asked.

"I don't know if it would bother me with him," Ava said. She lifted a shoulder. "He talks to me like I'm a person and not a kid. And he didn't get in the way when you came and picked me up yesterday. He seems like he wouldn't be too annoying."

"Well," Lauren said. "I guess that's the highest compliment that can possibly be paid."

"It's a pretty high compliment."

"I don't want to rush into anything. And I think I've

put you both through quite enough change as it is. I don't think you need me dating on top of it."

"He does make you smile," Grace said. "I like it best when you smile."

Lauren didn't know what to say to that, so she didn't say anything for the rest of the drive home. Her girls were apparently completely fine with Calder. And there was still a fluttery, panicked feeling in her chest. In fact, if anything it had increased. So apparently they were fine with her dating. They were fine with him.

And the question was, if Ava and Grace were okay with it…?

There were no more excuses except the ones that lived inside herself.

CHAPTER NINE

LAUREN TEXTED HIM the next day with the good news.

The house had passed inspection, and they had a close date. Furthermore, with the agreement she had with the previous owner, she would be able to move in before the official close date as long as she acknowledged the risks of not being covered by insurance during that time.

Calder didn't waste any time heading over there to wrap up any last-minute issues.

He felt... So damned accomplished. That he had actually fixed something.

He had always wanted to. To be of help. But it seemed like when he was a kid he had never done quite enough right. He'd never been enough.

But now... With this... He had been.

It was when it mattered, too. Because it was Lauren.

He helped her move all of her things out of storage for most of the day, and the house was nearly full by evening.

It would take days to get everything organized and put away. But for now, everything looked good.

"The girls can come over," she said.

He had just set up a big bed in her room, and he had other plans.

"Want to have the girls come over tomorrow morning?"

"Tomorrow morning?" she asked.

"I want to spend the night," he said.

He could see the fear flash through her eyes. The hesitance. He was willing to push it. He was willing to push it because this mattered. Because it was important.

"I don't know…"

"I've had you against a wall, on the floor and in a shower. I'd like you to see what I can do in a bed with nothing but time, babe. That's what I want."

She looked like she was going to protest again, but he brought his lips down on hers, kissing her deep and hard. He felt a rush. Like he was home. Like she might be home.

It was a strange thought, because he had lived in Gold Valley all of his life. If any one place was home, it was here. If any man had ever been home from the day he was born, it was Calder Reid.

But he had found something else with her. An escape and a refuge all at the same time. He didn't know how to explain it, not in the least. But he didn't really care to either. All that mattered was this. All that mattered was her. She kissed him back, tentative at first, and then growing bolder.

"I love you," he said. She froze completely.

He hadn't even known he was going to say it until that moment. But then, the words just kind of slipped out of his mouth, and at that point, he had known they were true. So there was no reason to fight it. No reason at all.

"You don't… You can't," she said.

"What part about wanting to be all in was ambiguous to you when I said that's what I wanted the other day?"

"It wasn't," she said. "But… But that doesn't mean…"

"Baby, it sure as hell does. I love you. I more than love you. I fucking need you."

"You need me? I've basically been one big... It's been some kind of strange role reversal. I've basically been your babysitting project for the past few weeks."

"No. I've been helping take care of you, because you needed me to. And I suspect that if I needed you to, you would take care of me."

She shook her head. "No," she said. "I wouldn't. Because I'm already taking care of enough people."

"Then just let me take care of you."

"No," she said. "That doesn't work either. I've been in one-sided relationships, Calder. They don't work. They don't work because they're not sustainable. Because somebody always ends up resenting someone else. And I just don't... You're going to end up resenting me."

"You're treating me like I'm an idiot," he bit out.

"I'm not. I ended up in a relationship with somebody that *I* resented. Because he couldn't give me what I needed. And we were miserable."

"You were miserable because he was an ass. You are not an ass."

"Calder..."

"Let me show you," he said. "Let me show you how good it can be."

He dipped his head to kiss her again, and this time she turned her face away.

"You don't want me to give to you. Because you don't want a one-sided relationship?" he pressed.

"Yes," she insisted.

"You're a liar," he said, anger pouring through him now. Because wasn't this just like his life had always been? "This has nothing to do with that. It has nothing to do with me. It's all about you, Lauren. I know that for sure and certain. This is about you. What is it, honey?

Let me tell you, my father lived his whole life trying to fill a void. He used marriages, he used all kinds of shit, piling it all up in front of him. But he had sons who would have loved him just like he was. If he would have let us. I would have fixed it if he would've let me. If you would let me, I would fix it."

"You can't," she said. "You can't because…"

Something turned over inside him, realization dawning on him like the sun over the mountains. "Because you think you don't deserve it."

"No," she said. "Don't turn this into you trying to fix my deep wound."

"I can't fix it," he said. "Until the day you decide that you deserve to have it fixed, I can't." He huffed out a breath. "I can't. You know what? You just made me realize that. I've spent my whole life wishing that I could fix this kind of thing for someone I care about. But I can't." He shook his head. "My father spent his whole life punishing himself because my mother left him. It wasn't until he married Chloe's mother that he got his shit even a little bit together. Until then, it was just… All these destructive relationships. He wouldn't let himself be happy. And it wasn't any better for us. He was bitter, and he was alone. And there was nothing any of us could do but watch him self-destruct over and over again. That's not what your girls want for you."

"Don't you dare," she said. "Don't you dare make this about me and my daughters."

"Why not? *You* are."

"Because *my life* is about my daughters," she said.

"And they'd be against you moving on from their father?"

She shook her head. "That has nothing to do with anything."

"I think it does. I think you're desperate for excuses so that you don't have to look down inside yourself and figure out what the hell the real problem is. But let me do you a favor. Right now, I don't want to please you," he said, emotion roaring up inside him.

"Right now, I want to please myself. You want me to be selfish. Then dammit, I'm going to take what I want, Lauren."

He hauled her up against his body, her soft curves crushed up against him. "I've been all about giving to you, because that's what you needed. And you know what? Something in me needed that, too. I wanted to take care of you, because I have been so desperate to fix things. But you're right. My life can't be all about that. So I want you to give something to me."

She was shaking, but he knew it wasn't from fear. She looked up at him, her lips parting slowly. Then, she placed her fingertips against his mouth. He parted his lips, sucking her fingertip in deep. He kept eye contact with her the whole time, his heart pounding out of control. A beast roaring through him.

He had always wondered what love would feel like. And now he knew. It was nothing like what he had imagined. It wasn't sweet. It wasn't quiet, or careful. It was desperate. And right now, it was brutal.

Ugly, and a little bit selfish.

But he wanted it. And she was right. He couldn't just care about her and expect nothing in return. He wanted. He needed.

He needed her to love him. With the same ferocity that he loved her. He needed her to care. He needed her to understand.

That this wasn't about anything she had ever experienced before. Whatever shit her husband had pulled with her… He wasn't the same man. But he was a man. Not a boy for her to protect. Whether she was protecting herself or himself, he wasn't entirely sure. But he was done with it. He swept her up into his arms, carried her back to the bedroom. She clung to him, her fingers wrapped tightly around his shirt.

She didn't protest.

He half expected her to.

After all, she had been in the middle of telling him all the reasons she couldn't love him. All the reasons they couldn't be. But apparently, she could still stand for him to fuck her.

That only made him angrier. Because he had given her something of himself. Not just his body. But something deep and real, and he had never done that with a woman before. She didn't want it. That was fine. He was just going to take now.

He threw her down onto the bed and she reclined there, her knees bent slightly, her elbows resting on the mattress, her gaze unreadable. She stared at him, and he didn't move. Not until she gave him a sign. Not until…

Her tongue darted out, slicked over her lips.

He wrenched his shirt over his head and began to work his belt through the loops. She stared at him, her gaze rapt. Sure. Because she could take his dick, but not his love. Or, his abs. She seemed particularly fixated on those.

He moved onto the bed, and he stripped her bare. So pretty and perfect. She sat up, pressing her palms against his bare stomach, parting the fabric of his jeans and drawing his cock out. She looked up at him as she

slid her hand over his length, her eyes meeting his. There
was no fight there, not now.

"Do it," he said. "That's what I want."

She lowered her head, obeying, taking him into the
wet heat of her mouth. The delicious suction was almost
too much for him to bear. She was so hot, and it was so
good. Every damn fantasy he'd ever had rolled up into
one. He didn't know if he could withstand it. Didn't think
he wanted to. She was just so damn hot. So damn perfect.

And she didn't love him.

He growled, bucking his hips, gripping her hair and
forcing her to take him deeper. And she did.

He'd tried to be nice. He was past that point. He'd
given her everything. And he hadn't wanted it to be a
transaction. He had wanted...

Suddenly, he couldn't think anymore, and he didn't
want to. Because it was just the two of them. Her mouth on
his body. She took him to the edge, and when he was about
to come, he pulled out, not ready for it to end like that.

"Get on your knees," he said.

"I already..."

"Turn around and get on your knees."

She looked up at him, something a little bit like awe
in those eyes as she stared at him. As if she were seeing
him, really seeing him for the first time.

She obeyed, turning her delicious ass toward him, her
face toward the headboard.

He shucked his jeans the rest of the way, taking care
to grab a condom before he ditched them completely,
and then he stroked himself twice before pressing himself against her damp, ready entrance.

He gripped her hips, pushing inside her, that tight, wet

heat threatening to overwhelm him as he went so deep he could barely breathe.

Could barely see straight.

If this was the last thing he ever did, he would be happy enough. He could die a damned happy man inside Lauren Bishop.

Except she didn't love him.

And that would burn. In his last moments, whether they were in sixty years or six minutes, that would burn.

He suspected it always would.

He didn't think about that. Not now. Instead, he lost himself. In the small sounds of encouragement she made. In the way that she moaned and arched against him. The way that she cried out when he pressed his hand between her legs and rubbed her clit hard, the way that she pressed her ass into him as he thrust deep.

He had never expected a declaration of love to come with such an animalistic physical expression. But that was because love didn't feel like he thought it would.

This was dangerous. It wasn't hearts and flowers, it was knives and bombs, and it had the power to destroy him.

It made him want to destroy her right back. Destroy them both.

Made him question what his motives were all along, and if he could trust himself, let alone if she could trust him.

He was turned around and tangled up. Inside out. Because of her. Only ever because of her.

When she came, it was sudden and welcome, because he didn't have the strength to hold on much longer. And when he cried out his own pleasure, that "I love you" was on his lips again. But this time, it sounded less like a promise and more like a curse. It satisfied something inside him. Something angry and needy and demanding. Something that was for him and not for her.

So he repeated it.

Over and over again until it was the only sound in the room. Those words, over and over again. Until they broke. Until his climax overtook him, and there weren't words anymore. Just a growl. One that came from deep inside him and seemed to say the exact same thing.

When it was over, she collapsed onto her stomach, rolling away from him, looking the opposite direction. And he...

He started to collect his clothes.

Because he didn't know what else to do. Because there was nothing else to do.

"Are you... Are you leaving?"

"I said that I loved you," he said. "You said..."

"You also said you were going to stay the night."

He shook his head, finding his jeans and pulling them on. "I can't."

"But you said..."

"Yes I did. And you said a lot of shit, too. You said that you couldn't be with me and just take. Well, I took something. And now I'm leaving. Lauren Bishop, I think I've loved you my whole life. It's stupid, because there's no way I could have any idea what love was when I was twelve years old. And obviously it wasn't this. But I'm offering myself to you. And I was never enough for my dad. He died never knowing that I felt like we didn't even know each other. Never knowing that all I wanted was more of a relationship with him. I'm not going to do that again. I love you. And I want more. I want everything. I want to fix your floorboards and go to sleep with you at night. I want to be your husband. I want to be a father to your girls. I want every damned thing, and I hope it scares you. Because it sure as hell scares me."

It was like his chest was being torn in two. It was torture. And she was just lying there. "There is nothing nice about feeling all of this. About feeling it deep in my soul and knowing that you don't feel it back. Nothing nice about it at all, babe. So you're right. It can't be half. And I won't take half. I thought to myself... I thought maybe I would be happy to just let myself be the fixer. But I can't be. Not now. Not anymore. So if you don't want everything, you don't get anything."

"You said you weren't doing all of this for anything. You said..."

"That was before I loved you. That was before I needed..." He shook his head. "I can't go only halfway. Not with you. I've half-assed a lot of things in my life, but I will be damned if you're one of them. Be my wife. Love me. Or let me go."

She curled in on herself, a look of desolation on her face, and for one moment he felt guilty. But he wasn't going to give. Not on this.

"I can't."

He nodded once. "I'm really happy that you got your house. And if you ever need anything... Well, you can call Tanner. He'll help out."

"You won't?"

"Until you know that you deserve it, until you can accept all this and not have me handing it to you, telling you to take it, we're never going to make it anywhere. And there's no point."

Then he turned and walked out, leaving a piece of himself behind.

CHAPTER TEN

LAUREN WAS MISERABLE. Absolutely, utterly miserable. And she was trying her best to be happy. She and her daughters were having their first breakfast in their brand-new house, in their brand-new life.

New life.

She had gone and messed that up. She had spent her very first night in her new house having sex with a man she couldn't have.

A man she wouldn't let herself have.

And the truth was she did love him.

She loved him like... She had never loved anyone like that, and that terrified her. It made her wonder what the hell her life even was.

Because if she thought of everything as choices and consequences, if she thought of Robert as a mistake... Did that mean that Calder had always been the one? But how is that even possible, when he had been too young all those years ago, and in that time Lauren had lived a whole life, and had her girls, and couldn't regret a single moment of it?

Who was the mistake? What should she have changed? Was this the mistake?

She honestly didn't know, and she didn't know where to go from there.

"Mom?" Ava asked. "Are you okay?"

"Yes," she lied. "I'm fine."

"You don't look fine."

"I'm fine," she insisted, while a piece of her heart broke off and tumbled down to her stomach.

"You look really upset."

"It's just… I'm thinking," she said. "I'm just thinking about our life."

"And it makes you sad?" Grace asked.

"No," Lauren protested. "I'm happy. I'm happy that we're here."

"I'm happy we're here," Ava said. "At least, I think I will be."

"What changed your mind?"

"Well, it was how you've been. In this house. What about Calder?"

Lauren blew out a harsh breath. "Why are you fixating on him?"

"You like him," Ava said.

"It doesn't matter if I like him," Lauren said. "I don't have time for that kind of thing. Not right now."

"Why not?"

"Because," she said.

"Because why?"

"Ava Marie," Lauren said. "It's not a discussion. I don't have time to date the man. I'm not going to… Marry him. It's ridiculous."

"I didn't say anything about marrying him."

"Well… I'm not going to."

"Did he ask you to marry him?" Ava asked. Grace was watching the exchange with an open mouth.

"He… It doesn't matter. I can't… How am I supposed to know that I'm making the right choice?"

"You always tell us to follow our heart," Grace said.

Well, her heart had been stupid, and how did she tell her girls that? Her heart didn't deserve...

Suddenly, it all hit her with more clarity than she cared for.

Her heart didn't deserve to be happy again. It had wasted its one chance.

She had broken her parents' hearts and run off with a man. She had been wrong about him. She had made her bed and lain in it determinedly. The consequence for her actions. She hadn't let him go to be with a woman who would be happier with him. She hadn't let herself go because she was so intent on punishing them both.

Because she couldn't let go.

And she was doing the same thing now. Holding on while pretending to let go. A new surrounding wasn't going to change her heart. She had to...

She had to let it go. Because as long as her heart was still staking its claim in the past, as long as it was still clinging to her mistakes, obsessing over right and wrong and what she deserved, she was never going to get anywhere.

And sitting there with her daughters staring at her asking her directly why she wouldn't let herself be happy, there was just no good answer to give.

All that self-sacrifice, all that trying to make up for bad decisions... It didn't make her better.

"Sometimes," she said, tears making her voice thick, "I think grown-ups forget the simple things that we tell our kids. And sometimes I think those simple things are the truest things. You're right, Grace. I would tell you to follow your heart. I've been scared of mine."

"Why?" Grace asked.

A tear slid down Lauren's cheek. "Because I think I love him. And because I'm afraid of getting hurt."

"Chloe said that when you fall off a horse you have to get back on it again. Maybe Calder is like a horse," Grace said.

Lauren slapped her hand over her mouth and tried not to laugh through her tears.

"Why is that funny?" Grace asked.

Ava looked slightly confused, but had that look on her face that said she suspected she understood why, even if the details were fuzzy, and was certain she didn't want to know more.

"Never mind," Lauren said. "You know, I'm supposed to be raising you and teaching you things. But, I think you teach me more every day."

"You teach us a lot," Ava said. "Even when I wish you wouldn't."

Lauren pulled her daughter in for a hug. "I think that's the best compliment you can give me."

"So, are you going to tell him that you love him?"

She released her hold on Ava, looking down at her pancakes. "I guess that would be the brave thing to do, wouldn't it?"

"I think so," her daughter said, her tone grave.

"You're really okay with it?" Lauren asked.

"It will be different," Ava said. "Maybe weird. But... This is already really different. So, maybe it's the best time."

Lauren laughed. "I guess I can't argue with the logic. Since I don't have any of my own."

"Then, I guess you need to go tell him."

"Can I finish my pancakes first?"

"That sounds reasonable," Ava said.

CHAPTER ELEVEN

CALDER HAD NEVER worked so hard chopping wood in his life. But, he wanted to destroy something, make it match his insides, so chopping wood seemed as good of an option as any.

"That bad, huh?" Tanner was there, looking him over like a smug son of a bitch.

"Don't you have somewhere better to be? I mean, honestly, you basically run the whole ranch, and I see you standing around snooping in my business more often than not."

"I don't have anywhere to be."

"I could use some help," Chloe said, coming out of the barn, with a horse on a lead. "There are stalls to muck," she said pointedly.

"And that's your job," Tanner said.

"Well, if you don't have anything to do, you could help me do it."

"As it happens," Tanner said, "I have a date."

Chloe's whole face turned red, and she turned on her heel, concealing her expression as quickly as possible. "Fine," she said. "I'll do it myself."

Calder watched Chloe leave, and he thought about asking Tanner if he realized just how messed up the situation with her was getting. It would derail the train Tanner had coming for him, that was for sure.

But he didn't want to make things tough for Chloe either.

"What the hell is up with you?" Tanner asked.

"I got dumped," he said. "I would have thought that was pretty obvious."

"Did you really want to take all that on?"

"Yeah," Calder said. "I really did. I love her. It didn't seem like a lot. It didn't seem like a burden. It just seemed… Right."

"Teenagers? A widow? That just seems like… A lot."

"Yeah, well, I always figured if I ever fell in love it was going to be easy. It was going to be nice. More like what Dad found with Chloe's mom. Not what he had with our mom. Not what he had with any of those other women he married. But this isn't like any of that. I'd kill someone for her. For those girls. I'm obsessed with her. I don't want anything but her. I want the hard stuff and the easy stuff. I want… Everything. And I didn't know feelings like that existed."

"I'd rather never have them."

Chloe appeared again, right when Tanner said that, her eyes looking determinedly anywhere but at Tanner.

"What?" she asked.

"Do you agree with him?" Calder asked, because he was in a mean mood. "No love?"

She lifted a shoulder. "If I did fall in love, it wouldn't be with a hardheaded rancher."

Maybe Chloe wasn't as much of a lost cause as he'd imagined.

Calder smiled, but Tanner's face remained blank. "Good choice."

He saw a car off in the distance, and when it drew closer, he recognized it.

His heart jumped up in his chest. Like he was a thirteen-year-old boy about to catch a glimpse of his crush.

Hell, when he had been a thirteen-year-old boy, the same woman had been his crush.

"Excuse me," he said, abandoning his ax and his brother and stepsister, jogging toward the house as fast as he could. By the time he got there, she was just pulling her car to a stop.

Lauren.

"What are you doing here?" he asked as she got out.

When she looked up at him, her eyes were full of tears, her expression pleading. "I'm here for everything," she said. "Because... That's what you said I had to take. And that's what I... It's what I want. I want everything, Calder. Everything."

"What changed?"

"Me. You're right. That's what needed to change. You are right that I—" she cleared her throat "—that I was punishing myself. I thought that I was just protecting myself, but it's more than that. It's deeper than that. I made a mistake, marrying Robert. Or maybe I didn't. Maybe life isn't that simple, and I'm trying to make it too simple. I almost melted my brain last night trying to figure out... If he was wrong for me and you were right, then was anyone the one? And was any of what happened with him supposed to happen? Was all of that a life I wasn't supposed to live?" She shook her head, a tear falling down her cheek. She didn't wipe it away.

"And then I just realized that it was that road that led me here. That marriage. It led me to this house, with my daughters. And it brought me to this point, as this woman." She cleared her throat. "I had a talk with Savannah the night of the birthday party. She said something that I didn't think about enough until last night. I have to trust that the woman I am now is different enough that I'm not repeating the same mistakes. But more than that, the woman I am now is the woman who was meant to love you. Who was meant to be loved by you. I'll never know if the woman I was would have been right for you. But this woman, this woman I am right now... She is. She wants you. I want you. I love you. And I have to stop living my life as a monument to my mistakes. And start being grateful for where my choices brought me. Because right now, with you, with Ava and Grace and the house, I'm happy. I'm whole."

"Lauren, your past matters to me. Because everything that built you matters to me. Everything you've been through, your pain, it matters to me. But what matters to me even more is your present. What matters even more is your future. Our future. It's one we can build together. You don't have to solve those questions by yourself. It doesn't have to be simple. Not if we're not alone."

On a sob, she launched herself toward him, and his own heart squeezed in response. Dipped in his chest.

He held her. Just held her. And then she whispered in his ear. "I love you. I love you. I love you."

Over and over and over.

Not a curse. A promise.

A promise for the both of them. A promise for the future. A promise for better.

"I love you, too," he said, brushing her hair out of her eyes.

"Is it too late for me to say yes?"

"It's not too late for you to say anything. But yes to what specifically?"

"To the proposal. I want to be your wife."

"That works out pretty well, then, because I want to be your husband."

She held on to him tightly. "Good," she said. "Because I wasn't going to let you spend the night with the girls there unless we had a commitment."

He laughed. "Is that the only reason that you said you'd marry me?"

"It's not the only reason. But, it's a damn compelling one, you have to admit."

"It is."

"How will that work? You live here, right? On the ranch?"

He nodded. "I do. But it's just a small cabin. And I like your place just fine."

"Well, you helped build it."

"We built it together."

Lauren smiled, and it made his heart feel full to bursting. "I have a feeling it's just the first of many things we'll build together."

"You can count on it," he said. "Whatever we do, we're partners."

"It'll never be one-sided with us."

He shook his head. "No. It's you and me. Always."

Lauren Bishop had been his ultimate fantasy when he was a boy. But she was better than a fantasy now, she was real.

And he wasn't a boy anymore. He was a man, and he was going to spend the rest of his life being the man she needed.

He'd always known that she was beautiful, but he'd never dreamed she would become his happily-ever-after.

But that's exactly what she was.

EPILOGUE

MUCH LATER, when Lauren and Calder were sitting together on the back porch, Calder pressed a kiss to her hand.

"It just occurred to me," he said. "I should probably ask permission before I marry you."

"I've been married before," she said. "And I'm thirty-five. You don't need to ask my father's permission."

He shook his head. "It's not your father I want to ask."

WHEN CALDER APPROACHED Ava and Grace, cowboy hat in hand, to ask them if he could marry their mother, Lauren didn't think she would ever stop crying.

They gave their permission, instantly and immediately. And she could tell that Calder was resisting offering a hug to both girls, probably waiting until they knew each other better. Another thing she appreciated about him. He never tried to force a relationship with them before they were ready.

And that was a trend that continued over the next several months. As they got settled in Gold Valley, and they got their lives settled with Calder in it.

It was Grace who called him Dad first.

One evening, while they were putting dishes away, two months after the wedding.

"Would you hand me that plate, Dad?"

Calder had stopped, frozen in the spot, and then he had handed it to her.

Then, he had pulled her in for a real hug. A long one.

And Lauren had been certain she'd seen tears in her husband's eyes.

He was a man who didn't take the gift of fatherhood for granted. Not at all. He didn't just keep pictures of the girls and show them around. He actually was around.

With Ava, things were slower. But one day when they were picking her up from school, Lauren heard her talking to her friends about upcoming slumber party plans.

"My dad's family has a ranch," she said. "My aunt Chloe can take us out riding, she said. And we can camp out in the barn."

Lauren looked back at Calder, whose face looked hard like granite. "Did you hear that?" she asked.

He nodded, his throat working. "I did."

"Do you think you made the right choice? Going all in with us?"

He slung his arm around her shoulder and pulled her in for a kiss. "I've never once regretted it. I went all in with you, but the three of you have gone all in with me. And that's a gift that I'll never be able to repay."

She looked up at him, her heart pounding. Because she had another little surprise for him. "Well, you're about to get in deeper, Calder Reid. Because you're going to be a father."

He froze, right there in the school parking lot, his eyes full of shock. He looked down at her stomach, then back up at her. And then he looked over at Ava and Grace, where they were talking to their group of friends.

Then he looked back at Lauren. "You made me a father already," he said. "And I'm happy to be one again."

Lauren threw her arms around her husband's neck.

"None of this was in my planner," she said, rising up on her toes for a kiss.

"Then it wasn't a very good planner."

"I guess not. Because this is a very good life."

* * * * *

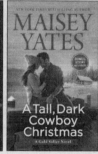

She was going to be interviewing Isaiah's potential wife.

The man she had been in love with since she was a teenage idiot, and was still in love with now that she was an idiot in her late twenties.

There were a whole host of reasons she'd never, ever let on about her feelings for him.

She loved her job. She loved Isaiah's family, who were the closest thing she had to a family of her own.

She was also living in the small town of Copper Ridge, Oregon, which was a bit strange for a girl from Seattle, but she did like it. It had a different pace. But that meant there was less opportunity for a social life. There were fewer people to interact with. By default she, and the other folks in town, ended up spending a lot of their free time with the people they worked with every day. There was nothing wrong with that. But it was just…

Mostly there wasn't enough of a break from Isaiah on any given day.

But then, she also didn't enforce one. Didn't take one. She supposed she couldn't really blame the small-town location when the likely culprit of the entire situation was her.

"Place whatever ad you need to," he said, his tone abrupt. "When you meet the right woman, you'll know."

"I'll know," she echoed lamely.

"Yes. Nobody knows me better than you do, Poppy. I have faith that you'll pick the right wife for me."

With those awful words still ringing in the room, Isaiah left her there, sitting at her desk, feeling numb.

The fact of the matter was, she probably could pick him a perfect wife. Someone who would facilitate his life, and give him space when he needed it. Someone who was beautiful and fabulous in bed.

Yes, she knew exactly what Isaiah Grayson would think made a woman the perfect wife for him.

The sad thing was, Poppy didn't possess very many of those qualities herself.

And what she so desperately wanted was for Isaiah's perfect wife to be her.

But dreams were for other women. They always had been. Which meant some other woman was going to end up with Poppy's dream.

While she played matchmaker to the whole affair.

Don't miss what happens when Isaiah decides it's Poppy who should be his convenient wife in
Want Me, Cowboy *by USA TODAY bestselling author Maisey Yates, part of her Copper Ridge series!*

Available November 2018 wherever
Harlequin® Desire books and ebooks are sold.

www.Harlequin.com

HDEXP1018

HARLEQUIN® *Desire*

Sensual dramas starring powerful heroes, scandalous secrets...and burning desires.

Save **$1.00**

on the purchase of ANY Harlequin® Desire book.

Available wherever books are sold, including most bookstores, supermarkets, drugstores and discount stores.

Save **$1.00**

on the purchase of any Harlequin® Desire book.

Coupon valid until November 30, 2018.
Redeemable at participating outlets in the U.S. and Canada only.
Not redeemable at Barnes & Noble stores. Limit one coupon per customer.

52616004

5 65373 00076 2 (8100)0 12384

HDCOUP0918

Get 4 FREE REWARDS!

We'll send you 2 FREE Books plus 2 FREE Mystery Gifts.

Both the **Romance** and **Suspense** collections feature compelling novels written by many of today's best-selling authors.

YES! Please send me 2 FREE novels from the Essential Romance or Essential Suspense Collection and my 2 FREE gifts (gifts are worth about $10 retail). After receiving them, if I don't wish to receive any more books, I can return the shipping statement marked "cancel." If I don't cancel, I will receive 4 brand-new novels every month and be billed just $6.74 each in the U.S. or $7.24 each in Canada. That's a savings of at least 16% off the cover price. It's quite a bargain! Shipping and handling is just 50¢ per book in the U.S. and 75¢ per book in Canada*. I understand that accepting the 2 free books and gifts places me under no obligation to buy anything. I can always return a shipment and cancel at any time. The free books and gifts are mine to keep no matter what I decide.

Choose one: ☐ **Essential Romance**   ☐ **Essential Suspense**
(194/394 MDN GMY7)   (191/391 MDN GMY7)

Name (please print)

Address   Apt. #

City   State/Province   Zip/Postal Code

Mail to the **Reader Service:**
IN U.S.A.: P.O. Box 1341, Buffalo, NY 14240-8531
IN CANADA: P.O. Box 603, Fort Erie, Ontario L2A 5X3

Want to try two free books from another series? Call 1-800-873-8635 or visit www.ReaderService.com.